Just Human

Kerry Heavens

*To Simone
Thank you for all the support you have given me!
Kerry Heavens*

Published by Kerry Heavens.
© 2013. Kerry Heavens.
Just Human
All Rights Reserved.

No part of this book may be reproduced or transmitted in any form or by any means, electronic or mechanical, including photocopying, recording, or by any information storage and retrieval system without the written permission of the author, except where permitted by law.

ISBN-13: 978-1492901426
ISBN-10: 1492901423

Editor: Kelly at Ultimate Proof Ltd.
Cover image used under license from Shuttertock.com
Cover Design: Kerry Heavens

I dedicate this book to

Renee Heavens
Virginia Tomkins
Joanne Rampersad

Three incredible women who have recently reminded me that life is short and precious and that I should follow my dreams.

One.

Vaguely queasy.

Liv.

I take a deep, cleansing breath. I never thought the smell of the rubbish tip would be so refreshing. With one final look at the heap through the hatch, I smile with satisfaction when I see that his mum's platter has smashed under the weight of someone else's discarded rubbish. Olivia Constance Harper, you are one vindictive woman. I dust off my hands and climb back into my car, blasting Cee Lo Green's 'Forget you', as I drive away.

He's gone to her and I really don't care. They're welcome to each other. My thoughts drift as I drive and snippets of the past three wasted years come to mind. No, I mustn't over think this; I was loving, loyal and happy. I will not let his selfishness take that away from me. I'm angry, sure, but he wasn't the world to me, I know that now. I have let go of 'us' too easily to claim I'm in that much pain.

I'm just pissed off that I devoted so long to someone who, in the end, I'm not even that sad about losing… and his punishment for his indiscretion is that he has nowhere to go but to her.

This makes me smirk, I doubt it's what he wants, but he has made his bed, now he has to lie in it. She's not that bad I suppose, as long as he doesn't mess up the towels in her bathroom, or light her just-for-display candles, or change the order of the cushions on her sofa. I'm sure she's no idea she has just taken on the houseguest from hell. God, I almost feel sorry for her. Well, almost.

Not for the first time this week, I wonder how the hell this even happened. I never saw it coming and not in a dense 'over trusting my man who is too wonderful' sort of way. Just in a 'him and her REALLY?' sort of way. He might scrub up well, all suited and booted for work. He holds down a respectable job, always smells nice, but, on the inside and sometimes at home the outside, he's, well... a Neanderthal. I would find my kitchen scissors on the edge of the bathroom sink and learn that they were misused for side-burn trimming or toenail clipping. The ensuing lecture would always fall on deaf ears. Not exactly the respectful gentleman I imagine she's looking for. He's a rugged alpha male. She's a fragile, wide-eyed, Bambi of a girl. Gorgeous, but a closet basket case. He'll find that out in time. They are, at best, unsuited.... Or maybe they are each exactly what the other one needs. Who am I to say? I clearly wasn't enough for him, perhaps she will be. It doesn't matter now. They no longer exist.

I'm grateful I saw it with my own eyes though.

I'd been down in the bar, wondering if he'd made it home from his meeting. If he had, he hadn't shown his face, so I planned to go and drag him down for something to eat and maybe a game of pool. He'd been working so hard I was worried. A lot had changed at work and no one's job was secure. He couldn't switch off when he got home, that was why he'd stopped coming down in the evenings. I got it, but I thought I would try and convince him just this once. Maybe we could... well, I'm sure Max won't miss me for half an hour or so...

"Mark, are you home?" I called as I came through the door, but I didn't even finish the sentence before I saw them, through the doorway, in MY bedroom. They can't have been at it long because they were still standing. He was removing her top slowly and kissing her neck. She yelped when she saw me, and when he spun round his flies were undone and his face was a picture. Weirdly, I almost laughed! I mean, Mark and Sarah, together? The concept was funny...well, if you ignore the betrayal.

He leapt away from her, shouting insincere, garbled apologies. Giving Sarah her due, she said nothing; I mean what can you say? She quietly covered herself and stood transfixed while he made a total idiot of himself. He got right up in my face, he was all "Babe I'm sorry" and "She means nothing to me" and "I love you." It was pathetic to watch. I'm sure she was flattered!

I stood, mute, wincing while he tried to touch my face and bring me back to him, holding me, begging for forgiveness. By the time I found the words I had misplaced in my brain, he was sitting on the corner of the bed with his head in his hands. Exhausted from the little scene he'd made.

"Have you finished?" I whispered, unsure if my voice would let me down. He looked up at me, bereft. "Get the fuck out," I said calmly and I really meant it. It was such an easy decision. Seeing him with her, with anyone, betraying my trust. Doing what my dad did. It was over, easy.

"No, don't do this Liv," he begged. He was clutching at straws though. He knew I would be unsentimental about it if he cheated. It was cut and dry for me. He knew I would never back down.

It didn't stop you though did it? Dickhead!

I shook my head and without raising my voice or getting emotional, I simply reminded him, "No second chances, not with this shit, you knew that. Now get out."

He drew in a deep breath and got to his feet. I stepped away just in case he had any ideas about touching me. I watched passively as he tucked in his shirt and did up his trousers. Pushing thoughts of how they came to be open out of my head.

I'm glad I arrived when I did. Any earlier and they might have got away with it. Any later and I would have a mental image I'm not sure I could live with. I wonder if I interrupted the first time? Or was it regular sex? Did I want to know? Would it help? No. I didn't need the details.

As he picked up his tie and jacket, I couldn't stop myself.

"How many times?" my mouth managed before my brain could shut it down.

"Liv," he whispered. I didn't want to know anymore and I couldn't trust myself not to ask. Waving my hand to stop him answering, I said, "I'm going back to work, be gone when I get home."

I turned to go and Sarah flinched, I'd almost forgotten she was there.

Why did she jump, maybe she thought I was going to hit her? I always had a nagging doubt that she was too prissy to be my friend. Maybe that's why he likes her; maybe that's what he wants. She is all sweet and feminine, vulnerable, not like me. Maybe I'm not his type at all.... Well, I don't have to worry about that now. For a start, she's no longer my friend and he's her problem now, if she will have him after that sickening display.

Back down in the bar, Max, my best friend, saw my blanched face and followed me into the kitchen.

"Hey, what happened?" he asked. He looked so concerned as he wrapped his arms around me that I broke into uncontrollable sobs. I could handle anything right then except Max's kindness. It was more shock than hurt, but in his caring embrace I really let go.

"Shhh, Liv. Tell me," he soothed.

"You were right about him," I wept.

He tried to pull away. "Where is he?" I pulled him back to me.

"Gone," I muttered meekly, I didn't want Max losing his cool. He can look after himself so I wasn't worried about that. But Mark isn't worth it. "Just leave it, please. I need you."

He held me until I was all cried out.

It's mid-morning when I go downstairs. My head is banging and I feel vaguely queasy, just how I deserve to feel after last night.

I know it was only four days ago that I caught Mark with her, but I'm moving on. I'll miss him; I'm not made of stone. He'd lived in my flat for couple of years. We were enjoying the 'now' but we really hadn't discussed the future. I've briefly analysed the part I may have played in our demise. I will admit to having no work/life separation, but I'm not taking responsibility for his wayward genitals and massive ego. If we had problems, there were a thousand other ways to address them. I'm hurt and furious, but this isn't a hopeless situation; it's a golden opportunity.

The overprotective dream team of Max and Connie, my aunt and self-assigned protector, are mollycoddling me. It's been exhausting. I'm trying to forge ahead and make the most of this phase of inspiration and they're trying to hold me down and force me to 'acknowledge my grief'. Grief?

Honestly. When I cleared out his stuff, they said I was being rash and not giving myself time. I've tried to explain to them that I feel good, clear headed and enthusiastic about my future. They think I'm bottling my feelings and suppressing my emotions. I literally can't win. I want to be up and they think I should be down. I'm going to have to ride it out; they both love me and think they're helping.

As for my behaviour last night…I'm trying to have some fun, I keep telling everyone. But in truth I am attempting to be promiscuous, something I am not. It's just not me. What I wanted to do after slinging Mark out on his ear was to loosen up and experience a little bit of life. I own a bar for goodness sake! I watch every day while people get drunk, flirt and then go home and have casual sex. Some of them don't even make it home; we have CCTV, we know!

But it's like I watch it through a window. For some reason, I've only ever managed to have non-casual sex. So I thought if I tried really hard to be not myself about it, I might just get laid… Well, I was wrong. Even if I fight all my natural instincts, I can't quite let go enough. What is my problem? I JUST WANT SEX! But the kind of sex that doesn't lead on to a relationship so that I can do it all again tomorrow. Is that really bad?

Max can see straight through my intentions and has lectured me about staying true to myself. I've told him, I've already had one more father than I need in my life, so butt out. But I'm going to have to admit soon that it's not really my style. Then he'll be all 'I told you so'. God, this is annoying, who would have thought I would turn out to be like this? I have attempted to defy convention every day of my adult life, but apparently not where sex is concerned.

The memory of last night is mortifying. But fortunately I went home alone, not my intention, but in all honesty a relief. I won't be admitting this to Max though; I won't give him the satisfaction. I try for nonchalant as I open the door that connects the stairs to my flat with the back of the diner. No one is around. Good. I ease myself into the booth at the back and open my laptop. I'll just sit here quietly and catch up on some bookwork. Hopefully Mr. Perfect won't notice me and I can avoid another lecture.

As I'm sifting through emails, a coffee slides across the table in front of me. I glance at the coffee and then guiltily up at Max who is wearing a look of disapproval.

"Thought you might need this," he says in a way that makes me feel about an inch tall.

"Okay," I sigh. "Can we just get this over with? I'm too hungover to deal with this right now."

"You'll need some breakfast too." He raises his eyebrows to silently convey the unspoken end to his sentence…to soak up all that alcohol.

Oh, this is going to be a long day.

Ten minutes later, he's back and I'm relieved to see a smile on his face as he slides in opposite me with two of our famous Grand Slam Breakfasts. It can't have been that bad last night if he's prepared to eat with me.

I drown my pancakes in maple syrup and dig in greedily. It's SO good; some days I love this place. We've worked so hard and I'm so proud of what we have achieved. The food is really great now that we have a good kitchen team. I managed to hire Jake, a bona fide American chef, last year and he has tweaked things to ensure authenticity. His pancakes are just a-maz-ing.

I glance at Max fondly, but he doesn't see. We eat in silence until Ali comes over with some juice. Apple juice for me and orange juice for Max. She knows I can't stand orange juice.

"Shall I get you another coffee?" she asks looking nervously back and forth between us, trying to assess the mood. Obviously news has travelled that I had a heavy night and Max is not amused, brilliant.

"Please Ali, and you'd better bring one for Mr. Grumpy Pants here too."

I turn to face Max and he shakes his head in amusement at me.

"So, how are you feeling this morning?" he finally says.

"Like I should. I'm sorry, I shouldn't have put you in that position, it won't happen again."

He takes my hand from across the table and gives it a squeeze.

"I just don't want you to be someone you are not," he frowns. "And I don't think it's a great idea to get so bombed in front of the staff." He shakes his head in disgust, although I can see the smile he is suppressing, playing on his lips. "Charlie had to carry you up to bed!"

"Don't laugh at me!" I pout, screwing up my napkin and hurling it at his head.

He ducks to the left and avoids the missile, laughing as he does.

"What? I'm just saying Charlie had to take your jeans off, he's traumatised!"

I wince at the memory. I was on a mission last night, trying to get the attention of this guy Will, who has been hanging around a lot recently. I know he's been flirting with me and I've been flirting back. I'm just not very good at the transition to the next bit. So, after too much Dutch courage, I think I made quite an exhibition of myself. There was dancing, I remember that, although I wish I didn't. I bumped into a table and knocked over some drinks. I think Max replaced them. He told me to go and get some fresh air.

Will followed me out into the garden and was more confident about taking the next step than me. He started kissing me. I remember thinking he was being a bit over the top, considering we were in public. But I reasoned that we saw this stuff all the time here and frankly, in my drunken state, I was quite pleased with myself.

Along with the customers in the garden, the doormen were treated to our little show and were in the awkward position of having to ask Max what to do. Ordinarily, in situations like this, they would allow things to go to a certain point and then they might ask the lovebirds to cool things down. They might even ask them to leave if they got out of hand. But as it was me, their boss, I don't think they knew how to handle it.

I shouldn't have put them or Max in that position. What I didn't stop to consider was that I'm the owner of this place and I owe it to my staff and myself to conduct myself in an appropriate manner. Something Max was quick to remind me once he had broken up our little tryst and hauled me into the privacy of the kitchen. He was pretty mad, but I was so drunk he wasn't getting anywhere. The bar was busy and he was needed, so he got Charlie to put me to bed. Poor Charlie! I'm mortified. I owe a few apologies.

"I'm really sorry, but can we please try and forget about it, it's mortifying."

"If only it were that easy for Charlie!" Max smirks as he wisely scurries away.

I sink my face into my hands and sigh. I'm never drinking again. All this hassle and I didn't even get lucky! Max comes back and I draw in a deep breath, rubbing my temples and lift my head for round two...and I'm looking straight into the hard disapproving eyes of Connie. Shit.

Connie is my great aunt, my maternal grandma's younger sister and since my grandma died long before I was born, she just naturally filled her role. When I was born and she came to see me in the hospital, Mum said it was like we were old friends, like I was born with a connection to her. That day, on her way home, Connie met her second husband, Jack. She couldn't believe her luck at finding such a lovely man out of the blue. She said I was her lucky charm. Connie and Jack married three months later and have been giddy with happiness ever since. It's still a little embarrassing sometimes to witness them together, but it keeps them young.

This morning, however, she looks stern. She flicks her eyebrows even higher and tilts her head before she starts.

"So, I hear we had an indulgent evening," she pauses, concern replacing disapproval. "What is this all about?"

"Connie, I just had a drink that's all. I admit I got a bit out of hand but it wasn't a real drama. Did he call you?" I glare at Max who is pretending to be busy behind the counter. I'll remember this.

"Sweetheart, I am worried about you. Is this because of Mark?"

Oh God, here we go, I'll be upstairs in my PJs, eating ice cream from the tub in five minutes if she has her way. I wish she could just accept that I'm not that sad about losing Mark, I'm just pissed off about what he did and how much of my time he wasted.

"Mark? No! I'm just enjoying myself."

"Darling, this isn't you. I...we, think you should talk about what's bothering you."

I shoot Max another look. Honestly, involving Connie is the lowest of the low. I don't need a pep talk, I need a good time! Why is this so difficult for people to accept?

Ah! This is so frustrating. I can talk to Connie about anything, but I can't admit to her that I'm trying to turn myself into more of a slut. Deep down, I know it is not right for me and if I can't convince myself, I won't be able to convince her. I do my best.

"I just want what everyone else seems to have. No strings fun. I guess I'm just missing the gene. I thought I could loosen up if I got a bit drunk, evidently it's a difficult balance."

"So this is about sex?"

"Well, yeah. I don't know how to have it without ending up in another relationship."

"Why don't you want another relationship?"

"Well for starters, I'm just out of one. Don't you think it would do me good to play the field for a while? I've never done that you know. I've gone from one long-term relationship to another. Four men…my whole life!" I raise my eyebrows. "I'm twenty-nine, people my age settle down, but I've always been settled down and look where it's got me. I want something else for a change. But I can't do it, is there something wrong with me?"

"No, of course there isn't, you're just an old romantic. You always need the happy ending. You can't pretend that you would be happy with one night stand after one night stand. You need to be invested in someone to get that far. I respect that about you, you should too."

"Huh! 'The happy ending' I never get it though, do I?" I scoff.

"You will, one day. But for now just relax, you can't force happiness and besides, from what I hear, you weren't at your most alluring last night, even if Prince Charming had come your way. Be yourself, you'll find someone wonderful. Anyway, there's no hurry and it's never too late, just look at me."

"But I really wanted to have some, you know, new experiences," I cringe, it turns out this is a little awkward to talk about with Connie.

"Well then, you'll just have to get yourself one of those friends with benefits." She winks and beams at me.

"CONNIE! What do you know about that?" Sometimes I really can't believe her; she is so cool, for almost seventy. But really, there are some conversations I should have with someone my own age.

"I know plenty. You kids think you wrote the book, honestly!"

She really is amazing. She never disapproves of younger generations, something older people so often do. She always admires new ideas and innovations; she enjoys new music, films and books. She is just cool.

"Do you have time to help me with something?"

"Anything," I smile. The lecture is over, for now.

"Well I want you to show me how to do this Facebook thingy."

Connie on Facebook, I shake my head with amusement.

"Come on then," and I shift over so that she can join me on my side of the booth. This should be fun!

An hour later, I'm feeling a bit more human. We've had such a laugh setting Connie up on Facebook and adding photos. She's now fully tagged in the photos on the Lady Luck's page. She has six friends and is awaiting responses from eighteen others. As I think we are wrapping up, she asks again, "So if I want to find someone, I just type their name up here and if they are on Facebook, they will be in the list?"

"Yes, that's right, who do you want to find? I'll help you."

"No one right now, but I want to know how in case I think of someone later. It won't do to only have six friends!" She frowns for a second. "Can you show me how to do that private message thing again?"

I smile lovingly and roll my eyes as I launch into the whole process again. This will take a while to stick, I know. But for Connie, I have all the time in the world.

I wander into the kitchen. I really should do something productive, so I set up to make some rhubarb syrup. This is the thing I am most proud of about Lady Luck's, our sodas. We make from scratch over twenty-five fruit-flavoured syrups along with some herb and spice flavours and serve them in any combination mixed with seltzer from traditional swan-necked soda pumps. The official name for a person who performs this task is a

Jerk. We have embraced this term at Lady Luck's and while every other so/so place in town has baristas or barmen, we're proud to be Jerks.

Then there are our milkshakes and malts, the menu is huge and everything is scratch made. I'm so passionate about it. I cannot stress how fantastic our team is. My team. I say 'our' because we're a family, but in reality it is mine, I'm blown away by that sometimes. I employ twenty-three people…okay, that scares me! But I've had so much great help and advice it has seemed reasonably easy. I no longer think of it as something that was handed to me on a plate. What I've now is a far cry from what Connie gave me; I genuinely feel that the success is deserved.

Five years ago, when I took over from Connie, I was able to finance the basic renovations. Everything else has been achieved over time. We took the whole place back to brick and then left some of it exposed. We completely transformed the place from Connie's – a quaint but very successful Surrey teashop – into Lady Luck's, an authentic American Diner. It has an industrial feel; a lot of the furniture is reclaimed. The walls are littered with vintage signs and Americana. It's a work in progress, but the fact that it evolves rather than having a complete and polished appearance makes it really homely.

I don't think it's big headed to say I've really made a success of it. Lady Luck's is buzzing; it's a popular place. It is everything I dreamed it would be. Great food and traditional beverages, done with a modern twist. Then, last year, I took it a step further when the Italian restaurant next door closed down. I took over the lease and opened a bar. My dream come true.

Max manages the bar for me; he's the best friend a girl could have. We were on the same course at uni and hit it off instantly, he's so much fun. I really fancied him at first, but then he told me he was gay so I got over it. He moved in with me not long into the first term. Connie had let me move into the empty flat upstairs and I was really grateful for the company. Having my own place seemed exciting, but it was a bit overwhelming and I was lonely. He helped with the bills and we looked after each other, grew up together. He still looks after me, although these days he lives with his husband, Charlie.

He was the perfect flat mate; I even got Connie to give him a job. Since we graduated, Max and I have never been apart. He's my right-hand man. He helped me get the diner off the ground, then the bar and I couldn't be without him. We are a great team, even if he can be a bit bossy and judgemental sometimes. He's helped me through the worst times and we have shared all the best times too. I love him.

Connie squeezes my shoulder as she comes to get her cupcakes out of the oven. She does know she doesn't work here anymore – I don't pay her. I pay an Executive Chef, a Sous Chef and five Line Cooks, one of whom has sole responsibility for desserts. But Connie's baking is second to none, so she remains the Pastry Chef at this address in an unofficial capacity. She has been on bloody Facebook on and off for two hours! I'm surprised she can tear herself away. She seems cheerful today, a bit too cheerful; maybe it's the spring air. I hope so, after such a depressing winter I really want to get our outside area looking fabulous.

Last year, when I took over the bar, we acquired a disused alleyway in between the old Italian and the diner. It was blocked off at the front by an old rusty gate and was just used as a dumping ground for broken furniture. It is quite wide as alleyways go, about twelve feet. At the bottom it opens out onto the delivery yard at the back. Max had the idea of turning it into a garden of sorts and in the end this saved our almost doomed application to the council. Apparently there was an issue with smokers causing noise when standing outside bars, so the fact that we had an enclosed area went in our favour and we were approved. We've closed off the front entrance to the bar and opened the front of the alley up. Now you have to turn down the alley, past the doormen to get into the bar. This keeps any trouble off the street, not that we have any. But it means the neighbours actually like us, a rarity I'm sure.

We've put some chairs and tables down one side and sectioned off some of the yard at the end to extend it a bit. Right now, it's a perfectly acceptable smoking area, but I have plans to make it a big draw to the bar over the summer…outdoor furniture, lighting, heaters, the lot. It might even be possible to connect the diner with the bar, we'll see. For now, we're using the kitchen in the bar for prep and bar snacks and the diner kitchen for meals. Food ordered in the bar is carried across at the moment, under a covered walkway, but I would love to end up with one big kitchen. There's so much to do.

My hangover, briefly sent packing by a Grand Slam Breakfast is getting its second wind and, as I am working tonight, I decide to go and put my head down for a bit. I take my freshly jerked soda, mango, my favourite, punch the code into the keypad and amble up the stairs to my flat. I really need to clean. Since Mark went, I've done nothing. I'm not miserable about being here on my own; I'm just in a bit of limbo about what to do next.

I stick Cocktail in the DVD player and flop down on the sofa. Films like this are just background noise to me now; I don't have to watch them to enjoy them. But they bring me comfort and I love them. I grab my laptop and open Facebook. I need to tell our followers that we'll be having a rib-eating contest next weekend. They love all that stuff. I'm just checking the photos from last night (in case there are any embarrassing ones of me) when I get a notification.

You have 1 new message from Danny Morgan.

Two.

That seems manageable.

Liv.

I blink at the screen for a minute. I have a new message...from Danny Morgan.

I let his name sink in...what the hell? A visit from the ghost of relationships past is not what I was expecting today.

Max had a number of short-lived 'relationships' on his path to self-discovery. Quite a large number actually. But not me. No, I've always found myself in 'proper' relationships. I've had four long-term relationships in the last fourteen years. I had been with Mark for four years, four nice but unremarkable years. Which is probably what I needed after Ryan. Jesus, he was a handful! That lasted almost a whole turbulent year and ended abruptly when Max caught him stealing the takings. I suppose I was preoccupied with starting the business and didn't notice him taking advantage of me. He was a total loser.

Before my Ryan disaster, I'd been dating Ed for a few years. We never lived together but it was quite serious. I met Ed at uni, he wasn't on my course but we all hung out together. He was in a band. I loved that about him. He seemed a bit dangerous, but he wasn't. Inevitably though I got more serious at about the same time that he decided it should just be fun. He was gigging further afield and clearly enjoying himself too much. It ended badly with me heartbroken. But we were young, it's how it goes. My vulnerable state after that explains why I fell for Ryan.

Ed wasn't my first though. Danny was my first.

I'm too stunned to know what to think. After twelve years, how am I supposed to react? I place the laptop to one side and sip my soda vacantly. I realise after a minute that I could actually read the message. I was so shocked by the existence of the message, it hadn't occurred to me to view its contents. I grab the laptop back and hover over the track pad. Wait, why do I feel so shaken by this? Do I want to know what he wants? Can I handle it? I just don't know. I spent so long pretending it was okay that he had gone, I believe it. Can I invite those feelings back in?

Okay, I'm getting a bit ahead of myself, he's just someone from my past, reconnecting via Facebook, from across the Atlantic. I'm probably safe from emotional turmoil if I open the message.

From: Danny Morgan   23rd March 2012

Hey! I was reminded of you today. How is life?
Add me if you feel like chatting to an old friend.

Danny x

Right…Okay… So, that seems manageable, chatting to an old friend…so that's how he sees us? Ignoring the disappointment his words make me feel, I think carefully. I know he meant more to me than I meant to him, way more. Should I risk stirring up my feelings now?

We were a couple at school, from the last year of our GCSEs and through A-levels, but it was much more than that. Danny moved here from America when we were six and moved in a couple of doors down from us. His mum, sorry 'mom', was a computer genius and was sent by her company to establish an office in the UK, so they could bring some new technology to the British market. They were able to make the move easily because his dad was British and was happy to bring his family back to his hometown. His mum's job was in London, so she commuted. His dad was an accountant and worked from home. Danny was an only child and he and his dad were really close.

At school, Mrs. MacWilliam put him in my group to help him settle in, as we were neighbours. I was in awe of the fact that he was American and I decided right then that he was my bestest friend. He really had no choice, but I think he was happy to follow along. Within no time at all we were inseparable. When my dad left, we moved to a smaller house a few roads streets away. It didn't make any difference; we still rode our bikes in my old road and did everything together.

We spent hours on end watching films. Hilarious eighties comedies, actions and, of course, romances. The film obsession was mine but Danny didn't mind indulging me. I was like a walking encyclopaedia. I could quote any film, I memorised every line. I think I watched them as a form of escape. Don't get me wrong, my family life wasn't awful, but it wasn't always easy either. I was ten when my dad left.

It's a tale as old as time – boy meets girl, boy knocks girl up, boy gets a bit fed up of girl, boy hands over control of his brain to his genitals – fuck everyone else.

Frankly, I'm ashamed my life is such a cliché. I'm a child from a broken home.

After my dad left, things were bad for a while. Mum was a mess and Grace started acting up. I was pretty angry about the whole thing, but what could anyone do? I used to watch films to switch off for a couple of hours and it became a habit. I could watch my favourites every day, hundreds of times over. I realise this probably wasn't healthy, but I wasn't crying all the time like Mum or throwing tantrums like Grace, I was just escaping. Harmless really. If we weren't at Connie's we were lost in movies. Danny never minded.

In the aftermath of a contentious divorce, my mum managed a moment of clarity and found herself a wonderful man. He's been a great dad, who loves my sister and me as if we were his own flesh and blood. We fight like father and daughter, so I know it's real. He's made us all happy again.

Dad continued to make a mess of things. Eventually, he and wife number three moved to Australia when I finished my GCSEs. They wanted to give her two little darlings a better life…lucky for them! Danny was my constant through all of that. Sadly, the pressure to give the perfect life to Ms. Unrealistic Expectations and her little bloodsuckers took its toll on Dad. Four years ago, he suffered a massive heart attack at work. He's buried in Australia. Grace and I weren't even told until after the funeral. I should have been angry with her for that, which of course I was. But I was mainly angry with him. I was bitterly disappointed with him and his weakness. If just once in his life he could have said no to a woman, he might still be alive, part of a family and loved. This all happened just before I met Mark. I missed Danny a lot through that time, even though I tried not to admit it. When we were together things were so easy and, despite years apart, at that time in my life, I'd never needed him more.

We never argued. In fact we laughed a lot. Over the years, our to-the-exclusion-of-all-others friendship very slowly became more. We held hands, hugged, and communicated in that barely audible way you do when you know each other inside out. In our bubble, we fell in love with each other.

I remember when we kissed for the first time. We were fifteen. I was making him watch Dirty Dancing for the 689th time, living it completely like I always did and I realised he was smirking at me. We had got some jam doughnuts from Connie's on the way home and had already had our usual jam or jelly debate. He calls it jelly, I call it jam. He always said I was wrong, which is ridiculous, because as I kept telling him, it's our language and if we say it's jam, then it's JAM. If they chose to borrow our language and then change it in places, they can't expect us to take it seriously. Anyway, I had some <u>jam</u> on my chin. He laughed at me then, when he finished rubbing it off, he leaned in and kissed me.

Things developed from there, the usual teenage stuff, nothing heavy. Except it was heavy because for so much of our lives we had given our friendship almost exclusively to each other and now we were giving each other all of these new first experiences. It meant so much. I really was in love with him.

When we went up to sixth form, the atmosphere among our peers subtly changed. Hormones I guess. Everyone seemed intently focused on losing their virginity – those who hadn't already. I think it was assumed that we had, I don't know, but there was undeniable pressure on everyone. I hated it.

Despite the external forces, I never felt pressure from him. We were always on the same page. Happy with how we were with each other. But the pressure was always there.

We built towards it slowly, but we both knew it was coming and that it would change everything. Strangely, I think we both felt it would ruin things. But we had come so far and experienced everything in life together. How could we not see it through?

Looking back, and comparing that innocent love to my relationships since, it still feels like the only real love I've ever experienced. I know you're supposed to learn and develop those feelings with each new experience but it has always felt like I gave him all my love then and he took some of it with him when he went away.

The news that Danny was leaving rocked everything. His parents sprang the news on him one day after school. Danny's mum had exceeded all expectations during her time in the UK and now she had been offered an amazing opportunity with her company to head up the new office in LA. They were taking it. They would leave when Danny's A-levels were finished. They wanted him to start looking at West Coast colleges.

We were both in shock. I tried to be positive about it. I was quite envious really. But we both knew it would be the end of us. It was so hard to comprehend, so in a way we ignored it and carried on. It was in this last, unravelling year of our relationship that we finally had sex. It was loving and tender, though tinged with sadness. We only did it a few times. We had lived without it before then and it seemed unnecessary to make it essential to our relationship at that point.

Danny embraced his new future. It was bright, just like him. He got accepted onto the Computer Science Undergraduate Program at UCLA. I was so happy for him, but then it would mean the end of us. Secretly, I looked into colleges in LA. I had this crazy plan that I could go with him and then we could be together. But Danny made no suggestion of keeping our relationship going and, in the end, I let go of the idea. I hoped he might at least want to try and make it work long distance, but he never suggested it. He wasn't willing to fight for us. Why would he when he had such wonderful opportunities to focus on? We were so young and a huge step like that would mean getting tied down at eighteen. I can see why he didn't want it. Looking back, I'm sure it was for the best, but it didn't feel like it at the time.

We carried on with the business of our final year, but things weren't the same. We didn't physically drift apart, we were stuck like magnets that only the Atlantic Ocean could separate. But we did sort of start to let each other go. I was accepted at The Surrey Institute of Art and Design. In any other circumstances, I would have been over the moon, but it was all so difficult to come to terms with. It was a really weird time. Our emotions were fractured. Every exciting piece of news had a negative shadow.

I can't remember the details of him leaving, they're too painful. I tried to make him think I would be okay and that he would be too. He seemed upset, I think, it was hard to tell what he was feeling when I couldn't even feel myself. I knew he wanted to go and I didn't want him to worry about how I would cope, so I worked hard to make him believe it was time for us to go our separate ways, that it was natural and would be best for us in the long run. I have no idea if I convinced him, I was numb. I couldn't tell if my feelings were real or just for show. I'd lost him and I'd tried to make him believe it was for the best. It was sickening.

The only thing I was certain of, was he didn't love me like I loved him and I had to try and move on. When I started at college that September, I was feeling slightly better. Danny had called a few times, but it was too hard. I tried to sound like I wasn't suffering at all. I suppose I was convincing. In the end he stopped calling and I was relieved. I had by default, not choice, begun to move on and his calls dragged me back. The whole thing was a living hell, but I've come a long way since then. I'm just floored to hear from him after all this time.

If he sees us as old friends I suppose I can live with it and if he wants to chat, I can do that surely? Nothing else could come of it anyway.

I click on his profile. It's only his basic info as I am not his friend, yet. I look to see if his photos are public, he has a few profile pictures that are, but no albums. I go through the profile pictures: a road sign, a can of beer, a dog, some sort of sculpture and then him.

Danny. Okay. Wow!

He's attractive, he always was, but now he's a man, tanned, and his brown hair is lighter from the California sun. The eyes are the same and he looks really happy, like he is fond of whoever took this photo. I scroll through his friends, no girls with the surname Morgan. Do any of the girls look like they might be his girlfriend? This is ridiculous, what am I doing?

I go back to the profile. The cover photo is of the beach, maybe where he lives? His date of birth, which of course I know. That's it. That is all I get unless I take the next step. I can't think straight.

On my TV, Tom Cruise drops all of his books and yells, "I'm doing the best I can. Okay?" and I allow the escape in.

I don't know how much time passes, but Tom Cruise turns to Elizabeth Shue as he is walking out of her father's apartment and says "and as for the way I feel about you, well I guess we'll never know". The sexiest line he's ever spoken. I've sat here for maybe an hour, I don't know. But as I come back from my Tom Cruise interlude, I'm aware that I still have a decision to make. I'll have a shower…that might help.

When I emerge, I feel much better. I'm still bemused but I'm resolved to add him and find out what he wants. I change into jeans and a Lady Luck's t-shirt. This one is black, fitted and shows our logo, which Max designed. I pull on my new Converse. I love them! They're leopard-print leather with studs up the back and around the laces, the best Converse I've ever had and I've had 'em all. I don't get excited about heels like most girls, but shoes like this, oh yeah!

Refreshed, I head downstairs. I need to grab a bite to eat before I start my shift and I need to bounce this off Max.

"Well, add him then!" Max is wide-eyed and excited. "I mean, how can you not? He was your first love, he didn't do anything to hurt you…well you know, apart from leaving…and now he wants to talk to you. You have to do this. Gimmie your phone!" He lunges towards my back pocket where he knows full well my iPhone is hiding.

"Hey! I wanted your opinion, not a wrestle." I defensively slap him away.

"Well my opinion is, do it, do it now!" God, he's like a hyper puppy.

"Okay, okay, I'll add him and see what he has to say." I try to walk away.

He steps across the doorway. "Nope! NOW! If you think you're walking away from this Liv, you're out of your mind." He folds his arms and gives me his best stern face.

"Alright, but I don't know what to say to him." Where do I even start?

"Just add him, put your phone away and see if he has anything to say."

"I can't just do that Max. It's been twelve years; I should say something to him. But I have no idea where to begin."

"Okay, well he says he was reminded of you today, ask him why. Here." He snatches my phone out of my pocket and holds it too high for me to reach. Damn it, I'm short!

He finds the message and begins typing a response. "MAX!" I yell, trying to climb him.

"I'll let you read it before I send it," he says as if he's speaking to a child. "There." Pleased with himself, he hands me back the phone.

From: Olivia Harper   23rd March 2012

Hey yourself! Reminded of me how?
I am reminded of you often.
Liv x

"Max! I can't say that, he might be married for God's sake!"

The idea of Danny being married briefly slices me in two. I recover quickly. I have thought of this scenario before, although then he was almost a mythical creature. Right now, via Facebook, he is alive and well and wants to 'chat'.

"He's not married," Max snorts.

"Well okay, maybe, but he just wants to chat. I can't say I think of him often, he'll think I'm a crazy person."

I ponder my choices whilst staring into the middle distance. Then, on impulse, I quickly delete the bit about thinking of him often and send the amended message before I can change my mind. Then I click on his name and hit + Add Friend. Fuck, I feel sick. I look up at Max, struck mute with anxiety.

"What did you do?" he asks, sensing my rash behaviour. I silently hand him the phone.

From: Olivia Harper						23rd March 2012

Hey yourself! Reminded of me how?

Liv x

I think I need to lie down again!

"Good girl!" He's almost giddy. "I can't wait to see what he has to say, this is brilliant."

"What makes you think I'll tell you? You're nothing but trouble. Look at what you've made me do already. This is a disaster!"

"Disaster, what are you talking about? He might still be in love with you, I might have helped."

"You have a vivid imagination Max, that was all over a long time ago. If he were in love with me he wouldn't have waited twelve years to tell me. Anyway, I think we are getting ahead of ourselves a little here." I have to end this conversation before I start to entertain the possibilities.

It is in the past. I'm over it. A relationship is not what I want right now. Even if it were a possibility. I really can't go back there again. Immediately I start to regret responding. Thankfully, it's time to start work, I put my phone on silent and stomp into the bar.

Mid-shift, the bar is packed. It's so busy in fact that we have stopped letting people in for now. The distraction is welcome. I realise that I haven't thought about Danny for a few hours. Oh God! Maybe he's responded! Suddenly my phone is burning a hole in my back pocket. I should have left it upstairs. Now I am fighting the urge to sneak a peek. I can't at the moment as it's too busy, but it's eating me up.

"Guinness is off," shouts Alex, one of the bar staff.

"I'll do it," I yell.

As I'm fumbling with the hose, I curse. I hate this job, it's what I pay the guys for. I only came out here to look at my phone, but my conscience makes me do the job at hand first.

There, I return to the bar and give Alex the thumbs up and then signal five fingers, telling him I'm taking a short break. He nods.

Out in the garden, I shiver, but the cool air feels great. I sit on the chair by the back door and finally take out my phone.

Danny Morgan has accepted your friend request.

You have 1 new message from Danny Morgan.

Oh crap!

The dread creeps in. I was excited to see his name, thrilled that he wanted to contact me. But the reality of the situation is that I've never loved anyone liked I loved him. No one has ever even come close. I made a good show of getting over him. But I know deep down, I never actually did.

I buried this whole situation years ago and outside of a relevant anecdote or two I've never spoken of it again. Max always suspected I was toughing it out, but I would tell him he was stirring and change the subject, and eventually it went away. Now it's back in all of its horrifying glory and I am going to have to deal with it. What does he want? I didn't realise I was still so affected by the thought of him and the realisation is unwelcome.

Trying not to hold any of this against him, I open the message.

From: Danny Morgan   23rd March 2012

Well hello stranger! I've never searched for you on here. I wasn't even sure it was you…Have you pierced your face??

Danny x

Shit! While I've been working the last few hours, I've given him unfettered access to my profile. It didn't even occur to me, what has he seen? I should have gone through it before I added him. Mind you, I don't have too much on there. I hardly use Facebook for me; I mainly use Lady Luck's profile. It says on my profile where I work, so if he was so inclined, he could learn more about me, through our open page. But my profile is quite minimal. Still, I am at a serious disadvantage now. Obviously, he is going to have had a good poke around everything he's had access to and I can't do the same. It's Friday night and I expect to be here until at least 2am. I glance at my watch, ugh! It's 10.20pm. This is going to be a long night. I must get back to the bar. I hit reply.

From: Olivia Harper   23rd March 2012

Yes it's me…and yes it's pierced…are you judging me? You have an unfair advantage, I'm at work. No more Facebook stalking until I can snoop around your profile!!!

Liv x

I re-read the message; I try to sound playful not panicked. Whether I succeeded is difficult to say. But I can't dwell on it, I have to work. I hit send and return to reality.

We stay busy until closing, mercifully. So the uncertainty I feel has no time to weigh heavy on my shoulders. But now the doors are closed and I'm a woman possessed. I whip the team into a frenzy, cleaning down for tomorrow. I need to get upstairs and not to sleep. I'm wired from the anxiety and too much caffeine, and I'm not working tomorrow. I'm going to spend the night reacquainting myself with my first love. I know from skype-ing Grace that when I finish a late one, it is evening in LA, so he might be free to respond.

Although I can hardly allow the thought, I'm thrilled at the prospect. What am I doing? This is not going to be good for me I just know it. But I'm committed now. I bound up the stairs in spite of the time and the eight-hour shift I've just pulled. Adrenaline pumping, I put my coffee down on the table and haul my laptop into my lap.

You have 1 new message from Danny Morgan.

From: Danny Morgan   23rd March 2012

If you say so ;-)

Danny x

Right, the gloves are off now, let the stalking commence! Clicking on his name, I'm rewarded with his full profile.

He works at Morgan Software, his own company. I click on the company name link and the browser takes me to his website. It's all pretty slick and I've no idea what it is he does exactly, but it looks like he's an Independent Software Developer undertaking a range of projects for some big companies. Some I know well and others just by name, but it's an impressive client list.

In the 'About Us' section, there's a short bio answering some of my questions. The headshot he uses is the same as his Facebook profile picture. In this context, his smile looks less like one of fondness and more like one solicited by a photographer. The fact that this is still the only photo I can see tells me that he doesn't fancy himself. I've no idea why, he's gorgeous.

Danny is the owner and there's no mention of other staff, it's a small operation started in 2006. Based in Santa Monica, they offer a baffling array of 'Bespoke Solutions' to problems I never knew existed. Then I am lost in tech spiel, this isn't going to tell me anything about him except that he's way smarter than me, so I navigate back to Facebook.

I look at the first few comments, surprisingly nothing that recent, obviously not addicted to social networking then? A girl called Brooke catches my eye, saying 'It was great to see you last night', but he didn't reply and that was over two months ago. He rarely posts status updates. Right, photos now...

Apart from the half dozen or so profile pictures I have already seen, there are a couple of albums of trips he has taken. One of which was to Vegas, the other a beach trip. The group of friends look roughly the same on both trips, about eight by the looks of it, half girls, half boys. One pretty blonde girl seems to always be near him. I immediately feel a pang of irrational jealousy. He is not mine, I remind myself.

Looking at the only other album, 'Jen and Scott's Wedding', I'm overcome with relief to find that the pretty blonde is Jen! This is so messed up. I've survived the last twelve years by hardly allowing him to cross my mind. Now here I am green with envy about a girl called Jen sitting too near to a man I have no claim over. I need to pull myself together.

His profile gives little away, probably much like my own. Neither of us were ever socialites, but I'm reasonably sure that he's not in a relationship. But why is he contacting me? Ugh! I sink back into the sofa and cover my eyes with my arm. I glance at the clock, 3.10am. What time is it in LA? My head is swimming and I can't even remember if they are ahead or behind. I search time differences on the internet and quickly find out that LA is eight hours behind the UK, so it's 7.10pm yesterday there. I decide to message him.

From: Olivia Harper   24th March 2012

Okay, so I've finished snooping. You don't give much away do you? I have to admit, I don't know what to say to you...How is life?

Liv x

Someone has to get this conversation started. I hit send.

I pour the remains of my coffee in the sink, rinse the cup and add it to the growing pile of diner crockery that must be returned at some point. In spite of the caffeine, I'm beginning to feel overcome with tiredness. I drag myself to the bathroom. While I'm brushing my teeth I hear the laptop 'bing', signalling a message. I hurriedly finish and change. Collecting my phone, laptop and a glass of water, I head to bed.

I get comfy under the covers and nervously reopen Facebook. This message has appeared in Chat, as we are both online. The thought of this live connection between us makes my stomach lurch. I'm about to talk to him, okay not hear his voice, but in real time…

Danny
I don't really know what to say to you either. This is weirder than I thought it would be…Life is great! I'm living in Santa Monica, near the beach. I work from home (computer stuff – yawn!) but it leaves me free to do whatever I like, mostly. My parents live nearby; they're still the same. There's nothing else to tell really. What about you? You give nothing away either. Apart from the facial piercings! I wasn't expecting that! What is happening in your life?

Olivia
There must be more to tell… My life is good. I'm still here, I never left. I'm a business owner. I have the diner of my dreams, which is doing really well. It's Connie's old teashop! I took it over when she retired and she and Jack helped me get it off the ground. I live upstairs, have done since my first term at college. Mum and Dave moved to Brighton with Dave's job and I didn't want to go. Connie let me have the place and I have never left. They've stayed in Brighton, it's lovely; it's like I've a holiday home. Not that I get any time off. It's pretty full-on running your own business. Grace lives in LA too, Venice. You should look her up!

Danny
Way to go you! I always knew you'd do it. I did look at where you worked while I was 'Facebook stalking', but I didn't realise you own the

place. Is it really Connie's? I wouldn't have recognised the place, it looks huge, way bigger than I remember. It's really amazing. I'd love to come and see it one day. You must be so proud of yourself. I might pass on Grace though, is she still a nightmare?

Ignoring his comment about seeing the bar one day, I press on, he was just being polite.

Olivia
Haha! No, she's settled right down. She married Andy. Do you remember him? They met at drama school. They have both done some TV acting in the UK, but Andy is doing really well. He was cast in a clichéd Brit mob film and his career took off. They live in LA now and while he has a steady stream of work, Grace has become a stay at home 'mom'. Baby No.2 is on the way. The diner has expanded; I have a bar too, next door, that's why it looks bigger.

Danny
Wow! Quite the entrepreneur! It looks as though you're busy, seriously, well done. So Grace is a mom? That is a turnaround! I remember Andy; I think he has been in a couple of movies I've seen. I was convinced I recognised him, but I couldn't think where from.

Olivia
That's him. Yes, she's a different person…I'm very much the same.

Danny
Except the piercings!

Olivia
You aren't going to drop this are you? Yes, five piercings!

Danny
FIVE???

Olivia
Lip, nose, ears…and some tattoos.

Minutes pass…I can't stand this! He's still online, why isn't he talking to me? He's obviously horrified.

Olivia
Have I frightened you away?

Danny
No, I was just looking at the pictures of you from your work page, trying to get a look at this rebel version of a girl I once knew!

Olivia
AND?

Why? WHY would I ask that?

Danny
Well she's quite…hot actually!

WHAT? Is he flirting with me? This is surreal. Time ticks by, I don't know what to say…

Danny
Are you still there?

Olivia
Yes.

Danny
The guy in the pictures, is he your boyfriend?
Olivia
Which guy?

Danny
The one who's always wearing a hat?

Olivia
Best friend.

Danny
But there is a boyfriend?

   I blow out a deep breath.

Olivia
Nope. What about you, are you not settled down?

Danny
Never found the right girl.

   Wow, I don't know whether to take that personally or not. This is going down a path that is too deep for almost 4am. I need to go to sleep; suddenly it is all too much.

Olivia
It's almost 4am here…I need to sleep!

Danny
Shit! Sorry, you should have said.
Olivia
I'd only just finished my shift, it's fine. But now I really need to sleep.

Danny
Maybe we could do this again?

Olivia

Sure. It was great to hear from you. Night x
Retreat! Retreat!

Danny
Night x

 I shut down my laptop and breathe a sigh of relief. I think that went okay. I think he flirted with me. That is not good. I've spent years trying to get past losing him, I can't let him reignite it all again. I must stay strong; he's too far away and too removed for it to come to anything. We can only be friends. I turn over and settle into my pillow. That's decided then, friends.

Three.

Many cats.

Liv.

I feel the weight of someone climbing onto my bed, I snap awake in a daze and then realise it's Max. Of course it's Max.

"Wakey, wakey!" he says in a singsong voice. "I've come for the gossip."

"Go away," I manage to croak as I disappear further under the covers.

"I have coffee," he offers, in an attempt to bribe me out of my cocoon.

"What time is it?"

"Gone eleven."

"Shit, I was up 'til four." In truth, I'm amazed I managed to sleep after our little Facebook chat, but I just blacked out and I feel surprisingly rested. It's Saturday and, as always, I'm supposed to be having brunch with Max and Charlie, so I haul myself up to sitting. "Alright, I'm up."

"So?" I can't help but smile when I see the excitement on his face, like a small child, but I'm not awake enough for an interrogation.

"What?" I tease.

"Don't try that, what did he say?"

"I don't know what you are talking about." I hop out of bed and scoot into the bathroom before he can catch me. *Take that nosey*, I laugh to myself as I turn on the shower.

"Downstairs, twenty minutes! Or I'll send Charlie up to drag you down," Max yells through the door.

Oooh! Bossy! I step under the hot water; I have twenty minutes to get my head together.

The diner is busy when I emerge twenty-five minutes later. It's always busy on a Saturday morning. Max has his back to me but I wave at Charlie to call off the dogs. I move behind the counter, checking in with everybody as I go, and pour myself a drink. I put it to one side as a customer approaches. They want two takeaway coffees, I can handle that.

I go into the kitchen. Jake is hard at work, so I try not to get in his way.

"Oh, Liv! You scared the crap out of me!" he yelps as he steps back into me.

"Sorry! I just want to grab something to eat. I don't want to get under your feet."

"What can I make you?"

"No, I'll just grab a sandwich. I can do it, you're busy."

"It's no trouble, what would you like?" He smiles sweetly. I think he wants me to clear off. Ever since I hired him, I've been pretty much redundant in the kitchen, but that is why I took him on and I quite like it really. The rest of the place is running so much better now I can step back and see what needs to be done.

"Some of your amazing Huevos Rancheros then please." I grin and head out to the boys, fetching my drink on the way.

"Okay, let's hear it, he's driving me mad!" laughs Charlie as I slide in.

I don't want my uncertainty about the situation to cloud their judgement, so I hand over my phone and wait quietly while they each pour over it in turn. This takes ages.

They look at each other in an unspoken dialogue.

"Erm, do you care to share?" I ask, my voice sounding uneasy and frustrated in equal measure. More reading. My food arrives and I tuck in while I wait for the verdict.

Another knowing look, a nod and Charlie speaks first. "Well, he still has feelings for you," he says in a measured tone, obviously knowing how it will be received. Clearly they agree and Charlie has been nominated as the messenger as they think I won't shoot him as readily as I would Max.

Well, I'm not having this from either of them.

"Bollocks!"

"No, seriously. Can't you see it?" Charlie asks in disbelief. In reality, Max has wound him up to the point that he's beginning to believe the nonsense.

"Not really," I mutter shaking my head. I have another mouthful of my breakfast and chew in silence.

Max is still looking at my phone.

"What about you? Do you have anything to add?"

He holds up his hands in a 'hey-don't-have-a-go-at-me' gesture. "I'm saying nothing," he says, putting my phone on the table.

Tapping his fingers and going back to his club sandwich, he shakes his head. Then, between bites, it gets the better of him.

"But he clearly *is* still in love with you," he whispers, afraid of the fallout.

"Oh God! You two need to get a grip," I snarl, with a little more venom that I intended. I reach for the Tabasco and we continue eating in silence.

When I finish, Max clears the plates and, when he's gone, Charlie leans over.

"You know, he only wants to see you happy. Don't get angry with him, I know he gets a bit overexcited."

"I'm not angry with him, I'm just…I don't know…" What is my problem exactly?

Max returns cautiously.

"Sorry," I mutter. "I'm just a bit frustrated. That's all. I mean, I was okay before this and now I don't know what to think. Even if he did have feelings for me, I'm here and I can't change that, I have all of this." I gesture at the surroundings. "He's in LA, I'm sure he is as rooted there as I am here." Sighing, I sink forward until my forehead rests on the table. "What if I end up in love with him again?" I mumble, muffled even further by my angle.

"Pft!" Max and Charlie exclaim simultaneously.

My head whips up. I narrow my eyes at Max and hold my stare as he works up the courage to say the words that I don't want him to say.

"You've never not been in love with him, you've just been able to ignore it for a decade or so." He breathes out like it's a relief to say it. He strokes my hair and smiles softly.

I drop my head back to the table surface and fake sob. So my worst fears are realised. I am not the strong, independent woman I envisaged, who doesn't want a boyfriend, just some casual sex. I am in fact, a sad little girl, still in love with my first boyfriend, who lives five and a half thousand miles away and can't be mine. I'm pathetic. I groan loudly.

"Listen," says Max softly, still stroking my hair, "You'll go and see Grace when the baby comes won't you?"

I nod, still stuck to the table.

"Well, perhaps you can see him then, in the meantime, chat to him. Get to know him again. Keep things light. You can't do anything else all those miles apart. Then, if you want to see him, you'll have your chance and if you don't, don't."

I know he's right. I draw in a deep, cleansing breath, lift myself up and drop my head on his shoulder. "What would I do without you?"

"You'd have cats," he teases. "Many cats!"

Okay, I can keep it light I think, besides it would be good to get to know him again, even if it never comes to anything. "Come on then!" They look at me quizzically. "I thought we were going shopping?" I say innocently. They both laugh and shake their heads as they get to their feet. Yes, I change like the wind and yes, this conversation is over, for now.

I don't find anything I want in town, so I have my nails done. My one concession to outright girliness, well apart from all the waxing, plucking and tinting, but I don't count those as girlie treats. I have my nails short for work, but they are fibreglass, as they are more durable than my natural nails and they're always painted. Today I've had a selection of pastels and for good measure I had my toes done too. While I'm drying, I think about talking to Danny last night, I decide to send him a message.

By mid-afternoon, I haven't heard anything back from Danny. But I guess it's first thing in the morning for him. I take my book and a coffee and sit at the table at the back of the bar. I don't really want to be upstairs I'm too fidgety. It is early so I can sit here for a while before it gets busy.

My iPhone buzzes on the table. He's online.

Danny
It just seemed like the right time. X

Well, that doesn't really answer my question, but if I probe more I will look needy. What can I ask him? I scroll through our conversation so far looking for inspiration. Not much to go on. I look through his profile again. Scrolling through his friends it occurs to me that he hasn't kept in contact with anybody from his time here.

Olivia
How come you haven't stayed in touch with anyone from school?

Danny
There didn't seem any point if I wasn't coming back.

Olivia
You're not missing much!

Danny
There wasn't anyone at school with enough personality to drag us away from each other back then. I couldn't think of a reason to be in touch with any of them now.

Olivia
Fair enough! We were pretty closed off.

Danny
I only had eyes for you.

God, are we going there already?

<u>Olivia</u>
Smoothie!

Okay, I'm flirting, but I'm trying to keep it light like Max suggested.

<u>Danny</u>
I wasn't back then!

<u>Olivia</u>
You did okay. Neither of us knew what we were doing.

<u>Danny</u>
OK?!? You know how to kill a man's confidence don't you! Also, FYI that is SO not what I was talking about! ONE-TRACK-MIND.

<u>Olivia</u>
Oh! Well, anyway it was lovely. I am sure we are both more confident now!

Shit I didn't just say that did I?

<u>Danny</u>
Lovely! This is awful, is that really what you think? You may as well say it was NICE!

<u>Olivia</u>
That's not what I meant, I wouldn't change things. I have good memories of that time you were so kind.

I wince at the turn this conversation has taken so quickly. I should be talking to him more like a stranger, but it's DANNY, there is nothing I can do but be drawn instantly back into our old rapport. This is how we speak to each other...spoke to each other! Oh GOD! I think of a subject change...think, think!...too late I realise as my phone buzzes again.

Danny
You're killing me here! God, I'd LOVE the chance to wipe that memory from your mind!! Can I have a do-over?

> Oh my God! What did he just say? Keep cool.

Olivia
Dream on!
> A bit harsh? Maybe. I quickly type a follow-up.

Olivia
For a start, you can't erase those memories. They are keepers! Besides even if you could have a do-over, there is the small matter of distance.

Danny
True. I just wish your most important memory of me wasn't just 'lovely', I want it to be fucking amazing!

Olivia
All my memories of you are amazing.

> Eeek! Too heavy!

Danny
I've missed you.

Olivia
I've missed you too.

> I have no idea what else to say. Obviously he feels the same because the messages stop. I busy myself to keep from over analysing it all. The worst that can happen at this point would be for him to say nothing more. But he's so far away, would it make a difference? He wouldn't just back

off now though would he? I read it again.

It's so embarrassing! But it isn't one-sided. Perhaps I WILL look him up when I visit Grace. Maybe he can have his do-over! I suppose if I'm ever going to have a fling, he's the best person to have it with. Urgh! Why am I letting myself go down this road? It's just a bit of flirting.

But I can't help glancing at my phone again. This sucks. Why has he vanished? I need something to do.

I've cleaned the flat, top to bottom. Eaten. Finished the wages. Checked on everyone downstairs. There is nothing left to do.

Dirty Dancing time…why has he vanished?

Two days have passed. I've kept busy, but it's eating away at me. Where has he gone? I won't be the one to break the silence. He contacted me for fuck's sake! I'm annoyed with myself for getting all worked up, when it's come to nothing so quickly. Hell, it couldn't come to anything anyway. He lives in sodding California! I'm pretty pissed off about the whole thing really, but even that in itself is making me furious.

I can't believe the rollercoaster I have been on recently. First Mark screws around and then I make a mortifying show of trying to 'have some fun'. Then, out of the blue, I am rudely reminded that I've possibly never stopped loving a man I can't have. Now, having taunted and teased me, he's fucked off!

Urgh! I'm so angry! As I force my mind back to the here and now, I realise that I'm slamming my way around the kitchen and Max is staring at me.

"WHAT?" I yell.

"Hey, don't bite my head off! You're like a bear with a sore head today. I know you're upset…"

"Upset? I'm not upset. I'm angry as hell. How dare he do this…" My eyes sting with tears which fall freely as Max closes his arms around me tightly. I breathe in his fresh, lovely smell.

"I know," he soothes. "I feel partly responsible. I think I got a bit carried away!"

"No, I'm just being stupid. Nothing can happen between us anyway. It just felt so nice to talk to him again. But it brought it all back. I'm just angry with myself for letting it all in."

Connie appears in the doorway, concern etched across her face. "What's wrong?" She comes over and wraps her arms around both of us.

"Oh, I'm just having a moment," I sniff, trying to make light of it as I wriggle out of their hold. I deliberately haven't told Connie that Danny has been in touch, because I didn't want her to tell me I shouldn't go back there. She would say that for sure, because she knows how hard it was for me to move on. I dry my eyes with my sleeve as I turn away to pull myself together. She'll be even more disapproving if she sees the effect it is having on me.

I move across the kitchen, collecting bits as I go, busying myself. But as I turn, I notice Max and Connie in a tense, whispered conversation. Connie shakes her head and I suddenly realise, Max is probably telling her about Danny. Bloody hell! I storm back over to them and stop, arms folded, attitude all over my face.

"Care to share?" I seethe. They both look instantly guilty. Connie turns and takes my elbow.

"Come, talk to me," she says firmly and leads me out into the diner and to the booth at the back. I shuffle in begrudgingly. "Tell me all about it."

I feel much better talking it all over with Connie. She surprises me by being very positive about our contact. She thinks I should have patience and see what happens. I told her, NOTHING will happen, he has vanished. But she seems sure that I will hear from him again. That's Connie I suppose. Expect the unexpected! I don't have as much faith as her, but I do at least feel less angry.

By the time the lunchtime rush has died down, I feel more positive. I'm still pissed off, but fuck him! Who does he think he is, messing with my emotions? I'm just wiping down some tables when my phone vibrates in my back pocket. I tense. No way will this be him, I'm certain. I grab it out and almost drop it as I fumble to turn it around. *LIV will you look at yourself! I thought you just said fuck him?* My heart is banging in my chest as I activate the screen...

You have 1 new message from Danny Morgan.
Brilliant, will this emotional rollercoaster ever end? Stop the ride, I want to get off!

From: Danny Morgan   29th March 2012

Liv,

I'm so sorry I haven't been in contact. I was suddenly called in to finish something that I started a long time ago. So I needed to finish up my current projects so that I can commit myself fully to it. I've been locked in for the last four days getting everything done, I'm almost there. When I'm done, I can't wait to pick up where we left off. I hope you haven't given up on me.

Danny x

Bugger! All of that torture I put myself through and he was at work. This is way out of control! I need help. I need a drink.

"Max!" I yell into the garden from the back door. Nothing. I move towards the door of the bar and, thank goodness, there he is. "Meeting," I say briskly and storm past him to the bar. Filling two glasses with ice, I discreetly pour a long slug of Bacardi into each, hurl in a wedge of lime and hose them both with Coke. Grabbing two straws, I stomp over to the table where Max eyes me warily. I hand him his drink. It's obviously my bar and I can do what I like, but we do have a 'no drinking on duty' policy, so I'm careful not to flaunt my abuse of power in front of the staff.

Max slowly takes a sip without breaking eye contact and as he does his eyes widen.

"What?" I ask, petulantly.

"Are you trying to get me sacked?"

I offer him a wry smile. "It's okay, I know your boss! She'll be cool."

"So?" he asks, knowing this is not a work-related meeting.

I slide him my phone. His face lights up and he places his hand carefully over his mouth to hide his grin.

"Oh!"

"Yes, oh!" I roll my eyes. "Look at what I've become! I speak to him twice and I turn into a bloody bunny-boiler. He's been fucking working."

Max bursts out laughing.

"Sorry," he chuckles, hiding his mouth again.

"Fuck off!"

"Have you replied?"

"No."

"You should."

"And say what? Oh that's okay, Danny, I thought you'd changed your mind about talking to me again, so I had a mini-nervous breakdown."

"I wouldn't open with that," Max splutters as he rolls around in his chair.

"I'm so fucking glad I amuse you."

"Sorry, sorry," he says as he tries to straighten up his face. Then, in a more serious tone, he manages. "You should just say something like 'No worries'. You know, sound breezy."

"No, I'm not going to reply. I mean, honestly what was I thinking? He didn't contact me for all this…madness. He just wanted to chat with an old friend. That's all I will ever be. If he does try to contact me again, I'll try to remember that. If he doesn't, I won't have to worry." Then I smile. "Now, finish your drink and get back to work, before I sack you!"

"Yes BOSS!"

"Oh and Max…I love you."

"Love you too," he says and gives me a playful smack on the bum as I walk away.

I feel better. So much so that I am not entirely sure I should reply if Danny does contact me again. I really don't think I need the stress. I want to go back to how I was before this.

By Thursday, I've heard nothing still. I'm relieved. Things have returned to normal. I'm busy in the kitchen making a batch of mint syrup, when I feel my phone. I have sticky hands, it'll have to wait, but the familiar, unwelcome churning begins in the pit of my stomach. *No! I must not let this happen again.* In fact I decide I'm not going to look. The eight other times this has happened today, it has just been texts and emails. This one can wait.

I bottle up the syrup and leave it to cool. I head out into the diner to see what's next and my favourite regulars distract me, Lily and her mum.

"Hi gorgeous!" I beam. "What can I get you today?"

She gives me a shy smile. She is so cute! They come in after nursery every Thursday for ice cream. A special treat.

"The usual?"

She nods.

"Sure." I roll up my sleeves as I head round the counter and open the sliding door of the ice cream case. Scooping three perfect balls of strawberry ice cream.

"Have you been a good girl?"

"Very," says her mum.

"Well, extra sauce for you then." I wink. She always gets extra sauce no matter who serves her because we all love her. "Anything else?"

"Please can Mummy have a latte?" she mutters shyly.

"Certainly, go and take a seat, I'll bring it over."

I place an overtly red cherry on top of the squirty cream I have just dispensed and deliver it to the waiting Lily.

Returning to the counter, I suddenly remember my phone. I scoop up some empties and head into the kitchen so I can have a moment to check it.

You have 1 new message from Danny Morgan

From: Danny Morgan   29th March 2012

Hey,
Did you get my message? I didn't hear back from you.
I hope you're okay. I'm free as a bird, if you feel like chatting.

Danny x

Oh, so now you're free? Well I am busy, I think to myself. Well…I can make myself busy, I know the coffee machine needs a thorough clean. I throw myself into that for a while.

By the time the coffee machine, the soda pumps and all of the blenders are sparkling it's nearly 5pm. I grab a tea and head upstairs for a break. I suppose I should reply to him. It isn't my style to be spiteful. Oh, there's another message from Danny…

From: Danny Morgan   29th March 2012

Have I blown it? I hope not.

Danny x

Well this changes things, he sounds as needy as I've been feeling. What to say…? Is this a time for keeping it light? I hate playing games but this slight shift of power proves too much. I take advantage…

From: Olivia Harper   29th March 2012

I got your message.
You are not the only one who has to work!

Busy, busy! X

It's stupid, I know. I'm shooting myself in the foot, because what I really want to do is talk to him, get to know him again. But the distance, the delay and the uncertainty create an almost competitive atmosphere. I rub my temples. This is ridiculous, I'm sitting here with nothing to do and I am being petty. I snatch up my phone.

From: Olivia Harper   29th March 2012

But I'm taking a break now…x

I sigh and stare at my phone. The screen lights up. He's online.

Danny
Wow, I thought I'd blown it for sure!

Olivia
Blown what?

Silence…. Seconds feel like hours, and then my screen tells me…

Danny is typing…

Danny
I don't know about you but talking to you has had a huge effect on me. I thought it would be easy, but…I was wrong.

Breathe! I need to think. Oh wait… Danny is typing…

Danny
That's why I had to shut myself away to finish this work. Thoughts of you were distracting me! When you didn't respond I thought you'd lost interest.

I need to process this; it's all too much.

Danny is typing…Shit…more?

Danny
Say something….

Okay think, think! How do I want this to go? I don't want to play games. But if I tell him how I've been feeling where will it get me? If I tell him, we will just be two people feeling shitty and uncertain on opposite sides of the Atlantic. How will that help? But then it occurs to me, that's what we already are. I've nothing to lose.

Olivia
It's had a huge effect on me too.
    Tears begin to fall silently down my cheeks. In for a penny, in for a pound…if he never talks to me again, he may as well at least know what he has done to me.

Olivia
I was OK you know. Then one message from you put me right back to that day. The day you left. I've realised I never got over it.

Danny is typing…

Danny
I didn't mean to hurt you. I just…I never got over it either. I had no idea you would feel like this. I thought if I made contact after all this time, we could be friends.

Olivia
We have no choice; I just don't know if I can do it.

    How has it come to this so quickly? At least he feels the same. Maybe we can find a way to be friends, over time. Right now, it's all a bit heavy. There's no way we can return to friendly banter from this. We'll just have to cool it and see what happens. I'm just about to say this when I notice…Danny is typing…

Danny
Please don't give up.

Olivia
Give up on what?

I say, surprised at the sudden anger I feel and I haven't finished.

Olivia
There's nothing to give up on. It doesn't matter how we feel when we are 5,000 miles apart. I can't do this right now, I have to work.

I shove my phone in my pocket and wipe my face with my sleeve. I need to get downstairs; if I'm up here alone for a second longer I will fall apart. I hurry downstairs and out into the welcoming thrum of the diner. I need a distraction, but I'm aware that I'm fuming; I must not slam around and frighten the customers. I take a quick deep breath and taking it as calmly as I can manage, I set about cleaning tables. This will keep me out of people's way. Deep in thought, I work my way around the empty tables, wiping, and restocking condiments. It is quite therapeutic. Mercifully he seems to have got the message…Oh no, I tense as my phone buzzes. Not here. I don't want to cry again. But there is no way I can ignore it.

Danny
It would help if I could see your face.

I scoff and shake my head. How is this helping?

Olivia
It would help if I could see yours, but I can't. That's my point!

I put my phone away, but it buzzes again instantly. I pull it out, getting really frustrated.

Danny
You could if you turned around…

Four.

Me in all my colours.

Liv.

I whirl round and see him sitting in the first booth. I am frozen to the spot. He holds my gaze; he looks apprehensive, but dead sexy. *God, look at him!* I can't take it all in. Time has stopped. I want to run to him, but in a distant part of my conscious I know if I do, I will be swept up in the heat of this Hollywood blockbuster-style moment. I feel weak. I need to sit down.

I manage to lower myself onto a chair and I drop my face into my hands. HE. IS. HERE! Isn't he? I raise my face so that my eyes peek above my fingertips, the rest of my face still hiding behind my trembling hands. I blink at him idly and watch as he slowly raises himself up out of his seat. He weaves his way over to where I'm sitting, never taking his eyes away from mine and lowers himself into the chair opposite me.

"Hi," he whispers.

"Hi," I murmur as I lower my hands. A tear escapes from my eye.

He raises a hand and then clenches it back, seemingly battling with himself. Then he relents and leans forward, wiping my tear away with his thumb.

At that precise moment a loud smash distracts us from our intimacy and we turn to see Max gaping at us, unable to acknowledge the mess he has created on the floor. One of the girls rushes over to help him and this snaps him out of his trance. He glances back at us as he hurriedly fetches the broom and collects the broken crockery.

I turn back to Danny, hardly able to connect with the situation.

"Best friend?" he asks.

I manage a nod. What is going on? He's really here; that much I know. Max just confirmed that he isn't a figment of my imagination. But how? I'm suddenly grateful for my stunned levelheadedness. If I'd run into his arms, I'd be completely lost by now and so many questions need to be asked. Not that I'm capable of forming them right now.

"How?" I manage.

"I needed to see you."

"But… I thought…Why aren't you in LA?"

"I told you I had to finish something I started a long time ago…so here I am."

I pull my eyes away from his, and stare off to the side. This is just too much. He reaches over and takes my hand. I look down at his hand holding mine, unable to connect the image with the feeling of his skin touching mine. It is like an out-of-body experience. I must be in shock. I look back at him, hoping for some guidance.

"I had to come. I had to see you. Once I started thinking about you, I couldn't shake you out of my head. Then when I looked you up, I had to know how you were…" He shifts nervously in his seat. "When you responded, I was blown away and I really wanted to get to know you again. Be friends." He shrugs almost apologetically. "I thought I could do it. But when we started talking I knew I was going to find it impossible. Then you made it seem like you felt the same way…"

"So you came?"

"I had to finish work stuff first, but yes, as soon as I could."

"When?"

"Last night, late. I was so anxious to see you, but it was late, so I went to bed. Then this morning when I saw that you still hadn't replied I messaged you again. But when you kept me waiting all day, I thought I'd made a huge mistake."

I continued to stare into his eyes, confused.

"I thought about going home, but I'd come all this way and I was desperate to see you. So I came here to find you, but I couldn't see you anywhere. I messaged you to find out if I'd blown it and...you were so angry."

Tears are now falling freely down my face; he pulls a napkin from the dispenser and hands it to me.

"I thought maybe I should leave, but then I saw you." He smiles a shy half smile. "Please don't cry."

He moves round to sit in the chair next to me and lifts his hand to my face.

"God, I've missed you," he whispers and closing his eyes he leans in and kisses me softly. A brief but tender kiss. Then he wraps his arms around me.

"I've missed you too," I croak, relaxing into his warm reassuring embrace.

It's like going home.

I realise after a moment that I'm at work and I sit up and glance around. As I do, all the staff hurriedly return to whatever they were doing. Trying not to seem like they were gawping.

"Sorry," says Danny, backing off.

"No, it's fine, I'm just supposed to be working."

We sit and stare at each other, the emotion of the last week...the last twelve years, hanging between us. What am I going to do now? I can't be here, I need time with him.

"Give me a sec," I say, getting to my feet.

Shakily, I walk to the counter, trying to compose myself. Max is fixated. He frowns, asking me with his eyes if I'm okay. I nod.

"Go!" he says with a glint in his eye, and signals upstairs with a sideways nod.

"Are you sure?"

He rolls his eyes and laughs. "No, I'm going to make you stay and polish glasses while your..." he lowers his voice, "...incredibly hot American sits and twiddles his thumbs!"

I narrow my eyes at him.

"Sarcasm, really?"

Max shrugs his shoulders playfully. "I could look at him all day, so if you want to stay, stay. But, frankly, if you don't take him upstairs, I WILL!"

"O-K! Keep your hair on!"

"And I don't want to see you back here tonight, do you hear me?"

I try to look disgusted at the insinuation, but I realise it's futile.

"Thank you," I mouth and, grinning, I blow him a kiss.

I turn back to Danny. He's staring intently at his hands. I take the opportunity to really look at him. It's surreal; it's him, but not quite. He isn't that different, still really good looking, but sexy, which I don't think I appreciated fully before. He was just my Danny then. Now he's tanned and vaguely muscular, or so it looks through his jacket. Like a 'super' version of the old Danny. Danny+. I've a sudden surge of worry. What does he make of me? I've changed, a lot. He's just grown up; I've become someone else entirely. I'm certainly not the plain, mousy schoolgirl I was when we last saw each other. He turns and catches me staring.

I blush, caught in the act, but quickly pull myself together enough to walk over to him and hold out my hand. Taking it, he gets up. My mouth is dry.

"Let's get out of here," I manage, with a weak smile. I turn and lead him towards the door to my flat. As I punch in the code, he looks at me quizzically, but his expression changes as I open the door to reveal a hall with stairs. Maybe he thought I was taking him into a store cupboard! We climb the stairs in silence and, as I open the door, I've absolutely no idea how to play this.

It's not something I have to dwell on for too long as he spins me round to face him. Pausing only for a second and fixing me with an intense look that communicates his intentions. I signal my permission with a barely perceptible smile and his lips find mine.

We kiss urgently and passionately. It's nothing like how we used to kiss. I can't even remember how that went now, but it wasn't like this. I'm not sure it's never been like this. Our hands are everywhere, exploring: mine in his hair, bringing him as close as he can be; his on my back, grasping and stroking. At once we pull away, breathless. We exchange a look and giggle.

"Sorry," he says, embarrassed. "I didn't intend to do that, I just couldn't help it."

"It's okay, I wanted you to," I smile. I need to do something to break the tension. "Give me your jacket, you look like you're not stopping," I demand, smiling at his surprise. *Yes that's right, I'm not as meek as I was either!*

He slips it off and hands it to me and I hang it on the hooks by the door. I'm so nervous, but I'm glad we haven't ripped each other's clothes off; I don't want to rush things or regret them. But now it's hanging in the air. We can't move past it. I turn to face him. His once brown hair is now almost blonde from the California sun and his skin is golden. The bright blue eyes are the same though. He moves towards me again and slips his arm around my waist, pausing just to gaze into my eyes. Oh God, this is only going to go one way...

We stand face to face, drinking each other in. I love the fact that he is more or less the same height as me. I am 5'6" and he is no more than two inches taller. I've been used to looking up at men and I'd forgotten how lovely it is to be on the same level. I smile at him and he smiles back.

"I can't believe you're here," he whispers.

"I never left."

"I can't believe *I'm* here then."

"Better," I smile. "Do you want a drink?"

"No." Danny lifts his hand and strokes it from my temple, down across my cheek to the corner of my mouth, pausing briefly to circle the tiny silver stud beneath my lip. "I like this," he whispers. Then placing a finger under my chin, he pulls my lips to his and kisses me deeply.

The kiss is less urgent this time, allowing me to take it in. He still tastes the same. I wonder if it's strange to remember how a person tastes.

"Mmm," I murmur involuntarily. This seems to ignite something in him and his tongue becomes more fervent as it caresses mine. Then he breaks our kiss. His eyes are alight.

"What?" I ask breathlessly.

"Do I get my do-over?" he asks, flashing me a wicked look.

My breath catches in my throat. Briefly, I wonder if it's too fast. But I know we can't get past it, we have to see it through. I need to relax, I've dreamed of this opportunity for years, now I have it, I must make it count.

Breathe.

I nod and take his hand turning away to lead him.

"Uh uh!" he exclaims and dragging me back to him, he scoops me up into his arms. "This is MY do-over! Bedroom?"

I gesture past the kitchen and he carries me quickly through the door. Clipping my ankle on the handle as we go!

"Shit! Sorry!"

"Ow! My way would have hurt less!"

He deposits me onto my feet and I take an exaggerated limp to the bed.

"Are you okay?" He sits beside me and lifts my foot into his lap, sliding my shoe off and examining it carefully.

I can't help laughing, his face is a picture!

"I'm teasing, you fool! But seriously, nice work with the do-over, I'm going to remember this for sure!"

"Right!" he growls, kicking off his shoes as he pushes my shoulders and I land on the bed giggling. He moves above me smiling.

"I'll have to give you something else to remember then. His knee moves between my legs and I feel his erection pressing into my hip.

Okay, now he has my attention.

His mouth is on mine in an instant, and my nervous hysteria is forgotten.

I pull at the hem of his t-shirt and yank it up. He grabs it from the back of his neck and whips it over his head. God, he smells so good.

He lifts himself enough to find the zip on my hoody and fumbles to get it undone. It falls open and he sits up, tugging at one sleeve. As my arm slips out, he catches my wrist and stares at me in disbelief. Briefly, I wonder what I'm wearing underneath if he is that surprised, then I realise. My tattoos! Self-consciously, I try to pull my sleeve back on. I haven't been with a man who's not into this, since, well, him. I'm not used to feeling like I want to hide them.

"No, don't," he says in wonder, carefully lifting the fabric away from my body. He assesses the ink on my arm. Then follows it from my wrist, up and under the short sleeve of my t-shirt onto my left shoulder searching for its end. He doesn't find it and he lifts an eyebrow. He looks back at me with glowing eyes.

"*Some* tattoos?"

"Uh-huh."

"That's a few more than some!"

I sigh.

"Are there more?"

"I'll save you some time," I sneer, pushing him off me. I feel angry at being judged, I am what I am out of choice. I'm not used to having to justify it to anyone. But if he's going to leave because of it, I want him to have the full picture. I love my tattoos and as I get to my feet I am ready to defend them. He sits back, resting on his hands and crosses his legs, waiting. He looks amused. I'm not laughing.

I slip my other arm out of my hoody, revealing that I've fewer tattoos this side, just one on the inside of my forearm, elbow to wrist. But then I lift the hem of my t-shirt up over my head and hear him take a sharp breath. The right side of my ribs is covered, wrapping round to my back. I drop my t-shirt and move to unbutton my jeans. Slowly peeling them off, I reveal my right leg inked across the thigh, ankle and foot. Then, yanking off my remaining shoe, I remove my jeans and wave my left foot, showing the only work I have had done on that leg. I hold my palms up in a mock 'ta-da!' gesture. Then I turn and show him that they go all the way round. *That's right take a look...this is me in all my colours!*

I bend to pick up my t-shirt as I turn back to him, suddenly anxious to put an end to the freak show. But he's on his feet, grabbing the t-shirt away and pulling my body against his. He kisses my neck and down onto my shoulder. I move to pull away.

"Hey! What's wrong?"

I turn my face away from him, unsure of what to say. Using his finger, he pulls my face back and raises an eyebrow, a huge smile spreading across his face. "I didn't say I didn't like them." He sits back on the bed and pulls me to straddle him. "You are beautiful..." he breathes against my ear "...and these..." he says tracing over a butterfly on my collar bone, "...are sexy!"

Oh... This is such mind fuck! I can't keep up. I smile a half smile, still feeling uncertain; my confidence took an unusual knock when I felt judged. It never happens and I feel unable to recover. But my dark cloud begins to disperse as he bites and sucks my earlobe.

"Mmm..."

He reaches around to unhook my bra. Tossing it away, he takes a nipple into his mouth and sucks hard, swirling his tongue around and tugging with his teeth.

I moan. Then he moves to the other side. My body responds even though my brain is still catching up, I pull his face up to mine and kiss him deeply. He twists and I find myself under him. He trails light kisses across my chest, over my tattoos, following them down, past my breasts and round my side, turning me to follow them as they disappear onto my back. He kisses and licks to where the trail ends at the base of my spine.

"So sexy," he breathes and I inhale sharply as I feel his warm breath against my skin. He turns me over, smiling briefly before moving lower out of view. I close my eyes as I feel him sliding my knickers down my legs.

He kneels between my legs and pulls me to the edge of the bed. I gasp as I feel his tongue at my knee; he slides it slowly up my leg and pauses. Despite sharing almost all of our first experiences, he's never done this to me. What is he waiting for? I feel his hot breath at the apex of my thighs and then suddenly his tongue is there, licking and circling, hard then soft, fast then slow, teasing. I groan and arch my back off the bed. Lifting my hips up to meet him.

Slowly, he slides a finger inside me, twisting it so that the pad of his finger is stroking my G-spot. He begins a steady rhythm with his tongue on my clit and moves his finger expertly. The feeling is so intense and he just keeps going. He knows his stuff. I must return the favour.

He sucks my clit every so often then returns to licking, giving me bursts of unbelievable pleasure. I'm rocking myself against his hand and face when he stills, pressing very firmly on my G-spot with his finger and not moving, not letting go. At the same time he increases the intensity with his tongue and I cry out. Wow! This is something different. So good! My desire overtakes my self-confidence and I thrust into his hand while he holds firm. I feel tension building within me and I know it won't be long, but I want to make it last and wait for him. I want us to come together.

I attempt to sit; he glances up at me without breaking his relentless rhythm. The sight of him, his face buried in me, combined with the intense feeling of his finger. *Oh!* It almost sends me over the edge…if I want to stop him, it needs to be now.

"My turn," I manage, breathless. Pulling his free hand, signalling I want him to get up.

He smiles, I can feel it! Giving me a wicked look, he ups his efforts suddenly. I cry out. The sudden intensity brings me nearer and then just as suddenly he is gone. Sitting back on his heels, he looks very pleased with himself. He stands up and leans over to kiss me, wanting me to taste myself on his lips, no doubt. As we kiss deeply, I place my hands on his defined arms and ease him back a step as I slide off the bed to my knees.

He's still wearing his jeans but I can see his erection straining at the denim. I trace along his length with my fingers and he gasps. Watching me intently, he pops his button fly open and slides his jeans and boxers down together, stepping out of them and kicking them to the side. I gaze up at him, eyeing his body. He clearly takes care of himself. My eyes move to his erection as I take it in my hand. He's so hard; large and thick. I suppose I didn't have the frame of reference before to fully appreciate these facts. I wrap my hand around him and stroke him, up and down. He gasps.

I remember the first time I touched him like this with a flush. But back then it was all under the covers. Now, here he stands naked in my bedroom. It's not exactly daring, but it feels brazen because it's us. Kneeling before him, I'm aware that the visual aspect of a blowjob is important to most men and I want to give him a great show. Considering my form, I bring my legs together, point my toes behind me and arch my back, lifting my face up to view him through my eyelashes. I know he will enjoy seeing my lips stretched around him.

I lick my lips and take him gently in my mouth. He lets out a deep, throaty moan as I start moving. I put pressure underneath with my tongue and take in as much of his length as I can. His breathing becomes ragged as I continue building my pace. Moaning, he drops his head back, tipping his face to the ceiling, losing himself to the sensation.

As the moments pass, I suck harder, keeping my pace steady. He moans again and grasps my head in his hands. Massaging his fingers through my scalp as my head moves back and forth, his touch is electrifying and I emit a low, stifled moan. He gasps as the sound vibrates on him and, in the heat of the moment, he pushes himself deep into my throat and pauses for…seconds, holding my head firm to keep himself there.

"*Ah!*" he cries and releases me.

I gag slightly as he withdraws, but I'm surprised that I was able to hold him for so long. Deep-throating is not something I've ever been a fan of, but this is carnal and not at all unpleasant. I seem suddenly to be, not only capable of taking him deep, so deep, but remarkably enjoying the experience. It's surprisingly rewarding.

Just knowing how much pleasure it gave him is empowering. So I place his hands back on either side of my head. I look him briefly in the eye, signalling my permission. I take him all in again, further still. He holds me firmly in place once more and this time he thrusts, once.

"Oh God, Liv!"

He releases my head, lifts me to my feet, and pushes me onto the bed. He gazes at me as he stoops to pick up his jeans. He pulls his wallet from his back pocket, opens it and produces a condom. I raise my eyebrows and he shrugs, amused.

Quickly rolling the condom on, he hooks his arms under my knees, lifting my legs up onto his shoulders and crawling between them. He enters me slowly, savouring the feeling. I moan loudly as he withdraws and pushes into me again, watching me all the time. His eyes reveal his desire and echo mine. I *need* him.

Nothing from my memory of us before matches this obviously, we were young and afraid. But even compared to my other experiences, this is something different. Our history maybe? But it means so much to have this second chance and that's making it so good. I groan as he picks up his pace. He leans down onto his hands increasing the friction between us.

"Yes!" I breathe as the friction reaches my clit. As we move together, we each moan in turn.

He lifts up slightly and looks into my eyes as he moves in and out of me. I can't believe this. I'm awash with sensation and pleasure, and Danny is the source. I reach up to touch his face, stroking his skin and sweeping my fingers through his hair. I watch my fingers for a moment, and then Danny turns his face to kiss my forearm, the closest part of me to his mouth. It brings my eyes back to him and as we reconnect he pushes harder and faster into me. Another loud moan escapes me. We're becoming breathless.

Withdrawing suddenly, he flips me over and deposits me kneeling in front of the headboard. I lean forward and grasp it as he lifts my hips to meet his. Filling me again, he groans and moves faster. Fucking me, urgently. He leans his chest onto my back. Reaching round, he uses one hand to massage my clit and the other to hold tight to my shoulder.

"Oh God, Danny!"

The sudden mix of sensations brings me close. It's just what I need, not something I automatically expect a man to know, or care enough about. He's panting at my ear and breathes, "Yes Liv...ah...yes!" and slams into me hard. I cry out, my orgasm thundering through me as he thrusts again and again, until he too cries out in release. It was worth holding back I think as we both climb down together.

Gasping, we still for a moment, then he pulls out of me and I sink to the bed, rolling over onto my back, panting. He removes the condom, ties it and holds it up.

"Trash?"

"Floor!" I laugh, almost drunk with pleasure. I pull him down to lie with me as he drops it. We wrap ourselves together and lie, face to face, still panting. I smile as he strokes my face, our breathing beginning to return to normal.

"Hi," he whispers.

"Hi," I whisper back.

"That was…"

"Fucking amazing," I finish.

"Yeah!" He smiles and reaches forward to kiss me.

"I'll definitely remember that," I tease.

"So will I."

A look of uncertainty passes across his face. "Sorry if I pushed my luck."

I can't think what he's referring to and then I remember him pushing himself deep into my throat.

"It was good actually." I'm a little surprised by this fact still, but I did like it. Before…Mark had tried it once, he always was one to push his luck. I felt it was degrading and selfish on his part, and I warned him not to try it again. But with Danny it was different; I'd do it again willingly.

"I just got carried away. I didn't even realise I was doing it until it was too late."

"I could have done it for longer," I admit shyly.

"I couldn't! One more and it would have been game over!"

"I'll have to remember that."

We sigh and lie entwined in silence, just looking. Then the worry creeps in filling the headspace that the silence creates. Amazingly, at no point during that did I think what we were doing was a bad idea. It was natural, but now…questions. How long is he here for? What does he want from this? How will I cope when he has to go? We've now established that he feels the same about the situation as I do. Have we just made it harder for ourselves?

My insides tie themselves into knots, but as I'm wondering how to broach these issues with him he opens his mouth.

"So," he says glancing down at my chest, "you had a couple of tattoos?"

Here we go. "I never said a couple, I said some *and* you said you liked them, though I don't quite believe you."

"I love them! I'll admit I was surprised. It's not how I expected you to turn out. But it's hot!"

This time I know it is the truth, his eyes give him away. He strokes my side across my ribs, watching his fingers as they trace the lines.

"Tell me about them."

"That'll take all night...and I'd rather talk about us. What are you doing here?"

He gives a resigned laugh. "I don't know what to tell you. I had to see you. I didn't think past that!"

"So you just got on a plane with nothing but a condom in your wallet and hoped for the best?"

"No, I did pack a bag."

"Full of condoms?"

"Clothes! When did you become a pervert?"

I laugh, but the humour evaporates quickly.

"How long are you here for?"

"Depends."

He's being deliberately vague because he thinks it's cute. But I've questions that need answers, questions that I should have been strong enough to ask before we went at it.

"Be serious!"

"Why?"

I prop my head up on my elbow, knowing that if I can form the words, the floodgates will open.

"Because the last few days have turned my world upside down and I need to know why you came and how long I have before I have to deal with you leaving again."

Too much? I sounded more vulnerable than I intended. But I *am* vulnerable going to kill me. At least if I know going in how long I have, I might be able to spare myself some of the heartache.

"Well, I don't have anywhere else to be right now. I want to get to know you to him. He's going to leave at some point and it's again."

"But what does that mean?"

"You're over thinking this, Liv. I'm here and I intend to stay around while we work this thing out."

I sigh, really frustrated. "Days? A week? Two? Give me an idea!"

"As long as we need. I told you, I don't have anywhere else to be right now."

"But what about work?"

He smiles. "I've cleared my desk."

"But…"

He puts his index finger over my lips. "Shhh…the beauty of my job Liv, is that I can do it anywhere. I just need a phone and an internet connection."

"So what, you'll stay?" I know I am getting way ahead of myself, but it's just self-preservation.

"Who knows?" he sighs, now he's getting frustrated. "Can't we just enjoy this?"

I think for a moment.

He's right, we need to see, but my feelings are much stronger than I realised and I'm looking to protect myself. I need to try and enjoy my time with him, who knows how and when it will end. Treat it as a fling, I tell myself.

"Okay," I kiss him lightly and jump up. "Shower?" I ask and hold out my hand.

Five.

Okay, that's enough questions for you.

Liv.

I step out of the hot water and wrap myself in a towel. Still a bit phased at the sight of Danny in my shower.

"Where are you staying?" I ask as I hand him a towel.

"Holiday Inn."

"Do you want to have dinner with me?" I can't believe how nervous I feel again having just shared my bed and then my shower with this man. He's so familiar, but this intimacy with him is not.

"Hell yeah, I don't plan on leaving you now!" he grins as he wraps his arms around me.

I feel giddy and I'm aware that I should at least try to keep my guard up. But right now he isn't going anywhere.

"What do you fancy?"

He flashes me a wicked look.

"To eat," I clarify.

He looks shy all of a sudden. "I'd really like to eat here."

"You want me to cook for you?"

"No, I want to eat in your restaurant." He smiles. "I really want to see what you've achieved…" He still looks uncertain, why? "…I just feel like I should take you out and treat you, it feels wrong."

Ego! Of course! "Don't be ridiculous, we can eat here. I'll give you a very reasonable rate."

He laughs. Recovering his confidence, he moves towards me and kisses me deeply, his fingers in my hair.

"I'm going to go and get changed, can you give me thirty minutes?" He turns and walks into the bedroom to get dressed.

"Sure," I say, rubbing my hair with my towel. I really want to tell him to bring all his things back with him, but I know I'll sound desperate and a little nuts. I'll just see what happens.

He finishes putting on his shoes and leans over to kiss me goodbye.

"I won't be long."

"At the bottom of the stairs, take the right-hand door. Then you won't have to do the walk of shame through the diner," I smirk. "Come back that way too, I'll buzz you in."

He throws me a charming smile and leaves.

I collapse onto the bed, almost hyperventilating. Gathering my thoughts, I grab my phone and text Max: 'MEETING!'

I let the phone drop and seconds later I hear Max bounding the stairs two at a time.

"Where is he?" he asks as he enters, anxious that he's intruding.

"Gone to get changed."

"So?"

I launch into the whole story as fast as I can and he's dizzy by the end. He hugs me excitedly.

"So when do I get to meet him?"

"Tonight, he wants to sample my wares."

"Sounds like he already has!"

I narrow my eyes. "I didn't call you up here for this, I need your help. What do I wear?" Max smiles as if I've answered his prayers.

Twenty minutes later, I'm wearing a black maxi dress and leopard-print cardigan. My hair is loose and I'm wearing a slightly exaggerated version of my already quite over the top smoky eye make-up. I apply red lipstick and he hands me my red ballet pumps. I'm deliberately not over dressed, this is carefully considered (by Max not me) so as to appear relaxed in his company, but also alluring, without being slutty. I push up my cardigan sleeves slightly as I'm flushed from the stress and I add two or three bangles. I'm ready.

I shoo Max away, thanking him. I promise we'll be down soon and he's gone, leaving me to stress.

The buzzer goes.

"Hello?"

"Hey beautiful," Danny says smoothly. The sound of his voice sends a jolt through me even though I know it's going to be him. I take a deep breath and then hold down the door release.

I stand at the top of the stairs as he comes through the door and I think we each gasp at the sight of the other. Breathe.

He's dressed in jeans, a pale blue shirt, and a navy jacket. He looks fresh and gorgeous. I can smell his aftershave already and it leaves me weak. I make my way down to his outstretched hand; he greedily drinks me in as I move. This whole situation is so highly charged. I feel embarrassed about taking it out into my diner. I reach the last step and put my hand in his. He kisses it.

"You look fabulous."

"Why thank you, so do you."

We stand for a moment staring at each other. Then I realise that we're going to eat and I'm really not hungry. I don't think I can sit and eat a meal right now.

"Can I give you the tour?"

He smiles widely. "Yes please." He turns and holds open the door for me.

We slide into the back of the diner. I pause, nervously. He slips his hand in mine and I feel myself relax.

I take him into the kitchen first, because it is closest. He shakes hands with Jake and the other guys as I introduce him. He chats warmly with Jake about football (the American one, which isn't football at all), apparently both support the same team. I don't care. I watch him because it's the most I've heard him say in twelve years. I feel inadequate because we haven't spoken at length about anything yet, but I snap out of it as their conversation drifts to me.

"She's done really well for herself," Danny says to Jake as he slips one arm around my waist and gestures at the surroundings.

"She sure has," Jake agrees, smiling. He shakes a pan of chips.

"It was good to meet you," Danny says, seeing that we're keeping him from his work.

I show him the rest of the kitchen and we head out to the front. He sits on a stool at the counter while I talk him through the soda bar. I tell him all about how we transformed the place. All the things I've collected and from where. I walk back around to him and stop in front of him. He's smiling in wonder. I turn and point to a sign on the wall. It's the word Lucky lit up in blue. As I do, he wraps his arms around my waist.

"That sign came from a bar in Venice Beach. I was out visiting Grace a couple of years ago and this lovely bar on the beach was closing. It was this local institution. When I told the guy all about this place, he gave it to me."

"I remember that place, we used to go there sometimes." Danny shakes his head, obviously processing the fact that we might have crossed paths sooner.

"Shall I show you the bar, or do you want to eat first?"

"Bar."

I lead him out of the front door and over to the entrance between the buildings. I could have gone through the back, but I want him to have the full tour. Pausing, I introduce him to the doormen. They look slightly uncomfortable.

"I won't be any trouble tonight, I promise!" I wink. They laugh nervously and this makes me laugh.

As I lead Danny into the garden, he eyes me quizzically.

"I got a bit drunk, the other day…very out of character," I laugh.

We step into the bar and immediately I relax. It's busy for a Thursday thanks to our new live music. That's why we need the doormen on a school night. The hum fills the air between us. Hopefully, in here we can talk without the silence being a problem. Although later, we may have to shout.

"Wow!" says Danny, taking in his surroundings.

I beam, he's really impressed. I watch him glance around with his mouth open. I don't think you can really see it from the street, but the bar is easily twice the size of the diner. It's darker in here and although the Americana theme runs through, it's more focused on music, art, tattoos, that kind of thing. Not so much of the cheerful Coca-Cola-ness of the diner. Max waves from behind the bar and makes his way towards us.

"Here comes Max."

"Max?"

"Best friend," I reply and he smiles and nods just as Max arrives before us.

"Danny, this is Max, my best friend and right-hand man." I smile, as I introduce the two most important men in my life to each other.

"Max," Danny says warmly, offering his hand to shake.

Max takes his hand, but pulls him into a hug.

"Great to finally meet you. What would you like to drink?"

Danny and I look at each other.

"Surprise me," he says. "Where are the restrooms?"

I point him in the right direction and, as he walks away, Max hugs me too and spins me round.

"He is *hot!*" he mouths and leaves his mouth hanging open to make his point.

"Alright, calm down, you'll have a heart attack!"

"No, but I mean he's gorgeous."

"Well eyes off Mr." I take his left hand and hold it up, pointing at his wedding ring.

"No, don't worry, he's all yours. Charlie is coming down later to get a look at him, we can both lust from a safe distance!" He flicks his eyebrows up.

"Knowing you two, it'll be an inappropriate distance."

"No promises," he says in my ear, just as Danny returns. "Well, let's get you two a drink." He says and returns to his position behind the bar.

Danny and I take the two stools to the side of the bar and sit half facing Max and half facing each other.

Without consulting us again, Max mixes us two Caipirinhas, which he knows I love, and gives us a moment.

"Cheers!" Danny says as he holds his drink up to clink with mine. We both take a sip and he seems happy with the choice.

"Do you want to eat?" I ask, still not sure I do.

"Can't we stay here for a while?"

"We can eat here, we do these sharing platters. Like menu samplers, do you fancy that?" He nods, smiling. "Do you mind what we get?" I ask, sliding off my stool. He shakes his head, still smiling and not taking his eyes off me. Tearing myself away from his gaze, I pop into the kitchen and catch the eye of Ray who works in the bar kitchen.

"Can you ask Jake to do me a sharer for two? Make it Mexican, loads of salsa and guacamole, he knows what I like." He nods and disappears off to the diner and I return to the bar to find Danny and Max in conversation. Hmm should I worry about this? I join them.

"So how long have you two known each other?" Danny asks.

"Since about two months after you left," Max replies. I wince at the bluntness of his response.

"A long time then," muses Danny. He seemed to take it well. Max serves a customer and Danny asks quietly, "So did you two ever…?"

"Max is married."

"But before that?"

"To a man!" I add with a smile. Men have to assume there's something more between Max and I; it's always been the same. Max doesn't wear his sexuality on his sleeve unless you have a well-trained eye and I've never met a guy that hasn't questioned us. In fact, I don't always think they believe me when I do explain. Ex-boyfriends included. I steel myself for this to be a problem.

"Oh!" he glances back at Max and then smiles. Hmm, he was almost jealous, but I think it won't be an issue. It makes me feel warm inside.

"You'll meet Charlie later, he's coming to look at you!"

He wrinkles his nose. "Am I that interesting?"

I laugh. "Not much happens around here."

Max returns, "So how long are you here for?"

Oh my God, straight in with the questions! I want to disappear into the floor, but I know he's done it for my benefit.

"Well I have no firm plans." Danny glances cautiously at me. "But I would like to think at least a couple of weeks, maybe more…I have an open-ended ticket." He looks like a deer in the headlights, but he has revealed more of his intentions to Max than he did to me.

"Don't you have to have a return date for immigration?" Don't hold back Max! I shoot him a look, which he ignores.

"Dual citizenship," Danny responds. "My father is British."

"Oh okay, so you could live here if you wanted?"

"Okay, that's enough questions for you," I say as brightly as I can manage, whilst assuring Max with my stare that I will do him harm if he doesn't back off. Max laughs and winks, then turns and goes back to work.

"Sorry."

"No, it's fine, he's just looking out for you," he says, seeing the humour. He places his hand just above my knee and leaves it there, causing me to take a deep, shaky breath. I need to get control over this, I'm not sure I like this weak side of me. I feel like a teenager and I've come a long way since then. No man gets me in a spin. I must keep control.

Our food arrives and we chat easily about work and our families. He's shocked to hear about my dad, but then in some ways he isn't that surprised. I don't let it turn our conversation somber though. I tell him all about this place and how Max helped me get it off the ground. The conversation turns to relationships and I discover that he's only had two serious girlfriends since us, but he's been single for a couple of years. I expect he's had a few casual girlfriends too, but I won't ask him. I admit that I'm just out of a relationship and fill him in on the circumstances that led to its demise. He frowns when I tell him how I found them together. But I explain that it made me realise he wasn't that important to me.

We talk about the old days and reminisce about all the films I made him watch. He tells me that he gets a lot of stick for his knowledge of 'chick movies'. Max has kept the drinks coming, we've tried a few different ones and I'm starting to feel a little tipsy. It's been great to sit with him and learn about his life since me. It sounds like he's been happy.

Charlie joins us for a drink and he and Danny hit it off. It turns out they do quite similar jobs. Looking at us from the outside, we're odd matches. Max and I look like we fit each other, our styles are similar, but Danny and Charlie both have a more wholesome image. I still can't get used to having him here in my world, having been the stuff of legends for so long.

Danny offers to pay for dinner but I refuse flat out. The music starts up so we fall quiet, the band is great and a few people are dancing, but we sit and watch. Dancing feels too intimate at the moment, I'm not comfortable enough in his presence yet. He obviously feels the same, as he doesn't suggest it. His hand strokes my leg for a while and then as the song finishes we both clap.

He leans into my ear during the lull between songs and whispers, "Can I stay?"

I smile and nod, relieved that I wasn't the one who had to ask. We watch another couple of songs and then his hand slips into mine and I know it's time to go.

We finish our drinks and say goodnight to Max and Charlie. Then I lead him through the back into the garden and across to the back entrance of the diner. As we cross the garden, he stops me and pulls me close.

"This..." he waves his hand, "is incredible! I'm so in awe of you." He plants a small kiss on my lips. I scoff as if he's being over the top. "Seriously, I can't get over it, you are so incredible, so strong and sexy." He smiles softly.

"Stop it," I blush.

"No," he whispers as he slides his fingers into my hair and leans to kiss me deeply.

I'm suddenly aware that I'm once again snogging a guy in the garden. The doormen are going to have kittens. I know it's the first time in my life this has happened twice in one week, but I still feel like a harlot. I break away and take his hand, pulling him into the diner and punch in my code.

Upstairs, he presses me into the back of the door as I close it and pushes himself against me, groping my breasts through my dress. He moans as his lips find mine, and the need I feel is mirrored in him as we lose ourselves in each other. The kiss is urgent and hurried; he hitches up my knee and grinds himself against me. I gasp, trying to gulp down some air, the intensity taking me by surprise. We pause, breathless and stand for a moment with our foreheads touching. A silent, mutual agreement that we should enjoy each other passes between us and the whole tempo changes to a slow, deliberate pace. My eyes are closed and when I open them, he's staring at me intently. Smiling, he takes my hand and leads me to the bedroom.

I unbutton his shirt and slip it onto the floor. He removes my cardigan and then sliding out of his jeans and boxers, he lifts my dress over my head. He moves back to kiss me tenderly, holding me close and guiding me down onto the bed. For a moment he pulls back, lifting away the covers so that I can shuffle into the centre of the bed. Then he gently lies beside me, but almost on top, so that the full length of his body is pressed against mine.

He slowly moves his hand into the lace of my knickers and slides a finger into me, moving in and out. I groan as a second finger enters me and the leisurely rhythm continues while he kisses me slowly and deeply. I feel his erection rubbing naked against my thigh and I reach around and grasp it while he thrusts slowly into my hand. I need to feel him inside me.

Releasing him for a moment, I hook my thumbs into my knickers. Danny gets the picture and helps me slide them down my legs. Stopping just short of my feet, he leaves them round my ankles then moves up to my bra. He expertly unhooks the clasp from under me and pulls the bra from my breasts. Taking one nipple in his mouth, he resumes his incredible fingering. I moan as his thumb circles my clit and his relentless fingers find their pace, moving in and out of me over and over again.

Minutes pass and he doesn't stop, my body sings from the sensation. I feel myself building and so does he, so he slowly slips his fingers out of me. I groan in protest. But he moves over me and kisses me deeply, he's perfectly lined up to give me what I want, but instead he begins to move himself against me, keeping our steady rhythm. He grinds on and on, his hands clasping my face as his tongue continues to dance with mine. I groan lazily into his mouth, the feeling is intense, our bodies pressed together head to toe, his mouth on mine, the slow grinding. My legs are held loosely together by my knickers, which, I now realise, were left in place deliberately.

It occurs to me that it's odd to be performing this relatively chaste act as an adult. It's more the stuff of teenage fumbling. I've done it before, with him, though we were fully clothed and inexperienced. But now, naked and confident in our sexuality, it is sensual. Once again I'm overcome with the urge to feel him inside me. I tilt my hips up to him, hoping he gets the message so that I don't have to break our sultry kiss.

But he pulls away from my face and fixes me with a carnal stare. Damn, his lips have left me. But this gaze is so intense it burns away the disappointment I feel. Making the best of this brief hiatus, I reach across the bed above my head, to the drawer beside my bed. Yanking the drawer open, I hold his eye contact while I grope around inside and pull out a string of condom packets. He raises his eyebrows in mock surprise and I shrug innocently as I tear one off and hurl the rest at the drawer.

We linger, staring into each other's eyes for a moment and then he grinds into me once more, bringing me back to the task at hand. I tear open the packet and reluctantly he breaks our body contact while I roll it on him. He sighs at my touch and presses himself back onto me. Moving his leg between mine, he pushes them apart until they strain lightly on my underwear. Settling himself between my thighs he enters me slowly, the feeling of fullness makes me gasp as he moves in and out.

He shifts up significantly and now his pelvis is rubbing directly on my clit as he works his way in and out of me.

"Oh, God!" I gasp at the sudden change of sensation. I realise he knows that I need this friction and I am briefly grateful for whatever experience taught him this precious fact.

Clasping the top of my head, he pushes himself as far into me as our bodies allow and with a slightly increased, though still deliciously easy pace, he keeps moving. I'm unable to really move my parted legs as they are kept somewhat straightened out, straining at my underwear and very much adding to my arousal. I begin to thrust my pelvis into his as he moves, taking control of my own gratification.

We increase the pace, both moaning at the pleasure we are creating. He shifts onto his elbows and thrusts harder and faster, while I meet him, keeping that luscious contact on my clit. Faster and faster we writhe, our bodies wrapped together, slick with sweat. Building and building towards a shared orgasm. I feel like I've waited all my life for this moment. I force my eyes open and find him looking straight into them. Nose to nose, we pant and gaze, then his lips engulf mine, tongues winding together, securing our complete bodily contact, sending us both over the edge.

We call out in mutual ecstasy as we come hard. My body wracked with wave after wave of blinding pleasure. I feel him juddering from his own release. We are both still panting, almost shouting, senseless, as we come down from the summit together. He buries his face in my neck and relaxes his weight onto me. We lie like this, breathless, for I don't know how long.

As we recover, he lifts his face up to mine and kisses me as he pulls out, discarding the condom. He lays his head on my chest and sighs, stroking his fingers down my arm until he reaches my hand. He spreads his fingers through mine and squeezes lightly. I lift my other hand and stroke his hair. We lie like this, sated. For a while I think he has drifted off to sleep, then he moves, slipping my underwear off my feet and pulling the covers over us, returning to the comfort of my chest and once again finding my hand.

Running my fingers through his golden hair, I gaze down at him; he is looking at our fingers linked together. In the old days, I would have known what he was thinking, or maybe I would not have needed to, I'm not sure. Right now, I feel so uncertain, as if I am balanced on a knife-edge and I could fall either side. I can hardly believe it is him, he is the same in so many ways, but in some ways like a stranger.

I would give anything to know what he is thinking.

Six.

I don't befriend blue-headed people.

Danny.

I sit back in my chair and rub my face. This has been a freaking long night; I've been locked in for…shit, fourteen hours! It's almost 7am. I need coffee and I need air. I hate this bullshit project. I've time still on the deadline, but the asshole I'm working for is driving me nuts and I really want him out of my hair. Plus I'm beginning to suspect that not everything about his business is entirely legal, that's probably why the money's so good. How do I get into these things? Well, I can't worry about that, my intentions are honest and I've put up with this jerk for too long not to get paid. I'll take my chances.

I need to get out. I grab my wallet and stuff it into the leg pocket of my cargo pants, pick up my Ray Bans and keys and head for the door. I'm still wrestling my shades onto my face as I open the door and the early morning sun blinds me. Shit! Shaking it off, I jump in my truck and head downtown. I grab a coffee and a bagel at a little place I like and sit outside, enjoying the cool morning. I have the life of a mole. I'm finishing this job, collecting my pay check and hitting the beach. I've nothing else lined up; maybe I should take a vacation? I need a vacation…. No, I need a shower. I glance at my reflection in the window beside me, I look like shit. I haven't shaved all week and I'm in yesterday's clothes. It's not exactly a great look, but it comes with the territory.

I take a look at my cell, 8:49am. What day is it? Friday. The maid comes for an hour on Friday mornings, if I hang back 'til 10am she'll be gone and I can shower and go straight to bed. Feeling guilty, I remind myself that having a maid is okay. I'm busy and would otherwise live in a pit. Plus, it's not like I can't afford it. Still, it feels weird and I'm always glad if I'm out when she comes. I check my emails to kill time; it's the usual crap so I set about deleting. I'm just closing my email down when the blue box pops up on the screen.

You have 1 new message from Connie Wilcox.

Who? I think, shrugging to myself as I open Facebook. I only know of one Connie and I doubt she'd be on Facebook. For a start, I haven't seen her in, like, twelve years and she's not exactly Facebook's target demographic. I mean, she would have to be at least seventy by now.

I check the signal as it takes its time loading; it seems to be fine, it's just so slow. I hate that. The message finally opens up and the profile picture of Connie is the generic Facebook blue head. I hate that too, seriously! I don't care who you are or what you think of yourself, get a photo. Even I have one and I hate photos of myself. Admittedly, it's the one and only useable headshot from an excruciating shoot for my website a few years ago and I use it for everything, but at least I don't have a blue head. It's my one rule of Facebook…I do not befriend blue-headed people.

From: Connie Wilcox   23rd March 2012

Dearest Danny,
It has been a long time! I hope you are well and life is good. I know this is out of the blue, but I think our darling girl Liv could do with an old friend right now. What do you think?
Forgive me if I have overstepped, I know I'm an interfering old bat! I have no idea what your situation is, but I suspect it could be the same as Liv's and if so then maybe you'll thank me for this one day. I only want

what is best. You know that girl is my world and I always thought the world of you too.

Think about it…that's all I ask.

All my love,

Connie.

I blow out a long breath. I hadn't realised I was holding and rubbing the deep furrow on my brow. It takes a moment to sink in. It is *that* Connie. Our darling girl…she used to say that. I slowly shake my head in disbelief. What is this all about? It *is* out of the blue, she's damned right.

Keeping control of my thoughts I try to process her message. Then, deliberately and carefully, I allow her to enter my head…Liv. It's been such a long time since I've allowed myself to think about her that I've no idea where to begin.

I stare at my cell for a while and then an idea strikes. Connie's friends…I click on Connie's name and find her basic info. I select friends; it's a very short list. Maybe she is new to Facebook? But there she's and my insides contract from just reading her name, Olivia Harper…still Harper. Shaking the emerging thought from my head, I select her name and wait. A small photo of my first love appears on my screen and my stomach lurches.

It's her.

I try to enlarge her face, but the resolution is too low and I lose her details. I need to do this at home really, but the maid will still be there. Picking up my keys, I shove my cell in my pocket and head back in to get two more coffees. I know what to do.

I pull up six blocks away behind the store and collect the coffees from the passenger seat. I try the door handle and am relieved to find it unlocked.

"Jen?" I call out. "Jen?"

"I'm here," Jen responds from where she's kneeling on the floor under the counter.

She emerges with an arm full of bags and stands blowing hair from her face. She dumps the bags on the counter top and turns to me.

"What is my favourite hermit doing here at this hour?"

"I bought you coffee," I smile.

Jen's parents are my parents' best friends. When we moved back here in 2000, they were quick to reconnect and Jen was encouraged to look out for me. We were the same age and although we had no recollection of it, we were reliably informed that we played together as small children. It was unbelievably awkward to begin with; I felt so sorry for her, having to cart me round out of a sense of duty. But slowly we became friends and when we both went to school and the social scene picked up, we often mixed our groups to hang out, as we attended nearby campuses.

Eventually, we became best friends and I looked out for her as much as she did for me. She's attractive, blonde, petite and girly; she often attracted the wrong type of guy. I'd be her 'boyfriend' when she needed to ward off sleaze bags, but nothing ever happened between us. We were just friends. Besides, I was in no fit state to be in a relationship. I was broken.

When we first became friends, I was a wreck. It was so good to have a girl to talk to; she really helped me get myself together. I made friends with guys too, but being close to a girl really helped me fill the void. Something about the nature of our friendship comforted me and, slowly, I pieced things back together. She was my rock and when I did finally start getting back out there, Jen was a great wingman.

Our friends and families couldn't understand why we never got it together. But we just didn't want it to be that way. We talked honestly about that stuff and it was mutual that there was no attraction between us. When we graduated and were both in the market for a roommate, we took the conscious decision not to live together. Although it would've been great to live with her, I didn't want to be constantly defending myself to jealous boyfriends, it was already a problem I had, even at separate addresses. She'd have also been a threat to any potential girlfriend, had there been many. So she moved in with her girlfriends and I moved in with my buddy, Scott.

We stayed close though and formed a small, tight group. I'd briefly dated one of Jen's friends and it didn't end well, so for a while, we had a rule that we wouldn't date each other's friends. Things changed, however, when I came home and discovered her and Scott asleep together in his bed. It turned out that they'd been carrying on for a while and it was serious. They were just waiting for the right time to tell me, worried I would be mad. I was anything but mad, it was great to see my two best friends together and the rule was just to protect our friendship against casual flings. This was something different. They were clearly in love and before long Jen was my roommate after all.

We lived happily together for a year and then, one night, Jen's birthday, when we were out celebrating, Scott popped the question and Jen said yes! I knew it was time to move out and let them be together. I'd been freelancing since graduation, making a name for myself. So I took the plunge, got my own place and set up my own software development company, working from home. Scott and Jen married a year later and I was best man.

Since then, not much has changed. Business has been good for me; I can pick and choose my projects, work when I want to, or when I need to. Scott does a similar job, but for a big corporation; he's more of a steady pay check kind of guy. Jen runs a clothes store with her mom. She and Scott haven't had any children, despite trying, so are now looking into their options. It's been hard to watch Jen's sadness at not achieving her dream of being a mom, but I'm certain they'll get there.

"Got time to chat?" I ask, handing her a coffee.

"Well I have to open up, but if you help me bring some boxes up from the basement, you have a deal."

Jen switches on the sound system and opens the door. I help her carry a small metal bench outside and place it in front of the window. She winds down a large blind to shade the window and as she busies herself with switching on a baffling array of lights around the place, I fetch the boxes from the basement. Once we've finished, we sit at the small couches by the changing area. In any other circumstances, I would be out of my comfort zone in this place, but I visit Jen here all the time and I've long overcome my macho worries about sitting on a pink sofa among vintage floral scatter cushions.

There are no customers; this part of town doesn't warm up until later. We have her laptop across our knees and are looking at the basic profile of one Olivia Harper.

"Is that her?"

"Yeah, she looks really different. She's pierced her nose...and lip! Wow."

"She's pretty."

"Yeah, she always was. She looks really different, but it's her."

I stare at her. I want to see more, but I can't unless I add her and she accepts. I've purposely never searched for her. In fact, I've never looked up anyone else I knew from England either, mainly because I wasn't bothered, but also in case they were friends with her.

"So?" asks Jen, looking at me expectantly.

"So, what do you think I should do?"

"Well, what do *you* think you should do?"

"God, Jen. I don't know. You know what it did to me, leaving her behind."

Jen looks at me pensively for a moment and then opens her mouth to say something. Closing it again, she changes her mind. I watch her, waiting. She starts again.

"Can I ask you something?"

"Anything."

"Why have you never settled down?"

I laugh. "I don't know, I've never met the right girl I guess."

"Maybe...maybe you have met the right girl...but you had to leave her behind." She finishes with her sweetest smile to soften the blow.

"Don't say that, I'm barely holding it together as it is!"

I rub my face. This can't be happening.

"She made it clear, she thought it was for the best that I leave. I wanted more, way more, you know that, but it wasn't what she wanted. I tried to stay in touch but she was obviously moving on, you know the rest, you were there. I can't do that again. Besides, if she wanted to find me she could have. It isn't her asking for contact. She probably hasn't thought about me in years."

"I don't believe that. This Connie woman obviously thinks you should get in touch. Maybe she never got over you either."

"I'd love to talk to her, find out how she is. But what if it isn't enough? What if…I can't risk it?"

"Danny, you know as well as I do that you'll do this. If not, it'll eat you up."

"Shit…Shit!"

I put my head in my hands, pausing for a moment, gathering my thoughts and breathing deeply. Then I sit up, grab the laptop and click 'Message' and hammer it out before I change my mind. She's right; it will eat me up if I don't.

From: Danny Morgan   23rd March 2012

Hey! I was reminded of you today. How's life?
Add me if you feel like chatting to an old friend.

Danny x

I hit send. Fuck!

"Good for you," says Jen, beaming from ear to ear.

"You know this is going to fuck with my head. I hope you can spare the time, it looks like you're going back into the therapy business," I grin. I'm terrified, but I can't deny it, it's a real buzz too. Liv. Christ! Suddenly she's real again. What is she like?

"What time is it?"

Jen cranes her neck and checks the clock on the wall.

"9:45."

"I'm going to go shower."

"That saves us a conversation!" she jokes. I jump up and as she stands I grab her and force her face into my armpit.

"Urgh! You are so gross! Get out of here!" she laughs.

I kiss her on the forehead and head out the back door to my truck.

"And don't come back 'til you smell better!" I wave my hand dismissively and I'm gone.

In the car, I try to focus, but I arrive home, not recalling any of my journey I'm so lost in thought. Robotically, I shower, shave and pull on some sweats. I flop down on the clean sheets of my freshly made bed. Right now, I don't feel bad about having a maid. I stare at my clock, 10.27am. I worked all night; I need to sleep. My eyes are heavy, but adrenaline spikes as I hear my cell buzz. I reach for it on the nightstand.

You have 1 new message from Olivia Harper.

As I'm dealing with the surge of adrenaline that revelation has delivered, it buzzes again.

You have 1 new friend request.

Oh hell! I dash to the computer, open Facebook and open her message. I need to do this on a big screen.

From: Olivia Harper   23rd March 2012

Hey yourself! Reminded of me how?

Liv x

Well, that gives nothing away. But she has added me. Maybe this won't be so bad. I click on her name and her full profile opens. I click on her photos, and sit and stare as photo after photo of my beautiful Liv appear. Seeing her face in detail instantly reopens the old wound and I already know I'm done for, but it's too late to do anything about it now. We've made contact. I just have to stay strong.

On quick inspection, it looks like she uses Facebook about as much as I do. But she seems to be tagged in a lot of photos. Always in bars, having fun, no…wait…it looks like she works in this place. I check on her info, she works at a place called Lady Luck's. Lives there would be more accurate.

There's no relationship status, and her name's still the same. In a lot of her photos there's this one guy, they look close, too close. He's all over her. I hate it. My impulse is to scoff at his fondness for hats, but I pull myself together. He might just be a friend, or an ex. Connie would not have put this out there if Liv was with someone, would she? Unless of course he is the boyfriend and Connie doesn't approve…who knows?

I need to respond. Where the hell do I start? I look back at her photo…what would I say if she were here now?

From: Danny Morgan   23rd March 2012

Well hello stranger! I've never searched for you on here. I wasn't even sure it was you…Have you pierced your face????

Danny x

There, it's a start. I'm so tired I must sleep. In a moment of extraordinary strength, I force myself to close the computer down. I fall into a restless sleep, dreaming of a girl I don't know, with Liv's face.

Seven.

This isn't sleepless in Seattle.

Danny.

I wake with a start. I've no idea what time it is. I feel around on the nightstand for my cell, but it's not there. I sit up and feel it on the bed next to me. I must have fallen asleep with it still in my hand. The screen comes to life and tells me it's 5:15pm. I'm surprised, I've managed about six hours' sleep...and I've a Facebook notification.

From: Olivia Harper

23rd March 2012

Yes, it's me...and yes it's pierced...are you judging me? You have an unfair advantage, I'm at work.
No more Facebook stalking until I can snoop around your profile!!!

Liv x

She sent it two hours ago, but I'm not awake enough to figure out what time it is in the UK. I get up and pull open the drapes in my room, squinting. I don't open them very often, but I need to sort out my body clock and I think daylight, even if it is fading, might be the only way. I wander into the kitchen and run the faucet until the water comes through good and cold. I drink straight from the stream of water and then splash some over my face. I stand up straight, dripping but refreshed, and push the water from my face back over my hair.

I fill a glass with water, taking it with me to the computer. As I wait for it to load, I wonder whether hearing from me has had the same effect on her as it has on me. I doubt that's possible. I open Facebook and re-read her message. She sounds almost panicked. It's funny, I did look round her profile, but she obviously thinks I'm stalking her! Maybe I should give her something to think about while she's working. I amuse myself for a moment and, smirking, I type a reply.

From: Danny Morgan   23rd March 2012

If you say so ;-)
Danny x

If I remember correctly, its eight hours ahead over there, so it's after midnight, maybe she's still at work if she works in a bar. Maybe she's asleep, who knows? My cell buzzes in my pocket. It's a text from Jen.

'Did you hear anything? X'

I dial her number and she answers in her usual way, no greeting, straight into the conversation.

"I hope you showered," she chirps.

I laugh.

"Listen," she continues, "I just got off and Scott has a late meeting, so I'm coming over. Shall I bring food?"

"No, we'll order in. See you in ten." I don't expect a reply, Jen is past pleasantries with me and she's gone.

I text Scott.

'Late meeting? Sucks to be you! You should strike out on your own then maybe YOU could buy your wife Chinese takeout, would save me a fortune!'

As I hear Jen's car, he texts back.

'If I struck out on my own I'd never see daylight like you! This way you pay for dinner and I don't have to listen to your love dilemmas. Be sure to send leftovers home with Jen'

I open the door, smirking.

"Something funny?" Jen asks as she breezes in and tosses her purse on the floor.

"Your husband," I reply as she heads straight for the drawer in the kitchen where I keep the menus and helps herself to a beer from the refrigerator. I raise an eyebrow at her when she closes the door. She smiles apologetically and grabs one for me too. We head out to the small terrace of my ground floor apartment and sit facing each other. She sips her beer and waits.

"Shall we order?" I ask.

"Not until you tell me what she said."

I fill Jen in on what little there is to know. But it isn't enough; she wants to snoop around her profile. It's pointless arguing with her, so I fetch the laptop. While she's satisfying her curiosity, I order dinner. We don't need to discuss what to have; it's comical that she still always gets out the menu. I hang up and return to my cold beer.

"Well, she's single," she says with authority.

"Thanks Nancy Drew! I reached the same conclusion." I tilt my head. "What about that guy though?"

"The hat guy? My guess is, he's gay."

"You think everyone's gay. Anyway, he's all over her, an ex maybe?"

"She'd have deleted the photos if he were an ex. He's nothing to worry about, trust me. So that's it, she hasn't responded?"

"No, she was working, so she might not get off yet. We sometimes worked 'til past 2am when we worked at Riley's didn't we? Anyway, I'm not waiting by the laptop." I don't sound convincing.

We talk about her day, and my project. Our food arrives and we talk and eat. We discuss Scott's job; he's up for a promotion, hence the extra meetings. Jen's worried about the tests she has next week.

"It's best to know, then you can make plans," I reassure her, finishing the last egg roll.

"I know. It's just stressful."

The simultaneous bing of the laptop and the buzz of my cell interrupts us. This is pathetic. I hardly ever use Facebook, and now I have all my devices trained on its every move. Jen launches herself at the laptop. It's a fight I won't win; so I let her look at the message. She graciously turns the laptop slightly towards me, so that I can look over her shoulder.

From: Olivia Harper   24th March 2012

Okay, so I've finished snooping. You don't give much away do you? I have to admit, I don't know what to say to you...How's life?

Liv x

Jen turns to me, grinning.

"What?"

"She is SO still into you!"

"How did you get that from...that?" I gesture at the screen. This is absurd! I shake my head.

"What are you going to say?"

"I've no idea."

"Well think of something, she's still online!"

"No!"

"Yep! I'll take that as my cue to leave." Jen grins and grabs the tray with the takeout containers, plants a kiss on the top of my head, and leaves.

I glance back at the laptop, the sun has just gone down and its bright white screen illuminates the table.

Fuck!

I take a deep breath and think. This is just unreal, she's online, right there, right now...and I can talk to her. Though what would I say? I'm not sure I can trust myself. Since she was put back in my head today, I've been reliving the whole mess, a mess I'd worked so hard to put behind me, What the hell was I even thinking getting into this? I'd like to say enough time has gone by and I'm a stronger person now, but where Liv is concerned, I don't think I'd ever have enough strength to make this a safe move. Frankly, whatever happens, I'm already screwed. Pulling the laptop across to face me, I look at her words. She says she doesn't know what to say to me. I know how she feels. Maybe it's best to go for honesty. I start typing.

Danny
I don't really know what to say to you either. This is weirder than I thought it would be...Life is great; I'm living in Santa Monica, near the beach. I work from home (computer stuff - yawn!) but it leaves me free to do whatever I like, mostly. My parents live nearby; they're still the same. There's nothing else to tell really. What about you? You give nothing away either. Apart from the facial piercings!!! I wasn't expecting that! What's happening in your life?

Hopefully, that sounds upbeat and doesn't give away my gut-wrenching panic.

Olivia
There must be more to tell... My life is good. I'm still here. I never left. I'm a business owner. I have the diner of my dreams, which is doing really well. It's Connie's old teashop! I took it over when she retired and she and Jack helped me get it off the ground. I live upstairs; have done since my first term at college. Mum and Dave moved to Brighton with Dave's job and I didn't want to go. Connie let me have the place and I've never left. They've stayed in Brighton, it's lovely. It's like I have a holiday home. Not that I get any time off. It's pretty full-on running your own business. Grace lives in LA too, Venice. You should look her up!

I can't get my head around the idea that Liv owns the place in her pictures. It looks great, the kind of place I would go with Jen and the guys. It looks nothing like the Connie's I remember, it's at least twice the size. Something that Liv confirms when she tells me she took on the old Italian place next door. That was my parents' favorite restaurant when we lived there. When she tells me her high maintenance sister lives in LA too, I'm floored. I couldn't care less about Grace, she's always been a total nightmare, but how many times has Liv visited her there? Just fifteen minutes from my apartment. How many times could our paths have crossed? I manage not to betray this when I reply. I don't think I'm ready for her to see that I am already freaking out over missed opportunities. Instead, I simply congratulate her on the bar. She always said that she wanted to do it and she did.

I casually tell her I'd love to see it someday. It seems nuts, but talking to her again makes me think that after all this time maybe we should try to know each other again. We were once everything to one another, I've missed her. Maybe I could visit some time, get my heart broken again for old time's sake! Immediately I regret saying it, but it's not like I would ever actually go. She has a life now and so do I.

She tries to tell me that she's still the same person, but from her photos I can see that that is so not true. She has piercings in places I never would have expected of her. I shut my mind down as soon as it starts to wonder to where else she might be pierced. I can't afford to think like that. She admits she has some tattoos and after searching I find an image of her wearing a short-sleeved shirt and a tattoo is visible on her inner forearm. I wonder how many she has? Most of the photos are of her face, but now I look at her in a different light, she definitely has more of a wild look to her than she used to.... Hot as fuck! I'm in real trouble. It suits her, this new image. Maybe it's not new, I realise with a sigh that it's been a really long time. Even though it feels like only yesterday she broke my heart.

She asks me if she's frightened me off and I realise I'd drifted away thinking about her, then in my infinite wisdom, I tell her she looks hot. Really? What the hell am I doing? I scrub my face and shake my head. I'm a danger to myself, I really am. To make matters worse, she then goes silent. I tentatively ask if she's still there, there are questions I'm afraid to ask. Questions that are really none of my business, but I need to know anyway. I decide I've got nothing to lose.

Danny
The guy in the pictures, is he your boyfriend?

Olivia
Which guy?

Danny
The one who's always wearing a hat.

Olivia
Best friend.

> Interesting, but she didn't say there wasn't a boyfriend.

Danny
But there is a boyfriend?

Olivia
Nope. What about you, are you not settled down?

Danny
Never found the right girl.

> Well perhaps I did, I just let her go too easily…SHUT UP DANNY! God, what am I doing?

Olivia
It's almost 4am here…I need to sleep!

> Excellent! I'll never hear from her again. She tries to cover herself by saying that she just got off work and she needs to sleep, but I'm sure she's

just eager to get away. I'm such an idiot. In a last desperate attempt not to let her completely slip away I add,

Danny
Maybe we could do this again?

Olivia
Sure. It was great to hear from you. Night x

    I fight the urge to hurl. What the hell just happened? I think, I just got way too heavy and fucked up my one and only chance to ever see Liv again. I bang my head on the table. Shit. She couldn't get away fast enough. I've truly messed this up. What I need to do now is get her out of my head.
    I check the time, almost 9pm. I should do some work, that'll help.
    I clear my head of distractions and work, hard.
    For five hours I manage to hammer away without entertaining thoughts of Liv and fall into bed fried at 2am.

    I'm woken at around 8am by my phone buzzing. I reach underneath my pillow and retrieve it. Turning it over, I assume it's Jen wanting info; I'm stunned to find that Liv has messaged me.

From: Olivia Harper   24th March 2012

It was great to talk to you yesterday.
Can I ask, why now? I'm not complaining, just confused.

Liv x

    Confused? You and me both! I'm surprised to hear from her again. I need to think about what to say. I thought I'd wrecked it yesterday; I really don't want to spend today feeling the same way. I shower then text Scott.

'I'm coming over for breakfast. Please don't be fucking when I get there!'

He instantly texts back
'Cock block! Jen says bring bacon.'

I have an open invitation for breakfast at the weekends, but I've walked in on one too many Saturday morning baby-making attempts, so I no longer take the risk. I stop at the market on my way and pick up the bacon. I also get newspapers and apple juice, they drink orange juice and I hate the stuff.

I walk through their side gate and into the yard, dump my keys and the newspapers on the table and head into the kitchen. Jen is mixing pancake batter in sweats and an old UCLA t-shirt. Scott is showering. I lean round and plant a kiss on Jen's cheek. She jumps out of her skin and it's only then I realise she is listening to her iPod.

"Fuck, you bastard!" she yells.

"Sorry, I thought you heard me." I cower as she slaps me hard on the shoulder.

"You scared the shit out of me," she laughs. I rub my shoulder, acting wounded.

She takes off her headphones and returns to her mixing.

"So, what happened after I left last night?"

I begin to give her the shorthand version and she tuts. "You'll miss all the good stuff, read it to me."

With a huff I pull my cell from my pocket and find the conversation. I read it out in a wooden monotone, hoping not to inject too much drama into it.

She's wide-eyed when I look up, just as Scott joins us.

"What have I missed?"

Jen scoffs, "Not much, just Romeo over here, practically telling his long lost love that he still wants her."

"I did not!"

She puts on a mocking tone as she says, "Oh Liv, do you have a boyfriend? I don't have a girlfriend because I still love you!" She bats her eyelids at me.

Scott rolls his eyes.

"She's probably running for the hills," laughs Jen.

"Thanks," I mutter, indignant. "Actually, it just so happens that she messaged me again this morning."

"What, after that performance! What did she say?"

I read the message out.

"I haven't responded. I wanted to think about my next move. So what do you think I should say?"

"Tell her it was just the right time."

"What and that's it?"

"Yeah, then see what she has to say."

Shaking my head at Jen, I turn towards the door. I sit at the table in the yard and stare at my cell. What do I say? I listen to the comforting sounds of my friends cooking breakfast and think. Jen has hit the nail on the head once again; there's really nothing else to say.

Danny
It just seemed like the right time. X

I sit in silence for what feels like forever then the rewarding buzz startles me. She's online.... She wants to know why I didn't stay in touch with anyone from the UK. I tell her there seemed little point, as there was no one that could drag us away from each other then, so I wasn't really interested enough to contact them now. The truth is, I did have friends I'd like to look up, but I could never run the risk of them still being friends with her. Not when I've tried so hard to forget. I've completely shot that to shit now haven't I!

Olivia
Fair enough! We were pretty closed off.

God, we were, but only because we were completely in love, well I was…I don't see what I have to lose in hinting at that.

Danny
I only had eyes for you.

Olivia
Smoothie!

> Oh, okay, I think I class that as flirting.

Danny
I wasn't back then!

Olivia
You did okay. Neither of us knew what we were doing.

> WHAT? Is she talking about sex right now?

Danny
OK?!? You know how to kill a man's confidence don't you! Also, FYI that is SO not what I was talking about! ONE-TRACK-MIND.

Olivia
Oh! Well, anyway it was lovely. I'm sure we're both more confident now!

> So we *are* talking about sex and as if that's not bad enough, she thinks it was 'lovely'.

Danny
Lovely! This is awful, is that really what you think? You may as well say it was NICE!

Olivia
That's not what I meant, I wouldn't change things. I've good memories of

that time. You were so kind.

I try not to think about that time, apart from being too painful, the vision of myself, as a fumbling idiot, is too embarrassing. Knowing she has that memory of me too is terrible. If I could have one wish right now, it would be to wipe those memories from her mind and give her something better to remember! I'm good at it now for fuck's sake. I don't want the one person that ever meant something to me to think of me at my worst. I need to find a way to say that so I offer something witty about having a do-over.

She completely shoots that down, fair enough. I don't know what the hell I was doing saying it! But it still stings. I absorb the crushing disappointment, then she starts typing again…

Olivia
For a start, you can't erase those memories. They are keepers! Besides, even if you could have a do-over, there is the small matter of distance.

Is she saying I could if I was there?

Danny
True. I just wish your most important memory of me wasn't just 'lovely'. I want it to be fucking amazing!

Olivia
All my memories of you are amazing.

Shit. Mine too…I decide I have nothing to lose by telling her that I miss her.

Olivia
I've missed you too.

Just then, Jen and Scott appear with breakfast and Jen notices my ashen face.

"What happened?"

I hand her my phone and even in my daze I note that Scott is unable to resist reading too.

Jen is beside herself with excitement.

"This is brilliant! She still wants you; you have to go to her!"

Oh hell, what is it with women and their Hollywood ideations?

"Get real! This isn't Sleepless in Seattle!"

Scott erupts with laughter, "You're such a girl. Why would you even know that?"

"Ignore him. But you should think about it," Jen says soothingly as she digs into her pancakes. Reluctantly, I eat too, I don't have any appetite, but it's only polite.

"You deserve a vacation," Jen continues. "Why don't you just go?" She'd love this to turn into something she could really get her teeth into.

"Because a) I live in the real world, and b) I have a ton of work."

"You're nearly done, you said so. Besides, she's talking about the two of you having sex, which means she's thinking about the two of you having sex."

Scott chimes in. "I don't like to encourage her man, but she has a point…"

"So, you're suggesting that after a mere two conversations, I fly 5,000 miles and try to rekindle a relationship with my first girlfriend, who probably isn't that interested…and then what? Fly home?" I frown at them both. "That sounds productive! I'm sure it won't be at all detrimental to either of us."

Jen thinks for a moment, "Can't you just go there for a break and not make it into something it's not?"

I drag my hands across my face, stretching my skin and then heave a huge sigh. "Ugh! At this point, I'm so screwed, maybe I have nothing to lose…"

"That's the spirit!" Scott laughs.

I sit and stare into the distance. Am I really entertaining this? I realise now that talking to her is never going to be enough. I was better off when

I didn't allow her into my head. Of course, now that I have, I either see where it goes, or try my best to forget about her. That could take years again. Damn it!

"Okay, I need to leave," I say scraping my chair as I stand.

"Don't think about it, just do it," pleads Jen. "You've never really moved on, this is your chance to either see it through, or put an end to it once and for all."

I turn and offer her a tight smile.

"I'll let you know," I say quietly, passing behind them as they sit at the table. Scott has his arm around Jen. "Thanks for breakfast."

"Good luck buddy," Scott says, tapping my hand as I pat his shoulder.

"Call me later," says Jen as I kiss the top of her head and walk away.

I realise as I'm driving that I didn't say anything else to Liv. I said I missed her, she said she missed me too and that is it. I feel terrible, but honestly, what would I say now? If I told her I was considering getting on a plane, she would have a restraining order in place before I touched down. This is ludicrous! I can't go to England. I just need to forget about her. I pound my fist against the steering wheel. Fucking pull yourself together! I'm just going to go home and get this work out of the way.

I breeze through the front door with renewed purpose; I'm going to finish this shitty job. Now more than ever, a vacation sounds like a great idea. Who knows where I will go, but like a light at the end of the tunnel, it drives me. I switch on my computer and get stuck in.

Eight.

Have I blown it?

Danny.

I hang up the phone. I've finally finished the job and got that asshole out of my life. It's Tuesday morning; I've been locked in for four days and nights. I need to shower. I pause for a moment and sigh. I'm beyond exhausted. Maybe I should go to bed? No, I'll feel and smell better after a shower. I head into the bathroom, turn on the water and return to the bedroom to empty my pockets.

I dump the contents on the bed and for a moment I think my cell lights up with a message. My stomach lurches but then I realise it's just a reflection from the window. Having shut it out for four days, my mind is clear now and it all rushes back in. I sit on the end of the bed and run my hands through my hair, feeling sick at the realisation that it's been four days and while I haven't contacted Liv again, I haven't heard anything from her either. I knew it was all just me. She's not interested. If she were, surely I would have heard from her, wouldn't she wonder why I made contact then vanished?

I throw myself back on the bed and close my eyes. I'm fighting back tears. This shocks me. Am I really that upset? It feels that way. I guess it's because I now know for sure that there's no chance of developing this into something more. Can I contact her again and keep it platonic? No way. So I'll just leave it. I'll move on. I guess it's what I have to do. Resigned, I hit the shower.

As I wash, I curse myself. I curse Connie and I curse Jen. How did I get swept up in this? Damn them and their romantic notions. Connie should have kept out of my life. Why did she do this? I begin to think of possible reasons Connie would have to turn my life on its head like this…then, like a bolt of lightning, it hits me.

She wants to make Liv happy.

That is the only reason she would have got involved like this. Because she thought it would make Liv happy…she thinks I could make Liv happy… she must…and if I take my head out of my ass long enough, I would realise that.

Seeing Liv would make me happy too. No two ways about it…then Jen's suggestion comes back to me.

I have to see her.

As crazy as it is and as damaging as it could be, I realise that there's nothing stopping me trying.

I jump out of the shower and grab a towel. I partially dry and stalk into the bedroom. Standing in the middle of the room, I look around, searching for inspiration. Obviously none of these inanimate objects are going to tell me what to do. Clasping my head, I inhale deeply. I need to get organised. I run to my nightstand and rifle through the drawer. My passports. Yes! I have two, one for the US and one for the UK because I have dual citizenship. Thank God they're both up to date, or this whole thing would be impossible. Legally, I have to leave the US as a US citizen, and enter the UK as a UK citizen.

My dad made us keep up our UK passports because we have right of abode in both countries and it keeps our options open. We have no family left in the UK, my grandparents both passed away years ago and my dad is an only child, like me. But he always wanted me to have the option of travelling. Because of his forethought, I can live, work and travel freely between the two countries. Right now I could kiss him, but he's in Mexico with Mom. I'll call them when they're back in a few days and let them know where I am. Who knows, I could be back by then?

Shaking off that negativity, I go to the closet and reach up to the top shelf, drag down my suitcase and fill it with everything I can find that is clean and warm. It won't be warm there I know. I dress and go to the bathroom, gathering everything I'll need from in there and return to the bedroom. As I put the things in my suitcase, I realise I'm grinning. I try to pull myself together, long enough to shut everything off and lock everything up. My heart is pounding.

I pick up my rucksack and fill it with the important stuff: laptop, cell, passports. I return to my suitcase and drop in my hard drive and all the wires and chargers I'll need. I have no idea how long I'll be. This is so impulsive; I hope I've thought of everything. I zip the case closed and look around nervously. Then, when I'm as sure as I can be, I call a cab. I can't believe how fast I've thrown this together. My hair isn't even dry. I just know I have to go.

I lock the door behind me, instinctively check my truck door to make sure it's locked and head out to the waiting cab.

"LAX," I say as I sit in the backseat. "But can we just make one quick stop first."

We pull up outside Jen's store and I jump out. Bursting in the door, I see Jen as she comes from the back. She looks at me with concern.

"Danny? What's up?"

"I just came by to ask you to look in on my place."

"Why, where are you going?"

"On vacation!"

She takes in this information and then slowly her face changes in realisation.

"Liv?" she whispers, breaking into a smile when I nod. She throws her arms around my neck and I spin her round.

"Does she know?"

I shake my head.

"What time is your flight?"

I shrug.

"I'll take the first one out."

"Oh my God, Danny. You're so romantic!"

I grin.

"So will you keep an eye on things for me?"

"Of course, how long will you be?"
I shrug, still smiling like an idiot. "I'll call you."
Kissing her square on the lips. I turn and head for the door.
"Good luck!" she calls after me.

At LAX, I practically run through the door searching for a departure screen. I scan down the list, direct will be expensive and most likely full, so I need to get to the East Coast then get a connection to London. The first one I can see is a Delta to JFK direct. It takes off in three hours. I head to the Delta desk.

Ticket in hand, I pass through Passport Control. Now I have to wait. Yeah, like it's that easy! I mean, sure I'll sit still for three hours thinking about what could be waiting for me in London. If I'm this bad now, I'll be like a caged beast on the airplane. To occupy myself, I indulge in a spot of window shopping. I buy some candy and a bottle of water and wander into an electronics store. I'm buzzing from the excitement and nerves. As I browse the iPads, I decide on a whim to buy one.

It's a rash decision, but I realise that I've barely seen the light of day for weeks. I've more than earned the big payday I've just received…and I'm on vacation. The helpful clerk agrees to charge it for me and even lets me sit at one of the demonstration desks to sync it with my laptop. Thirty minutes later, I'm set it all up, but it's still charging. I have an hour to kill. I glance around and the clerk, Megan, comes by to find out how I'm doing. We get chatting.

She asks where I'm going and I tell her the whole thing. Telling a stranger, I realise how exciting and romantic it really is. She wishes me well and says she hopes, one day, someone will come and sweep her off her feet like that. I thank her for her help and head to the gate.

I scroll through my apps and decide to download a book for the flight. I can't remember the last time I found the time to read. Then, tapping Facebook, I take a deep breath and compose a message to Liv, telling her that I'm sorry I haven't been in contact. Unsure of what to say that won't ruin the surprise of me flying in, I tap my knee restlessly. Then I decide to just be vague and tell her I have to finish something I started a long time ago. Hopefully she'll think it's cute when she finds out what I mean. I ask her not to give up on me before I sign off.

Hopefully that will hold her until I get there. I hope it's enough. I've no idea how she is, or what she's thinking, and I can't wait for a response as the flight begins boarding. I switch to airplane mode and head on board. I sink into my seat in first class…hey, this is my first vacation in three years! I could have used the first class lounge but I couldn't relax for that amount of time, I thought shopping would keep me busy. Arranging my things in the luxurious surroundings, I'm amused to find an electrical outlet, I could have charged here! I also see that I can pay to use in-flight Wi-Fi, but sleep is the only thing on my mind. I've worked for four days, snatching only cat naps and I've got myself here purely on adrenaline. I need to sleep. I plug in my headphones and close my eyes, drifting away before other passengers are even on board. The flight attendant asking me to turn off my electrical devices stirs me and I oblige. I'm so tired, but now I have about six hours' uninterrupted sleep ahead of me. As soon as we are in the air, I arrange the blanket and pillow, tip my seat back and I'm gone.

My sleep is blissful. I'm aware of my surroundings, but I feel cocooned, like I'm in exactly the right place. I dream of Liv and me as kids. I feel so content. The flight attendant wakes me to put my seat up and we land. It's like no time has gone by, yet I'm rested. At JFK, while I wait for my BA flight in the first class lounge, I check Facebook, but she hasn't replied. I'm too disoriented to work out the time difference; I don't even know which time zone I'm in right now.

The second leg of my journey is more stressful. I watch a couple of in-flight movies and drift in and out of sleep, but mostly, I worry. What if she doesn't want to see me, she hasn't replied to my last message. In fact I haven't heard from her in days. What if she isn't interested at all and backing off is her way of telling me. I worry that I'll see her and go right back to the awful place I was before.

As we come into land at Heathrow. I stare out of the window, it's been twelve years since I left this place behind and I feel anxious about what I'll find here now. It's late, according to the captain 23:43 local time. I need to find a hotel.

The taxi pulls up outside the Holiday Inn. It's new, but just like any other. I pad wearily over to the desk and fifteen minutes later I'm entering my room. I've booked in for three nights. Hopefully by then I'll know if I have a chance. I check Facebook again. Nothing. Is she ignoring me? It's late; I'll deal with it in the morning. I crawl into bed, feeling daunted by the fact that I'm less than a mile away from the only girl I've ever loved...and she has no idea!

I wake to the sounds from the street. The hotel is on a busy road on the edge of town, it sounds like everyone else is up and at 'em. I reach for my cell, 11.49am. Unbelievable! I obviously needed the sleep. I stretch out and take a deep breath. Now I have to figure out my plan. I check Facebook, still nothing. I need to get in touch or this will all be wasted, but I want to speak to her, assess her mood before I just show up. What if she never returns my messages? Maybe this is all a mistake. I have to know. I hit new message and tell her I'm free to talk.

I wait...and wait. Nothing. I get up, shower and dress. I head out for lunch, revisiting my old town, avoiding the area I know she'll be. Much of it is just the same on the surface, but so much has changed. I go into the mall and head to a Starbucks. I have all the time in the world to explore and reacquaint myself, but right now, I need food and coffee and I've a head full of issues, so Starbucks suits me perfectly.

After I have eaten, I wander around. I explore everywhere and before long I'm in the street where Connie's once was. I won't take the chance of being seen, not until I know where she stands, but I can see it from here. It looks like the kind of place I would go to at home. I turn away before I'm tempted to get closer and ruin it. How long is she going to keep me waiting? Perhaps she's making a point. I send another message asking her if I've blown it.

It's around 3pm. Not knowing what else to do, I decide to go and see a movie to keep busy. I wander back to the mall and head up the escalator to the movie theatre. I choose a Mark Wahlberg movie about smuggling or something. The film doesn't matter. The point is, if she hasn't replied by the time it has finished, I'll go there and find out what's going on.

Two hours later, I emerge and straight away I check my cell, nothing. Then, like a miracle, it lights up.... My heart stops for a moment. I open the message.

From: Olivia Harper   29th March 2012

I got your message. You're not the only one who has to work!
Busy, busy! X

She's mad; I've made a huge mistake. I should have been honest with her. What was I thinking? Perhaps I shouldn't be here. But we can't finish it like this; I've come all this way. I have to see her before I leave or I'll never forgive myself. I set off, determined. I'm going to put an end to this now, even if she throws me out.

I slow as I reach the entrance and act like I'm reading the menu. Looking through the window, I don't see her. Moments pass and staff are coming and going, but she isn't here. My phone buzzes again.

From: Olivia Harper   29th March 2012

But I'm taking a break now...X

She wants to talk. Glancing back into the diner, confirming she's not there, I go in and ease myself into the first booth. With my back to the window, I can see everything. I'm sweating! She might be in the back somewhere and walk out at any moment. I glance at my screen, she's still online. I start typing...

Danny
Wow, I thought I'd blown it for sure!

Olivia
Blown what?

Is she playing games with me, surely this isn't one-sided? It's turned my life upside down, to the point where I've crossed the Atlantic, she can't be unaffected by this, can she?

Danny
I don't know about you but talking to you has had a huge effect on me. I thought it would be easy, but…it's not.

I send another message, explaining why I disappeared. Still she says nothing. I force myself to wait. A girl comes over to take my order. I order a coffee, purely so that I can sit here.

Olivia
It's had a huge effect on me too.

Oh thank God! She's typing again...

Olivia
I was OK you know. Then one message from you put me right back to that day. The day you left. I've realised I never got over it.

Shit, I didn't want to leave, why doesn't she see that? I wanted to stay and be with her. She pushed me to go. I certainly didn't think this would be the result of me contacting her again. I'm so confused.

Danny
I didn't mean to hurt you. I just…I never got over it either. I had no idea you'd feel like this. I thought if I made contact after all this time, we could be friends.

Olivia
We have no choice; I just don't know if I can do it.

No, no!

Danny
Please don't give up.

Olivia
Give up on what?

Olivia is typing...

Olivia
There's nothing to give up on. It doesn't matter how we feel when we're 5,000 miles apart. I can't do this right now, I have to work.

Fuck! She's coming and she seems really pissed. I sink lower in my booth and watch anxiously.

Suddenly, my heart is in my mouth, there she is! Fuck! She's so beautiful. She's completely changed, the Liv I left behind was attractive but not in the head-turningly sexy way that confronts me now. She isn't a girl you could not notice; you can see even from a glance that she's really different. She's effortless. Her uniform of jeans, Converse and a hooded sweatshirt with the logo of the place on it would have you wanting to work here, especially if you got to look at her all day! I want to really take in all the details of her, but she moves so quickly.

She looks upset and I've caused it. It takes everything I have not to go to her. But I can't, I'm not her safe place anymore. I've caused this. She doesn't see me as she starts wiping tables. Her back is turned, but I can see the tension in her body, she's mad as hell. I look at my cell and I know what to do.

Danny
It would help if I could see your face.

I watch as she pulls out her cell and reads it, her shoulders slump then she replies and puts her cell back in her pocket. Her message comes through.

Olivia
It would help if I could see yours, but I can't. That's my point!

    This is my chance...

Danny
You could if you turned around...

    I wait. She snatches her cell out...then she spins around.

Nine.
Did you two ever…?

Danny.

Fucking amazing sex is one thing, but fucking amazing sex with Liv is just…there are no words.

You can't put into ordinary words what it feels like to want something so badly for half of your life and then when you get it, it's more than you could've ever hoped for. Sex I realise, now, has just been sex with everyone else. This 'thing' that Liv and I have is something else. I don't know if I can acknowledge what that means just yet, but I do know I'm in pretty serious fucking trouble!

After showering and reaching an agreement about eating in her restaurant, one I'm not entirely happy with since it'll mean me not paying. I went back to the hotel to change. I was in and out in five minutes, desperate to get back to Liv. I enjoy the cooling air as I walk back. I've just had sex with Liv Harper…and it was out of this world.

I've fantasised about what it would be like to come back here and be with her again, although not for a long time, I couldn't keep torturing myself. But even when I did, I couldn't have imagined it would feel like this. It's surreal, we haven't talked yet and we have a mountain of stuff to deal with, but we are together and I can't ask for more.

I want to stop at the store on the way back. I've used my only condom. I can't just assume she'll have some and I'm certainly not going to miss out.

I text Jen.

'I've seen her, it's going well! Going for dinner now. I'll call you x'

At the store, I toy with the idea of buying Liv flowers, but convenience store flowers apparently suck wherever you are in the world. I make a mental note to find some nice ones tomorrow.

I arrive back at her place and push the buzzer.

"Hello?"

"Hey beautiful," I respond and she releases the door.

She's standing at the top of the stairs and I catch my breath. She looks incredible. I almost bolt up the stairs to get my hands on her, but I know I need to be a gentleman, I can't tear her clothes off every time I lay eyes on her. As she makes her way down to me, I study her. She's wearing a floor-length black dress and a leopard-print sweater. The thing I'm most drawn to is the red lipstick. It goes with her red shoes, but I know it's just for me.

Girls only wear lipstick like that to get guys' attention, according to Jen. If a girl has tried this trick on me before, I haven't noticed. But right now, Liv has my attention. I hold my hand out. I want to kiss her, but I don't want to smear that lipstick, I'd rather watch it on her mouth all night, thinking what it would look like smeared on parts of me...do we really need to go out? Breaking my thoughts, she reaches the bottom of the stairs and gives me her hand; I kiss it as I can't kiss her beautiful lips. Yet. She stares at me. I've no idea what she's thinking, but I just stare at those full red lips. I have to do something before I'm so hard I can't walk straight.

"You look fabulous," I manage. My voice must sound strained.

"Why thank you, so do you.". She just stares at me., I have no idea what she' is thinking, but I just stare at those lovely red lips. It is looking less and less like I will be able to stop myself jumping her right here when she speaks.

"Can I give you the tour?"

I'm relieved. I desperately want her, but it can't be all about sex. We need more. More was all we had before, sex wasn't important. Obviously it's more appealing to us both now, but I want to get some of the old us back too. At least out in public we can make a start. Hoping to break the tension as soon as possible, I accept and open the door to the real world. I feel uncertain, so I hold her hand for comfort and when I do she seems to relax too.

She shows me around with passion and enthusiasm and I feel proud. She's done all of this and she's only twenty-nine. My girl has accomplished her dreams. My girl...I allow this concept to float through my mind. She was once, I wonder if she can be again?

She tells me about this Lucky sign on the wall. The owner of a bar I have been to many times in Venice Beach gave her it. She went there just before they closed down and the guy gave it to her. I'm speechless; I could have seen her there. I could have had this sooner. It's like a one-in-a-million chance I know, but I kick myself for not drinking there more.

"Shall I show you the bar, or do you want to eat first?"

"Bar," I reply, I don't want to interrupt the flow with food. I follow her out of the front door, down a side entrance and into a garden of sorts, between the two buildings. Two doormen greet us and she looks sheepish, promising to behave herself tonight. I wonder what the deal is, just as she explains.

"I got a bit drunk, the other day...very out of character."

I smirk, *that* I'd like to see. Inside, the bar is lively and it changes the charged atmosphere between us, we instantly become more relaxed. I'm seriously impressed. I would definitely be a regular here.

"Wow." I murmur.

She looks pleased with herself and she should be. Liv leans closer and says, "Here comes Max."

"Max?"

"Best friend," Liv replies as he approaches.

I'm introduced to Max. The guy bear hugs me, taking me completely by surprise. Whatever their relationship, he's certainly at ease with me.

"Great to finally meet you," he says. "What would you like to drink?"

I can't think of anything, my head is full of questions, so I look to Liv.

"Surprise me. Where are the restrooms?"

When I come back to them, Max beats a hasty retreat. Liv and I sit at the bar and before long we are handed our drinks. It's strong and tastes like lime, I like it.

"Cheers" I toast, clinking glasses with Liv. She asks if I want to eat, but I just want to sit here with her. The diner is quieter and we both seem more relaxed. She says we can eat here though, so I agree. She goes to the back to place our order and as soon as she's gone, Max approaches. Here we go.

"Did you tell Connie you're here?" he asks. I'm taken aback by his knowledge of the situation.

"No, I came on a whim. Does Liv know she contacted me?"

He shakes his head and answers my next question with a look...she would be mad if she knew. We understand each other.

"I'm glad you're here," he smiles and then leaves me once again confused about what he is to Liv, just as she returns.

"So how long have you two known each other?" I ask, hoping to get a better idea.

"Since about two months after you left."

"A long time then." As he turns to fix some drinks I ask Liv, "So did you two ever...?"

"Max is married," she replies with a wry smile.

Married? Okay, but that doesn't answer my question.

"But before that?"

"Married to a man!"

"Oh!" I look over at Max, How the hell does Jen do it? She called it from a photo! I see the ring now too. It all falls into place. I smile with relief. I know she's not mine, but I feel better knowing this guy isn't after her.

He starts asking me about my plans. He clearly wants information for his friend.

"Well I've no firm plans, but I'd like to think at least a couple of weeks, maybe more...I have an open ticket." I should be saying this to Liv, but I avoided the subject earlier.

"Don't you have to have a return date for immigration?" It's funny, I could see myself doing this for Jen, so I appreciate where he's coming from.

"Dual citizenship," I explain. "My father's British."

"Oh okay, so you could live here if you wanted?" Wow. Don't hold back buddy!

"Okay, that's enough questions for you," Liv interjects, trying to rescue me. "Sorry," she whispers as he moves away laughing.

"No, it's fine, he's just looking out for you."

When the food arrives, I realise I'm starving. I haven't eaten a proper meal in days and Max has already given us a second round of drinks, different ones. I tuck in and it's delicious.

We talk about everything. Liv tells me how much Max has helped her and their relationship makes perfect sense to me now. Like Jen and me. We each needed to fill the chasm left by the other.

I'm stunned to hear that her dad passed away in Australia and Liv wasn't told until after the funeral. Who would do that? Then, in retrospect, I admit that the kind of women he was involved with strike me as selfish enough to bury a man without informing his children. Liv sweeps quickly past this, not wanting to give it space in our conversation. She's very philosophical about it, I admire her for that.

She tells me about her relationships, which I find difficult to hear. Especially as the last guy cheated on her recently. She caught them, which makes me sick. Why would anyone do that to her? I want to inflict harm on this asshole and I will if I ever find him. She tells me that it made her realise she didn't really care for him that much after all. In fact she seems unsentimental about her past relationships in general, like me.

I tell her about mine, well the two that stuck for a while. I leave out the casual ones; she must have done the same. I was fooling around with someone until recently, but she was just a friend really and it was a convenience thing for both of us. I haven't talked to her in a while, which usually means she's hooked up with someone else. There is no romance between us. But I don't tell Liv because it doesn't make me look great.

The drinks flow and so does the conversation. I tell her all about home and work. Max's husband arrives; he's cool. We are in a similar line of work, but we can't get too into discussing it because the bar has filled up and live music starts. I watch Liv listening to the band. She looks happy and I reach out to stroke her leg. Just touching her sends my body into overdrive, I have to get a handle on this, I'm going to burn out pretty fast if we have to do it five times a day.

Speaking of burning out, I'm absolutely beat. But there's no way I'm going back to that hotel, not while there is a chance I can stay here with her. In between songs, I pluck up the courage to ask Liv if I can stay. She nods with a grin.

Ten minutes later, we've said goodnight to Max and Charlie and are crossing the garden. I feel the need to stop her and pull her close.

"This..." I gesture at our surroundings, "is incredible! I'm so in awe of you." I kiss her lightly. "Seriously, I can't get over it; you are so incredible, so strong and sexy."

"Stop it," she insists.

"No," I whisper as I lean in to kiss her. We kiss deeply for a moment, then she pulls away. At first I think something is wrong, but she drags me quickly into the diner and upstairs. It's so swift that my blood is pumping hard by the time she opens her door. I push her against it as it closes, moaning as I find her breasts and mouth. My kiss is hurried and my hands are desperate with need. I almost lift her and take her here, but I stop. I need to control myself! We are both gasping for air. There's a time and a place for sex like that, but after so long apart, we should take time and enjoy it.

There's a shift between us and I look at her. Her eyes are closed, she's still recovering her breathing and then she opens her eyes right into mine. Her beautiful dark brown eyes look deep inside me, knowing me, like no one else ever has. I take her into the bedroom and close the door.

We undress each other and kiss skin to skin. I want to feel all of her, touching all of me. I'm naked, but she's still wearing her lace underwear. I guide her down to the bed, lifting the covers to one side as I go. She moves up to the centre of the bed and I move over her, so that the entire length of our bodies are touching.

I slide my hand into her underwear, pushing my finger slowly into her. I add a second finger and she lets out a moan. I move them in and out, again and again, as I kiss her. She moves her hand to where I'm pushing my hard-on into her and wraps her hand around me. I push myself in and out of her hand while she grasps tight. Then she lets go to take off her underwear. I lift off to help her slide them down, but I leave them round her ankles. They're sexy lace panties and knowing they are restraining her a little turns me on. I go back to free her from her bra and then put my fingers back where they belong, inside her, moving in and out. I suck on her nipple and she sighs as my thumb begins circling her clit.

I could watch her like this all night, moaning with pleasure. I keep going at a steady rhythm, kissing her mouth, then her nipple in turn, my fingers constantly moving, until I feel her start to tense slightly. I slide my hand out of her, before she comes; I want to be inside her when she does. She protests slightly but I push myself against her, deliberately not inside her, and begin to move. The friction on us both is gratifying. We move like this for a while, grinding like teenagers; my tongue finds hers, it feels so good.

She lifts her hips up further, firing my need to be inside her. I break the kiss and stare at her. I'm about to get up to grab a condom when she pulls open the drawer on the nightstand revealing a whole string. I'll pretend she just bought those, for my own sanity. Pushing the image of Liv with another man out of my head, I shift slightly and watch her roll the condom onto me. Her hands feel amazing on me; I have to have her right now.

Moving over her again, I open her legs with my knee, feeling as they strain against her lacy underwear, although I can't see it I'm turned on by the idea. I enter her slowly, my breathing affected by the warmth and pressure. I keep going until I'm buried fully inside her, then trying desperately not to think too much about the circumstances for fear of unravelling, I begin to move. Once we've established a rhythm, I shift higher over her so that I rub against her clit as I move. I want her to come and I know she will if I hit the right spots. I hold onto her head and as she starts to thrust, I know the friction has found its mark.

I could watch her all night, sighing and rocking. But after a short while, I pick up the pace and we both groan, thrusting faster, building.

We're sweaty and tangled, she's straining to move her legs, but they are held down as my legs pin her underwear to the bed. I watch her, my face touching hers. She's lost, her eyes closed. I'm so close now I feel it building. She suddenly opens her eyes and, holding my gaze, we kiss deeply. It finishes me and I come loudly inside her, staring into her eyes as she comes too. I shake as my body contracts with pleasure and I can feel her body doing the same.

As we still, I relax onto her and nuzzle into her neck. We lie like this for a while. My hand finds hers and I mingle our fingers, holding her tight, while she begins to stroke my hair.

I want to stay like this all night; I never want to let her go. I kick off her underwear and wrap us in the covers then return to my place on her chest, her hand in mine and once again she strokes my hair. I've never felt so close to anyone. I realise now, I've never let anyone but her in.

Ten.

Two magic weeks.

Liv.

I'm woken by the familiar sounds of the kitchen staff starting the day. They get in at 6am and we open for breakfast at seven. I feel like I've woken from a beautiful dream, I'm so relaxed and content. It takes me a sleepy minute to realise that the source of my happiness is asleep next to me. I sigh, Danny. He isn't a dream, he's a breathtaking reality and he's sleeping peacefully beside me. I turn and watch him softly breathing. His face hasn't really changed, a bit fuller in places I suppose. There are one or two lines that are new, but that's all really, except maybe a general bronzing you can't escape living in California, my sister's the same. He has thick golden brown hair, cut quite short, but a bit dishevelled. His hairline has receded slightly, which I find quite attractive. His hair's shiny and smells so good, I want to touch it, but I don't want to disturb him.

He must be jet-lagged, but I've no idea if it'll make him sleep late or wake up early. I decide to let him sleep for as long as he needs. He doesn't have to wake up for any reason and I'll be at work in a few minutes anyway. Sighing at having to leave him, I tiptoe out of bed and run the shower. As I glance back to the bedroom, he's turned over, but not woken. He obviously needs the sleep. I shower and then dress in silence. I wish I could stay with him in bed, but I have to be downstairs this morning. Resigned, I creep out and close the door quietly behind me, feeling sad and detached as I make my way downstairs. If I knew how long he was going to stay, I'd feel better.

I make coffee for the kitchen guys and myself and potter around. I want to get ahead this morning so that I can spend the middle of the day with Danny before I have to work tonight. It's going to be hard having him here and having to work, not knowing how long I will have him. I could be wasting precious time. On the plus side, he's only upstairs, not in California. I'll take this any day over the nothing we had before. Maybe I can take a few days off; I'll look at the rota later.

It's Friday and tonight will be full-on in the bar. I don't know what he'll do while I'm working all night, I guess go back to the hotel. I should tell him he can stay upstairs, but that's a conversation we need to have. He's welcome to stay here, I want him to. It just feels like a huge step that I shouldn't be ready to take. But the fact is, he's spent so long away from me, now that he's here, I want him to be right here with me. I need to talk to Max about it, but he worked late last night. I could ring Connie, but it's a bit early. I'll ring her at seven.

I busy myself with prep for the day. I just need to get through breakfast, then I have cover from eleven, leaving me free until six tonight, so I can spend the day with him. Hopefully we will talk, we definitely should.

I'm putting the blind down, when Connie arrives.

"Hello, what are you doing here so early?" I ask. Instantly suspicious that Max has been on the phone, reporting my visitor.

"Jack was out fishing early, so I thought I would come and help my darling girl. Coffee?"

"I've got one, but do one for yourself and we'll sit down, I could do with a chat."

"A chat? Everything alright?"

"Yeah. I'll be in, in a minute."

She disappears and puts her bag away then she makes her coffee while I put the tables and chairs outside. We have a few coffee regulars at this time, but it's an hour before the breakfast crowd usually hits, so I have a few minutes to talk.

She sits on the end stool, while I fill sugar jars. How do I go about this?

"I talked to Danny again," I begin.

"Good, I told you, you would…and?"

"Well, he was working, that's why I didn't hear from him."

"See, it wasn't as bad as you feared," she smiles, satisfied. "So, are you going to talk to him again?"

"I hope so. He's upstairs!" I wince as I land this huge fact on her.

"Here?" She seems genuinely stunned. I nod, beaming from ear to ear.

"He's here, right now? Danny?"

"Yes!"

"For heaven's sake, sit down and tell me…how?"

I roll my eyes and come round to sit with her. She takes my hand and waits. So I launch into the whole story. Well, I leave out the sex details, but I tell her everything else.

"Darling, that's wonderful. So what now?"

"I don't know, that's the thing. He won't tell me how long he plans to be here. He has an open ticket and he says he wants to stay as long as we need to sort things out. But I can't get my head round it. If he stays until we sort things out, then goes, what will we have sorted out?"

"Darling, you should be asking him all of this."

"I know, but we haven't really talked yet and if I press the issue, I might put him off."

"Well, then, just see what happens." She thinks for a minute. "Have a few days off, go away with him."

"I know, I'll try."

"Where is he staying?"

"Well, last night he stayed here, but his things are at the Holiday Inn. I want him to stay here if I only have him for a short time. But is it too forward of me to ask him?"

"Ooh, darling, that's a tough one. Though you could say that he has been rather forward himself by flying thousands of miles to see you, so if you want to ask him to stay, ask him."

"Hmm, I didn't think of it like that."

"He can't have come all this way, hoping to stay in a hotel down the road from you."

"I know, I just feel uncertain." I rub my temple, while I give it some thought. I'm interrupted by an American accent.

"Mind if I join you two beautiful ladies?"

"Danny!" Connie jumps up to greet him. They hug and Danny kisses her cheek. Then she holds him at arm's length. "Let me look at you."

"How are you?" he asks, politely.

I stand up to let them talk. I pass behind Connie's back and mouth 'Coffee' at him, he nods slightly and winks at me. Such things don't normally affect me, but my legs almost buckle. I shake my head. He's really getting to me. I look him over as I make the coffee. He's wearing last night's clothes and I decide that I will ask him to stay here with me. The worst that can happen is that he says no. The best that can happen is that he does stay and instead of coming down in last night's clothes, he comes down in, say, loose track suit bottoms and a tight t-shirt…you know, just off the top of my head!

They chat so easily that I'm once again green with envy that the most he has said since he arrived is to someone else. He sips his coffee while they chat; he's very at ease this morning. I return to the sugar, whilst listening. They drink their coffee and he tells her about his work. He has a meeting scheduled for May for something new because he thought the last project would take him longer. But he will only take the job if it suits him. The last job wasn't great, but the money was good so he can take some time off now. He says he'll be more selective in the future. He normally enjoys his work. I wander into the kitchen, leaving them deep in conversation and start a batch of ice cream.

I'm pouring the finished mix into the ice cream machine when I feel his hands on my hips. I relish his touch as his arms close around my waist and he sinks a kiss into my neck.

"You're going to make me spill this," I whisper, as he lingers at my neck and sways slightly at my hips.

"Sorry," he lifts his head, but keeps a loose hold on my waist. "What is it?"

"Ice cream."

"Can I help?"

"We have to wait twenty-four minutes for it to pasteurise and then freeze."

"What do we do for twenty-four minutes?" he grins and kisses my neck again.

I nudge him away with my hip.

"Clean!" I admonish, throwing my tools into the container I'm holding and carrying it all to the sinks.

"What can I do?"

I nod my head towards a roll of blue tissue mounted on the wall.

"Dry."

He obediently pulls off a metre or so and uses it to dry the utensils I've washed. I pull the hose down from its cradle and wash out the container, turning it upside down when I'm done.

"Leave that to dry," I say, pulling blue tissue out for my hands and then tossing it in the bin from where I stand. It lands bang on target and he raises an eyebrow. I pretend not to notice. He follows me back to where I'm working and watches as I wipe down the surfaces.

"I should go back and change."

I stop wiping and turn around.

"I don't want you to."

He looks at me quizzically.

"You like me dirty?"

I stifle a giggle; I'm not usually a giggler.

"No, I mean I don't want you to keep going back and forth to the hotel." I'm suddenly serious and insecure. I need to pull myself together before I look at him. "Can't you just stay here?" I hold my breath, waiting for his reaction.

He frowns, but then comes over to me, placing his hands on my hips and holding me face to face.

"I would love to, but I don't want you to get sick of me."

"I won't."

"I've just arrived; don't you want to see what happens?"

"How long are you booked in for?"

He looks sheepish.

"Until tomorrow morning."

"You said you'd stay around."

"I will, but when I came, I didn't even know if you'd want to see me. So I checked in for three nights hoping I could figure out what I should do in that time."

"And?"

"And I think we can agree, three days won't be long enough!" he grins.

"So how long *are* you staying then?" I think it's a fair question and my face tells him, I seriously want an answer.

"Until you tell me to go," he whispers against my cheek, but he pauses and doesn't kiss me.

"Well then, you can't afford the hotel." I offer a tight smile. "Now kiss me, then go and get your things."

He pulls back from me and laughs.

"Not in that order, I haven't brushed my teeth." But he looks troubled.

"What is it?"

"I don't want to lose you before I really have you back."

His face is pained. I put my arms around his neck and smile.

He wants me back! I use all my willpower to prevent myself doing a little dance and maintain a serious expression. When I'm sure I have control, I speak.

"Okay, how about you stay here for two weeks and if it gets too intense or starts to go wrong in any way, you go back to the hotel while we figure it out."

"What happens after two weeks?"

I shrug. "We'll review."

He thinks about it and then smiles.

"Deal?"

"Deal!"

He kisses my forehead.

"Good, now go and brush your teeth, I have to work!"

I crack on while he's gone, getting all my jobs done. I've given him my key so that he can go in from the other door, rather than wheel his suitcase through the diner. But now, I have no idea if he's back or not, the suspense is killing me. It's almost ten, so I text Max.

'Wakey wakey! He's bringing his stuff from the hotel…Eeek!'

He texts back straight away:

'HOW LONG HAVE I BEEN ASLEEP?'

I laugh out loud and reply, 'Very funny.'

I put my phone in my back pocket. Connie thinks it's great, I remind myself, before I begin to doubt the decision. Max does too, he's just teasing. Danny has been gone ages. What is he doing? But I press on. If I can just do the wages, I will be free in an hour. Providing he hasn't run back to America. I settle myself into the back booth and spread my paperwork across the table. PAYE is quite simple, but now that I do it for twenty-three people, it takes some time. I open my laptop and get stuck in.

I'm plodding through the task when a lady carrying a huge bunch of flowers comes through the door and approaches the counter. I watch with mild interest as she speaks to Connie, but I'm shocked when Connie points at me. I flush with embarrassment when the lady approaches me.

"Liv Harper?"

"Yes?" I manage meekly.

"For you," she smiles handing the beautiful arrangement to me.

"Thank you." I blush.

Mercifully, she keeps it brief and leaves, but as I stare at the flowers, I'm mobbed.... Well, okay, Connie and Ali rush over to have a look.

"Is there a note?" Connie asks.

I examine the bouquet and find a small white envelope tucked with a sachet in the centre. I hastily open it.

Beautiful flowers for a beautiful girl.
I have missed you.

Danny x

The three of us swoon. I've never been sent flowers before. I've received the odd bunch from the supermarket, but nobody has ever had them delivered to me by an actual florist. I've also never seen such a beautiful display in all my life and I need two hands to hold it. Bright magenta tulips and delicate lilac tulips with frilly petals, mixed with purpley hyacinths and some other flowers I don't know the names of, in all possible shades of purple. They are so beautiful, I almost cry.

"I'll get something to put them in," offers Connie, hurrying off to the bar.

Just then Danny appears from upstairs. He beams when he sees the flowers in my hand.

"Secret admirer?"

I smile as he approaches and puts his arms around me, being careful not to squash the flowers. He smells great. His hair is damp and he's wearing jeans and a white long-sleeved t-shirt.

"Thank you, they're beautiful."

He kisses my temple. "Like you," he murmurs into my skin.

Connie reappears and takes the flowers from me. She sets to work and I leave her to it.

"So did you check out?"

"Yeah, my bags are upstairs…. It feels weird!" He smiles shyly.

"Two weeks remember, nothing to freak out about.".

"That's true."

He hovers, looking unsure what to do with himself.

"Listen, I'll be done down here by eleven. Can you keep busy until then?"

"Yeah, d'you have Wi-Fi?"

"Of course, I'll get you the code," I say heading to the till. I copy it down for him. "It works, here, upstairs and in the bar. Make yourself at home."

"Thanks."

"Do you want a coffee to take up?"

"I can't keep taking your coffee, can't I make one upstairs?"

I look at him as if he has suggested growing the coffee beans himself. "Why would you want to do that? It's nowhere near as nice. Besides, staff soft drinks are free."

"I'm not staff."

I shake my head and make him a coffee. As I hand it to him, he sighs.

"Look," I say in a lowered voice. "When I first started this place, Max and I lived rent-free upstairs and only had to share the bills. We took a low wage to get things off the ground and ate here every day to save money. It kind of stuck!" I check no one is listening. "The rest of the staff get soft drinks free and fifty percent off everything else. Max and I still mainly eat here, because we can. By default, Charlie does too." He looks at me like he's not going to give in.

"Listen, it'll cost me more to stock my kitchen than feed you here. If you're going to be my guest for two weeks, you'll have to accept that. No one here will take your money!" I smile sweetly..

He raises his eyebrows and sighs. "Fine, but I'm taking you out this afternoon." Then he turns and takes his coffee upstairs.

I sigh. Egos! Pfft!

At 11am, I head upstairs and find Danny asleep on the sofa, with an iPad lying on his chest. He must be really tired; I don't want to wake him. But then again, I've been downstairs counting the minutes until I could see him again and it's no fun if he sleeps all day. I sit on the edge of the coffee table next to him and gently lift the iPad off him. He opens his eyes.

"Sorry," I whisper.

"It's fine," he yawns, rubbing his face. "I didn't mean to fall asleep. I guess it just caught up with me." He stretches and puts his hand on my knee. "Have you finished?"

"Until six."

"So do you want to go out with me?"

"What did you have in mind?"

"Get ready, it's a surprise," he grins.

"Get ready for what?" I frown. I hate surprises. I'm prepared to admit

I'm a control freak. He must remember this about me. "What shall I wear?"

He smiles. "Just jeans and a sweater, we'll be walking."

I do as I'm told and he fishes a jumper out of his case, puts his wallet in his pocket and takes my hand, flashing me a grin.

"Where are you taking me? You don't know where anything is."

"I did live here for twelve years, you know, it can't have changed that much."

"Well the only place we ever went was Connie's…and that's gone!"

"It's not the only place we went."

We walk through town and out onto the park, holding hands. It feels like it used to be, for the first time since he arrived. Maybe because we've done this walk so many times before. I can't figure out where we're going when we walk all the way through the park and out onto the road. We cross over and the only thing left in town is the leisure centre. As we walk up towards it, I'm confused. I thought we were eating.

He holds open the door for me and leads me over to the glass wall.

"What do you think?" he says, nodding his head towards the ice rink below us. I look down and then look back up at him, amused.

"The last time I went down there was with you." I can't believe he has brought me here, this place is *so* us.

"Would you do me the honour of accompanying me again?" he asks, holding out his arm in a comically overblown chivalrous gesture. I happily link my arm through his.

As we reach the lower level, the smell of the ice hits me like a shot of nostalgia. I'm glad I never came here after he left because I think this would have killed me. I've butterflies in my stomach as we wait for our skates and I can't help but stare at him. He's happy, excited like a teenager. Just being here with him makes me feel the same way.

We lace up our skates in silence. It's busier than I thought it would be on a weekday lunchtime, but still quiet compared to the old days at the ice disco. We used to come here a lot. In those days they used to play a few chart songs on a loop and hearing Barbie Girl still brings me back here. They don't call it the ice disco anymore; according to the poster in front of me it's now ICE XTREME! But I feel old just reading the poster, so I won't suggest we go for old time's sake. This is perfect.

We stand and teeter towards the ice; he steps out first and turns to help me. My body tenses as it adjusts to the loss of traction underfoot. I hold onto the side with my other hand.

"I've forgotten how!" I giggle.

"You'll remember," he says, completely at ease. "Come."

He leads me away from the handrail and we're off.

I try to remember how to do this in a fluid, relaxed style. I used to be quite good, but any skill I had seems to have left the building. I can remember feeling this free: forwards, backwards, pirouettes, I could do it all. I try to loosen all my joints and get my muscles to remember, but I'm rigid. The muscles in my bum are already pleading for mercy. I come to a stop, laughing.

"What's wrong? You used to be so natural," he laughs. "It's like I'm dragging an ironing board around!"

I'm laughing so hard, I'm at risk of doing a windmill and landing on my arse.

"I know! What's happened?"

"Just relax. Here, bend your knees." I oblige. "Now bounce," he insists, demonstrating. I copy him. Then he takes both of my hands and wobbles my arms like a caterpillar, to make sure they are nice and relaxed too. He gives his whole body a shake and I do the same.

Then he takes my hands again and expertly sets off backwards, leading me. I must admit it feels better already. I relax into it and before long we are whizzing round holding hands, it feels amazing. My body eventually loosens up and I start to feel free again.

We venture into the middle and slow down. The middle is the haunt of the cool kids and the couples. He spins us slightly as we come to a stop and I put my arms around his neck. He kisses me and I melt. It feels like I'm in a film. I feel like Kate Moseley kissing Doug Dorsey in The Cutting Edge.

"Do you remember that awful ice skating film you made me watch a thousand times?"

I laugh. "The Cutting Edge."

"That's it. He was a hockey player who got injured and cut from the Olympic team. Wasn't he blinded?"

"He lost some of his peripheral vision," I correct. I could tell him that it was eighteen percent but I feel this knowledge doesn't reflect well on me.

"Sorry! Then she turns him into a figure skater and they win gold. God, it was awful!" He shakes his head, amused.

I slap him playfully.

"I loved that film."

"Don't I know it?"

I kiss him deeply as he gently spins us.

"This is brilliant, thank you for bringing me."

"Come on," he says, taking my hand. "Let's eat."

We sit in a gorgeous little pub. I've been here before, it used to be awful. It has recently been done up, but as I hardly get out, I didn't realise. Sat on a comfy sofa, we face each other, having eaten a satisfying lunch. We both had fish and chips, which he views as a delicacy. This tickles me, but apparently they just can't get it right in the States.

We've talked about his life at home, his friends. He tells me about 'pretty blonde girl, Jen'. She sounds lovely; he hopes I'll meet her one day. He tells me she was partly responsible for him coming here to see me.

"So why now?" I ask, hoping it will open the door for about five thousand-or-so of my other questions.

He hesitates, like he's deciding whether to tell me.

"Something made you enter my head. Once you had, I couldn't shake you out." He smiles shyly.

"Did you think about me much?" It's not a question I would want to answer, but I'm only thinking about myself when I ask it. I want to know if I was ever on his mind.

"At first," he sighs. "But I had to move on. I was torturing myself."

"So you shut it out?"

"I had no choice."

I nod in empathy; it's exactly what I did.

"I know," I whisper. How do we get so deep so quickly?

"Once you were back in my head though, I either had to look you up, or start trying to shut you out all over again. It seemed like the right time, so I took the risk."

"Big risk. I might have been married!"

He laughs, like somehow he knew it wasn't the case.

"When I found you, it seemed like you were unattached…you know the rest."

"But what if I hadn't seemed unattached?"

"I would have left you alone," he looks away, like this idea pains him. He recovers quickly though and turns on me. "What about you, did you ever try to look me up?"

"Never." But not because I didn't want to, I want to say. Because I couldn't stand it. Even though he has just admitted the same thing, I just can't reciprocate. I feel too vulnerable.

"Yet, here we are," he muses.

"I know. Is this all a little weird?"

"What do you mean?"

"Well, I think most people would have tried to be friends to begin with."

"Most people didn't have what we had in the past."

"I know, but…I'm nervous about us falling back into it without addressing some issues."

"What issues?"

"Erm, our geography stands out as the most obvious thing," I joke, but there is little humour in my voice.

"I'm here."

God this is infuriating. Is he trying to make me ask him to stay? I'm not doing it! He couldn't possibly promise me something like that yet and I wouldn't expect him to.

"Yes, but not for good," I dodge the inevitable.

"Why?"

Shit, really? No way! I shake my head in exasperation. He doesn't know what he is saying. He leans forward and takes my hand. It sends my insides into a frenzy. What is he going to say? He looks serious.

"Listen, here is what I know. Nothing went wrong between us, just circumstances tore us apart. If I hadn't left, who knows, we might still be together. I've tried very hard since then, to not hold everything up against what we had, but it's impossible. There has been something missing in my life ever since that day and last week, for the first time in twelve years, something changed. The missing piece came into view and I had to come see if I could put myself back together."

He breathes...I don't.

WHOA!

If I don't breathe soon, I'm going to die. I expel the air from my lungs and heave in some more. I swallow hard. What am I supposed to say? I feel like I've been hit by a lorry. I haven't allowed myself to fully examine my feelings for him yet out of self-preservation. But here he is talking about missing pieces. I must have my mouth hanging open. I make an effort to communicate with my body. I think it responds, but I can't be sure.

To fill the silence, he continues. He stares at me intently.

"We couldn't pretend to be friends even if we wanted to. It's still there, and you know it." He smiles a tiny smile. "I know it's fast and I know it's scary, but I can't be any other way with you. Not when I still…"

My hands leap up, one goes straight to my mouth, the other fleetingly opens palm out imploring him to stop speaking before shakily joining the other at my face.

He presses his lips together, abruptly ending the sentence and looks down at his hands. I feel awful for stopping him, but I can't hear what I think he was about to say.

"Sorry. Too soon, I know."

I try to steady myself to speak, still not sure what to say. I have to give him something. Deep down inside, the part of me that secretly still thinks about him all the time, is yelling, TELL HIM YOU FEEL EXACTLY

THE SAME WAY! But all the other layers on top...fear, doubt, pain, insecurity...are muffling the scream. I have been cheated on twice, stolen from and I didn't even trust my own father. I'm not a girl who believes in 'happily ever afters' anymore. He is the only guy who has never done a number on me. My main fear is that if he is no longer a myth, he's here, then he might let me down too.

    I force myself to look into his eyes. He looks despondent. This relaxes me slightly; he feels uncertain too.

    "I'm scared."

Eleven.

Long-range foreplay.

Liv.

The bar is heaving. I caught sight of Danny once or twice in between pouring drinks, but we're slammed and I can't even tell if he's still down here now. I wouldn't blame him for heading upstairs to get away. I wish I could be with him, it feels like such a waste. A hand slides around my backside, and it isn't Max who is in front of me so I swing round in surprise, wondering which of my staff is groping me. Danny grins and holds up a handful of glasses.

"I can't just watch; where do I put these?"

I grab his face in my wet hands and kiss him square on the lips. What a sweetie! I point to Josh who is collecting empties on the other side of the bar.

"Talk to Josh, he'll sort you out," I yell over the din. "Thank you, so much," I call as he disappears. I turn back to take the next order, buoyed by his gesture. Shaking my head, I realise that in four years together, Mark didn't even bring his own glass up to the bar at closing, never mind help out a little, and Danny pitches in on his first night here. I try not to get swept away by his chivalry.

Max sidles up to me whilst waiting for a card payment to authorise and, when I face him, he raises his eyebrows at me.

"Ten out of ten for lover boy!"

"Stop!" I laugh, but I can't help blushing slightly.

I watch as Danny loads up a basket and heads to the kitchen. Swoon is more the word. It's like seeing a good-looking guy with a baby. You would have noticed the guy for sure, but the baby is the deal breaker. Helping out in the bar tonight is like an aphrodisiac, as if I needed one! Max catches my eye again and we both fall about laughing. I'm such a sap, he knows it and I know it. Danny may as well have burst in like Patrick Swayze and said, "No one puts Baby in a corner."

As things settle down slightly, I look for him in the bar. I'm going to take a quick break and I want to see him. He isn't here, maybe he's gone upstairs. I pass the kitchen and then have to stop and backtrack. Danny is being shown how the dishwasher works by Josh and they both look up as I enter.

"You should get him on the payroll, Liv," quips Josh.

"Can he take a break?" I ask Josh, but looking Danny straight in the eye.

"Five minutes!" Josh jokes and takes his leave. I never take my eyes off Danny.

We stand in the kitchen, a counter between us, holding each other's gaze. His lips curl up in a wry smile and he moves around to me. I meet him and he wraps me in his arms. We just look at each other. I can feel the change in the tension between us, but I'm trying to ignore it.

"We have a no-sex-in-the-kitchen policy here."

"Hmm, the boss is a real ballbuster, I've heard."

He leans forward and kisses the end of my nose. It's a tiny kiss, very chaste but intimate, and it lights a fire in me. Apart from him before, I haven't really had this sort of intimacy with anyone else. The men in my past have all been selfish. I've forgotten how it can be. I'd even begun to find it annoying in other couples, like it was some kind of weakness. I'd have scoffed if I'd witnessed us as a bystander.

Suddenly, I see what I've become, a bit hard around the edges and dismissive of romance, but only because I haven't had it. At heart, I'm a serious romantic, but I've separated that from reality and learned to live with the type of romance the men in my life delivered. I'm forced to admit, Danny has the moves, I'm not sure he realises it though. He really doesn't seem to be overly trying to impress me, it just comes naturally. But he is good! Flying here, great sex, dinner, more great sex, flowers, ice skating, lunch, a walk in the park and now helping out in the bar. Not bad for twenty-four hours!

I swallow my pride and go weak at the knees, like I'm supposed to. It can't hurt can it?

"What are you smiling at?" he asks, bringing me back to him.

"You and your moves."

"My moves?"

"Helping out tonight."

His eyes widen.

"That's not a move!...I'm hurt." He reels back, clutching his chest in mock agony.

I laugh and pull him back to me. "It's okay, I'm impressed."

"I couldn't just sit there, you were so busy. I can't believe you would think that I had ulterior motives."

"Well motives or not, thank you."

"What else can I do? I don't want to go upstairs yet. I want to be near you…and I want to earn my keep."

"Do you have any experience?" I question, suggestively.

"Actually, yes. I worked in a bar for four years."

"Well then, there's loads you can do. Now kiss me, before my break's over."

He places his hand over my hair and draws me in to a deep kiss. I know I shouldn't be doing this here, but I don't care. Everyone will just have to get used to the new me if Danny is around.

I lead Danny behind the bar and over to Max.

"A new recruit for you, apparently he has bar experience," I tell him. Max looks surprised.

"Well then, let's see what we can do with you," he provocatively muses and I leave them to it. I'm sure Max will be gentle with him and I'm hopeful Danny can take it if he's not. Either way, I can't have anything to do with it if we want to get anything done tonight. I look back and Danny smiles at me. God, he's handsome.

I try very hard to get back to work. The lull doesn't last and we're busy right until the end. I keep my head down and just keep serving. Danny passes back and forth behind me, restocking drinks, collecting empties and such. Occasionally, he brushes me as he goes by, reminding me he's there. I can't believe how happy I am that he's here. He seems to get into it and it looks like he's really helping. Max gives me the thumbs up, and he's notoriously hard to impress, so he must be doing okay.

I'm excited about this weekend. I grabbed five minutes with Max earlier and he's got me covered, so I can take the weekend off. I feel bad, but when do I take time off? It wasn't that hard to cover, Max hasn't got to work any extra, which makes it easier. But I live and breathe this place; it's hard to step away. I'm thinking of taking Danny to Brighton. We can see my parents and relax. I still have to run this by him.

After closing, Danny helps me bottle up for tomorrow. We let the staff go as we are almost done and Max makes us all a rum and Coke, we take them to sit in the garden so we can cool off while we drink.

"Thanks for letting me pitch in tonight," Danny says enthusiastically. He obviously still has adrenaline pumping. The Bacardi will sort him out. It's our routine.

"Well you have a job here any time. We could do with the help," replies Max with a smile.

"Wow, you must have really impressed Max, he isn't usually so enthusiastic about newbies."

Danny stretches out. "I'd forgotten what a buzz it can be. I sit and stare at a screen all day, it's nothing compared to this."

"Are you tired?" I ask.

"Exhausted, but my brain hasn't taken the hint." He rolls his head round on his shoulders.

"Drink up, it'll help you sleep," says Max.

We all sip our drinks.

I look at my phone; it's 1:45am. I sigh; I'm tired from my eventful day. Danny looks shattered, but he's here, I'm here and I'm not tense for the first time in a week.

"This is bliss," I say, almost to myself.

"I could get used to it," agrees Danny.

Max shoots me a look that says did-you-hear-that? I haven't had time to tell him all of Danny's revelations from today; I think if I had, he would be out hat shopping right now. I make a mental note to fill him in when I get him to myself, for now I settle with rolling my eyes at him.

"Well I think I'll leave you kids to it," he smirks, draining his drink. "I'll lock up."

"Thanks," I wink at him.

"Night," adds Danny and we watch him walk away.

I put my feet up on the arm of Danny's chair, and a few moments later Max comes back into view at the front door. He locks it and then pulls the gate closed, locking us in for the night. He waves as he walks away. I look back to Danny.

"Did you have a good night?"

"Great. Just to be with you was great.... Are we doing it again tomorrow?"

"Well, I thought I'd take the weekend off." His face lights up. "We could go somewhere, maybe Brighton?" I add, with a hint of apprehension. I don't want him to think I'm pushing it.

"Liv, are you going to introduce me to your parents?" he teases.

"Well..."

"As your old friend, or something more?"

I think for a moment.

"It'll have to be as something more. I'm not having you sleeping in the spare room. Or we could stay in a hotel if you'd rather keep it quiet?"

His eyes widen and a huge smile spreads across his face.

"I think I like your first suggestion."

"What? Stay at my parents, over a hotel?"

"If you're going to tell them about us and sleep in the same bed with me at their house...sure!"

"Why?"

"Because telling them makes it real," he says shyly. "If you're prepared to do that, it means you're giving us a chance."

I look down at my hands to avoid his intense gaze. I'm trying to give us a chance, I'm just afraid. Telling my parents didn't seem like a huge deal, but I suppose it does make it real. I've no intention of hiding it though, whatever it is we have going on.

"It'll be great to see them again," he says, taking my feet into his lap. "What will they say?"

"About us? Fuck knows! I don't even know what to say!" I laugh. "Did you tell your parents you were coming?"

"No, they're on vacation, but I'll call them when they get home. Jen knows where I am."

"You'll tell them why you came?"

"I'll tell them I came to find you and I can't leave."

"Just like that? Won't they be worried you've gone mad?"

He laughs. "No, I think they'll be relieved actually." I furrow my brow and he answers my unspoken question. "You have been the unfinished business in my life for twelve years, Liv. They saw it. Jen saw it. I just refused to see it. They'll be glad I'm doing something about it."

"But what if it doesn't work out?" This is my biggest question.

"Then I'll know…but I refuse to think like that." He can see my doubt. "Two weeks, remember?"

I offer him a tiny smile and then shiver.

"Are you cold?"

I nod. He puts my legs down on the floor and pulls himself up out of his chair. Holding out his hand, he stands over me. I place my hand in his and he lifts me up onto my aching feet. He collects our glasses from the table in his free hand and we drift back into the bar together. I check the doors and switch off the lights; he puts the glasses away in the kitchen. We head back out into the garden and I lock the back door.

As I turn, he's right there and I bump into him. I laugh until I see the intense look in his eyes; he pulls me close, his lips hovering over mine. Somewhere within the aching exhaustion I feel, I have a desire to be touched…I inhale sharply, hoping the chilly air will wake my body up enough to find the energy. He looks deep into my eyes and brushes his lips against mine.

"I'm going to take you upstairs," he whispers, "lie down beside you and hold you while we both fall asleep."

Oh. My. God! That may just be the sexiest thing anyone has ever said to me.

"You know just what to say to a girl." I grin into his lips and they press against mine. It's a passionate kiss, but I can surrender to it because I know he doesn't intend to take it further. I give my all, pouring the last of today's energy into my connection with him. When we break away from each other, my eyelids are heavy.

He leads me across the garden, tucked safely under his arm. I rest my head on his chest as I allow him to guide me. Inside, I summon enough energy to secure the door and enter the code. Behind me, he places his hands on my bottom and pushes slightly, propelling me up the stairs. I giggle sleepily. Once inside, I drop my keys, missing the table and dragging my feet, pour a glass of water and head into the bedroom. Danny picks out a couple of things from his case and I quickly use the bathroom.

When I emerge, he's changed, wearing jogging bottoms and a t-shirt. He looks so hot, but my body is now asleep from the neck down, so it has little effect. I sit on the bed and begin to undress while he uses the bathroom. I'm not usually this tired; I've been doing this for a long time. Maybe it's the mental exhaustion of the last few days, catching up with me.

I've made little progress when he returns, so he helps me to my feet and undresses me like a child. Then, when I'm down to my underwear, he skims his fingers across my stomach, running them up my ribcage and turning me to face away from him. He unhooks my bra and slips it off and then he lightly kisses me at the nape of my neck. A shiver runs down my spine.

I feel him removing his t-shirt behind me and he turns me around. For a moment I think we are about to go back on what he said downstairs, but instead, he slips his t-shirt over my head and pulls it down over me. I smile a sleepy smile and kiss him.

"You might just be perfect," I mutter, as I let him put me to bed.

He slips in beside me and wraps himself around me. I feel so safe, so content. I've no idea how he came to understand me so well, I think as I drift off. But being this sensitive, not demanding sex when I'm so tired, understanding me completely, is basically foreplay, long-range foreplay, because sleep is calling, but it still counts. I'll remember this. I'm aware of his breathing changing…he is drifting too.

I ease back into consciousness and for a moment I'm disorientated. I squeeze my eyes together tightly and then pry one open. Blinking against the light, I realise it must be late. The light is bright mid-morning light and the sounds of life drift up to me from downstairs. I'm draped across Danny, who is still sleeping soundly. I can't see the time without moving and I don't want to wake him.

I sigh happily; this is insane. Danny is back in my life. Staying with me, hinting that he might stick around, helping out in the bar. Telling me, well almost telling me that he has feelings for me still. It's hard to take stock of these facts. It feels like a dream and I don't want to wake up. That's why I want to head to my parents, I think. Put it in some context. Mum might have some pearl of wisdom that can help me.

Danny shifts slightly, still fast asleep. Where my leg is draped across his, something hard presses into my inner thigh. Morning glory! I smirk, nuzzling his chest and lightly kissing his skin. Mark comes unwelcome into my mind. He always used to say that being woken up by sex is the best thing that can ever happen to a man. He was always remarking on the fact that I never did it, but he never deserved it. He had no idea how to put a woman in the mood; he only cared about himself.

I shake him out of my head, reminding myself that I'm lying across a man who doesn't just care about himself. He seems to care about me, a great deal. I shift slightly, feeling him hard against me once more. I could just slide on top of him and do it right now. I pause to consider this, what's stopping me? Gently, I lift my head; he's so beautiful. I kiss his chest again, but this time I trail kisses down his sculpted abdomen, pausing at his waistband.

He moans slightly in his sleep but doesn't wake. I delicately lift the elastic up and stretch it back, holding it in place with my hand below his impressive erection. He stirs slightly, I position my mouth over him, before he wakes and lick him. He stirs again, moaning. I want him to wake up in my mouth, so before it's too late I take him between my lips, rolling my tongue around the tip and then plunging down onto him. He moans loudly, shifting beneath me as he becomes aware of what's happening.

"Oh!" he sighs as I gently suck on him. I watch as his eyelids flick open and shock registers on his face. He lifts his head to see what's going on and laughs when he confirms his suspicions.

"Oh God, Liv. That's incredible," he breathes, still grinning like the Cheshire Cat.

I smile and continue, taking him in all the way. I move up and down while he groans and strokes my hair.

After minute or two, I decide that I want in on the action, so I stop abruptly, pulling him out of his reverie. I ignore the look of mild disappointment on his face and lean over to my drawer and pull out a condom. Holding it between my teeth I wriggle out of my knickers. I pull down his tracksuit bottoms and he kicks them off. He seems amused at the matter-of-fact way I'm going about this; he puts his hands behind his head and watches patiently.

I straddle his legs; taking the condom from between my teeth and dipping my head low over him. I lick him lightly, and he gasps. I smile with satisfaction and sink my mouth down onto him again. He throws his head back and moans. It's the most gratifying sound and it spurs me on. I move faster, sucking him in. He's lost again his breathing becomes more rapid. I slow before he gets too close and, sucking hard, I pull my mouth away.

His hand touches my cheek in appreciation and I lean my face into his touch as he strokes my face. Then I sit back up and look for the condom. He holds it out to me and, as I reach to take it, he pulls it away, circling my waist with his arm and pulling me down onto him. He kisses me deeply, while he presses himself hard against me. He lets out a low groan, almost a growl into my mouth and the primal sound pushes me on. While our tongues still wind together, I search for his hand with mine. Finding it, I pluck the condom from his fingers and sit abruptly, wiping my mouth and tearing open the wrapper.

He inhales sharply as I roll it over him and watches as I position myself. I slowly lower myself onto him, pushing down until every last inch of him is buried in me. We both moan, and then I rock. "*Ah!*" he breathes, as I begin to move. Not up and down, but backwards and forwards, with him deep inside me. My hands move from his chest up to my own, feeling my hard nipples through the fabric of his t-shirt. They travel up to my hair and my eyes close, as I become lost in the sensation.

I feel his hands glide up my thighs and lift the hem of the t-shirt up, pulling it over my head and letting it fall. His hands go straight to my nipples, simultaneously pinching and pulling them. This is so good, I love having my nipples played with, and I hope he won't be too gentle. I moan loudly as he pinches harder, making sure he gets the message that this is what I like.

Tentatively, I slide my hand down and stroke myself. I don't know why I feel self-conscious about this, but some men like to think they are enough. Women are just not built that way. He begins to thrust into me as I keep up my rocking motion.

"*Oh,*" I moan as our pace increases.

He holds out his hands for me to lean on and I take them, using the leverage to rock faster. Then I drop forward, pinning his hands against the bed either side of his head.

We both moan at the change of position. He seems quite turned on by me holding him down and the new angle is hitting the spot inside and my clit is rubbing against him perfectly. He strains at my hands holding him down and writhes under me, thrusting into me, clearly enjoying his wake-up call. I twist slightly, forcing my breast into his face whilst still holding his hands down. He lifts his head and willingly, greedily, sucks hard on my nipple. I cry out, this is just amazing. I keep moving back and forth, watching him suck in my nipple again and again. He bites it briefly and this drives me wild.

"*Yes!*" I hiss, rocking harder and faster. He moves to the other nipple and goes in hard. I cry out again and while I'm distracted he frees his arms and grabs my hips. Keeping tight hold of my nipple between his teeth, he takes more control and slams into me. I'm right on the edge, when he tenses and lets out a muffled cry into my breast. He bites down as he tenses and, with one final slam, I come hard around him, calling out as I collapse onto his chest.

We lay gasping against each other. I realise I'm drenched in sweat and try to move myself off him, but he stops me and settles me back down. He laughs breathlessly.

"What?" I pant.

He says nothing, just laughs again.

"What?" I lift my head up and look at him; his eyes are shut and he's got a huge smile on his face. Aware that I'm looking at him, he opens one eye.

"Good morning."

"Good morning. What's so funny?"

"Nothing…Just, WOW! I'm a lucky bastard," he grins and pulls me towards him until our lips meet. He kisses me lightly. "What did I do to deserve that?"

"Well I woke up with something sticking into me, I thought it was a hint," I tease, rolling onto my side.

He follows me so that we are facing.

"I'd never be so forward," he flirts, stroking my hair behind my ear.

"Well, my mistake, it won't happen again."

"Hey, let's not be hasty," he laughs, pulling me into his arms. "That's officially my favourite wake-up call of all time." He kisses me again. I grin, feeling very pleased with myself.

"I have to move," I say, wriggling free.

"No, no, no!" he pleads, trying to pull me back.

"I need the loo," I laugh. He lets me go and I scurry naked into the bathroom.

When I return, he holds the covers open and pulls me in with him. He kisses me deeply and then lies down beside me.

"These are incredible," he says, kissing my tattooed shoulder. "How bad does it hurt?"

"Some hurt more than others."

"Why did you get them?"

I laugh and turn to face him. "You mean what was I thinking?"

He frowns. "No!" Then his face softens when he sees realises that I'm teasing him. "No, I mean, do they all have a story or are they just because?"

I shrug. "Both I suppose. Some have meaning; some are just what I wanted at the time. It's like the history of me."

"Colourful history," he smiles, rising up over me. "So which one hurt the most?" He looks at me and then begins inspecting my skin. "This one?" he asks, stroking over a bird on my collarbone.

"No, that one wasn't too bad. The side of the rib cage hurts the most," I say unthinking and then just as he moves down to take a closer look at what I have there, it hits me. That's where I have my 'Danny tattoo'. I cringe, it's not like it says his name or anything, but if our past means anything at all to him. He will know without a doubt that it could only be about him.

When we were kids, we had a hurricane here. It was noteworthy because we never get such extreme weather and also because that night, the weather man stated categorically that there would not be a storm! Anyway, we did have one hell of a storm. The Great Storm as it is now known. We lost a lot of trees in the south of England that night, many fell on cars and houses, it was pretty major! Anyway, in the Royal parks around here, the trees are hundreds and hundreds of years old and are huge. So many big trees fell that night, it took a long time to cut them into pieces and take them away. Some lay where they fell for months in remote places.

As kids, we played inside a beautiful weeping willow in the park at the end of our street. It was vast, with a widespread, dense canopy that hung all the way to the ground, making it the ideal hiding place for us to play. It sat by the edge of a pond and it was 'our place'. When we went back to it after the storm we were devastated to find it lying on its side, its roots torn out of the ground. We sat side by side on its trunk, mourning the loss of such a mighty tree that had been our special place.

Over the weeks and months the men with their chainsaws worked. The hazardous trees were removed first, the roads were cleared. Then they moved into the parks, clearing footpaths. As their work progressed, we would sit on our trunk, waiting for the day when our special tree would be taken away. The day never came.

Unlike a lot of the trees that fell, our tree's leaves stayed green. Miraculously, the tiny portion of the root system still in the ground was sustaining the whole tree and, as it was not dangerous, it was just left. Over the years new branches grew up towards the sky and our willow began to weep again. By the time Danny left, the canopy was full again and hidden inside was still our special place, just a little more horizontal. It was on that tree trunk that we'd made all our plans and it was there that I told him he had to leave.

Lots of my tattoos are symbolic references or tributes to people and things I've loved. So it was natural to mark such an important person in my life in some way. Equally, I was never certain it was a good idea to have a reminder permanently etched on me of someone I tried so hard not to think about. But I was feeling a bit low after I'd heard my dad had died. It was before I met Mark, I'd been single for a while and wasn't really sure what was next for me. Feeling lost one day, I found myself sitting on our trunk. It was somewhere I no longer went, the memories were too potent, but sometimes I missed him so much and when I needed him most, I went there. I realised that it was such a symbol of us that I took some photos and had this beautiful tattoo, something to remind me of our time together and keep him with me.

There is no mistaking what it is, it is 'our' tree and I had the words 'you are always rooted here with me' inked beneath it. It was bad enough that the words had always got to Mark's jealous streak, but now that Danny is actually reading them, I'm really questioning my choice. I'm mortified, as any hopes I had of playing down how I feel about him evaporate. Danny inspects it quietly, but doesn't say a word.

"What time are we meeting Max and Charlie?" he asks, after a thoughtful pause.

I don't know if he's changing the subject because he wants to spare me the awkwardness. Or whether he doesn't realise what it is. Either way,

I'm relieved I don't have to explain.

I shower and then let him use the bathroom. He takes his bag of toiletries in with him. I want him to feel at home, so I clear some of the shelf to put it on. He smiles uncertainly. It's too soon to make space for him in my bathroom, I know.

I dry myself and pull on my jeans and a top, then with the towel wrapped around my hair, head into the living room and pick up the phone.

"Hi Mum."

"Liv, darling! I haven't spoken to you all week. How are you?"

"I've been busy, sorry. I was thinking of coming down to see you today, do you have plans?"

"No, we're free. It will be so lovely to see you. Do you have the weekend off?"

"Yes, Max has covered it. I just feel like getting away for the weekend."

"Will Max not be coming?" She sounds disappointed. She loves Max and Charlie.

"Not this time."

"Oh well, maybe we could kick Dave out and have a girls' night!"

"Erm...well, I was hoping you wouldn't mind if I brought someone else with me."

"What?" she gasps. "You haven't taken Mark back have you?"

"No Mother! Of course not."

"Well, that's something. So it's someone new? And you already want to bring him here? It must be serious."

"You don't mind do you?"

"No darling, not at all. As long as you're happy...how did you meet him?"

"It's a long story. We'll tell you all about it when we get there."

"Have you been seeing him long?"

"No, not really."

"And he's happy to meet the folks so soon?"

"Mum, it's fine, you'll see. We'll be down about 3pm. Maybe we can all go out for dinner?"

"Lovely, drive safely," she says, trying to sound convinced.

"Bye Mum."

"Bye darling."

I hang up and then in record time dial Connie. It rings. YES! I've beaten her to it.

"Hello?"

"Connie, it's me."

"Liv!"

"Listen, I just called Mum, I'm taking Danny down to see them later, but I didn't tell her it's him I'm bringing. She sounded concerned, so she'll call you to get the info. Can you just be vague? I want to surprise her."

"My lips are sealed darling. How is the lovely man?"

"Just lovely," I sigh. I have to get a hold of the mushiness.

"Good, well you enjoy…yourselves." As she's speaking, the line cuts out for a second, She has a call waiting.

"Ooh, there's the beeps, it must be Mum," laughs Connie. "I'll be the soul of discretion."

"Thanks Connie." And she's gone.

I turn around smiling and Danny is watching me. He's wet from the shower and cleanly shaved, wearing only a white towel round his waist. He looks amused.

"Why didn't you just tell her?"

I shrug. "More fun this way."

He narrows his eyes at me and smiles.

Twelve.

Quiet!

Liv.

We enjoy a lovely brunch with Max and Charlie. I considered blowing it out just this once, but Danny may as well be part of it. Mark never was and it made things difficult. Danny seems at ease with them and I think they genuinely like him. He has loads in common with Charlie and, unlike previous men in my life, he fully understands my relationship with Max. His relationship with Jen is the same. It's a shame they're not here, I'm sure we would all get along.

As they chat, I sit back and assess the situation. On paper, this could really work. I know it's early days, but I trust him more than I'd trust anyone else. He seems utterly unfazed by the fact that I live here and clearly don't plan to leave, so maybe he could see himself here too. I'm not nearly as freaked out as I was at first. Something changed yesterday, when he helped out in the bar. I compared him to Mark and suddenly it opened my eyes.

He said to me in the pub, he wouldn't tell me how he felt, he would show me, and so far I think he has. He's made me feel much more relaxed and secure since…was that yesterday? I'm losing track. Yes, it was only yesterday. In fact he hasn't yet been here forty-eight hours and look how much my life has changed. It's ridiculous really, to be feeling how I feel and considering so much after such a short time. I have to keep reminding myself this is not a new relationship and the normal rules don't apply.

I'm so happy right now and given that I'm newly single and supposed to be dealing with the hurt of infidelity, I couldn't be better. I was determined not to get into another long-term relationship. But I wasn't prepared for this little curve ball. I just have to see what the next two weeks bring. After that, who knows. Right now, I'm going to pack a bag and take Danny to my parents. I hope they're as happy about his return as I am.

We say goodbye to the boys and pack a few bits in a bag. We're sharing a bag of mine as his case is too big and his backpack is too small. It feels like a big deal. We both gloss over the weirdness, it's practical. But it's yet another questionable leap into domesticity.

We throw the bag into my Mini and I drive us out of town. We chat as I drive and listen to music. But he'

s quiet as we join the M23.

"Are you okay?"

"Just worried that your parents won't like it, that's all. I wish you'd told them."

"They'll be fine, trust me." My mum thought Danny was the best thing since sliced bread, she was almost as cut up about him leaving as I was. She's going to be blown away. I smile, glancing at him. "You'll see."

"I just don't want them to put doubts in your head."

"Just relax, that's why we're going."

He takes a deep breath and seems to snap himself out of it.

"This is a great car," he says, running his hand along the inside of the door. "Very you."

I smirk. It's very me. It's only three years old and was my first 'new, new' car. It's the red one with the union jack on the roof and the white stripes on the bonnet and I love it.

"What do you drive?"

He squirms with embarrassment.

"A Ford F-150."

"What's that? One of those huge great pickup trucks?"

"Yep."

"No Prius?"

"Um, no."

"How very anti-establishment of you."

"That's just my run around," he says quietly.

"What, you have more than one car?"

"Yeah, a few years ago I got my dream car, but she's a classic."

"She? Oh God, is she my competition?" I laugh. "What is *she*?"

"A 1967 Ford Shelby Mustang GT500."

I gawp at him.

"Eleanor?"

He laughs hard at my 'Gone in 60 Seconds' reference.

"Only you would know that Liv!" he says, running his hand up my leg. "That's why I…" he trails off, catching himself about to break his promise.

I ignore it.

"That is amazing, is it…sorry 'she', in good condition?"

"She is now," he says with pride.

"I would love to drive a proper muscle car. I bet it's incredible."

"Well you can drive her anytime."

"Really? That's possibly the coolest car ever made. The sound they make...ugh!"

"Yeah, she's got some lungs."

"Wow, I can't wait to meet her." I laugh. "I hope she likes me!"

Danny shakes his head at my disrespect.

"I would love a vintage car, but I couldn't be arsed with the upkeep."

"What would you have? No wait, I bet I can guess. Knowing you I would be a DeLorean."

I steel a sideways glance at him, tutting. "As if! There is nothing sexy about a DeLorean. No, it would be a 1950s Porsche Speedster Convertible. Not that I've given it any thought. I think they changed the spec after '56 or something, so one before that." I laugh.

"Nice." Danny nods appreciatively.

I signal to come off onto the A23. We're almost there and I begin to feel nervous. I hope this goes well. We drive in silence until we get into

Brighton and Danny takes my hand, for comfort I suspect. I give it a little squeeze.

I pull into my parents' driveway and stop the car. We exchange a tense glance as we climb out. Why am I so nervous? Danny takes my hand and I lead him down the side of the house, ignoring the front door. We come to the back door.

"Ready?" I ask. He nods, then smiles and shakes his head. "We could still go to a hotel," I joke, starting to turn away.

He pulls me back.

"No! Let's do it." He smiles.

I open the door and we walk in.

"Hello?" I call.

"Liv?" My mum yells from upstairs. "Dave, they're here!"

I hear clumping around above us and then they both come down the stairs. We stand hand in hand in the kitchen and as they round the corner and see us, they both freeze.

"Oh my God!...Danny?" Mum comes forward first, a look of amazed wonder on her face. "Shit, look at you." She smiles and goes up to him. For a minute I think she's going to grab his face to check if he's real, but she seems satisfied without molesting him. She laughs and hugs him. He laughs too.

"It's great to see you again, Helen." Danny hugs her back. Then she releases him and turns to me with a look of 'what the hell?' on her face before hugging me. Danny steps forward and shakes a dumbfounded Dave's hand. Mum steps back and looks at us both.

"What on earth is going on? You two have some explaining to do. I think I'll need a tea." She shakes her head and puts the kettle on. "Dave, get the mugs," she bosses. This is mum caught off guard, flustered.

Danny and Dave exchange pleasantries and move away from us slightly. Mum and I get the tea things ready and while the men are out of earshot, she hisses, "What's going on?"

I laugh. "I don't really know." She frowns at me, not happy with the lack of information.

"So Danny," Mum says loudly interrupting his chat with Dave. "How have you been? What do you do with yourself?"

"I've been great thanks. I live in Santa Monica. I design computer software. I work from home, it's quite dull really. But life is good," he replies; tension etched on his face. His eyes catch mine almost asking, did I do ok? I give him a reassuring smile.

We move into the living room. Mum doesn't even wait for us to sit down before she continues.

"So what brings you back to dreary old England then?"

I shoot her a look. Easy Mum.

Danny takes a deep breath, sitting beside me on the sofa.

"I was thinking about Liv and decided to look her up, so I found her on Facebook and we talked a couple of times." He takes my hand. "It was obvious right away that we missed each other. It really affected me, talking to her again after all these years, more than I thought it would. So I felt I should come and find out if there was still anything between us. I needed a vacation, so I came and surprised her." I laugh; this is the understatement of the century.

She passes us our teas.

"And now you two are, you know, an item?"

"Helen!" Dave admonishes. Mum tuts and waves him away.

"I think we are." Danny smiles at me.

Mum grins; I knew she would like it.

"So when did this all happen?" she asks, casually taking a sip of her tea.

"Thursday."

Mum splutters. "Thursday? As in two days ago?"

Danny winces, as do I. We're both very aware that our relationship, or whatever you would call it, won't stand up to much scrutiny at this point.

"I know it's fast," Danny says in defence, "but we have a past...and it's not like we broke up, we just couldn't be together anymore." He pauses and looks to me for reassurance, backup, some kind of support. I can feel how desperate he is for their approval, because they matter. He sighs; "I can't be any other way around her."

He's almost apologetic. I feel for him, maybe it's a bit soon to bring my parents into it.

"I feel the same," I manage. "It's just natural...you know? How it should be."

"A week ago, I had no idea this would happen," Danny shrugs. "When it did, I thought it would be nice to talk to an old friend. I never thought I would be here now."

"But we are being realistic," I add. "Danny is here for a holiday right now. So although we can't help how we feel, we're giving it two weeks, then we'll see." An unwelcome wave of panic sweeps over me when I contemplate what will happen after two weeks. I fight it back, here and now, is what I have to tell myself. Here and now.

Mum thinks about this for a minute.

"Well as long as you look after each other like you used to, I won't have anything to worry about," she says and smiles fondly. Danny gives my hand a little squeeze and I feel him smile, although I can't look at him because I feel like I might cry all of a sudden.

Breaking the emotional silence and rescuing Danny, Dave speaks up.

"So Danny, how are your parents?"

"They're doing great thanks," he gushes, grateful for the change of subject. "Dad retired last summer. He's taking classes and 'taking time to smell the roses' he says. Mom's not ready to give it up just yet, but she has slowed down. She doesn't work as painfully hard as she used to. Right now, they are on vacation in Cabo. They're looking to buy a place there."

"Ah retirement!" sighs Dave wistfully.

"Oh stop it, Dave!" Mum jests. "You wouldn't know what to do with yourself if you had all that time on your hands."

"You manage. Although, you do seem to have the responsibility of keeping Brighton's retail trade afloat, single-handedly. That seems to consume a lot of your time," Dave retorts. Mum narrows her eyes at him and shakes her head. We all laugh.

The conversation moves on and becomes easier. Tuning it out, I reflect on what we have established here today. We've told my parents; in fact, I've heard Danny say that he thinks we're an item. I'm trying not to get carried away; we need to see what will happen. But I do now understand why he was so enthusiastic about coming here. It does feel great to receive approval. It does make it real. However, how we will approach the future after this 'holiday' period remains to be seen. I'm on an emotional knife-edge. I feel like I could fall either way. Here and now is all I can hang onto.

We walk into Kemptown for dinner at a little bistro owned by a friend of Dave's. Danny is trying to explain to Dave what it is he does for a living and Dave is really interested. But frankly, he can't work a remote control, so there's not a chance of him grasping the technical details of software development. As Danny is patiently explaining the mechanics to him, Mum links arms with me and steers me towards a shop window on the pretence of looking at something.

"So?" she hisses.

"So what?"

"Well? Are you okay with this?"

"Yeah, I am. Nervous, but really happy." I shrug.

"You won't get hurt again will you?"

"Who knows, Mum? But isn't it at least worth a try? I know it was a lifetime ago, but I loved him and I think he loved me."

"He still does," she says matter-of-factly.

"Mum, don't!"

"It's so obvious, Liv. You must see it."

I shake my head. "He's tried to say it already and I stopped him. It's too soon."

"And you feel the same way?"

Sighing, I nod. "I can't go there yet. I'm afraid of what will happen to me if he leaves again."

"But it's best to be honest darling."

"Not if it leaves me vulnerable."

She purses her lips. "Well don't play games, he deserves your honesty."

"I know. I just want to see what will happen when his holiday is over. If he wants to try, I will give it a go."

"I hope you do sweetheart!" She grins at me and goes all silly. "I can't believe he's here." She leans in and whispers, "And he's gorgeous!"

"Mum!" I laugh, but I can't disagree. I watch him chatting to Dave. He's so good looking. I don't know whether it's age or just that the nineties were kind to no one, but he has something different about him now. Something that I'm sure lots of girls must notice.

We walk on, slowly catching up with the boys. Their conversation has moved on to golf and I'm relieved to hear that Danny has nothing more than a passing interest. We arrive at the restaurant and Danny and I are subjected to a series of gushy introductions. Steve, the owner, has heard all about me and the success of my restaurant. He wishes he had the confidence and the opportunity to start as early in life as me. Mum introduces Danny as if he is a returning war hero. He blushes at her flattery as he shakes hands with Steve and Sandra, Steve's wife who appeared among us.

Once all of the introductions are finished and we've made a sufficiently loud entrance into the restaurant, we're shown to a table in a quiet corner. It's cosy, with reclaimed dining furniture that has all been rubbed down to bare wood. The built-in seating against the wall is upholstered in a vibrant pink-striped fabric, which is the restaurant's main feature. Otherwise the decor is fairly rustic and natural. I like it; it really makes you feel at home. We're sitting in the best corner and the tea lights on the table provide a warm glow.

Danny and I sit on the pink sofa seat, he gestures for me to go in first, then sits close to me. I'm feeling warm and pink-cheeked by the time we settle in. It's mainly from all the wine we had at Mum's before we left, but the ambiance here and the proximity of Danny is adding to the effect. Wine is really not my drink. I enjoy a nice amateur rosé, nothing too professional. But it makes me quite drunk, so I generally avoid it. I always end up like this with Mum and Dave though, because they only drink wine.

Before I have time to think about perhaps not drinking too much more, Dave has ordered us a bottle. So instead I strip off my jumper and give way to the relaxed vibe. Danny places his arm around me while he listens to Dave telling him about Steve's association with some vineyards in France. This is obviously very impressive to Danny because he hangs onto Dave's every word.

When the waiter comes to take our orders and everyone is distracted, Danny asks me if I'm okay.

"Yeah, I just shouldn't drink wine," I admit…gratuitous honesty, an effect of the wine. "It makes me really drunk."

"Oh, me too!" he laughs. "I'm past my comfort level already. I'm so glad it's not just me, I've been listening rather than speaking to keep from making an ass of myself…Have I been an ass?"

"No, not that I've noticed," I smile. This information puts me immediately at ease. He isn't likely to notice how drunk I am if he's well on the way himself. We glance at each other and giggle.

"What are you two giggling about?" quizzes Mum.

"Nothing!" I reply innocently. Mum eyes us suspiciously. Once we're both more at ease, the conversation flows freely. The food is wonderful, I start with the duck liver parfait with brioche toast and greengage chutney. Danny and Mum both have the smoked mackerel pate and Dave has spicy pork balls. For main course, we all have the steak. It's the reason we're here, apparently the best steak ever, so we hardly even look at the rest of the menu. The rumours are true. It's melt-in-the-mouth-amazing and the 'dripping' chips were without doubt the best chips I have ever had.

The heartiness and quantity of the meal has a slightly sobering effect on me, so I have another glass of wine. I've lost track now of how much I've had to drink, but I'm not worried about my behaviour. I feel at ease, I'm with my family. Mum, Dave and Danny. He's been touching me constantly since we sat down. Either his arm is around me or his hand is on my leg or he's holding my hand or even just sitting so close that our bodies are touching. Coming here was the right thing to do; Mum and Dave's acceptance of our hasty union has put my mind at rest.

Mum is a bit drunk too by the time we get the bill and she giggles as Dave and Danny squabble over paying. Dave wins, when I distract Danny with a kiss. We bid our hosts a fond farewell, I insist that Steve and Sandra must come up with Mum and Dave and eat at my place. Steve promises to arrange it and we set off noisily into the night. The cool air is welcome, although it does highlight the drunkenness. I link arms with Danny for support as much as affection. He squeezes my arm against his body and kisses the end of my nose lightly.

"Thanks for this," he whispers.

"What?"

"Bringing me here. I've had a great night."

"Me too."

Then with Mum and Dave walking slightly ahead, he steers me towards a little gift shop with a recessed doorway. He pushes me against the shop door and takes my face in his hands, kissing me deeply.

"Danny!" I giggle, pulling away. "My parents are just there!"

"So?" he grins, wickedly, and kisses me again. Placing his hands on my bum and pulling me in close to him, he stares into my eyes. "I want you," he whispers. "We should have gone to a hotel."

My lips curl into a wry smile. "We'll just have to be really quiet."

His eyes widen. "We can't! It wouldn't be right."

"Oh come on. We've done it before," I tease. He raises an eyebrow. We need to catch up before they notice, so I push past him, taking his hand and march to close the distance with Mum and Dave.

"Oh there you are," Mum says.

"Just looking in a shop window," I maintain. Mum chuckles, knowingly.

Danny puts his arm around me and pulls me close, and we follow Mum and Dave the rest of the way home. When we get in, Dave begins the protracted process of making coffee from his machine. He loves the bloody thing and I instantly regret buying it for him for his birthday. If it was just a cup of instant, we could probably decline, but Dave will be disappointed if we turn this down. I exchange a look with Danny; I know he wants to go to bed as much as I do. But we don't want to be too obvious, or rude, so we politely accept a coffee and dutifully sit and drink it with them.

"You two are quiet," remarks Mum, a little too pointedly.

"Just tired," I reply tersely.

"I guess I'm still a little jet-lagged," offers Danny, picking up on the hidden dialogue between Mum and I. "I suppose I should turn in," he murmurs and yawns, to prove his point. He looks at me for backup, so I stand and collect our coffee cups.

"Thanks for a lovely evening," I say.

"Yes, it was great," adds Danny. "Thanks."

"You are most welcome," says Mum as she struggles to get up out of her chair. "Leave those in the sink."

We carry the cups out to the kitchen and, ignoring Mum's request, I rinse them and place them on the draining board. Purely out of habit, I bang the coffee grounds out of the filter and clean the machine ready for tomorrow. It's a La Spaziale machine, like we have at the diner, only smaller. Ever since I showed Dave mine, he has lusted after one, so Mum, Grace and I got it for him for his sixtieth birthday.

Mum looks back into the living room and tuts in exasperation.

"He's asleep!" She turns to us and says, "If you'll excuse me, I need to get my husband to bed! Goodnight."

Danny smirks at me…we are alone. Standing on opposite sides of the kitchen, minutes pass. We listen as they both get ready for bed, then the bedroom door shuts. Danny moves towards me, backing me against the pantry door. He strokes my hair and pushes it behind my ear, then he kisses my exposed neck. I sigh. The touch of his lips sends a rush of excitement through my body. His lips travel upwards to my earlobe, sucking and kissing, then his hand curls around the back of my neck as he finds my tongue with his.

I push him back.

"Can you be quiet?" I ask.

"I can. Can you?" he teases.

"I don't know, let's see shall we?" I smile with a raised eyebrow, taking his hand as I switch off the lights. As we quietly walk up the stairs, he gently runs his index finger up my inside leg, making me gasp as he reaches his target. I wriggle away and giggle.

"Stop it," I hiss and hold my finger to my lips. His eyes glint in the half-light, his smile telling me this is going to be fun. He hooks the back of my jeans with his finger and pulls me close to him as we reach the landing, pressing his front into my back. He kisses my neck again while his hand wanders across my stomach to the top of my jeans.

We are right outside my parent's bedroom, when his hand slides into my jeans, past my knickers and his finger slowly enters me. I breathe out a quiet "*Oh!*"

"*Shh!*" he whispers, his lips pressed against my ear. I can feel his grin. His free hand urges me on and with his finger still in place, we move towards our room. I was pleased earlier when Mum put us in the room furthest from theirs. Once inside, he pulls his hand away and closes the door. I switch on the bedside light while he unzips the bag and rummages round for something. Condoms, he reveals, holding them up triumphantly. I smile.

He moves over to me and pulls my jumper and top up over my head, in one go. His hands travel quickly over my bare skin, caressing my breasts through my bra, before unhooking the clasp and casting it aside. He moves back then to my jeans, unzipping them but not removing them. He pauses to pull off his top then slips his hand back past my jeans and underwear and plunges two fingers into me.

"Now this is something we have done before with your parents next door," he whispers, close to my ear as his other hand slides into my hair, pulling me close for a kiss.

We kiss while his fingers do their magic inside me, so I pull at the button fly on his Levis and reach into his boxers. He is hard already and he gasps when I wrap my hand around him and begin to move. We stand in the middle of the room, half naked, kissing and touching, building our pace and both becoming breathless until finally a little moan escapes from my lips.

"*Shhh!*" he breathes, withdrawing his hand. I sag with disappointment. Okay, maybe it wasn't such a little moan, he probably has a point. We need to keep quiet.

I kiss him again, occupying my lips before they let me down again. Then I slide both my hands into his jeans and push them down to the floor, following them with clear intentions. He stops me as I stoop and brings me back up to standing, shaking his head. He clearly has a different plan. He quickly kisses me and then spins me around until I'm facing away from him. He takes a couple of steps forward, in spite of his jeans around his legs. We stop in front of the small sofa and he bends me over it. I wasn't expecting this and I look at him quizzically.

"I sat on the bed earlier and it creaks so loud," he whispers. Then he suddenly yanks down my jeans and rips open a condom, he puts it on in record time. He flashes me a wicked smile and then fills me in one swift motion, taking me by surprise and delivering a wave of pleasure. Watching him over my shoulder the whole time, I can hardly stifle my moan.

He shakes his head, withdrawing and fixes me with his intense stare.

"You need to be quiet!" he says, with mischief in his eyes and a wry smile on his lips. I nod, so desperate now, I'll do anything. I need him inside me again. He seems satisfied and suddenly pushes into me again. This time I respond with a suppressed groan and he continues. He holds onto my hips as I stand bent at the waist, my hands resting on the seat of the sofa. He draws back, then thrusts into me again and again, finding a rhythm. This is going to be fast.

I'm in ecstasy. I desperately try to keep quiet, but as he drives deeper and faster into me, I'm unable to prevent another small sound from escaping. He leans forwards over me and clasps his hand around my mouth.

"Quiet!" he hisses close to my ear. I don't think I've ever been so turned on. He keeps his hand in place and picks up speed. I breathe heavily into his hand and feel his hot breath against my ear. He's hitting my G-spot, hard, and I can feel myself getting close. Our breathing becomes more irregular as we can both contain our orgasms no more. I haven't even touched myself. My hands are planted firmly on the sofa, but this is a case of mind over matter. I'm so turned on by his forceful nature and the urgency. I'm coming hard before I even know what has happened.

I cry, almost silently, into his hand as the intense pleasure hits me. He keeps going, nearing his own climax and just as the final waves of my orgasm are subsiding, I feel him tense. His breathing halts from the tension of his body, then he breathes out a huge sigh of release in my ear and I feel his whole body shuddering. As he comes back down to earth, he takes his hand away from my mouth and turns my face to meet his lips. It's an awkward angle, but it's an emotional kiss.

That was risky, being forceful like that, but I'm in heaven. Being told to shut up obviously floats my boat, who knew? He slides out of me as the kiss becomes more sensual and gently lifts me to standing and turns me to face him. He holds my face between his hands and gazes contentedly into my eyes. A slight smile touches his face as he closes his eyes and kisses me once more.

Thirteen.

Get rid of him, whoever he is.

Liv.

We spent the rest of the weekend relaxed and happy with my parents. We walked around Brighton, took in the sights, sat on the beach and did a spot of shopping. We brought the relaxed vibe home with us as well; the past week has been wonderful. My concerns have all but gone and, although we haven't addressed it, we're getting really cosy. I'm well aware that Danny has only been here for ten days, but our relationship doesn't reflect that at all. From the outside looking in, we seem like any other established couple of our age.

We have, as Danny pointed out, been together for years; albeit with an extended hiatus, and it's feeling like that too. Except he's like no man I've ever been with. He cleans, he helps out and he considers me. I know he has nothing else to do right now, but it feels like it's in his nature to be this way. When my flowers were looking a bit sad on Friday, I went up to see him at lunch time and found that they had gone and the vase was washed and on the draining board. I probably would have left them for another week until the water was all smelly, but he cared enough to do it for me. Later on, I was astounded to have a second visit from the florist with another gorgeous bouquet.

AND the sex is amazing!

It has been surreal, but I'm thinking about it less and less. We're in our two-week bubble and I'm determined to enjoy every minute. Things have been perfect, then a couple of days ago, I got a text from Mark which said, 'Can we talk? x'. It came through while I was curled up on the sofa with Danny watching a film. I showed him. He surprised me by not being jealous or overprotective, he simply asked me what I was going to do. I told him I would do nothing, I don't owe Mark anything and I don't have anything to say to him. So I deleted it in the hope that he'd get the message.

Danny's parents got home from their holiday, so he called them to let them know where he was. They were naturally shocked, but supportive. He told them that right now he was just visiting and he'd let them know if he planned to fly back at any point. He's also spoken to Jen a few times. I've no idea what she's like, but from the one-sided parts of conversation I've heard, they seem to have a lovely friendship.

He has hooked up his laptop and an array of other equipment that I don't understand and has made one end of my dining table his temporary office. He has no work right now, but still has to check his email every day. Jen passed on a few messages from his machine at home, so he hasn't missed anything so far. He's been keeping himself busy and I notice he's been on Facebook a lot. Over the last week he's liked the bar's page and I've tagged him in the few photos he appears in. I also noticed that he's now friends with Max, Charlie, Connie and a couple of the bar staff. I guess he has nothing to do.

He's been helping out every day, wherever I'm working. I told him to relax and enjoy his holiday, but he says he's here to be with me, not sit in my empty flat. Right now I'm grateful for his help because it's Easter Sunday and we're really busy with a late lunch crowd. He's helping me with some glasses in the bar kitchen, when my phone buzzes in my back pocket. I pull it out and frown…Mark.

'Please, I need to see you. x'

"What's up?" Danny asks.
"It's Mark again," I sigh. I thought he would just go away.
"What does he want?" he asks, looking concerned. Like me, he

assumed that Mark would not be an issue.

"He wants to see me." I glance up at Danny. "Well he can fuck off," I say decisively and shove my phone back in my pocket.

Danny continues loading glasses into the dishwasher.

"Maybe you should talk to him, see what he wants," he says without looking up.

"What for?"

"Well he won't go away until you tell him to. If you say nothing, the door is still open."

"Trust me, he knows the door is very closed."

"Well obviously not, or he'd leave you alone."

"I've no interest in anything he has to say." I shake my head and carry on stacking glasses.

"Okay," Danny says, backing off. We continue to work in silence. I'm so furious with Mark for daring to penetrate the bubble. Not that he realises that is what he's doing. He has no idea how my life has changed since he left. He probably imagines that I'm all broken. He knows I was angry, perhaps that's why he has let the dust settle before getting in touch. But maybe now he expects to find me vulnerable and ready for reconciliation. Well whatever, I'm not interested. I finish up and stalk back into the bar, grateful, that we're busy.

At about 5pm the rush is over and Danny and I have taken a break. Tonight will be busy with the younger crowd, tomorrow is a Bank Holiday, so they will be making the most of the extra drinking time. We've eaten and showered. I laugh when he emerges from the bedroom wearing a staff shirt. He ruined another t-shirt today helping out, so I gave him one of our shirts to save the rest of his wardrobe.

"I hope you know, I'm not paying you!" I joke. He raises an eyebrow at me; I ignore his suggestiveness and slip my arms around his waist.

"You couldn't afford me anyway." He leans in and kisses me. He holds me close to him and fixes me with his intense stare. "Can I take you away?"

"Away?"

"Yeah, can you get a few days off? I want to take you away for a romantic trip."

"When?"

"I don't know, this weekend?"

I frown at him. "Where will we be going?"

"It's a surprise. Can we do it?"

"Well I'm not working this weekend, so yeah!"

"Great!" he says and kisses me. "Come on," he says patting my bum. "Back to work."

"Ooh, I love it when you're all forceful" I tease and turn to head back downstairs.

After I've checked in on the diner staff, wiped a few tables and served some drinks, I head next door. Danny is already pitching in with Max behind the bar and I watch them for a minute. They have a sweet rapport. The fondness I feel for them both overwhelms me. Just then, my thoughts are interrupted by a familiar voice behind me.

"Liv."

I turn to find Mark standing behind me. Shit. I'm aware that my expression is stony, which is a relief because inside, I flounder for something to say.

"What do you want Mark?"

He looks sheepish, but also a bit lost. Come to think of it, he looks like shit, untidy and unshaven. He sighs, "Please, I just want to talk."

"There is nothing to say," I say, keeping my cool.

"I miss you," he whispers, attempting to take my hand.

I jump back, shocked by the over-familiar intrusion. Three weeks ago I was sharing my bed with this man, now the thought of him touching me makes my skin crawl.

"Don't."

I'm suddenly aware that Max has joined me and that Danny can't be far away.

"This has nothing to do with you Max," sneers Mark, before Max even opens his mouth.

I hold my hands up to both of them and usher Mark to sit down at a nearby table. The bar is quiet; I would rather deal with this now, in public.

I turn to Max, who is hovering behind me and tell him I'm fine. He looks doubtful, but backs off and goes back to the bar. Danny is still working, although he's also watching. I smile weakly at him and then return to Mark.

Sitting down with Mark at the table, I'm filled with dread. I don't want to give him my time, but really he won't go away unless I do. He looks up at me with hope in his eyes, oh God; this is going to be brutal.

"You look great," he says with a smile. I resist the urge to hurl. I may be stupid, but I never imagined seeing him again and it has knocked me for six.

"I can't say the same about you."

"I'm a mess. I don't know what to do without you."

I shrug and shake my head. "You had me…but you made your choice."

He grabs my hand across the table and I flinch, but I don't immediately snatch it back.

"Please give me another chance."

I sit and look at him. If there was no Danny, I would be furious with him right now. I would yell and scream at him, for what he did and for having the audacity to come here asking me for another chance. But I've completely moved on, there seems no point in getting angry or emotional, even though he deserves it. It would make it seem like he still means something to me and he doesn't. I take a deep breath and pull my hand away calmly.

"It's over Mark."

"I know I messed up, but I love you. Please, don't throw this away."

I have to stifle a laugh. "You threw it away, not me. But you did me a favour."

He looks at me as though I've just driven a knife through his heart.

"Don't say that. Why are you being so cold?"

"Mark, I…" I don't know how to put this into words. I don't care enough about what he did to fight with him. He means nothing to me. I'm just going to have to tell him about Danny. "I'm with someone else."

Mark's jaw hits the floor, his vulnerable demeanour hardens and his eyes turn cold.

"What?" he spits. "Why are you doing this? Are you just trying to hurt me?" His stance changes. "Who is it? Get rid of him, whoever he is. It can't be that serious. Did you just meet him?"

"Actually I've known him for years and it's pretty serious. Go home Mark. It's over, there is nothing more to say." I glance over at the bar and Mark sees me looking in the direction of Max and Danny. Before I know what is happening, Mark's chair is scraping on the floor and he is stalking over to the bar towards Max, who is still standing customer side, ready to throw Mark out if anything kicks off. I jump up and follow him.

"It's him isn't it," Mark accuses, pointing at Max.

"Max is gay," I remind him, through gritted teeth. I want to yell, but this is not a private conversation and I'd be screaming Max's business across the bar.

"No, he's been all over you for years. I've never trusted him."

Max can't take any more and starts towards Mark. Then, behind him, I see Danny vault the bar in one swift fluid motion, land square on his feet and pull Max back.

"Leave it Max, it's not worth it."

"Oh, pull yourself together Mark, it isn't Max," I say, putting myself between them.

"Well who is it then? Probably half the weekend crowd...slut!"

I turn to Max to stop him defending me and I see that Danny has put himself in between them. Just as relief sets in, I watch in slow motion as Danny lands a punch right on Mark's jaw, knocking him to the ground.

Mark touches his mouth and finds it bleeding. I look back to Danny, who is standing shoulder to shoulder with Max. Both are satisfied that someone has finally put Mark in his place, but they're ready for more if it's required.

Ben, one of the doormen, walks through the door just then, arriving early for his shift, and takes in the scene. He looks to me, then at Mark on the floor.

Mark staggers to his feet, looking between us all in disgust.

"Who is this joker?" he spits, sneering at Danny. Danny flinches towards Mark and Max stops him.

"Go home, Mark," I growl. "We're done." I turn to Ben. "He's barred."

We watch as a disgruntled Mark is escorted from the premises. Turning back to the boys, I see Danny rubbing his hand and Max slapping him on the back, one comrade to another. In any other circumstances I would have been angry about the violence in the bar...or indeed anywhere. But I've wanted to smack Mark in his smug face ever since I caught him. I regretted stopping Max at the time, so I'm secretly pleased he got what was coming. I can't lie, it was kind of a turn on to see Danny jump the bar and defend me.

I scan the bar and am relieved to see only one couple that we know quite well. Everyone else is either in the diner or the garden, but as it's six-ish, a lot of punters have either finished for the day or haven't even started. I think we got away with it. I head over to the couple and apologise, offering them a drink on the house. I also fix three rum and cokes and go in search of the boys.

I find them sitting at a table in the garden. After I put down the drinks, Danny holds his hand out and pulls me into his lap. I curl my arms around his neck.

"I'm sorry, I shouldn't have lost it," he says sincerely. "I just couldn't let him call you that."

I smile at him and kiss him lightly on the lips.

"He deserved it. Thank you." Turning to Max I add, "And you. Sorry about what he said."

Max laughs it off. "Well, to be fair, I have been all over you for years," he mocks and we all laugh.

The rest of the night went without incident. The Bank Holiday is a good one for the business; I think we can afford to go ahead with the outdoor revamp, which is brilliant. The weekend has been brilliant for me and Danny as well, I'm really getting used to having him here. I left him earlier, sorting out his washing and finding space in my room for his stuff, because I'm sick of tripping over his suitcase. I need to go out with Max and start looking at garden furniture and there's a trade show at the NEC, so we head off early and leave Danny having a day at home. I haven't made a big deal out of clearing him a drawer or anything. Things are so relaxed between us; I just left him to it.

I return home at gone 6pm to find him in the kitchen, cooking. I pause in the doorway to watch him, as he hasn't noticed me yet. The radio is on and he's kind of dancing as he moves around. There's a beautiful, fragrant smell filling the flat. It's Thai for sure. I drink him in, while he adds something to the pot, watching his hips rock to the beat. He's so sexy, freshly showered and wearing his trackies and a black t-shirt. He flips a tea towel over his shoulder as he turns and freezes when he sees me. He looks slightly embarrassed as I beam at him, but he recovers quickly and crosses over to greet me.

"Hey!" he says folding me into an embrace. Lifting me effortlessly as we kiss, he places me down on the counter, next to the chopping board. His arms release me and his hands trail down my sides and onto my thighs as they withdraw. He pulls away from our kiss and returns casually to his chopping. I steal a piece of red pepper and crunch as I watch him. He continues chopping and stirring in silence, stealing the odd glance. He's so hot in the kitchen!

"So did you find anything?"

"Yeah, it's going to look great." He turns and catches my eye. "What is all this?" I ask, waving my hand at the food.

"I wanted to do something nice for you. Do you like Thai?"

I smile and nod, putting him at ease. "You didn't need to do this, you're spoiling me." I capture him in my arms as he tries to pass me. I pull him between my legs and hook my ankles together to hold him close. Resting my elbows on his shoulders, I run my fingers through his shiny hair.

"I want to spoil you," he whispers.

"Careful," I warn, "I'll get used to it."

"You should," he pulls away and I don't try to stop him. He moves backwards and forwards, creating this wonderful-smelling dinner for me and he cooks as we chat. When he's finished adding ingredients and started a pot of rice, he returns to his place between my legs.

"Did you find space for your things?" I ask, stroking his face.

"Yep," he replies with a wry smile. I wonder briefly what the knowing look is about, but he interrupts my train of thought.

"Would you like a drink?" he asks, on his way to the fridge before I answer.

"Please," I reply and as he collects two glasses from a cupboard, I notice for the first time, just how familiar with everything he is. Then as I glance around, I realise.

"You've cleaned!"

"Well I didn't have anything else to do."

"Yes but you didn't have to clean. I feel really bad now, swanning in to a lovely dinner and a clean flat." I pull him back to me and kiss him. "I'll have to make it up to you."

"Hmm, not now though," he insists, laughing as he wriggles away. "I'm cooking."

I huff. How does he have so much control? I slide down off the kitchen side and peer into the pot on the cooker. I stir the pot and lift the spoon for a taste.

"Do I have time to shower?"

"Oh, no you don't," he admonishes, grabbing the spoon from my hand. "Go, have your shower, dinner will be in fifteen minutes."

I shower and change into my soft black jogging bottoms and I'm wearing nothing under them, which makes me smile, thinking about Danny discovering that later. I root around for a vest but I see a freshly washed and ironed stack of his t-shirts. On the top is a well-worn Guns 'n' Roses t-shirt. I run my fingers over the faded design. This can't be 'THE' Guns 'n' Roses t-shirt, the one I got him for his fifteenth birthday. They aren't hard to come by; it must be a different one. I slip it on and head out to the kitchen. Danny has finished in there and is waiting at the dining table for me. Two candles are burning, my latest flowers are in the centre of the table and fresh drinks have been poured.

"This is amazing, thank you." I say, sitting down. "What are we having?"

"Massaman Curry," he says as he loads my plate.

"It smells delicious." I take the plate and wait for him to serve his own. It feels odd being cooked for in my own home. I rarely cook for myself, and I can't think of a time when anyone was selfless enough to do this for me. He digs straight in, so I do too. It's a heavenly coconuty, peanuty chicken curry with potatoes.

"This is so good," I murmur with food still in my mouth. "Where did you learn to cook like this?"

"I just like food," he shrugs.

"Well, you can do this anytime."

We eat and chat. He has enjoyed his day of domesticity and got loads done, including packing for our weekend away. We're off in the morning and I hate not knowing where we're going. I try probing for clues but it's futile.

"You know I hate surprises," I pout.

"Only because you're a control freak."

"But how will I know what to take with me if I don't know where we're going?"

"I'll pack for you. Just let it go." He smiles, "I see you found my stuff."

"Yeah, I hope you don't mind, it just looked too comfortable to resist," I say, looking down at the t-shirt I'm wearing. "Do you remember I bought you one of these?"

"That *is* the one you bought me."

"No way!"

Danny shrugs. "I couldn't throw it out. It reminded me of us."

"I can't believe it hasn't fallen apart after fifteen years."

"I don't really wear it, I just keep it."

I suddenly feel awful for helping myself. "Oh God, I'm sorry, shall I take it off?"

"No! It looks great on you, and besides, I only kept it because I didn't have you."

I smile back at him. Wow! All this time he's kept a bit of our history. I never expected him to be sentimental about us.

"But why did you bring it, if you don't really wear it?"

He suddenly looks embarrassed. "It's my lucky charm."

I lean over and kiss him. I feel so lucky and I'm struggling to keep down all the serious feelings I have. Neither of us has mentioned it, but tomorrow it has been two weeks. The 'magic' two weeks is almost over and we need to discuss what happens next. That's what this weekend is really about. I hope we'll sit down and talk about the terrifying concept of our future. We are, so far, really happy together and I can't even think of how I would cope if he went home, but then I can't see him wanting to at the moment. Although it is his home, so who knows what he'll want to do. I've managed not to think about it too much over the last two weeks, but the fear is building again now.

I clear away the dinner things, insisting that he doesn't help seeing as he cooked. I nip down to get us coffee, ducking into the kitchen, so that I don't have to go out onto the floor in my current get up. It's really busy with the Thursday late night shoppers, so I have to hover for a minute until one of the waitresses comes into the kitchen.

"Carla, could you do me two lattes please?" I ask, gesturing at my outfit by way of explanation. She laughs and goes off to make them, while I raid the freezer for a tub of ice cream. I keep small tubs of leftovers, for the staff and myself. I take a vanilla and a black cherry. Carla returns with the coffees and I grab a tray to take it all back up. As I'm typing the code into the door, a customer comes through to use the toilets. I smile meekly as he passes, mortified by my appearance.

"Well that was embarrassing," I tell Danny as I get back up to the flat. "A customer saw me!"

"So?"

"So, I'm not wearing any underwear!" Cringing, I put the tray down on the coffee table.

Danny pulls me down into his lap and slides his hand under the Guns 'n' Roses t-shirt. "If I'd known that, I wouldn't have let you out of my sight," he says as he caresses my bare skin.

"Stop it," I shoo him away and sit up, passing him a coffee. I settle back down with my legs across his lap and sip my coffee whilst staring at Danny's profile. "Why won't you tell me where we're going?"

"Why won't you just let me surprise you?" he counters, holding firm.

"It's the Isle of Wight isn't it?" I look up at him and we both laugh. I can't stop. When I finally breathe, he slaps my leg and gets up.

"Come on, let's get you packed."

Fourteen.

I love you.

Liv.

Waiting in the Eurostar departure lounge at Kings Cross, I notice how many kids there are waiting to catch the train to Disneyland Paris. Fleetingly, I wonder if that's where we're going, but I really don't think Mickey Mouse and a million kids is Danny's idea of a romantic weekend away. When we caught the train to London, I automatically assumed that we were staying here, but that changed when we arrived at the Eurostar check-in. I suddenly panicked about my passport, until Danny produced it from his pocket. He was going to have ask me to bring it, but then he found it while he was cleaning, so he decided to keep the whole surprise to himself.

Now we're sitting waiting to be called for our train to who knows where. I like being in control, especially where travel is concerned, mainly because I fear things like not having my passport when I need it. But now that we've crossed that particular bridge smoothly, I'm relaxing. It's quite nice to be whisked away and you can't be whisked if you know the ins and outs.

Danny looks like the cat that caught the canary, sitting beside me. He gives my hand a little squeeze.

"You're pretty pleased with yourself aren't you?"

"I sure am!" He laughs, pulls me against him and kisses the top of my head. "Do you want to know where we're going?"

"Nope." At this point it makes no difference.

"I'm impressed. But you'll find out soon enough anyway."

Just then the voice from above announces the Eurostar to Brussels Midi and Danny gets to his feet.

"That's us." He holds his hand out for me. We collect our things. Danny wheels our small, shared suitcase and I carry the breakfast and coffee we've just picked up from the patisserie on the concourse.

Once we're settled into our seats, I have to ask him.

"Brussels?"

"Bruges."

Hmm, I've never thought of going there.

"I've heard it's beautiful, what made you choose it?"

"I called my dad. He and Mom toured Europe for a month, a couple of years ago. I knew he'd have a recommendation. He said it was their favourite stop on the tour. It's not too busy or touristy like the big cities, perfect for a quiet weekend. He even told me the name of a hotel. Is it okay?"

"It sounds perfect. Thank you." I lean over to kiss him. It becomes a deep, long kiss and when I regain my senses I check around me to see if we have any spectators. Thankfully the carriage is only half full and we are several rows away from the next passengers.

"Breakfast?" Danny asks, as he begins to open the bag.

I sip my coffee and flip through the seat-back magazine, until I come across an article about Bruges. Danny hands me my ham and cheese croissant and I read him the article between bites.

"I'm excited to see it now," I say as I finish reading.

"I'm just excited to have you to myself for three days. Do you realise how much you work?"

"I know. I've actually been quite slack since you arrived, I normally work more." I'm aware that I have no work/life separation, but I haven't ever really needed any. Sorry." I add regretfully.

"Don't be silly. I kind of sprang myself on you. Besides, I've loved helping out. It's a real buzz when it's busy. I have to keep reminding myself it's your place. You're incredible." He leans in again and kisses me. "I'll have to do some work myself soon. I can't stay on vacation forever."

My stomach lurches. Does he mean he's going home?

"Don't look so panicked! I'm not going anywhere." He takes my hand, turns to face me and fixes me with that intense stare of his. The train goes dark as we shoot into the tunnel, but we don't really notice.

"It's just that we haven't talked about it," I manage, trying to disguise the growing sense of dread I'm feeling.

"Well let's talk about it now. We have…" he looks at his watch, "…two hours." His gentle smile softens his face and puts me more at ease. "You can't go anywhere, or stop me from saying anything here. You're trapped!"

I laugh, nervously. "So that was your plan? Trap me under the English Channel and then say whatever you like."

Danny shrugs and grins.

"Maybe."

I sigh and rub my face. I don't think I'm ready for this. Over the last two weeks being with Danny has become normal. I don't want anything to change. He's looking at me. I have to say something.

"So what do you want to say?" I want to throw up.

He thinks for a minute. "I guess I want to say that I'm happy. Really happy and I don't want that to change."

Oh thank God!

"I'm really happy too." I gush. "But what do we do now?"

Danny leans back slightly, assessing me.

"Do you like me being here?"

"Of course. I don't want you to leave."

He breathes a quiet sigh of relief.

"Then I won't."

"But is it really that easy? What about your apartment? Your family and friends, your car, work? You can't just walk away from all of that."

"I know, I know." He shakes his head. "It's crazy, but I know if I go back I'll never be happy. I have to try, I want to be with you."

A shiver runs all over me, this is what I want to hear him say but I have so many doubts.

"But how can it work, if you give up everything to be with me and I give nothing?" Once again, we have gone from zero to intense and life changing in a matter of minutes.

"It won't be like that."

"But that's exactly how it will be," I counter. Frustrated that he only sees the romantic side of everything, I'm trying to be a realist and protect myself from pain. But then, I have to admit to myself that the only reason I have him now is because he followed his heart. I would never have taken the risk.

"Okay, hear me out..." he holds my hands as he starts to present his argument. "My parents are going to be spending more and more time in Mexico. They've found a place they love and Mom is going to retire. I'm an only child and I have no grandparents left. Nothing is keeping me anywhere."

"But what about your friends?"

"It's only Jen and Scott that I really care about and they want me to be happy. I'll still see them. Grace lives like, fifteen minutes from them, you go see her, we'll combine visits. Besides, they'll visit me too."

"What about your apartment?"

"I'll give notice when we get back."

"But, that's your home."

"I don't care about that. If you could see it you'd see, it's just a place to sleep. I'm...I was... a single guy. I haven't made it a home. I don't have any attachment to it. I'll get rid of it."

"Just like that? What if it doesn't work out?"

"Why do you have to always doubt? It will work out. If I have to go back, I'll stay at Jen's or my parent's. My parent's house will probably be empty for months at a time anyway. But it will work I know it, if you give it a chance."

"And work?"

"I can literally work anywhere."

"You've really thought about this haven't you?"

He smiles. "I've thought about nothing else." He lets go of my hands and folds his arms. "You can't come up with any obstacle I haven't thought of already." We sit quietly, racing through the darkness for a while.

"Have you talked to your parents about this?"

"Yeah, Dad's psyched about having a reason to visit the motherland more often. The question is, will you have me?"

I can't believe he'd need to ask that question.

"I want nothing more," I say sincerely. "I'm just so scared."

"Of what?"

I fall silent while I search for the explanation. Staring into the darkness I wonder what I'm really afraid of. I'm not exactly sure myself, so how I can try to explain it to him, I don't know.

"The thing is, I've been hurt by men before. Men, I realise now, I never truly loved anyway. I see now that you are the only person I've ever really loved and while losing you broke my heart, you never actually hurt me. You left, but that wasn't your fault. So you've stayed perfect in my memory. I guess my fear is, if I let myself love you, you might turn out to be just human. And if you're just human, you could easily hurt me too. I couldn't survive being hurt by you Danny." I sigh, feeling relieved to finally voice my fears, but extremely vulnerable now that I have.

Leaning against the window, he stares at me, taking it all in.

"But I *am* just human," he frowns. "It broke my heart too and I'm just as likely to get hurt here as you, but I still have to try."

We sit in silence again. A passenger passes us and reminds us that we are still on the planet. The pitch-black surroundings and the artificial lighting, combined with the consuming white noise of the train thundering along have cocooned us in our pair of high-backed seats. We are sitting in the last two seats in our carriage and unless I lean out into the aisle, I can't actually see or hear any other passengers.

Danny suddenly shifts and once again holds my hand to focus my attention while he talks.

"I don't have any idea what I want for my future, but I know I want you. I'm twenty-nine years old and I haven't had a relationship with anyone that's even come close to having a lifelong future, except with you, but we were too young. We're adults now and I have you back, I can't pass up a second chance like this. I can see my future with you Liv, and if you feel the same way, then we have to try."

"I do," I whisper.

Danny takes a deep breath and pulls me into his chest. I wrap my arms around him, returning the embrace. He gives me a tighter squeeze in acknowledgement and we speed under the sea, wrapped around each other. It feels almost like a promise, to keep me safe. I realise then, things have to be less one-sided between us. He's giving up so much to make this work, I have to trust him and be more forthcoming with my feelings. I should be honest about how I feel…if only I was brave enough to admit it to myself.

I pull back from him and realise I have tears running down my face. Danny brushes one away and lifts my chin.

"I won't hurt you, you know," he says looking me straight in the eye. "I love you."

"I know. I love you too," I say without hesitation. This time I wanted to hear it and I wanted to say it. I have no choice, it's true. He closes his eyes and kisses me. Then he takes my hand and spreads his fingers between mine. I rest my head on his shoulder and we sit like this for some time until suddenly the train is filled with light again. When I lift my head to look at Danny, he is staring out of the window.

"Penny for your thoughts."

He turns to me and smiles. "I was just thinking about where we go from here."

"Me too. So what did you come up with?"

"Well I have to go back to LA next month for a meeting. I was thinking you could come with me."

"Grace's baby is due on the 14th of May, so, as soon as she's had it, Connie and I are going to fly out for two weeks. But obviously we don't know yet exactly when that will be. Mum is going out the week before and is staying at least a month. When's your meeting?"

"May 10th." He laughs. "Like it was meant to be."

"So when will you fly out?"

"I don't know."

I think for a second.

"How about, if the baby comes early, we all fly out together. But if she's late, you go ahead and we'll follow? I just don't want to go until she arrives, so I get to have the maximum time with her."

"Okay, but you'll stay with me, won't you?"

"Of course." I watch the French countryside whizzing by, while I think about what it will be like to be in Danny's world. "Will I get to meet Jen and Scott?"

"Trust me, Jen will insist on it. I think I'll have a tough job getting you to myself. Oh and Mom and Dad will want to see you…" he laughs. "On second thoughts, maybe we should just stay here!"

"Oh stop!" I slap him playfully. "I can't wait. You'll have me all to yourself when we get back; it's only a couple of weeks. Let's not forget my mum will be there and then there's Grace and Andy. Connie too…maybe we can all get together!"

Danny rolls his eyes in a dramatic fashion and bangs his head repeatedly on the window. I try to look offended that he hates the idea, but we both end up laughing.

Then my mind starts filling with questions again. "What will you do after that?"

"Come home with you," he says and looks at me quizzically as if to say 'what else would I do?'

"You know what I mean. Your apartment, your stuff. How are you going to go about this?"

"I haven't really thought about it. I guess, I'll give notice on my apartment and bring my stuff back to England with me."

"And that's it?" I marvel. Why isn't he fretting over this?

"What else?"

"Aren't you freaking out? It's so fast and you're moving countries."

Danny shakes his head wearily. "Why don't you get it, I just want to be wherever you are. I don't care where that is."

"But it's only been two weeks."

"Yes that's right, two weeks, plus our entire childhood," he says, as though he is explaining it to an elderly relative. "But it will be another month by then, will you believe me when it has been six weeks, plus our entire childhood? What is the accepted length of time before you change your life to be with the person you love? A day was all I needed." He gives me a wry smile. "I love you. Just let me be with you. Please?"

I relax, I believe him. My last defence has fallen and I'm exposed, but I trust him completely. "I love you too."

While we wait on the train for a prolonged stop in Lille, we discuss his plans to continue to work with companies in the US as well as companies in the UK. That way, he can keep touching base in LA and we can both maximise the opportunity to visit our loved ones. He has it all worked out. He even thinks he can charge the flights as expenses, so it won't always cost us the earth.

"Will clients really pay to fly you over? There must be other people who do what you do."

"I'm quite in demand you know."

"Oh, I don't doubt that," I tease. He grins and strokes my cheek with the side of his hand.

"So these clients won't mind that you're living across the Atlantic?"

"That's up to them. But it won't make any difference to the service I provide. Often I don't even meet with them face to face anyway." He shrugs. "I'll try to establish myself in the UK too. But I work with international clients, purely over the phone all the time. The US clients will just have to become the international ones."

I squeeze his thigh. "I can't believe what you're prepared to give up, for me."

"It's not for you, it's for me. I wish you would see that."

Good God, he has all the lines, I think as my stomach does a back flip. The old me would happily slap the new me for getting sucked in by the romance of it all. But it's pretty damn romantic; my lost love is back, like something from my precious films. This is what I've wanted all along. The train lurches forward once more and I sit back and daydream about what life will be like now that I have Danny.

After changing trains at Brussels Midi and a short ride on a local train, we arrive in Bruges. Champagne and chocolate-dipped strawberries were waiting for us in our room at the charming Hotel Aragon, which, for some reason, I find so funny. It is way too clichéd. Danny assures me it was part of the package, not something he requested specifically. I feed him a strawberry, which he bites while trying to stifle his own laughter. He backs into the bed and I fall down onto him still holding the strawberry, laughing hysterically.

I look down into his eyes beneath me and then kiss his strawberry-tasting lips.

"Thank you," I whisper.

Danny grabs the strawberry from my hand and hooking his arm around me, flips us quickly so that I'm under him. He pauses briefly, his face just above mine; I feel his shallow, ragged breath. He feeds me a bite of the strawberry and then kisses me and we share the sweet taste as our tongues explore. When he pulls away I'm breathless, wanting more. But he has other ideas and jumps to his feet. He pops the rest of his strawberry in his mouth.

"Come on," he says as he chews. "We can do it later, I want to go out."

"No fair, I'm all turned on," I moan as I sit up.

He smiles then shrugs one shoulder, before leaning forward to kiss me again.

"Later," he whispers in a more sensual tone that leaves me giddy. Then he turns and disappears into the bathroom. I fall back on the bed with a huff. God, I want him!

Nevertheless, ten minutes later we are walking down the short cobbled street that leads from our hotel to the main square. It opens up before us and we are taken aback. What greets us is a large, open square lined with imposing gothic-style buildings on one side and on the other, in contrast, gingerbread-looking houses each with their own bustling restaurant in the front, under cover of canvas blinds. Standing proudly above it all is the impressive belfry, which is staggeringly high compared to everything else. All around us, people are taking in the sights and relaxing in the spring sunshine.

I look at Danny and he smiles.

"What do you want to do first?" I ask.

"I have a list from Dad."

He rolls his eyes and then pulls a crumpled piece of paper from his back pocket. I laugh. I remember Danny's dad; the list shouldn't surprise me. I can picture Danny, asking him for any suggestions for this trip and his dad saying 'are you taking this down?' He's a particularly methodical man. Danny reads me the list.

1. Climb the tower
2. Eat moules frites on the market square
3. Drink the beer. Kwak & Kriek Boon
4. Carriage ride
5. Canal boat
6. Waffles
7. Fries & mayonnaise from the frietkotjes (vans in the square)
8. The old chocolate house or Bittersweet – for hot chocolate

"Your dad is a man after my own heart, it's all food related."

I take the list from him and study the scrawl, then with a quick glance around the square I look back to Danny, who is watching me with interest.

"Well we can do…" I tap my finger down the points counting, "…four of these right now." I glance around again. "But first I need money. We need to find a cashpoint."

Danny narrows his eyes at me.

"I have all the money we'll need."

I'm not bothered, we are here to enjoy ourselves not argue about who is paying for what. I shock myself with this attitude, but he has been staying with me and I have been insisting he is looked after. If he wants to treat me, let him knock himself out. I shrug. For a second Danny doesn't know what to do with my reaction, but I begin to walk away so he follows. I peep at him and he's shaking his head in disbelief. I smile inwardly. I like the new me.

We start by buying a little cardboard tray of chips with mayonnaise from the van on the square to keep our hunger at bay. Then we share them while we wait in line to go up the tower. The chips are really good. Danny is sceptical of the mayonnaise, but he's won over. So far, the chips were 3€ and the belfry was 5€ each, if he insists on paying, at least I'm a cheap date.

It's some time later that we climb the last of the 366 steps to the top of the tower. The number of people allowed up at one time is limited, so we were glad we had chips to keep us going during the wait. In the area at the top, we are treated to a 360-degree view of the city. Each of the tall archways is open and it's reasonably windy up so high. In the centre is a huge bell, enclosed by a metal cage and looking down the centre you can see smaller bells below. We were treated to the quarter-hourly peel of the bells while we were climbing; it was quite an awesome sound. But for now they are silent.

I head to a window at the front and rest my arms on the cold stone ledge. The ledge is well over a foot deep, so there is no way you could lean out of the window, but I lean right forward to get a good view.

"It's beautiful," I turn and say to Danny, but I realise he's not behind me. He's still standing in the middle looking at me in mild horror. "What?" I ask, worrying that I have ignored some sort of etiquette or something.

"I don't think you should lean out like that."

I laugh at him and then clap my hand over my mouth.

"Are you afraid?"

"Well I'm not a big fan of heights and I'd feel more comfortable if you didn't lean right out like that."

"Oh don't be so silly! The wall is about two feet deep, come on I'll protect you." I take his rigid hand and slowly lead him to the window. I stand in front of him and he wraps his arm around my waist, but he is not very relaxed, so I don't push it by leaning out again. We stand for a while and enjoy the view...at least I do. Then we move around to look at different aspects. The canals are gorgeous; I look forward to taking a boat trip. When I can see Danny has had enough, I suggest we go down. He looks relieved, but before we start the climb down, he turns me to him and kisses me lightly.

"I love you, you know," I tell him as his lips leave mine, determined to say it first this time. I don't want to always be the one saying I love you too.

He looks very happy and simply answers, "I know."

I turn to lead him down the steps, but his arm swoops around my waist pulling me back to him and from behind me he whispers in my ear, "I have always loved you, Liv."

My hair stands on end and I stand stock sill while my whole body responds to his words. Thank goodness he's holding me up. I have no words. I catch myself about to cry, so I try to pull myself together as I turn to face him again.

"You're going to make me cry."

"I don't want you to cry, but I want you to know that I've never stopped loving you...and I never will."

I gulp and fight the sting in my eyes. I can't speak, so I just nod. I hug him. It's the best I can do. I don't want to sob in public. But I'm sure he realises I feel the same way.

"Let's go eat," he says, trying to distract me from my overwhelming emotions and we start on the steps back down to earth.

We've chosen at random one of the seemingly identical restaurants on the square. Bob, Danny's dad, told him they were overpriced and for the tourists, but he thought we would enjoy sitting on the square. We scanned the vast menu of beers and found both of his recommendations. I'm not a huge fan of beer, but I sometimes enjoy a Hoegaarden, so I thought I would give another Belgian beer a go. I have opted for the Kriek Boon, which we discovered is a cherry beer. It's quite enjoyable.

Danny went for the Kwak, for the comedy value of the name alone. But when it was delivered, I was beside myself. It comes in a hilariously huge glass, with a round bottom. It's like giant chemistry equipment and it sits in a large wooden holder, because it can't stand up on its bulbous bottom. It screams 'I'M A TOURIST' and has had me in fits ever since. I've already taken photos and posted them on Facebook. It's brilliant. Danny took it on the chin and is enjoying it. It would be worse if he was the only one, but looking around there is at least one now on every table.

We both order the moules frites and sit enjoying our comedy beers and huge steaming pots of mussels. We while away the afternoon people watching and drinking funny beers. I'm experimenting with fruit beers, Danny is sticking resolutely to Kwak and it's a good three hours until we test our legs and then we realise just how strong Belgian beer is.

Giggling, we walk arm in arm back to the hotel. It's about 4pm and we've decided to head back for a snooze before a night on the town. We collapse onto the comfy bed fully clothed and despite a few minutes spent kissing and stroking, it has been an emotionally exhausting day and we both drift off to sleep quickly.

Fifteen.

Friend of yours?

Liv.

I wake up to darkness and take a moment to find my bearings. Danny is sound asleep next to me and I've no idea what time it is. I stumble to the bathroom and turn on the light and I'm relieved when I look at my watch to find it is only 7:15pm.

I open the bathroom door and throw light across the bed. Danny is curled up sleeping and I just want to stand here and watch him, but we're only here for forty-eight more hours and we should go out. I crawl onto the bed next him and kiss his cheek softly.

"Danny." I whisper. He stirs slightly so I kiss him twice more. "Danny." I say with a bit more volume.

He rolls onto his back and pulls me onto him with his eyes still closed.

"Mmmm, what time is it?" he mutters sleepily, his eye peeping open and squinting at the light from the bathroom.

"Quarter past seven."

"Hmm, I love the way you say that."

"Say what?"

"Quarter past seven," he says wrapping his arms around me.

"How else would you say it?"

"Seven fifteen. The way you say it is so British."

"Are you still drunk?"

"No, but I am hungry." He rolls me off him so that he can get up. As he walks to the bathroom he rubs his head. "Ugh, I shouldn't drink during the day."

"It's a holiday perk, enjoy it. We'll go out and drink some more, it'll be fine."

When he emerges from the bathroom, he retorts, "We don't all have livers like you."

I pretend to be wounded, but in all fairness, he is quite right. Wine gets me and these beers are strong, but at my own game, I can play pretty hard.

We get changed and, on the way out, we ask the man on the reception desk to recommend somewhere for dinner. He gives us a few leaflets, one of which is a map. He emphatically recommends Bierbrasserie Cambrinus and circles it on the map for us. We take the other leaflets to look through and head out for dinner.

The Cambrinus is a welcoming bar with a relaxed atmosphere. Some diners are eating others are just drinking. This is my kind of place; we can eat and then stay all night. It's buzzing and warm inside and we find a table. A waiter brings us menus and phone directory of a beer list. He briefly discusses beer with us in perfect English and leaves us to decide.

I'm sitting with my back to the window, facing into the room and Danny is opposite me so he can't see the party behind him, but they are drinking beer in glasses even more ridiculous than Kwak's effort.

"Don't look now, but I've found your next beer!" I whisper across the table.

Danny leans in to listen to me and looks all excited about the prospect of more silly beer.

"What? Tell me."

"Well...It's in a wooden stand like Kwak but the glass is shaped like a horn with a pointy bottom." Trying not to stare at the men I can just about make out the name on one of the wooden stands. I flip through the menu and find it. "It's this one, La Corne du Bois des Pendus. You have to get it, I need a picture!"

"Okay," he laughs, enjoying the 'in' joke. We have so many of these stories from our history. The do-you-remember-when anecdotes. But we are both relishing the first of hopefully many more to come. The waiter comes back and Danny orders his Corne. I go for a raspberry beer, as I enjoyed the cherry so much. We both order chicken with mushrooms in Flemish beer.

Our drinks arrive and Danny sees his next funny beer for the first time. We are beside ourselves, but I manage to compose myself long enough to take the obligatory Facebook photo. I post it and tag us both and this time I put our location. While I have my phone out, I quickly jot a text out to Max checking on everything at home. Then look up guiltily to find Danny watching me.

"Sorry, just checking everything's okay."

"It's fine, I just want you to relax," he says, taking my hand across the table.

My phone lights up on the table and I look to read Max's report. But it's Facebook. Someone called Brooke Ellis has commented on my photo. I open the message and read it aloud.

"What's with all the weird drinks Morgan? I haven't seen you lately, let's get together xxx"

Danny looks uncomfortable and my insides lurch. But I trust Danny completely so I make light of it.

"Friend of yours?"

Danny shifts in his seat and draws in a deep breath. "We have a little history."

Hmm. Okay, that's fine. I had another boyfriend until recently, so I can't hold that against him. But Danny sent him packing last week AND he knew about him from the start. The question is how recent is this history?

Knowing full well what I'm thinking, he begins to explain.

"We kind of had a casual thing. But I haven't seen her in months." He offers me a tight smile, obviously hoping that this won't change anything between us. I feel uneasy about it, but he hasn't done anything wrong.

"It's fine. I have exes too."

"She's not really an ex. But I'll make sure she knows I am in a relationship now," he says, and gives my hand a squeeze. "What?" he asks as I shake my head.

"Nothing, it's just hearing you say you're in a relationship now. It's nice."

"We are though, aren't we?"

"Yes, we are. It's just the first time I've heard it out loud like that. I'm still getting used to it."

"Well get used to it. I'm really serious about this Liv, I love you."

Our dinner arrives and interrupts our serious moment. I'm glad we don't have the chance to dwell on the Facebook comment. It seems of little significance and Danny will deal with it.

"Whoa!" Danny and I look at each other in total disbelief, our meals are obscenely big.

"Look at the size of this thing!" Danny exclaims, as he slides his ginormous oval plate from side to side inspecting the impressive dish from all angles.

Our chicken is served in meaty beer gravy, with onions and mushrooms and a towering wedge of potato dauphinoise. The whole thing is to die for and we greedily tuck in.

Grateful for the distraction, I change the subject completely and we begin discussing the diner menu. I am eager to know what Danny thinks of my take on American cuisine. Apparently I have done well and we enjoy our meal while discussing my ideas for improvement.

"I did notice you mislabelled the doughnuts though. If it's American you're going for then they should be *JELLY* doughnuts!" He takes another mouthful, chuckling to himself.

I put down my cutlery.

"My language, my diner!" But I love that he remembers our old debate.

"I'm just saying, it's not right, that's all."

I shake my head and carry on eating.

After another lovely couple of hours, we have once again consumed a good meal and a few beers and despite the pull to stay in the cosy atmosphere of the Cambrinus, we only have the weekend, so we head out to explore Bruges by night. We take a touristy carriage ride from the market square, which is quite romantic despite the driver barking occasional facts at us as we trot along. We are certain that his English only covers the bizarre bombardment of information we are subjected to, so we don't bother to tell him we just want a quiet canoodle in the back whilst seeing the night sights.

By the time our comedy tour is complete, we both have the giggles and all the beer we have consumed today is making it worse. We walk along a few tiny streets gazing in windows and laughing. Danny has his arm around my shoulders and I've tucked my hand in his back pocket. I give his bum a cheeky squeeze and he stops walking and pulls me in front of him. He steps back until he is leaning against a shop window and slips his free arm under my jacket and gropes my bottom, while he kisses me slowly.

"I think I've seen enough of Bruges tonight…" I murmur in his ear while he kisses down my neck. "I want to see more of you."

"I like the sound of that," he breathes.

I take hold of his jacket collar in both hands and pull him forwards until our lips are touching. The arm around my shoulders slides down to my bum as well and he draws me tight against him, pressing his erection into me. I take a sharp breath in surprise and he gives me a knowing look. Looking each way down the street to check we're alone, I casually stroke my hand across the front of his jeans. Danny quietly moans and captures me in a deep kiss.

"Come on," he grunts as he breaks the kiss. "Or I'll have to have you here."

I raise one eyebrow. "*I* like the sound of *that*."

"God, don't tempt me," he says, grabbing my hand and heading off towards the hotel.

We burst through our door, kissing and touching. My hands stroke the bulge in his jeans. Danny tears his jacket off, letting it fall to the floor and then does the same to mine. Our lips hardly parting, I free my arms and go back to fondling him through his jeans, before tearing the button fly apart and dipping past the waistband of his boxers. He lets out a moan when I grasp his hard-on and he moans loudly.

"Sshh!" I giggle, tempted briefly to turn the tables on him and play the same control game he used on me at my parents. But I want to let myself go tonight and the alcohol is making me unconcerned about our surroundings.

I love Danny's response to my touch; he's completely lost in the sensation of me stroking him. He stops kissing me and gasps; resting his forehead on my shoulder he is briefly incapable of managing his pleasure and his motor skills at the same time. I continue to stroke my hand up and down, feeling him fall to pieces as I move. He won't last long like this, I can feel it. I don't know whether to stop and allow us to savour the experience or carry on and have the satisfaction of making him come, hard and fast.

His hand suddenly halts mine and he catches his breath while staring into my eyes. Apparently, he wants to go for savouring. We stand eye to eye in our room, my hand still wrapped around him. He gently takes my hand away and straightens up. He takes my face in both of his hands and kisses me tenderly, but with such passion that I'm instantly rendered useless. My hands hang limply by my sides while he takes his turn.

One hand moves behind my neck, keeping our mouths connected while his tongue does the business. His other hand slips down and his fingers run along the top of my jeans, following it around to my back and sliding inside until his fingers are splayed across my right bottom cheek. He gives it a gentle squeeze, which I find mildly amusing in my beery haze. But it barely registers through this mind-blowing kiss. It's hot and breathy; our tongues are hardly contained within our mouths. I'm so turned on.

He stops abruptly and yanks my jeans down, following them until he is on his knees in front of me. He lifts my feet one at a time, first slipping off my shoes, then freeing my feet from my jeans and casting them aside. Then he pulls my underwear down too and tosses them over his shoulder. He pulls his face back and inspects what is before him. I'm naked from the waist down and would be extremely self-conscious about the situation, but for the extensive wax I had before we came. Plus I've had a fair amount to drink today and I am filled with lust. Right now I couldn't give two hoots about whether I'm preened and scrubbed, I just want him to reach his mouth forward and do what his current position promises.

Danny obliges willingly and I feel his tongue slide into me. He holds my thighs to steady me as he licks and sucks. It's a bad angle for access, but he certainly makes the best of it. His fingers slide into me then and he begins working them inside me as he gets to his feet. Standing face to face is however, a great angle for his fingers to find my G-spot.

"*Ah!*" I cry, shocked by the sudden intensity. Danny is using such force; I think he could lift me off the ground. I'm hardly aware of my loud moans. He doesn't relent; I'm completely incoherent, awash with sensation. I'm so wet. I just can't get a hold of my thoughts, I've no idea how many fingers he's using, and he's moving so fast. Suddenly, he stops thrusting his fingers in and out and presses them deep inside me, rubbing his fingertips back and forth over my G-spot while his thumb does magic things to my clit.

I hardly see it coming, but suddenly I tense and then practically double over as I experience the strongest, most intense orgasm of my life. Crying out in ecstasy, I fight for breath, I'm so overwhelmed with pleasure and the speed with which it has hit me. The aftershocks of my climax continue to course through my body, leaving me helpless. So while I rock back on my heels and hold onto Danny's shoulder to keep myself upright, I don't notice him whipping a condom out of his back pocket and rolling it on, he doesn't even take the time to push his jeans down.

He lifts my right leg and holds me like a rag doll as he strides the couple of feet to the wall. Pressing me hard against it, he hitches up my other leg and has slammed inside me before I realise I am no longer standing in the middle of the room. My body is still dealing with the waves of pleasure and my insides contract against his hard length, over and over. I cry out again. I can't keep track of what's happening to me. It's all pure pleasure and I have no control over the next move. Danny moans and throws his head back as he fucks me hard and fast against the wall.

I can't believe this is him...I can't believe this is me! This is what I meant by experiencing things a bit more, I just never imagined it being quite so spectacular…or with Danny. I manage to regain enough of my senses to put my arms around his neck, pulling him forward until our foreheads are touching. He has my legs in his arms and my back is pressed firmly against the wall. His thrusts are hard and constant, forcing involuntary moans out of me with each stroke and in no time at all, I find myself building again.

I can't really tell if it's truly another climax or whether I'm still experiencing an extended version of the last one. It's unbelievable. I literally scream, into Danny's neck as my body crashes into my second earthmoving climax. Danny follows and lets out a long loud moan, which forms into the words "I love you Liv."

" I. Love. You. Too." I pant. "So. Much." Then I kiss him while he continues to hold me up. Gradually, we begin to get our breath back and he lets my legs down slowly, sliding out of me as I take my own weight once again.

Returning to planet earth, I laugh, giddy from the change of pace.

"My God!" I exclaim, still breathless. "That was incredible."

"Hmmm." he says, nuzzling into my neck, pushing me back against the wall. "You're incredible." He kisses the spot where his face rests against me. Rousing himself, he pushes away from me and tugs the condom off, then pecks me on the lips before disappearing into the bathroom, leaving the door open. I suddenly get a flush of self-consciousness, realising that I am leaning against the wall, naked from the waist down. I quickly whip my top and bra off and rummage around in the case for something to wear. Danny's Guns 'n' Roses t-shirt slides over my head as he emerges from the bathroom.

"I think I've lost that shirt haven't I?" he smiles warmly.

I just shrug in response.

"It never looked this good on me anyway." He crosses over to me and slides his hand underneath the hem, raising his eyebrows in appreciation when he finds that I don't have any underwear on.

"I was thinking of running a bath," I tell him. "Do you want to join me?"

"Sure. But let me do it, you just relax."

As I sit down on the edge of the bed, he empties his pockets onto the bedside table. Then, he sits to unlace his shoes...we were in such a hurry, he was still completely dressed. As he folds his clothes and puts them on the chair, I notice the screen of his phone is alight. I'm just about to point this out when it goes dark again.

"I think you have a message."

Danny frowns and heads to the bedside table. I watch as he activates the screen and a troubled look creeps across his face. He taps his way around the menus for a moment, shaking his head.

"Problem?" I ask wearily, feeling uneasy.

He opens his mouth to speak, then closes it again. As if he doesn't know how to tell me what it is.

"What?"

"Err..." he pauses. "It's Brooke."

"Brooke?" I ask innocently. I know who she is; I just don't want him to think I have given her a single thought.

"The girl who commented on the photo tonight."

"What's up?".

"Well, I'm not sure. She seems mad." He's still looking at the phone and seems bemused.

"About what?"

"I can't tell...she's called me a couple of times." Then he looks up at me in mild horror. "She's calling me again!"

"You'd better answer it then. I'll run the bath." I say, hopping up and fleeing to the bathroom with my insecurities in tow.

I leave the bathroom door ajar, not in an attempt to eavesdrop, but I feel if I close it, it's making too much of the situation. I can hear him answering the call.

"Hey Brooke, what's up?"..."Yeah, Bruges."... "No, it's in Brussels"..."No I wasn't in LA I was in London."..."Yeah"... "Taking a vacation."... "What's with all the questions?"... "Well I haven't talked to you in weeks."...

He's beginning to sound agitated, then I realise, I'm listening and not running the bath. I quickly flush the toilet to make it seem like that's what I was doing and turn on the taps. The bathroom is filled with the sound of the cascading water and all background noise is cut out. I don't think I would hear him if he called me. God this is infuriating. I want to know what's going on. I know it's nothing bad, but the untrusting side of me would rather hear things first hand, than rely on his version of it later. Even as I think that, I know it's ridiculous. No matter what, I can trust Danny. I know I can.

I busy myself adjusting the temperature and adding some of the complementary bubble bath, which is a nice one in a large glass bottle. Then I set about laying out the bath mat, getting towels, organising what little we have brought with us in terms of toiletries. Then, when there is nothing else to do, I peer back into the bedroom. Danny is pacing the floor looking angry, but I still can't hear what he is saying. I'm in an awkward position now. I can either sit in here, hiding, with blatantly nothing to do, until he finishes or, I can go back out there, as if it's no skin off my nose who he's talking to. I decide to test the water.

I breeze back into the room, throwing him a casual smile and go straight for the bag. I determinedly pull out fresh underwear and finding my make-up remover and moisturiser. I look up at Danny, who hasn't said much since I entered the room. He smiles at me apologetically and I mouth "sorry" at him before heading back to the sanctuary of the bathroom.

As I disappear, I hear him saying, "Well I'm sorry you feel that way." Then all sound is lost in the roar of the running bath. My mind is racing. What can they be saying? I take off my make-up, turn off the taps in the bath, then as I sink into the water, I hear him wrapping up the conversation.

"Not for a while, no."..."No!"... "Look, I'm sorry, but that's just how it is."... "I'll talk to you soon."... "Goodbye." Then he's silent. A minute or two passes and then the bathroom door opens slightly.

"Can I come in?" he asks softly. His tone is completely different with me.

"Of course. Everything okay?"

Danny comes in and perches on the edge of the bath, still wearing only his boxers, he sighs heavily at my question.

"Fine, sorry about that." In a daze, he stirs the water with his fingers. Then he snaps out of it and asks, "Can I get in?"

"I was hoping you would."

He slips off his boxers and settles into the hot water at the other end of the bath, his feet slide under my legs and rest either side of me and he takes my right foot in his hands and strokes it. He's in another world. I watch him for what seems like an eternity, but it gets the better of me. I withdraw my foot and sit forward, engaging his eye contact. "Okay, what's happened?"

He smirks, realising then that he has been on another planet.

"Sorry, I owe you an explanation." He rests his arms along the rim of the huge bath and sighs again. I sit back, mirroring him and wait.

"That was Brooke, obviously. She was all worked up because after she saw the photos on Facebook, she noticed that I was overseas. Then she was at the mall and ran into some friends who told her I had gone off chasing some girl in England." I wait. 'Some girl' rings in my ears, this can't be as bad as it sounds. But he says nothing else.

Eventually, I have to ask, "Why was that a problem?"

He rubs warm water on his face and hair.

"Oh, I don't know," he says, exasperated. "She's jealous."

"But I thought you hadn't heard from her in months. She can't care that much."

"I know, I guess she's just not used to me being unavailable." He winces saying this and pauses, waiting for my reaction, I think. I give nothing away. My mind is racing, but I can't make sense of what he's saying. I look puzzled, so he continues. "When I don't hear from her for a while, it usually means she's dating someone."

"So this has been happening for a while?" This is none of my business and isn't actually a problem. It just seemed like it was a short-lived thing when it came up before, now it sounds like more.

Danny nods, almost regretfully.

"A couple of years on and off. But it was mutual. I wasn't really looking for a relationship and she likes to come and go. But we never overlapped, if she met someone, she would stop calling. There was never a promise of more, it was always temporary." He inhales deeply.

"But it must have meant more to her, or she wouldn't be angry now," I suggest, trying to sound impartial.

Danny shakes his head. "I don't think so, I just think she's used to being able to call me and I'm there, so she was mad that I wasn't around and now she is madder still that I am involved with someone. She likes to get her way." Thinking for a moment, he pauses. "She has a temper, I guess…She isn't really the sort of person I would hang around with, she's just a friend of friends…it was just physical and I'm not proud of it."

God, what do I say to that? It's not for me to judge. I'm a bit gutted that he didn't tell me about this in the beginning. Then when it came up tonight, he made it seem like it was less significant than it was. But he's told her straight and he's being upfront with me about it now. It's not really an issue, I suppose.

"So what now?"

"Nothing, she needs to get used to the fact that I am not available. That's it. I'm with you now." He smiles at me fondly and strokes my leg.

And it's over, just like that. I'm relieved that it's not a big deal, but I'm uncertain whether or not it should have been. In the end, the beer wins and I let it go. Danny sits up abruptly and beckons with a subtle tilt of his head that he wants me to do the same. Sitting up straight, we are much closer to one another and he reaches forward and pulls me to him, sliding me along until my legs are wrapped behind him and we're pressing up against each other. I close my eyes as we kiss.

Sixteen.

War path.

Liv.

After the first two whirlwind weeks, things have settled down. Danny took some freelance work from Charlie to keep busy and we've got into a routine. Grace's baby is due in two weeks; so she could have it any day now. Danny plans to go ahead to LA next weekend and spend some time with his parents before Connie and I arrive, then, as planned, he'll come back here, to stay. Tomorrow, it's one month since he came to find me and, to celebrate, I'm cooking us dinner.

I've left him in his little computer world, sat at what used to be my dining table, pouring over two screens. I don't get it, how can you use two screens to perform one task? Whatever it is he's doing, he does it for hours at a time and sometimes I miss him. I liked it in the beginning when he was around all the time, but that's not realistic in the long term. I feel less guilty about working now at least and he's always there when I finish.

I stroll through the farmers' market, picking up vegetables for our dinner tomorrow. I'm making him something that he hasn't had in years, a good old English roast. Rib of beef, Yorkshire puddings, the lot! He mentioned it a couple of weeks ago, so I'm going to make it for our one-month anniversary. I pop into the butchers to pick up the joint I ordered and head back.

Danny isn't at his desk when I get home, so I stow the food away and

pop downstairs. No one has seen him. I pull out my phone to text him.
'Where have you gone? X'

While I wait for a response, I go and look for Max. Nobody knows where he is either. Those two have been thick as thieves lately; I only went out for an hour, who knows what they could get up to in that time. Shrugging, I head for the diner, I'll do some work until they turn up. We're seeing Max and Charlie tonight in the bar, so I should get some stuff done now.

As I decant the latest syrup batch into bottles, I hear my phone beep.

'Surprise! X'

It says. I shake my head and carry on. Not even wanting to think what that could mean. When I finish, I text him back.

'I don't like the sound of this x'

'You'll love it I promise. X'

I start making the next flavour, to keep my mind off what could be going on and hours go by. It's 5pm before I know it, so I go up for a shower. I text him again.

'Showering, when will you be back? Is Max with you?'

There's no answer so I jump in the shower. I start to get annoyed. What the hell can they be doing? Then, just as I'm rinsing the conditioner out of my hair, I hear them talking in the kitchen. The shower is too loud for me to hear what's being said, but they sound rowdy. I hope they're not drunk, it's Max's birthday drinks tonight. I've organised a sort of 'thing' for him and I'll be furious if they've ruined it. I get out of the shower with a black cloud over my head. I know I should just chill out, but until I know what's going on, I can't.

I stomp out of the bathroom in my towel, dripping water on the carpet, and meet them coming out of the kitchen, laughing and talking excitedly.

"Where have you been?"

"Whoa!" Max says, turns to Danny and murmurs in conspiracy. "War path…"

I narrow my eyes at the pair of them.

"Have you been drinking?"

"Uh oh!" laughs Max.

Danny approaches me and holds me at arm's length; he looks goofy, like he just rode a rollercoaster. His face is flushed and I can smell a hint of alcohol.

"You have! We're supposed to be doing that tonight. I can't believe you go off…"

I don't finish because Danny shushes me, laughing as he presses his finger into my lips.

"Shhh. Relax. We just had one, to celebrate."

"Celebrate what?" I snap, feeling increasingly annoyed about being the only one not in on the secret.

Max pipes up from the background, "I think I'll leave you guys to it." Then he heads for the door, adding, "Eight o'clock in the bar," before he closes the door behind him.

I turn back to Danny. It's hard to be irritated by him when he looks so excited; I soften slightly and turn up the corner of my mouth in the slightest of smiles.

"So what's going on?"

"I asked Max to help me with something after we got back from Bruges." He pauses, allowing for maximum dramatic effect. "Something I've wanted to do for a really long time."

"AND?"

Danny steps back and lifts up his top, which mystifies me until I see his right arm is cling-filmed down to his elbow and up onto his shoulder. A tattoo! My face lights up. I find very little sexier than a guy with a great tattoo. Danny with a tattoo might just make me combust.

Staring in amazement, I step forward, glancing at Danny's eyes. They're glittering with excitement.

"Can I look?" I approach with caution. Danny nods, so I gently peel off the masking tape and carefully unwrap the cling film. I'm blown away by what I find underneath. Max has taken him to the right guy for the job. A local guy we've both been to on many occasions, it can be really hard to book him because he travels, but it's worth the wait if you do. He specialises in dot work and produces the most beautiful intricate geometric work I've ever seen. Danny has really gone for it and had a half sleeve. It's so incredibly sexy!

I study it for ages. I'm just stunned.

"Do you like it?" he asks, snapping me out of my trance.

"It's amazing." I grin, taking his face in my hands and drawing him in to a passionate kiss. I want to jump him right now, but he is probably sore and I'm fresh from the shower. There'll be plenty of time for that. Fleetingly, I think about kissing it once it's healed, it makes my hairs stand on end. I know it's bizarre, but it does something to me. I pull away before I go too far.

"Did he tell you not to leave this on?" I ask, holding up the balled-up cling film.

"Yeah, he told me you'd show me how to take care of it."

"You've certainly come to the right place." I wink. "Come on." Taking his hand, I lead him to the bedroom and from my bedside drawer I produce my ointment of choice. Very gently, I rub it into his skin, loving the opportunity to touch it. He winces slightly as I cover the skin on the inside of his arm. "Hurts there doesn't it."

"A little."

"There!" I exclaim, finishing my duties. I kiss him on the cheek, resisting the urge to kiss his raw skin. "All done."

"Thanks. So, you like it then?"

"I love it, very jealous actually. I'll have to make an appointment now. How did you get in with him so easily?"

"Max gave me his slot. He got another one for while we're in LA."

"Wow! Max must *really* think the world of you."

"He's a good guy. We've really bonded."

I chuckle. "Quite the little bromance you've got going on."

"Oh, stop!" he jokes. Then he gets serious. "I really like him and I love that he loves you. Besides, it makes it easier to stay here if I have friends." I smile to myself, it's true and I am so glad the most important two people in my life seem genuinely fond of each other. I know too well how hard it can be when that isn't the case. Max and Mark despised each other.

At just before eight, I come out of the bedroom, ready for our big night out…well in, we live here. But it's Max's birthday on Monday, so tonight we're hitting the bar. We could go somewhere else, but why not stay where we're treated like royalty and everyone knows where to find us. Besides, it's Saturday night and I've no interest in fighting for drinks at some other bar when I can just snap my fingers here (metaphorically of course, I treat my staff very well). I've set up a V.I.P. area and put on some food. A few friends are coming and we have a friend's band playing. Max's ideal night.

"You look beautiful," Danny says from his vantage point at the table. He's been working while I got ready. He closes down his computers and comes over. "Ready?" he asks, offering his arm. I hook my arm under his and grin.

"Ready."

As we go past the kitchen, I check on everything and see the cake that they've made for Max. Everything is perfect and we walk out into the bar, just as they arrive. Danny greets them warmly and while Charlie talks shop with Danny, I catch Max.

"Thank you," I whisper in his ear.

"Hey it was all him, I just got him in."

"Yeah but you gave up your birthday appointment."

"Anything for you. How's he finding it?"

"Sore I think, but I love it," I reply, watching Danny chat with Charlie. "I wish I'd been there."

"Hot is the only word for it," jokes Max. I feign shock and slap him, but I know he's right. I pout, envious that Max got to see it. "Hey, you can have the next one." He winks.

Danny and Charlie join us and, as the food comes out, some other friends arrive. Before long the band is playing and everyone is having a great time. I can't remember being this happy, ever. I've watched as my friends interact with Danny. He fits here perfectly and I'll do anything to make sure he stays. Max and I have been having a good old dance and I need some air. I head out to the garden and find Danny, sitting on his own looking at his phone.

"Everything okay?"

"That was Jen. Just checking my flight details, she's picking me up Friday." He holds his arms out and I perch on his knee, careful not to lean on his tattooed arm. "She can't wait to meet you."

"I can't wait either. But I hate not going with you. I haven't let you out of my sight since you came back into my life; it's going to be really weird here without you."

He pulls his arm tight around me, and nuzzles into my neck. "It's only for a short time, then you'll be with me. I need to do this, wrap things up. Then I'm all yours." I smile inwardly. I love how that sounds.

"Is it too early to bail on Max?" I murmur in his ear, biting his earlobe.

He laughs. "Yes! It's his birthday, where's your loyalty?"

"Oh, he won't mind." I run my index finger up his free thigh. Danny snatches my hand and pulls it away.

"You're so horny! Now get back in there, before your friend misses you. We have plenty of time for what you have in mind." He commands, pushing me off his lap and standing to follow me. I hang my head in disappointment and he tuts and shakes his head. Then we both laugh and head back inside.

When I finally do get Danny up the stairs, he's had so much to drink that there's no hope. He makes a drunken attempt at foreplay, but it's simply comical. I flop him into bed in his boxers and get ready for bed myself. Before I climb in with him, I lovingly rub ointment into his tattoo. It really is beautiful. I study it in detail while he's out cold, following the lines with my greasy fingers. When I am satisfied that it's sufficiently moisturised, I slip into bed next to him, hugging him close.

"I love you," I whisper.

"Hey sleepy head." I bounce on the bed to stir him.

"Mmm," he stirs.

"Time to get up." I bounce again, a little too enthusiastically. "You're leaving today and I want to see you before you go." I can't believe how fast Friday came around and now he's leaving me.

"Ugh, get off!" Danny mumbles in a sleepy daze. "Why are you doing this to me?"

"Come on," I order, pulling back the covers.

Suddenly he's wide awake.

"Oh it's on now!" he growls with a wicked smile. He grabs me and pulls me down. I struggle, but he wraps himself around me and grabs the covers again, pulling them completely over us. I scream as he begins to tickle me and we wrestle around until he has me pinned beneath him.

He hovers over me in the half-light under the covers.

"I have you right where I want you."

"Come on then tough guy, what are you going to do with me," I challenge.

He flicks his eyebrows up and wrinkles his nose.

"Get up and catch a flight," he says, whipping back the covers and leaping up.

"Hey, no fair!" I pout. "You can't get me all excited then leave me hanging."

"You got yours last night," he reminds me, with smile.

I drop my head back onto his pillow and recall last night.

"Mmmm...I did. Fancy a repeat performance?"

"No can do. Gotta fly!" he quips, tossing his t-shirt over his shoulder and heading into the bathroom.

I huff, but reluctantly get up. I'd already been and got us coffee and pancakes from downstairs; at least they won't get cold now.

I set us places at one end of the table, which is significantly clearer now that Danny has packed. His laptop, the hard drive and all the wires have gone. All that remains is the desktop Mac he bought a couple of weeks ago. He's obviously leaving that here. He'll need it until he ships his stuff over.

Danny comes out of the bathroom and sits at the table.

"Thanks, I'll need this, it'll save me from airplane food."

We eat in silence. I'm dreading dropping him off and I guess he's dreading leaving. I know it's only for a few days, maybe a week, but I don't want him to go. Danny's phone lights up and he glances at it, then clears the screen. He looks up at me.

"Just Mom wishing me a safe flight," he says and puts it in his pocket.

Once Danny has finished, I clear our plates. I don't have much of an appetite, so I scrape most of mine into the bin. I stack up the plates to go back downstairs and finish my coffee. Danny is pottering around getting his last bits ready.

"Ready when you are," he says as he appears in the kitchen doorway.

"Never then," I smile, watching him as he moves towards me.

"It's going to go so fast you know. And I'll call you every day."

"I know."

"I'll miss you, so much."

"I'll miss you too."

"Come on. We can do this at the airport."

"Okay," I reluctantly agree.

We park at the short stay and walk across to the terminal, hand in hand. I wait with him while he queues to check in and then we head for Passport Control.

"I love you," he says with a smile. "And I'm never going to let you go."

I go weak at his words.

"I love you too," I whisper, fighting tears. This is so stupid I reason; in a few days I'll be here catching a flight to join him. I have a stern word with myself and manage not to sob when we kiss deeply and lingeringly. Hurried passengers move around us, while we are oblivious. The airport is one of the few places where such PDAs are acceptable.

"See you, beautiful," Danny murmurs in my ear as we hug one last time and then he turns and heads through Passport Control, waving briefly before he disappears.

I drag my feet back to the car and drive home in silence. Pulling up to the back of the diner, I feel so depressed knowing he won't be there when I get in. I turn off the engine and reach for my phone to text him.

'I love you x''

Then I text my sister.

'Hurry up and have this baby, I just dropped Danny at the airport and I need a reason to follow him ASAP! ;-) X'

Straight from the car, I head into the kitchen and find myself something to do. This is going to suck!

Seventeen.

Just friends ;-)

Danny.

I zip up my case and sit back on the bed. I'm looking forward to seeing everyone, but I really don't want to leave. I think I have everything organised, I wanted to finish it before Liv gets in, so we can be together with no interruptions until I have to leave in the morning. It's already after nine, but there was no one to cover, so she had to work. Hopefully she will be finished soon. Just one last thing to do, text my flight number to Jen. I was pretty drunk when she called the other night, so I promised to text the exact details when I sobered up. I reach for the email I printed off this morning and send the text.

'LAX, Tom Bradley International Terminal, 15:05, Flight BA0283. Xxx"

Liv gets in as I finish typing and I watch her through the doorway, she drops her things on the table and begins to take off her shirt as she crosses the living room, pulling her hair tie out so that her hair falls loose around her shoulders. She gives me that 'you're gonna get it' look as she reaches the door. Without a word, she climbs straight on top of me, straddling my legs and grinds herself against me. I take a sharp breath and kiss her while she pulls at my shirt.

Wow! I knew we'd do it tonight, but I wasn't expecting her to be so charged, right out of the gate. I take a moment to process what's happening. Once she's lifted my shirt over my head, I wrap her in my arms and we kiss like this for a while. Of course we both want more, but tomorrow we will be apart for the first time in a month and we'll miss every part of being together. I want to savour everything we do tonight and not rush. Despite the fact that she came in and got right down to it, I know she feels the same way.

I run my tongue around her mouth for a second more, before withdrawing from the kiss and exploring her face with my lips. She sighs as I trail light kisses around her temple and down to her ear. I continue down her neck and pause for a second, breathing heavily against her skin, while I free her from her bra. She leans back to encourage me and I happily suck on one of her nipples, lightly pinching the other. I've found that she loves it when I am rough with them, but I'm taking it slow tonight.

Liv moans as I suck harder and begins to move against me again. I'm rock hard and a little uncomfortable in my jeans, so I slide my hand between us, yanking at the buttons, but Liv tries to get up. I stop her, pulling her back, my mouth still working on her breast. I refuse to break contact, so I stand quickly, lifting her with me. Holding her up with one arm, I push down my jeans with the other and sit again before we lose contact. I switch breasts, causing Liv to moan again, and pay as much attention to this side, while I kick off my jeans and boxers beneath us. Now it's only her underwear between us.

She sways her hips and teases me through the thin cotton of her panties, I want to rip them off, but I let her have her fun. I need a condom anyway, but to get one from the drawer means stopping, so I put it off a while, surrendering to her seduction. She kisses my neck and then moves down my shoulder to the top of my new tattoo. She can't keep away from it, especially now that it's healing. I didn't do it just for her, I've always thought about it, but I couldn't have hoped for a better reaction. It's still a little uncomfortable, but she knows that better than anyone and is very careful around it. Stopping herself, she returns to my lips, but I know she can't wait until she can kiss it, touch it and lick it, like I do to hers.

I start to push myself against her, she groans at the pressure, but soon I'll need to stop and grab a rubber. Liv lifts slightly and before I realise what's happening, she's pulled her panties to one side and positioned herself so that I am just inside her. I look at her in panic; she just smiles as she very slowly starts to sink down onto me.

"Wait," I tell her.

"It's okay, I went back on the pill last week. Today's the first day I'm protected."

I frown. "Why didn't you tell me?"

She shrugs. "A week is a long time to wait. I thought it would drag if you were waiting too."

"Are you sure about this?"

She nods and smiles. I relax and moan loudly as she lets me all the way in. The feel of bare skin inside her is incredible, most of my relationships have been short-lived or casual, so I've only gone bareback with one other girl, a long time ago. She was on the pill and we were together over a year. Since then, I got used to rubbers, but this…this is unbelievable. As Liv begins to ride me, I put my hands behind me on the bed to keep us upright. The sensation is overwhelming, I can't imagine ever going back to rubbers now that I've had this. I'll always want to experience her this way. She's incredible.

She loves it like this, me sitting with my feet on the floor and her on top; it pushes all the right buttons. I watch her as she gets more and more into it. She's so beautiful. She starts rocking back while she holds onto my shoulders. I sit forward a little and wrap my arms around her, pressing our bodies together. She lets out a long, low sound as the friction changes and then starts to rock faster. I help her by lifting her slightly, but she's in control. She keeps going, her eyes are closed, but I can't take mine away from her. She tips her head back, extending her neck and I accept the invitation and kiss and bite her there. She gasps as my teeth sink into her skin, but I know she loves it. I trail my gentle bites of her skin lower and lower, until I reach her breasts. I pause while Liv keeps moving.

She knows I'm making her wait, so she grabs her breast and feeds her nipple to me. I grin as I suck it hard, knowing this will really put her over the edge. She moans loudly as I bite down on it and really picks up her pace. She's lost now and it's just a matter of how long she can hold out. She slams onto me and I bite down again, finishing her off and she cries out my name as she spirals down from her orgasm. She breathlessly continues to rock gently and I feel her clenching inside, until she slows to a stop.

She looks at me and smiles. I sweep her hair away from her face and kiss her. I press into her again, causing her to moan and reminding her that I'm still hard inside her. She kisses me and with one last tilt of her hips, she stands up, dropping straight to her knees between my legs and takes me in her hand. I sigh as she works her hand up and down. It feels so amazing, wet from being inside her, to be stroked like that. Her hand glides smoothly over the slick skin.

Liv holds my gaze as she lowers her head and takes me in her mouth and I moan as I feel her tongue swirl around me. She glides up and down, sucking me deeper and deeper. She's getting so into going really deep and she's great at it too. I've never met a girl like her before; she seems to actually like it. While she works her magic, I watch her. I'm able to hold back a little now, since the shock value has subsided, but watching her is still a huge part of the experience. Her hair has fallen around her face and I want to see her mouth stretched wide around me, so I scoop all her hair and hold it behind her in a ponytail, following her up and down. I moan with each stroke now and I want to push myself hard into her, but I let her control the depth..

Then, just as I am dreaming of it, she pushes down hard on me and I feel the resistance at the back of her throat. I push slightly on the back of her head and briefly go further still down her throat. She gags; the magical sound, but I hold her there. She has told me she likes this loss of control and I'm only too happy to oblige. She pulls back slightly and I push her down again, then, gagging, she rips her face away, gasping for air. She gives me a sly satisfied smile. She gets to her feet. She's been in control, now it's my turn.

I grab her wrist and toss her onto the bed, climbing on top of her as she lands. She's pinned on her front beneath me and while she wriggles until she is comfortable, I lick from the base of her spine up to her neck, she groans with pleasure. Moving back so that I'm kneeling over her legs, I slide my arm under her waist and lift her onto her knees. I sit back on my heels and stroke my hands over her perfect ass, slipping my fingers between her legs and slowly into her. I smile as she lets out a long moan at the feeling of my fingers moving inside her. I spend some time teasing her this way. She's unbelievably wet.

I remember, suddenly that I don't need a condom, why am I stalling when I could be inside her, skin to skin. I pull my fingers out abruptly, causing her to gasp, and position myself behind her. Sinking slowly into her, I savor every single inch until I am buried in her all the way, then I draw in and out of her with long strokes, the sensation is amazing. I change my position, so that my legs are on the outside of Liv's, encouraging her to close hers some. As her thighs press together around me, the sensation changes, she feels so incredibly tight.

Dropping down onto my hands and knees over her, I naturally increase my pace, pushing Liv lower under me. Before long she's lying almost flat beneath me and I'm lying with my full weight on her. Her legs are closed together, making her even tighter. I reach forward and grab her wrists, pinning her to the bed, leaving her helpless, while I drive myself into her. She moans loudly, letting me know she likes it, so I don't hold back. Suddenly, she gets tighter, I don't know how or why but this makes it impossible for me to hold back anymore and I explode into her, moaning incoherently.

I come to rest breathlessly on top of her, as she too calms down from her garbled moans. We pant together for a few seconds until I realise I'm still holding her down. I release her wrists and take some of my weight on my elbows. I smooth her hair away from her face and kiss her cheek. She smiles.

"I love you," I whisper.

"I love you too," she whispers back.

I know I'm going to have to move, or I'll squash her, but I'm so drained and I'm still inside her. Taking a deep breath I force myself to roll off her, pulling out as I go. I fall into my pillow and moan, my breathing still ragged. Liv sighs beside me but doesn't move.

"That was incredible.".

She turns to face me. "I know!" she giggles.

"I don't know what happened at the end there, but you were like a fucking vice! What did you do?"

"Sorry, I crossed my legs to make it tighter."

"Don't apologise, it was fabulous. You were already tight, but that was another level."

"I've got another trick like that. I'll show you sometime," she says with a wicked smile.

"Hmmm." I turn onto my front so that our faces are almost touching. "I can't wait."

"I have to move," she sighs, not moving at all.

I watch her, having an internal battle, then reluctantly, she drags herself up and disappears to the bathroom. I grin to myself; I'm a lucky guy.

I am almost asleep when she returns.

"Hey!" she exclaims, slapping my bare butt. "You're sleeping!"

"No I'm not." I grin, closing my eyes tighter. She pokes my side, I ignore it. She climbs on top of me, I ignore that too. Then she tickles me, she has me pinned, so she has the advantage for a moment and I can't help my laughter as I fight to defend myself. But then I manage to take back control and I turn the tables on her, while she shrieks with laughter. I notice with slight disappointment that she has underwear on.

"Hey, why did you put panties on?"

"Panties," she says, testing the word. "I love the way you say that."

"How else would I say it?"

"Knickers," she says bluntly. So British. "I love that way you say it." She smiles. "And I love you."

I sink back down beside her. "I'm going to miss you, even if it's only for a few days."

"I'll miss you too, but you should spend some time with Jen and your parents before you come back, I'll get in the way of that. Besides I have a feeling the baby will come soon, Andy says Grace is the size of a house!"

She laughs at the thought of that. From what I remember of Grace, I imagine she's a nightmare pregnant.

Liv sits up. "Come on, let's have a shower."

I drop my head back onto the bed. How can she be so energetic?

"Come on," she calls from the door.

I wave my hand dismissively.

"I'll be right behind you," I say to humour her. I so don't want to get up, I think I might just stay here a while. From the dresser, my cell rings. I sigh and reluctantly drag myself off the bed.

I groan when I see the caller ID. It's Brooke. Why is she calling? I reject the call. I'm sure I'll find out what she wants when I get back. I just know she won't have good intentions and I won't have her ruin this for me. I think back to Jen and Scott warning me off her in the beginning. Jen in particular has always detested her, and I ignored them…what harm could friends with benefits do? Except, without the benefits, I don't think I would want to be friends. Liv has given me the clarity to see that Brooke has been a huge lack of judgement on my part. Now I just have to make sure that Brooke gets the message and keeps away from me from now on.

I also have a Facebook notification.

> Jennifer Hendricks tagged you in a post.

I open Facebook to see what she said.

> Picking up my boy Danny Morgan tomorrow from LAX. So excited to see him!

So maybe Brooke saw that, and that's why she called. Oh well, I shrug to myself, she would have found out I was back in town from someone. Shaking it off, I join Liv in the shower.

I wake to Liv bouncing on the bed, waking me up. She tempts me with some more of last night's action, but I need to get ready for the flight so she makes me breakfast instead. We're quiet as we eat, both thinking about being apart.

My cell, which has been on silent since Brooke called last night, lights up on the table beside me. Shit, it's a message from Brooke! I snatch it up and scan the message quickly, before clearing it off.

Hey! I tried calling you. I hear you're coming back. Can I see you? Just friends ;-) xxx

I glance up and Liv is watching me. I know it's bad but I lie and tell her it's from Mom. It's bad enough that I won't be with her; I don't want her worrying about Brooke, especially as there's nothing to worry about. I'll take care of it. I put my cell in my pocket before it causes any more trouble.

I finish up and start getting my things ready to go, while Liv clears the dishes. She didn't eat much, I hope it's just because I'm going away and not because she's suspicious. Now I feel guilty and I haven't done anything wrong. Okay, I just lied, but only to protect her. Fucking Brooke, Jen was so right about her, she's trouble.

I hold Liv's hand as we walk into the terminal building and we wait in line for check in together. We don't say much; we're both a little off today. I keep having to remind myself that we will be together again in a few days, it's not the end of the world. But with this Brooke shit hanging over my head and the fact that I won't have Liv with me, I am dreading going home.

We reach Passport Control and Liv can't go any further. So I stop and look at her.

"I love you," I smile. "And I'm never going to let you go."

Maybe it is going away from her, I don't know, but I get the urge to say more…Offer her more commitment. Feeling panic rising in me, I slam the brakes on that thought and try to remain calm enough to finish saying goodbye.

"I love you too," she whispers, fighting tears. I kiss her and pour everything I feel for her into it, not caring who sees.

"See you, beautiful," I say managing to keep my voice steady as we hug. Then I head through security, waving before she's out of sight.

I wait in line at security and go through the motions in a daze. I'm rattled by my sudden urge to offer her a huge commitment. What was I proposing? Proposing? Sweat has formed on my brow. There's no way I can allow myself to think like that. Look what happened last time, I remind myself.

I settle into a seat looking out across the airport with a coffee and stare unseeing into the distance. Of course I know I want to marry her, I always have, I just haven't thought about it for a long time. Not since we were kids. I know now it was crazy, but I bought a ring and had a plan. A terrible plan, but a plan nonetheless. I didn't want to lose her. I was being made to leave England and I couldn't stand the thought of a future without her. I wanted her to come with me, or I wanted to stay, I don't know. But I thought our parents would take us more seriously if we were engaged. Looking back, I realise they probably would have taken us less seriously. But I was certain it was the answer.

I went to Liv and tried to talk to her about not wanting to go, but she was emphatic about it, she said it would be the best thing for us. She said young relationships rarely last a lifetime and that we should go our separate ways and experience life. I was devastated. I spent the rest of my time in the UK drifting around like a zombie. I realised then that she didn't love me like I loved her. I never told her about the ring and I clung on to the rest of our time together, because I knew I would never see her again once I left.

I've never loved anyone else, not even close. I still have the ring. I just don't think there's any way I could bring myself to go there again. The thought of the heartache brings the shutters down. Now that I have her again, I'm in it for the long haul; whatever comes along, nothing will faze me. I'm committed, I'm moving to be with her and I've had no doubts whatsoever. But just then, I felt like I wanted to offer something more and that really has freaked me out. My worst fear, rational or not, has always been that she knew what I was going to do and was pushing me away to stop me from proposing, so that she didn't have to say no. Jen thinks I'm nuts, but then, she's afraid of moths. Moths can't actually hurt you, but the agony of that sort of rejection stays with you for life.

I take a sip of my coffee and it's stone cold. I've sat here for an hour and all I know is that I love Liv, I want to spend the rest of my life with her and I don't know if I'll ever have the courage to seal the deal. My cell beeps.

'I love you x"

I love you too I think, more than you'll ever know.

Eighteen.

There's no need to get nasty.

Danny.

Walking through the doors at LAX, I scan the faces, looking for Jen. I don't see her, so I walk slowly through the roped-off section exclusively for 'arrivers', flanked on both sides by 'collectors'. I always feel scrutinised at this point in the travel experience. You don't want to look too needy; people look at you and think, 'Aw he was expecting someone that didn't come.' Then again, if you saunter through not making eye contact, you could miss the love of your life or your mother, waving furiously at you over the barrier. It's a fine line.

Just as I'm feeling like my over-eyeing of the crowd is putting me in the desperate category, I see her. Hiding behind a sign, which reads,…'Danny Boy'…I shake my head and walk over to her. She doesn't realise I've seen her and when she peeks out from behind the stupid sign, I'm standing right in front of her with my eyebrows raised. She cracks up and squeals, excited to see me, much to the dismay of the elderly man standing next to her. She moves away from the barrier and we both walk to the end until we are no longer separated and then she jumps me.

She leaps into my arms and I spin her round. When I put her down and kiss her forehead, she holds me at arm's length and inspects me.

"You look different," she says with a grin.

"I'm great. Happy."

Jen squeals again and puts her arms back around my neck. "I'm so glad you're back."

"I missed you."

"I missed you too. Come on, let's get out of here."

We pull up outside my apartment and Jen comes inside with me. She's been in and put the AC on, put some drinks in the refrigerator and collected my mail. I put my case in the bedroom and when I come out she's fixed us a drink and is sitting out on the terrace.

"So, how's it all going?" she asks.

I smile then sigh. "It's going great, perfect. Liv's incredible. Thank you for putting the idea in my head to go."

"Well you never would have gone off your own back."

"No, I owe it all to you." I tease. "Where would I be if I didn't have you telling me what to do?"

She laughs. "I dread to think."

We sit for a moment in silence.

"So you're set on moving?"

I nod. I know she wants me to be happy, but living on different continents will be hard on both of us.

"It's going to suck here without you, you know."

"I know," I reply, deadpan. "You could always come too."

"You know how much of a baby Scott is about the cold."

"Who needs him?" I joke.

Jen laughs.

"So what's new?" I ask.

"Nothing much, it's been real quiet here without you."

"Brooke's been calling me.".

"Really? I didn't think you'd seen anything of her recently."

"I haven't, but she's obviously available and that's when she calls me. The problem is, she isn't accustomed to finding me unavailable. She didn't take it well."

"I hope you told her to take a hike."

"I did, but she isn't taking no for an answer."

"I don't want to say I told you so, but she had bunny-boiler written all over her from the start."

"I can't have her screwing this up for me. In a couple of weeks, I'll be out of here and it won't matter. But while Liv is here, I don't want her messing with things." I shake my head in frustration. "The problem is, I know she will."

"Have you told Liv about her?"

"Yeah, but if I tell her that I think she's going to go all Fatal Attraction on us, Liv might run for the hills."

"It won't get that bad."

"Oh no? She comments on a photo posted by Liv and blatantly asks to hook up. Then the same night she calls, while I'm on a romantic break and I have to spell it out for her, with Liv in the next room. Then last night she saw your status about picking me up and calls me again."

"What did you say?"

"I didn't answer. But then this morning, while I'm eating breakfast with Liv, she texts me." I show Jen the text.

Jen can't believe it. "Just friends eh?"

"That's not all, while I was waiting for my bag at reclaim, I get this." I show her my cell again.

'Why are you ignoring me?'

"Wow!" Jen says, rolling her eyes. "You've got problems."

"You don't say."

"What are you going to do?"

I sigh. "I want to say nothing, but I'll have to make sure she gets the message before Liv arrives."

"Well, I don't envy you."

"Thanks!"

Jen heads off to let me unpack and get ready to see my folks. As soon as I close the door, I pull out my cell and text Liv.

'Landed, safe and sound. Miss you like crazy. I love you and I can't wait till you get here xxx'

The doorbell rings and I wonder what Jen has forgotten. I open the door and Brooke is standing there.

"Hi," she grins and moves in to kiss or hug me, I'm not sure which, but I don't wait to see. I step back.

"What do you want Brooke?" I ask as calmly as possible.

"There's no need to get nasty."

"I'm not getting nasty, but I've told you, I'm with someone now."

"Okay, but you're back, it can't be that serious. I came to keep you company," she purrs, seductively, reaching out to place her hand on my chest.

Ugh! It makes my skin crawl to think I've been with her, many times. She's hideous, not looks-wise, just as a person.

"No," I say firmly, grabbing her hand and moving it away. "I'm only back to pack up. I'm moving to England."

She looks completely disgusted by the idea.

"But you've known her, like, a month."

I laugh. "Not that it matters, but I've known her practically my whole life." I pull the door half closed next to me. "Now, you need to hear this. What we had was nothing serious and it was only when we were both available. I. AM. IN. LOVE. WITH. SOMEONE. NOW. And I'm asking you to please respect that."

She looks at me in shock for a moment and then bursts into tears. Jesus! Why is this happening to me?

"Don't cry Brooke." I half warn, half beg. I remain firmly on my side of the door and while I strongly suspect it's all an act, the nice guy in me hates to see a girl crying on the doorstep.

"Sorry," she sniffs, wiping carefully under her eye, so as not to mess up her make-up. "I just missed you, I hadn't seen you around in a while and then I heard you'd left. It made me realise that we had something pretty special and it was gone."

"Brooke, what we were doing wasn't anything but convenient for both of us. It was fun while it lasted, but it's over."

She continues to wipe at her eyes with her plastic-nailed fingers, trying to save her overdone make-up and, I'm no expert, but I suspect, probably false eyelashes. She's wearing a short tight skirt and a low-cut tight top. Looking at her now, Liv fresh in my mind, I've no idea what I was ever thinking! She's kind of a tramp.

"Do you have a Kleenex?" she asks.

"Sure," I reply, leaving her on the doorstep to find some. When I return, I'm irritated to find that she's stepped inside. I offer her a tissue from the box. She takes a couple and dabs at her eyes.

"I'm sorry," she says. "I just thought if I came here, you might, you know." She shrugs.

"What?" I ask, exasperated.

"Want to hook up, for old time's sake."

"Well that's where you and I are two very different people. "I don't operate that way."

"Okay," she says, nodding. "Okay. I'm sorry. I won't bother you again, I can see you're really serious about this girl."

"She's the love of my life."

"Well I'm glad you're happy." Brooke opens the door, then pauses and turns and puts her arms around me. I stand rigid and unresponsive, while she gives me a squeeze and a peck on the cheek. I'm repulsed but I want to get her out of here the fastest way possible. She eventually let's go when I give nothing in return and steps outside.

"Goodbye Danny."

"Goodbye Brooke."

I close the door and take a deep breath. That was creepy and perhaps too easy. I drag myself away from the door and flop down on my bed. I need a nap. I look at the clock. I can fit a couple of hours in before dinner at Mom and Dad's. I set the alarm on my cell and immediately drift off.

I pull my truck into the driveway at my parents' house and the front door opens. Dad comes out to meet me with a warm hug.

"Isn't anyone going to let me in on this?"

We both open an arm to include Mom in the hug and she settles between us. We are not usually so affectionate as a family, but I've been away a while, when they weren't expecting me to go. Plus I've told them

I'm going back for good. We just hold each other for a while.

"Come inside," Mom says, patting us both to end the hug. "Your father is making one of his specialties."

I look to Dad. "Uh oh, this isn't from another of your 'World Food' classes is it? I've never recovered from Ethiopian week."

Dad defensively replies, "Ethiopian cuisine is delicious and I'll have you know, very popular."

"I know Dad." I laugh as we walk into the house. "Just not the way you cook it!"

Dad shakes his head slowly and jokes. "Such disrespect…and from my only child."

We head into the kitchen and I get two beers and settle at the counter. Dad pours Mom a wine.

"So how are things going with Liv?" he asks as he hands her the glass.

I swallow my beer. "Great, really great."

"And you're sure about this move?" Mom asks, with maternal concern in her voice.

"I'm certain." I assure her. "I'll miss you guys and Jen, but I really want to do this. I love her."

"We know you do son," says Dad. "You always have. We're really happy you're finally doing something about it."

I offer Dad a small, appreciative smile. I'm glad he understands.

We eat a Mexican feast. Luckily, a cuisine my father excels at. Dad and I put away a few beers and talk about England and how it has changed since we left. We talk about what I'll do for work and about Liv's business. They both seem impressed by what she's done with the old tearoom. I show them some pictures. Dad wants to hear all about people I've seen, places we've been. He's keen to come and spend some time with us, once I have settled in. After Mom goes to bed, he turns the conversation back to Liv.

"I always wondered why you didn't try to stay behind when we left," he muses, which throws me a little.

I frown. "Why?"

"Well, when we decided to come back, your mother and I thought you'd be very resistant to the idea. We'd thought up all sorts of strategies, to make you come with us, but in the end you just came quietly."

"I guess I wasn't ready." I shrug. I could tell him about my failed plan, but I don't want him to lose respect for me.

"You did the right thing, you know. Showed a lot of maturity." He reaches forward and pats my hand. "And look at you now, well respected in your field, got the pick of work and got the girl in the end too." He smiles and raises his beer. "I'm really proud of you."

"Thanks Dad," I say, raising my beer. "But I have you to thank that I can just up and move so easily."

"I always wanted you to have the choice. I know you talk like an American, but you're a Brit too. You promise me you'll do the same for your kids one day."

"Whoa, Dad, one step at a time," I say almost choking on my beer. I feel so transparent. It's unnerving. I want all those things with Liv. Dad gives me a knowing smile. Swigging back the rest of my beer I say, "I think I'll turn in." I get up and collect our empties. "Thanks for tonight."

"Glad to have you back," he replies. "Sleep well."

"Night," I say over my shoulder as I head up the stairs to the guest room. Mom has left the bedside light on for me. Once I'm ready for bed, I take my cell and crawl under the covers. I check my messages. But there has been nothing new since the reply from Liv that came while I was sleeping earlier. I check the world clock app; it's 11pm here, so it is 7am there. Will she be up? I decide to take the risk, she won't mind if I wake her. I just want to hear her voice.

It rings twice and she picks up.

"Hello?"

She sounds wide awake.

"I didn't wake you did I?"

"No, I'm awake. Mum called me half an hour ago and woke me up, Grace's contractions have started."

"Really?" I sound happy, when really I couldn't care less about Grace's contractions. It just means I'll have Liv here soon. "That's great, so when are you flying in?"

"I don't know, I'll talk to Connie this morning, probably a couple of days, weekend flights are really expensive."

I sigh. "Just come now, I'll pay," I plead only half joking.

She laughs. "I know, I miss you too. But I'll be there soon. Spend some time with everyone, before I get there."

"Screw them," I joke. "I want you."

"Me too, I hate this, the bed feels big without you."

"I'm all alone in a big bed right now…Fancy some phone action?"

"Oh stop!"

"God I want you," I sigh.

"So how are your parents?" she asks, changing the subject.

"Really good, I'm in their guest room, actually. I had a few beers with Dad."

"Good. I'm worried about seeing them. Do they think I'm stealing you away?"

"No! They're really happy for us. Dad is already planning a visit."

"That's a relief. So what do you have planned?"

"I'm going to go to sleep now, then on Saturday mornings I usually have breakfast with Scott and Jen."

"Just like me and Max."

"I know."

"Well, you should get some sleep and I have to get up."

"Okay," I say reluctantly. "Call me when you know your flights."

"Will do. I love you."

"I love you too."

"Bye."

"Bye."

The line goes dead and I sigh. My blood is racing and I have an overwhelming feeling of panic. I know deep down it is because of my worrying urge at the airport today. I need to talk to Jen about this. She's the only person I ever told about the ring. She'll get overexcited and tell me to propose. But she's the only person that knows the full history; I've no choice but talk to her about it.

I drop a grocery bag on Jen's counter and pull out juice for them and juice for me. I start a pot of coffee and tip the rest of the groceries out and organise them. I grab Jen's mixing bowl and cup measures from the cabinet and start measuring out flour for the pancakes. I clatter around my friend's kitchen for a few minutes more before Jen emerges blinking in the light, dressed in her faded Green Day t-shirt that I believe may have once been mine. I shake my head, what is it with women; all their clothes are so uncomfortable, that to relax, they have to steal ours.

"Jet-lag or crisis?" she asks, getting coffee cups down and rubbing her eyes.

"A little from column A, a little from column B," I huff, dumping milk into the bowl with a splash. I start stirring the batter like it's insulted my mom,. Jen watches quietly, waiting.

"I couldn't sleep, so I started thinking," I say, beating furiously.

"Oh, that's never good."

I ignore her tone and carry on.

"I love her Jen, so much." I stop beating and pull a baking pan out of the oven, turning it on as I shut the door. "I'm so happy. I want to spend the rest of my life with her." I start putting bacon on the pan as I speak. "But…" I pause, trying to put my fears into words.

"But, you're afraid that if you go buy a ring, you'll end up heartbroken and alone again."

I freeze, how can Jen see straight through me like that?

"Well I would have put it a little less bluntly, but, yes, that's about the size of it."

Jen thinks for a moment. "Then don't do it."

I step back and stare at her.

"What?"

"Leave things as they are. Don't push it. You're only just back together and besides, you can be happy together without all that stress."

I go back to putting the bacon in the oven, not knowing how to react to that.

"Disappointing, isn't it," she challenges.

"What?" I ask, baffled by this whole conversation.

"The thought of a steady future with no risks," she says, revealing the point she was making with this little game.

I drop my shoulders, keeping my back to her and rest both hands on the counter. "I see what you're doing, but you don't understand."

"Danny, I get it, you're afraid of rejection, but she loves you."

"The thing is, I know we can be happy together without all that stress…But…I took forever to get over never seeing her again and not fighting hard enough to keep her. I've spent my whole adult life not loving anyone, because no one was Liv. I feel I owe it to myself and to Liv, now we're together and it's adult and real and I can fight for it…Don't you think I should make it everything it can be?'

"YES!" she says, exasperated. "Of course I do."

"So you think I should."

"What? Propose?"

I shrug, looking to her in desperation for some guidance.

"I don't see why not, but you don't have to do it now, do you?"

"No, I guess not. But when we were saying goodbye at the airport, I told her I was never going to let her go. Then I got this overwhelming urge to cement that somehow, promise her something. It felt so right." I pause, shuddering at the memory it brought back. "But then I remembered how I felt that day, when she told me it would be the best thing for us both if I came here and we got on with our lives. I was ready to give up everything for us to be together and she didn't want me to. I can't deal with that a second time."

"But she would probably say yes," Jen reassures.

"I know."

"So what's the problem?"

"I'm freaking out!" I laugh a little. I know how ridiculous this is. Calming slightly, I reason, "I know I don't have to think about this now, but I have. I've got her back Jen, something I never thought would be possible. I should make up for lost time right?"

"I think you should just calm down, you'll give yourself a heart attack," she laughs. "Let me meet her. I'll tell you where I think she's at. You know it's my special skill."

"Would you?"

God I sound pathetic! I need to pull myself together. Liv would freak if she knew what I was thinking. Vaguely, I recall the last time I was standing in this kitchen. I was a mess then too, having crazy thoughts about jumping on an airplane. That risk came off, maybe it's worth taking another. I busy myself with breakfast while Jen pours the coffee.

Scott emerges from his pit.

"Glad you could join us," I call as he stumbles across the living room. He sits at the table and Jen puts a coffee down in front of him.

Scott has never been a morning person. He sips his coffee. In my experience, he can't function before the caffeine hits.

"When I said, we'll see you in the morning for breakfast, I meant the morning for us, here in A-MER-I-CA," he grumbles.

Jen laughs. "Don't listen to him. I'm glad you're here. We need to make the most of you while we can."

"So when is the big move?" Scott asks.

"Couple of weeks, maybe three, I don't know. There's nothing to it really, I'll pack my stuff and take it with me, give notice on the apartment and store my furniture at my folks. We don't need it but it might be handy one day. Dad's talking about moving some of their furniture to Cabo, so he'll use it." I flip a pancake. "That just leaves my car, Dad will sell it for me. There's no rush."

Scott thinks for a minute.

"I could put a memo round the office for you, see what that does."

"Thanks."

He clears his throat, "So…um…what about the Shelby?"

I laugh hard. "Forget it! I'll get it shipped." He's had his eyes on that car ever since I got it finished. He wasn't interested when it was a wreck; he thought I'd lost my mind. But when he saw her all shiny, he changed his tune. I think he was jealous that I had the disposable income when he was buying a house. But he isn't having her. Scott pouts.

My cell vibrates in my pocket, so I hastily wipe pancake batter off my hands and grab it.

"Hi." I answer.

"Hi!" says Liv. I mouth LIV to Jen and step out into their yard.

"It's so good to hear your voice."

She laughs. "You've only been gone a day."

"I know," I sigh. "But it sucks."

"Well then, I have good news."

"Yeah?"

"Connie and I are coming tomorrow!"

"That's fantastic. What time?"

"We land at 19:05."

"Can I pick you up?"

"Are you sure? We can get a cab."

"Liv, I literally have nothing to do here but wait for you to arrive, please let me meet you at the airport."

"Thanks, that would be great."

"So what's going on with Grace?" I ask, more interested now it's bringing Liv to me.

"She's at the hospital now with Andy. Mum is waiting at their house, looking after Matthew, she thinks it will be really soon. We just decided to book a flight, the baby will come in the next few hours and we can help out when we get there."

"Are you still going to stay with me?" It's what we agreed, but now we're apart I need the reassurance.

"If it's still okay with you."

"Are you crazy? Of course it's okay."

"I can't wait to see you," she says.

"Me too."

"I'd better go and pack then."

"Okay, text me your flight details," I remind her.

"Will do, love you."

"Love you too."

I return to the kitchen with a big smile on my face.

"She's coming tomorrow," I tell them. Feeling so much better, now I know when she is definitely coming. I don't need to worry about all that other stuff yet; I can just enjoy being with her.

"We should go out tonight." I suggest.

"You've cheered up," remarks Jen with a smile.

Nineteen.

Home turf advantage.

Liv.

At 3:30am my phone beeps loudly from the bedside table. It's a text from Mum.

'Mia Helen Turner has arrived! Sat 5th May, 19:53pm (LA time), 7lbs 6oz. She can't wait to meet her Auntie Liv and Great-great-Auntie Connie. See you tomorrow. Xxx'

I smile sleepily and type a reply.

'Give them all big kisses from me and get some rest, help is on its way! Xxx'

I smile and snuggle into my pillow. Tomorrow, I'll meet my new niece, see my gorgeous nephew and be with Danny. Tomorrow is going to be a great day I grin as I try to get back to sleep.

I spot Danny at the end of the arrivals hall. He's standing apart from the crowd, so we will see him easily and I grin from ear to ear walking towards him. He looks amazing, dressed for summer, his tattoo partly visible and sexy as hell. I notice some young girls near him, checking him out and smile to myself that he's mine. I walk straight up to him and, without a word, we kiss, not for too long, as Connie is right next to me.

He breaks away and breathes, "My God, I've missed you so much." Then he greets Connie in his charming way that always encourages her to flirt with him.

The evening is warm, hotter than a warm daytime at home. It's lovely. Danny insists on wheeling the cases and as we follow him to the car, he tells us that it's exceptionally warm for the time of year. He loads them into the enormous car and helps Connie up into the backseat. I'm hovering behind him and once he closes the door on Connie he smiles and kisses me lightly on the lips.

"I hate being apart from you," he says.

"Me too," I smile.

He opens the front passenger door for me and closes it once I'm safely inside. While he's walking round to his door, Connie reaches forward and squeezes my shoulder.

"I'm so happy for you darling," she says, leaving her hand in place.

I stroke her hand.

"Thanks, I'm happy too."

Watching Danny negotiate the evening traffic from the wrong side of the car is an alien experience. Despite the fact that the setup is all wrong, he looks so natural. His confidence is alluring and I could just watch him for hours, but he and Connie have been chatting easily so I try to join in the conversation. Danny is telling Connie that his mum would love to see us all while we're in town and is going to call my mum to arrange dinner at their house.

It's 9pm when we pull into Grace and Andy's driveway. Mum greets us at the door; she's so starved of adult conversation, she launches into a long stream of consciousness about how things have been over the last couple of days. When she comes up for air, she offers us tea and while I am dying to go home with Danny, we indulge her because she's been on her own with a toddler for two days.

Grace and Mia are doing well, Andy has been with them, but they are expected to stay in hospital at least another couple of nights. Mia had a slight temperature when she was born, so she has to see out a three-day course of antibiotics before they will discharge her. It's just a precaution.

Mum and Andy are taking Matty up to meet her tomorrow. We arrange to talk in the morning, so that we can all get some proper sleep tonight.

Danny brings Connie's case in from the car, while I say goodnight. I feel guilty about staying at Danny's, but, in reality, once they are home from the hospital, there'll be too many houseguests. We've made it work before, but it's nice to be able to take the pressure off. Danny and I hop into the car and meet in the middle as we both buckle up. He places his hand under my chin and draws me into a sensual kiss; I close my eyes and enjoy the taste of him.

"Let's go," he says, pulling away from my lips, leaving me wanting. I sit back in my seat and sigh. "Tired?"

"A bit."

"Hungry?"

"Um, yes." Actually, I'm unbelievably tired. My body thinks it's early tomorrow morning, but in order to be awake and possibly expend some serious energy with Danny in bed tonight, I could do with some food.

"Let's get you home and we'll order in, I don't want to share you with anyone else tonight." He glances at me and smiles sweetly. Yep, I'm going to need some energy!

We pull up to Danny's apartment about fifteen minutes later. I can't believe how close I've been to him on so many occasions over the years. I've always found it difficult, coming here knowing this is where he might be. I had no idea of course, he could have moved on, but it was always on my mind. I used to worry if I was shopping that I might run into him. I really didn't want that to happen, because I couldn't stand the thought of bumping into him with his wife and children. How stupid. I should have been out looking for him.

"This is it," Danny says almost apologetically, as he switches off the engine. I reach out and stroke his thigh, working my hand up his leg and holding his stare. He briefly closes his eyes, savouring the moment.

"Come on," he says, snapping back to reality. "Let's get you inside."

He opens the door and shows me inside. It's bigger than I imagined and nicer. He made it sound like a neglected boy's pad or student digs, but it's clean and spacious. He has photos, lamps and cushions, a plant or two; it's nice and homely. The lamps were even already switched on to welcome us.

"It's lovely, Danny."

"It's fine," he shrugs. He goes and puts my case in the bedroom and I follow him. The bed is huge; we both look at it and then each other and smile.

"Why don't you take a shower?" he says to stop that line of thought. He points to the en-suite bathroom. "I'll order some food."

"Danny, it's late, we don't really have to eat."

"Hey, no. I'm starving and I want you to eat," he insists. He runs the shower for me while I get some stuff from my case, then goes to order the food.

I step into his spacious shower and let the hot water revive me after my long trip. It's surreal being here. For years I've imagined what his life was like. I thought it would be just like Grace and Andy's; it was my only point of reference. Then he came back, so I've got used to having him in my world. He's so familiar, but being with him here is totally different. I suppose it's a reverse of the control, I'm the guest here. It will do us good to do it this way round, I don't want him coming back with me still feeling like a guest. When we go back, it's for good I hope; I want us to be equal.

Feeling more human, I pull on my comfy trackies and a vest and go looking for Danny. He is sitting outside on a small patio, drinking a Coke. Turning his head when he hears me coming, he says, "I got you a Coke, but I have juice and stuff. I didn't know what you'd want."

"That's fine, thanks."

I sit in the chair next to him. Danny opens the can of Coke and pours it over ice for me.

"Do you feel better?"

"Much. Thanks."

As he sits back, I lift my feet onto his lap. He strokes them and we just sit. The relaxing rhythm of his fingers on the soles of my feet threatens to make me just a bit too relaxed in my exhausted state. Fortunately, the food arrives before tiredness takes hold. Danny emerges with a tray of food in those brilliant Chinese takeaway boxes that they have over here. I don't know why we haven't adopted this at home, but they are *so* American. The food is delicious, Danny has chosen well; apparently this is what he and Jen ritually have.

"I'm still really nervous about meeting Jen" I admit. "And your parents. They can't all be that happy that you're leaving the country to be with me."

He laughs. "All I can tell you is what they've told me, they're happy for us. If any of them corner you and say bad things, or threaten to rearrange your face, tell me about it and they'll sleep with the fishes."

"Don't laugh at me. If someone was taking Max away from me, I would hate them forever!"

"Ah yes, but my friends are reasonable."

"Hey!" I pout.

"Listen, I've seen them all and they all say that they love the difference in me, I'm happy and relaxed. They all genuinely want good things for us. Okay?"

"Okay," I relent.

"Now, can we go to bed?" he asks, innocently flashing me his amazing smile.

I giggle. Pathetic! But that's who I am now.

"Only if I can have a cuddle."

"Well...okay deal."

Danny grins and jumps to his feet. In thirty seconds flat, the food has gone, the door is locked and Danny is leading me into his bedroom.

"I'm pleased you're letting me walk this time, my ankle couldn't take another knock," I joke.

He turns to me and narrows his eyes. I accidentally laugh even though I'm trying to keep a straight face.

"Right!" he shouts, grabbing my thighs and throwing me over his shoulders in a fireman's lift. I shriek.

"Put me down," I giggle.

He obliges and drops me on the bed and I flop back laughing. The bed is really high; the possibilities of this do not escape my attention, even in my hysteria. Danny leans over me and waits for my laughter to subside. Silent anticipation hangs between us as I wait for him to make his move. He smiles softly and moves forward to kiss me. My lips part and our tongues take over as he crawls onto the bed above me. He whips his t-shirt off and comes back to my lips, holding me to him firmly with his hand grasping behind my neck.

I moan into his mouth when his hand slips gently around my throat, clutching my chin and forcing my head to turn away from his kiss. I sigh as his lips glide down my neck. I love masterful Danny. He catches his breath and settles between my legs, hitching my knees up either side of him and pulling me closer to him, then traces kisses down until he reaches my vest. He pulls the neckline down sharply, revealing my naked breasts, and causing me to gasp. He squeezes them together, licking and biting them in turn.

He slides his hands underneath me and lifts me to sitting, long enough for me to lift my vest over my head. I throw it off the bed as he lies me back down again, returning to my breasts with a new fervour. I lift my head to watch him and as he licks upwards, our mouths almost meet. He begins licking over my nipples and brushing my lips at the top of each stroke. I try to reach forward to meet him, but he's tantalisingly out of my reach and remains in control. I run my fingers through his hair, holding him close and pushing him into my chest, while I writhe with pleasure beneath him.

He draws back, tugging at my bottoms. They slide easily down my legs and I hear him exhale at the realisation that I'm not wearing underwear. He plunges his tongue straight into me before he has managed to remove my trousers completely; he struggles slightly with the multi-tasking. I don't want him to stop the incredible thing he's doing inside me with his tongue so I kick them off. He moves his hands under my bottom and lifts my hips off the bed while he remains with his tongue working deep inside me. I groan loudly, unable to control the volume, the pleasure is so intense.

As he switches to sucking hard on my clit, I squirm to get away, not certain if I want to stop him or beg him to carry on forever. I claw at the bed, moaning, almost laughing, unable to control myself. He continues regardless and holds my hips down firmly to the bed, causing me to thrash around more. My attempts to pull away have worked me further up the bed and Danny breaks contact for a moment to drag me back to him like a rag doll. I put up no resistance and I know, from his dominant demeanour, tonight is going to be all for me. He stands quickly and pulls down his shorts, stepping out of them and crawling back between my legs.

Gathering my legs up, Danny pushes himself quickly into me, and drives his tongue back into my mouth in one motion. He thrusts, once, then twice and as he finds a rhythm he moves my legs down and around his back and rolls us onto our sides. Moaning together, we both move, the pace quickening.

He stares deep into my eyes, amplifying the intensity. One arm is underneath me, wrapped around my back, holding me tightly by my hair. The other hand moves over me, never settling in one place too long. He pinches my clit, sending a shockwave through me. Then he pinches hard on each of my nipples, before brushing his hand across my throat, fingers splayed, but never tightening his grip. His actions are gentle, though unmistakably domineering. I've never been so turned on.

Then he slows everything down. He brings my knees up under his arms and releases my hair, pulling me tight to him in his strong arms. I lose my leverage and lie still while he glides in and out of me slowly. He starts kissing me, really taking his time. He strokes his fingers up and down my face, with such tenderness, I want to cry. I'm overwhelmed by the love I feel from him. I touch his face and he looks deep into my eyes, pressing his forehead into mine and leaving our lips, just barely brushing while still thrusting in and out of me.

Our breathing is ragged and warm between us. Then Danny takes his hand away from my face, forcing it between us and rubs my clit with surprising determination. I convulse as he attacks the most sensitive part of my body with so much force, and I cry out. Danny holds me tight with the arm that is wrapped around me, stopping me from escaping and forcing me to accept the mind-blowing pleasure that has me so close to the edge. It's almost unbearable, but I can't tell him to stop

Just when I think I can't take it anymore, he releases me, turning me on to my other side and entering me from behind. He continues his assault on my clit and has to hold me tight to him to keep me under control. Then he slows his hand, allowing me to get a hold on what I'm feeling. I turn my face to his and as we kiss, his fingers send me freefalling over the edge. I call out. There are no words, only pure feeling and Danny breathing hard in my ear as he nears his climax.

"I love you," I whisper and feel him tense at my words.

"Oh God," he groans as he releases himself into me, holding me tight and continuing to thrust gently.

We're both in pieces, panting, slick with sweat and barely a coherent thought between us. Danny's hand slides around my neck, grasping me gently while he presses his lips against mine. His tongue parts my lips and we kiss forever, he wraps me in his arms and we keep this intimate, sensual moment alive for as long as we can.

"I love you so much," he whispers.

I smile. "Thank you."

"For what?"

"For loving me, for finding me, for giving me more pleasure than I knew I could have," I reply, kissing him again.

"The pleasure is all mine."

The bright sunshine wakes me and I stretch sleepily and smile to myself when Danny curls around me.

"Good morning," he says.

"Mmm morning," I reply stroking his fingers.

"I let you sleep. I though you needed it." I hear the smile in his voice as he recalls last night.

"I did," I purr. Then it occurs to me he's let me sleep late and I panic.

"Wait, what time is it?"

"It's okay. It's only 10am."

"I realise Danny is dressed in shorts and a t-shirt, and I can smell coffee.

"You're dressed," I say with a hint of disappointment.

"I went to the bakery to get breakfast." He sits up, holding out his hand to me. "Come on dirty girl, you need a shower."

"Me, dirty? You were doing all the dirty things last night." I sit up and indignantly ignore his proffered hand as I get off the bed.

"I didn't hear any complaints."

No, well, he's got me there. I laugh, and turn back to face him.

"When did you get so dominant?"

Danny laughs, "Home turf advantage, I guess. I thought you were really into it…was I wrong?"

I raise my eyebrows; he knows I was.

"No. I like the new you," I say as he pulls me against him. I comply, submissively and allow him to pull my hair back so that my neck is exposed to his lips, pausing as he gently bites. I gasp. His teeth relinquish the flesh and his lips soothe the skin. I really like this side to him and I grin. He loosens his grasp on my hair and I straighten up.

"Make sure some of this Danny…" I say, gesturing to all of him, "…comes home with me." Then I grab him behind the head and pull him to my lips, my turn to be in control. I run my other hand down his chest, to his waist and without pausing I feel for his erection. It's as hard as I expected and I grope it through his shorts. Danny moans and I instantly let go. Looking him in the eyes, I leave the suspense hanging for a second.

I flash a devious smile. "Now, let's shower, I want to meet my niece."

Turning on my heel, I march into the bathroom, leaving him standing in his bedroom with a hard-on.

"Oh. Come. On!" I hear him object. Ignoring the protests, I turn on the shower and step under the water, laughing.

Danny pulls his truck into the car park at the hospital and I check my watch. We arranged to come at 3pm, so that they could have some time with just Matty and the new baby. We're ten minutes early so we sit for a minute. Danny is quiet. I wonder if all this baby stuff is too much for him. I said I was happy to go on my own, but he insisted on coming. Grace said everyone was welcome, so that's not the problem. I just think, like most men, Danny merely catches sight of a baby-gro and comes over in a cold sweat.

We've just been shopping and I went 'Auntie Liv crazy' in a baby shop. Don't get me wrong, I'm not broody; I'm just an excited auntie. Danny went into himself in the shop and has been quiet ever since. I need to find a way to convince him that this isn't going to turn me into an obsessed clucky nightmare. I'm just not that girl. He'll see.

"There's your mom and Connie," he says pointing. I look over and see them stepping out of a cab.

"I'll go and tell them we're here," I say opening the door.

Danny fetches the presents from the boot and emerges with balloons and a big gift bag. He walks towards us with reluctance.

"Here, let me carry that," I offer, "you look ridiculous."

He hands them to me gratefully, not holding my eye contact and fidgeting nervously. I really need to discuss this with him, I'll do it after this, or it will start affecting things.

We walk through the sparkling corridors to Grace's room. We're greeted at the door by Matty, full of exuberance.

"Have you come to meet my sister?" he asks. Once he's satisfied that we have presents, he lets us into the spacious room. Grace is sitting on the bed, looking radiant and relaxed. Andy is sitting in one of the chairs holding tiny Mia.

"This is her," Matty says standing next to his dad. "She's a baby." We all laugh. Then while Connie and Mum mob Andy and coo over little Mia, Grace gets up and comes over to Danny and me with a huge smile.

"Hi, you two," she says with a grin that says she has a million questions. She hugs me tight, then let's go and hugs Danny, kissing him on the cheek. He's quite taken aback, because I doubt they've said more than a few words to each other their whole lives.

"How are you doing?" I ask.

"Oh fine," Grace says dismissing the idea that she would be anything but fine. "Much easier the second time. But never mind about that, I want to know all about you two."

Just then Andy appears at her side and leans over to kiss me then, seeing Danny, he shakes his hand and engages him in conversation.

"So?" asks an unrelenting Grace.

"Grace!" I hiss. "Can we talk about this later?"

"Okay, but I want all the details."

"Grace," My mum calls from across the room. "I think Matty wants to open the presents."

Grace rolls her eyes and turns to attend to Matty.

We all move into the room and sit in the seats set out for us. Grace sits on the bed with Matty and Andy stands, while they arrange the presents and balloons.

"I don't think these presents are for you," warns Grace gently. "But I will need some help opening them. Do you know anyone who is good at opening presents?"

"Me!" shouts an impatient Matty.

Everyone is smiling as they begin opening presents from Connie. Connie gets up from her cuddle and places Mia in my arms. She is so perfect. I just stare at her. She wraps her tiny fingers around mine and I'm in love. She breathes softly and sleeps, while I stroke my thumb across her knuckles. I realise that I've been mesmerised, which won't help Danny and his misplaced 'man-panic'. I look at him and he smiles, putting his arm around me and leaning over slightly to get a closer look. He looks more relaxed now, so I go back to idolising my niece and try not to worry about the repercussions.

Next they open the big bag of gifts from me, well us. Matty pulls out pink thing after pink thing, getting further into the bag until he pulls his head out with a very confused look on his face.

"Livvy, I don't think this is for babies," he says frowning and holding up a Spiderman toy.

"Oh, really? Sorry, I thought babies liked Spiderman."

"No," he says with such authority. "Spiderman is for big boys."

"Oh. Well, do you know any big boys who would like a Spiderman?"

He looks at me, realising I'm pulling his leg and smiles. He turns to Grace and asks for confirmation.

"Is it for me?"

Grace nods.

"It's for me," he says to me, as if I was stupid to suggest otherwise.

"Say thank you," Grace says with a nudge.

"Thanks Livvy!" he shouts, then hands it to Andy, who sets about the protracted process of extracting a toy from a box.

Everyone starts chatting and I feel like I'm hogging the baby. But everyone else is doing things, so I keep hold of her.

Danny leans in again.

"She's so small," he says with wonder.

"I know," I agree. I watch him as he takes in every detail of her. "Do you want to hold her?"

To my surprise, Danny nods.

"Can I?"

"Of course," I say, taken aback. I turn in my chair and pass her into his waiting arms. He's cautious, but surprisingly at ease with her. I stare at them; baby Mia opens her eyes and Danny mouths 'Hello' to her. Something inside me clenches, I'm certain it must be my ovaries or some other reproductive part of me jumping to attention. They are beautiful together and despite myself, all my hairs stand on end. I pull myself together before he notices and remind myself that although I want children, I've never heard the ticking of an internal clock. I've found the man of my dreams and I'm more than satisfied with that right now. Danny looks at me and smiles nervously, he seems just as surprised by all this as I am, and maybe he isn't going to freak out about it after all.

Eventually, it's my mum's turn again and she relieves Danny of little Mia. Danny holds my hand and strokes his thumb back and forth. We sit quietly listening to Grace and Andy filling Connie in on the events that brought Mia into the world. I glance at Danny and catch him staring at me. He gives me a small, shy smile and squeezes my hand. During a lull in conversation, Andy offers to get everyone a coffee. Danny offers to help him and he kisses my knuckles and lets me go, following Andy out of the room.

I watch as he disappears from view and linger a moment longer, thinking how amazing he is, When I turn away, I realise Grace is staring at me, her jaw is hanging open and she's fanning herself with an envelope. I roll my eyes at her and she laughs. She comes over and settles into the chair beside me, while Mum and Connie are distracted with Mia and Matty.

"Oh my God, Liv! If I'd have known he was living round the corner, looking like that, I might have ditched Andy and looked him up myself."

"Stop it!" I laugh, slapping her arm. "You've just given birth, what's the matter with you?"

"I know but, *hello!*" she jokes. "And did you see him with Mia?"

"Yes, I saw him with Mia," I say taking a deep breath while a shiver of desire washes over me at the memory.

"It's like that black and white poster I used to have, of the hot man with the baby!"

"Don't," I warn, barely holding it together, I don't need encouragement.

"I always thought he was pretty ordinary, but he's gorgeous now, how did that happen? And head over heels for you, I can tell."

Matty comes to my rescue and distracts Grace and I have a moment to reflect. When the boys get back with trays of coffee and cakes, Grace leans in and says under her breath, "When I get out of here, I want to know *everything*."

We stay a while longer, then Andy takes Mum, Matty and Connie home and Danny and I leave too so that Grace can rest.

We drive away from the hospital in silence; my stomach is in knots because Danny has gone back into weird silent mode again, since going off with Andy. I don't know what's eating him, but I'm afraid to ask. I still think it's just that he assumes I'll get all broody. But it might be something worse. I'm running through all the possibilities when he pulls the car over on a quiet street and switches off the engine. He turns in the seat so that he's facing me.

"Why have we stopped?" I ask, at a loss.

"We need to talk."

"Couldn't it wait 'til we got home?"

"No." He looks so serious.

Panic rises in me; I feel I have to get in first.

"Danny, if this is because of being at the hospital, you have to know…"

"I want us to have a baby," he blurts.

Silence falls in the car as the dust settles from this revelation. I'm completely without words. I look at him, and he looks terrified.

"I…" I try to form a sentence and fail miserably.

"I know it's such early days. But at the hospital, I just..."

I can't believe what I'm hearing, I thought he was freaking out because he didn't want a baby, instead he was freaking out because he *did* want one, with me! I can't think of anything to say. I was so ready to defend myself and assure him I'm not one of these girls, I'm finding it difficult to change gears and entertain this sudden concept.

I look around us; we're sat on a quiet residential street, sitting at the curb, changing our lives. This is crazy; we need to talk about this, but not here.

"Can we go somewhere and talk about this?" I ask.

"Home?"

Not there, I think, we need to keep sex out of this.

"A bar or something, where we can sit in a corner and talk."

Danny nods sullenly and starts the engine.

Twenty.

You're such a girl!

Danny.

I'm such a fucking idiot, I curse myself as I drive. Liv sits silently beside me, probably planning her escape. I drive us to a quiet bar I know of, where we won't see any of my friends. At the door to the bar, we have an awkward moment where we both insist the other goes first. In the end, I hold the door open and follow her in. We choose a corner with sofas to sit down and I leave her to get us drinks without asking what she'll have. I know she'll have a rum and Coke and I have the same. I've already decided I'm leaving the car here; I need to get really drunk.

Sitting at a safe distance from Liv on the same sofa, I hand her, her drink and take a good slug of mine. She isn't talking and if she was I'm certain I don't want to hear what she'll have to say. I've screwed this up big time. There I was worrying about the fact that I was thinking about marriage again. Then we went to the baby store today and I got to thinking, about babies and our future. I watched how she got with all the small clothes and I just really wanted it to be us, marriage or not. I realised that I want our future to start as soon as possible. Then when she had the baby in her arms at the hospital, I almost said it there, in front of everyone. At least then I showed some restraint.

But driving home, I couldn't put it off any longer, I could hardly look at her, so I pulled over and got myself into this mess. I tried to go easy; I didn't want to reveal it all in one go. I was going to say something like,

I've been thinking about our future blah, blah'. But she started saying something and I thought she was shutting me down, so it just came out. 'I WANT US TO HAVE A BABY'...I blurted out...to Liv! Maybe deep down I want this to fail, why else would I scare her like that. I close my eyes and sigh. This is so bad. I couldn't have done anything more stupid. But all the buildup since that moment at the airport has made me crazy. I just started thinking, what if she doesn't give me the chance to tell her what I want or how I feel again. I could spend the rest of my life with the same regrets I have lived with the last twelve years. I couldn't let that happen. A marriage proposal is my irrational fear, so for some reason, in my panic, I felt like proposing to start a family would terrify her less.

I feel a shifting on the sofa next to me; Liv has moved closer and is looking at me expectantly.

"A baby?" she asks. Her tone softer than I imagined it would be.

I nod, regretting my impulsiveness. I've put her in an awkward situation now, she feels like she needs to let me down gently.

"Now?"

"No. But, you know, one day," I mumble, sounding like I'm backtracking. I shouldn't backtrack completely. I should say what I mean. It can't make things worse. "I was hoping, one day soon, though," I add, knowing I'm sealing my fate.

Liv sighs heavily and drops back against the sofa. Here it comes. Then, from nowhere, she throws her arm across her eyes and starts to laugh. I watch her. What the hell is this about?

Her laughter eventually subsides and she looks at me.

"Of course, one day soon," she says and laughs again.

I rub my temples. Then look up at her again as it sinks in.

"Wait...of course?"

She nods. "Of course."

"You want to have a baby?"

"I want to have a baby...with you...one day...soon," she says still laughing.

"You do? Really?" I try not to sound like an overexcited kid.

"Why would I not? I love you, you love me, and we are together forever as far as I'm concerned. Of course I want kids and I don't want to wait long, I'm thirty soon." She climbs across my lap and settles herself against the arm of the sofa with her legs over mine. Our faces are close and now our conversation is more intimate.

I shake my head, trying to take this in.

"So why was that so funny?"

"Because," she says, "you went all quiet earlier while we were shopping and then again at the hospital and I thought you were freaking out that I was going to get all broody and want a baby." She laughs. "I thought I was going to have a hard time convincing you that that isn't who I am."

"So you don't want baby?" I'm confused again.

"No, I do! I want the works, but not in a pressure-y, maniac way. Just as it comes."

"So, sorry, I need to get my head around this. Why did we need to come here and talk?"

"Because I didn't want to decide our future on a curb-side." She touches my face.

"And why couldn't we go home?"

"Because I thought you'd want to jump my bones and I wanted to talk."

Now I laugh.

"I always want to jump your bones." I wrap my hand around her neck and bring her face even closer to mine. "So…are we deciding our future?" I ask, marvelling at how we've got here from where we were five minutes ago.

"I'd say it's pretty decided, wouldn't you?" she smiles.

"I have no idea," I admit. "I thought we were breaking up."

"Why on earth would we be breaking up?"

"Because I freaked you out."

"I'm not freaked out. I want what you want, I'm happy as long as we're together."

I kiss her, so relieved that I haven't just thrown it all away.

"Let's go home," I say into her lips. "I want to jump your bones."

"You always want to jump my bones," she grins, kissing me back. She swings her legs round and reaches for her drink. "Aren't you going to finish your drink?"

"I don't need it now," I say, standing to take her home.

While Liv sleeps, I creep out onto the terrace and sit in the afternoon sun. I feel so energised, but then I have a lot to think about. We just decided something vague but very important about our future and then had amazing sex. How can I sleep after that? I text Jen.

'Are you guys free for dinner tonight? x'

'With you? Always. J x'

'Meet at 8pm, the usual? x'

'Great. Is tonight the night I get to meet Liv?'

'If you're good. ;-) x'

We ease in through the crowd at the bar; it's less busy as we move down. Jen is sitting at a table, checking her cell. She looks up as we approach.

"Hey!" she cries, her face lighting up. She hugs and kisses me and then turns to Liv. "I can't believe I am finally meeting you!" She grabs Liv in a huge hug. "I feel like I already know you!"

I shake my head, peeling them apart. "Okay, leave her alone, she gets the picture." Then Scott appears.

"Can anyone join in?" he jokes and wraps his arms around us all.

"Liv, this is Jen and this is Scott," I say reluctantly.

"It's lovely to meet you both," Liv says as we sit down.

Everyone settles down and the conversation flows easily. Liv fits naturally in with us. I stop worrying about Scott's terrible jokes or Jen revealing too much about me. Now I know, although I needed no more reassurance, that she's the one and only girl for me. Scott and I bring drinks back to the girls who are deep in conversation.

"So Liv, Danny was telling us about your bar and restaurant. It sounds wonderful," Jen says.

"It's hard work, but I love it," replies Liv. "It's quite a lot like this place." They talk, like old friends. Scott and I listen for a while, but eventually, we tune out and talk football. We choose some food and I go up to the bar to order. Jen joins me for the half-time team talk.

"I love her," she whispers, conspiratorially.

"Of course you do, she's perfect," I say, glancing back at the table. "I need your help," I whisper, turning back to her, my face serious.

"With?"

"Choosing a ring," I say and then slowly smile.

Jen's face breaks into a huge smile and she almost jumps up and down. I look at her in wide-eyed horror.

"Keep cool!" I warn her through gritted teeth.

"Sorry!" she whispers, looking back to see if she has given it away, but Liv and Scott are deep in conversation.

"Oooh! I'm so excited for you! So what are we talking here? Tiffany, Harry Winston?"

"Something unconventional. That's all I have," I shrug apologetically.

"It's okay, I can work with that. Budget? Never mind, you can afford what she deserves."

"Okay, now I'm worried," I laugh, but in truth, I can and I want her to have the earth. She would be over the moon with that little chip I bought her twelve years ago and I'm sure she doesn't really class herself as the kind of girl who would need 'the rock'. But I want to spoil her; she deserves 'the rock', just not the type of rock all the other girls have, something 'Liv'.

Jen smiles. "I'm so proud of you," she says rubbing my shoulder.

"I'm just grateful I have you to tell me what to do, or I'd still be the wreck I was when we met."

"So when are we doing this. Tomorrow?" she asks enthusiastically.

"Well Liv is looking after her nephew in the afternoon, can you get away?"

"Sure, Mom can cover."

I look back to the table. "There's only one problem."

"What?"

"I don't know her size."

"Oh, that's no problem." Jen says and grabs two of the drinks from the bar and marches back to the table, like a woman possessed. Holy shit, what's she going to do? I follow her as she sits down, trying to catch her eye. Terrified, I have no choice but to spectate, as she refuses to meet my stare.

Jen hands Liv her drink and as she takes it, Jen smoothly says, "Wow, I love your ring."

As I'm having a mini-heart attack, Liv casually replies, "Thanks, it was made by a friend of mine." She offers her hand forward for Jen to have a closer look.

Jen takes Liv's hand and turns it gently, inspecting the ring. "It's so unusual, why is the metal black?"

"It's oxidised silver, you can have it this way or shiny. I liked it this way, it's more unusual."

"Does your friend do this for a living?"

"Yes, she sells them on Etsy," replies Liv.

"I LOVE Etsy!"

"Me too."

"Are they expensive?"

"No, they're about..." Liv thinks for a moment as she does the conversion, "$45."

"Seriously?"

Liv nods enthusiastically. "And you can have any stone you like."

"Wow!" She turns to Scott. "Can I ask Santa for one of these please?" Scott rolls his eyes.

"I can get you one, no problem," offers Liv. "Don't bother waiting for Santa," she adds with a wink at Scott,

"I'd love it if you could. What other stones?" enquires Jen.

"Amethyst, Peridot, Topaz, Moonstone like this..."

"Is that moonstone?"

"Yes, but it's faceted, you don't normally see it like this."

"It's so beautiful, but I'll have to go with Amethyst, it's my birth stone."

"Okay. So do you want it black like this, or shiny silver?"

"Definitely black, I've never seen anything like that."

"And what size?"

"Oooh," says Jen with uncertainty. "I don't know."

"Here," says Liv, passing her ring to Jen. I'd almost forgotten what the purpose of the elaborate ruse was, so my heart stops briefly as I watch the exchange take place. Jen casually slips the ring onto the ring finger of her right hand, the same finger Liv wears it on.

"It fits!" she exclaims triumphantly. "That's the size I need." She hands the ring back to Liv and I watch as she replaces it on her hand.

"So, can you get me one made?" asks Jen enthusiastically. "Exactly like that but with Amethyst."

"Sure. I'll text her tomorrow, she'll be thrilled."

"Do you want me to pay you now?" asks Jen reaching for her purse.

"Oh, no," says Liv, "we'll sort it out once it's made. She'll probably send you a PayPal bill or something."

"Yay!" says Jen clapping her hands together. She casually picks up her drink and takes a sip, glancing at me for a nano-second with a look of total satisfaction. I have to hand it to her, that was smooth. Elaborate, but smooth. I need to lie down.

Later, after we've eaten and a few other friends have shown up, I leave Liv deep in conversation about her tattoos with a couple of the guys and find Jen at the bar. I slide my arms around her from behind and kiss her cheek.

"I love you," I tell her.

"I know," she says, patting my face and turning. "I am very wonderful," she adds sarcastically. I laugh at her typical humour.

"I nearly died," I laugh. "I didn't know what the hell you we're going to do. But I have to admit, that was the work of a true pro."

"I'm glad you enjoyed the show. Now, you'd better move some

money around, because tomorrow, we shop!" she giggles. We turn and watch Liv, showing some of her arm to our friend Jim.

"Do they go all the way up?" asks Jen, watching.

"All the way up and all the way down," I tell her with a huge grin.

"Wow!"

"Uh huh."

"I still can't believe this," she says, running he fingers up my left arm. I shrug then I notice someone new has joined our group.

"Shit! Brooke. What's she doing here?"

"Causing trouble no doubt," says Jen under her breath.

I don't wait for the 'I told you so' conversation; I weave my way back to the group and sit protectively beside Liv. Jen rejoins us and I try to relax. She's still talking to some other people and I don't even know if she has seen us. I want to leave, but Liv is having a good time and I may not see a lot of these friends again for a long time. For a while, Brooke disappears and I breathe easy, then out of the corner of my eye, I see her passing us to go to the restroom. I inadvertently look up and she glares at me. It's a stony look that leaves a nasty feeling in the pit of my stomach. The girl is unhinged. I instantly regret sitting right by Liv, now she knows her adversary's face. It worries me.

"Danny," Liv gets my attention. "You have to take me to Jen's shop. It sounds great."

"Yeah," I say a little absently. Liv looks at me concerned, but quickly resumes her conversation.

When she extracts herself a little while later, she turns to me and puts her hand on my knee.

"What's wrong?" she asks lovingly. "Something's been bothering you tonight and I'm not sure if it's me."

I take her hand.

"Oh God no." I tell her, giving her my full attention.

"Well what is it then?"

I take a deep breath.

"It's that girl, Brooke," I say, glancing at the bar. "She's here."

"Oh." Liv looks around. "Are you worried I'll be jealous?" she giggles.

"No, I'm worried she'll cause a scene."

"Well don't worry about it. You haven't done anything wrong."

I cringe at the thought of Brooke crying on my doorstep the other night. I didn't tell Liv because I thought it wasn't important, but now if it comes out, it might look like I have something to hide.

"No, I know."

Jen and Scott interrupt us. "We're leaving," says Jen.

"Sorry, I have an early meeting," adds Scott.

I laugh and say to Liv, "Scott here loves the rat race. We do the same job, but he wears a suit and has breakfast meetings."

"At least I get dressed in the morning, man!" he ribs. "Anyway, Liv, it was great to finally meet you," he says giving her a hug.

I look to Liv. "I think we'll follow you out." Liv nods.

We say goodbye to a few of the others and find our way outside. Brooke deliberately ignores us as we walk by, which is fine with me. On the sidewalk, we finish saying goodnight to Scott and Jen.

"I'll pick you up from the store tomorrow," I say to Jen. "Say 1pm?"

"Great and Liv, you'll join us for breakfast on Saturday won't you? It's tradition."

"Thanks," Liv says. "I'd love to."

"Maybe we could hit the beach after?" suggests Jen.

We hug and kiss and walk away in opposite directions. Liv hooks her arm through mine and we walk the couple of blocks to my apartment.

"I enjoyed tonight," she says. "Jen is exactly how I expected. You're exactly like me and Max." She gives my arm a squeeze. "I'm so glad you get it, I'm sick of defending our friendship to guys."

"I know what you mean."

"So what are you and Jen up to tomorrow?"

"Just lunch, then shopping. I promised I'd help her pick out a new purse," I joke. There's no way she'd guess what we're really doing.

"You're such a girl,," she laughs digging me in the ribs with her elbow.

"Guilty as charged," I admit, holding up my hands. I'm relaxed now that we're away from Brooke and I stop in the street and take Liv into my arms. I love this girl so much and soon I'll be able to make her mine forever.

Twenty-one.

You're such a guy!

Danny.

"Okay, so I've done some research," Jen begins, all business-like, producing wads of paper from her purse.

"Whoa! What's all that for?" I recoil, glancing between Jen's notes and the road.

"Well, I figured you'd just be thinking we'd go to 'the ring store' and pick out something that is just Liv's kind of thing."

I wince, "Is that not what we're doing?"

She scoffs and shakes her head disapprovingly. "Danny, you're such a guy!"

I laugh. "Last night Liv said I was such a girl. I told her I was picking you out a new purse today."

"Okay, well try to keep that frame of mind."

I pull into a parking lot and we find an outside table for lunch. Jen spreads her pages out and begins her eliminations.

"Now, first of all, these aren't actual rings for you to choose from, I just need an idea of what you mean by unconventional so I know where to take you."

"Yes sir!"

"Okay, so, first we have unconventional materials." Holding out a sheet with rings made from Perspex, teeth (yes *teeth*), wood and a whole host of things I can't identify at a glance. I pull a face and shake my head, shuddering at the thought of a tooth ring.

"Right, not *that* unconventional. Good!" she says balling up the sheet and tossing it onto the table.

"Next, we have an unconventional style of ring, not usually associated with engagements." She holds out a sheet with skull rings, fingerprint rings, huge knuckle covering, biker chic type rings.

"Not special enough to say how I feel," I say politely.

"Great," she says, screwing up the page. "Correct answer. Next we have more conventional engagement-type rings in unusual cuts." She shows me pointy diamonds and square diamonds and just about every shape you can think of. I nod slowly, considering this option. She lays this sheet on the table.

"These are rings where the traditional diamond is replaced with a coloured stone." I nod a bit more enthusiastically at this idea. She sets this sheet beside the other one.

"So, now all I have left is vintage or super-conventional," she says adding these sheets to the table in front of me.

I blow out. "Are you sure there's not just one store?" I tease. She responds with stony silence. Okay, we're not kidding about this, fair enough. I keep my head down and pour over the pictures.

"Well I think the vintage is out, they all look a bit fiddly, not really her style," I say removing the sheet. "And there's no way any of these are her thing." I pull out the boring conventional page. "So this is what I think we should look at."

"Alright, we're getting somewhere. I know a couple of places to start."

We eat a quick lunch and we are back on the road. My stomach is in knots as we pull into the parking garage; I can't help remembering the feeling of doing this before. Back then I was nervous about getting laughed out of the store, now I'm just worried about finding her the perfect ring and actually getting to give it to her this time around.

After striking out in two places, we enter a third and are greeted by a friendly woman named Victoria. She sits us down in the plush surroundings, and offers us champagne, Jen accepts and I have a coffee.

While we wait, I realise I feel slightly more at ease in this place, than the last two. She begins by discussing our requirements. Jen explains that we are buying for a very alternative girl.

After asking a few more questions, Victoria sums up her interpretation of what we are looking for.

"So you want to get her something really different, but without cheating her out of the engagement ring experience?"

"That's it!" I'm excited that this girl really gets it.

"Okay, so give me a few minutes and I'll bring you a selection of cuts and colours so that we can start to discuss ideas." Before she leaves she says, "Don't forget, we can make virtually anything for you. Don't worry, we'll find you the perfect ring." She touches my arm warmly and then scurries away, pulling keys from her waist. I turn to Jen, she looks excited and at last, that's how I feel too.

Victoria returns with two trays, one with an array of rings of all different colours and the other with plain-coloured rings in all shapes and sizes. I quickly rule out all the bright colours and anything pinkish and turn my attention to the shapes. I pull out a long pointy one, a square and one that is like a rounded square.

"Alright," says Victoria enthusiastically. "That was easy, most of my clients have a much harder time narrowing it down." She shuffles the rings around so that we are left with a tray with the three shapes I like and the colours I didn't object to. "So you like the greys and violets, but nothing too strong, or pink, and these are the cuts you would consider." She slips her hand under the table and brings out an iPad. "Give me a moment to check our inventory and I'll have someone refresh your drinks." Then she collects the trays and disappears again.

"What do you think?" whispers Jen.

"I think we are getting somewhere, don't you?"

"Absolutely!"

Our drinks are replaced and Victoria returns with a new tray and her iPad. This tray is covered, I assume to add suspense. It works!

"So I've pulled out a few rings I think you might like," she says, pulling back the cover. Jen and I lean in. Victoria continues, "Now it's a case of budget. I have a selection of options for you, but they range hugely in price."

She explains in great detail why one costs more than another, even though it's smaller and why some colours are more expensive than others. Then she suggests Jen try a few on. Interestingly, our opinions change once we see the rings on her finger. My first thought is, they are all a little small and plain. I express this and Victoria obligingly changes the selection, this time some are significantly bigger and some have stones around the band of the ring. I like this tray better.

We discuss the details of these rings and Victoria quietly lists the prices we have jumped to. I glance at Jen and she giggles.

"Don't look at me, it's your money."

"How much are you supposed to spend on these things?" I ask, openly to both women.

"Well there are no rules you must obey, obviously it's a personal choice," replies Victoria. "But some people adhere to the salary rule."

"Go on," I urge, dreading her answer.

"Well some say, you should spend a month's salary, some say three months. Then there is the car rule."

"The car rule?" asks Jen.

"Yes, some say you should spend what you spent on your car."

"Uh oh!" laughs Jen. "Looks like you'll be parting with a fair amount of cash then."

Victoria continues. "There is also size to consider. The national average carat weight of an engagement ring is 0.4 carats. Whereas here in Los Angeles the average is 1.8 to 2.0 carats."

"Well we live in London now," I laugh nervously.

"I always say, buy what you can afford," Victoria concludes, coming to my rescue.

"Well I want to buy the right ring, so I'm flexible to a point, but I was thinking $20,000." I turn to Jen. She's wide-eyed. "What? I talked to Scott this morning, he gave me a reality check."

"Yeah but, he wouldn't spend that on a ring."

"No, I figured I should at least double whatever he suggested," I tease, winking at her. "Besides, we're older than you guys were."

Victoria smiles. "Well there are a few options and I can show you through a few options on here," she says opening the iPad and scrolling through the menus. She leaves us with a slideshow and goes to find a couple more rings.

She joins us again and shows us two more rings. "I thought it would be worth trying these on, but there is one I know of that I think could be just what you are looking for. However, it is marked for transfer to our Las Vegas branch. I have a colleague finding out if it has left and if it was for a sale, or just a change of display."

"Thank you so much," I say.

Just then a girl hurries in from the back with another tray, which she places on the table. "It was just a change over, not a sale and I managed to stop the courier," she puffs, out of breath.

"Thanks Holly. Well, let's hope it's as good as I remember," says Victoria as she pulls back the cover.

She reveals 'the' ring. She lifts it up and Jen puts her hand to her mouth. Victoria talks us through it.

"It's a gray, cushion cut, 2.04 carat diamond, set in platinum. The band is set with approximately .60 carats of matching gray diamonds. It's very rare; most diamonds that are classed as gray are yellowish or greenish grays. This is a true gray. I have never seen one like it before." She hands it to me and I turn it in the impressive light. It's perfect.

"Is the metal darker than the others?"

"No, but I think the colour of the stones would have it seem that way." I hand it to Jen and she tries it on.

"This is the one Danny."

"I know, she'll love it."

"This one is $26,000," says Victoria in the background. I don't care.

"We'll take it." I tell her. "How long does it take to have it sized? I'm returning to the UK on May 20th."

"That will be no problem. I'll get the paperwork," she replies.

Half an hour later, we step out into the fresh air and Jen lets out a little squeal and hugs me. "Well done."

"Thanks. I couldn't have done it without you."

"Now you just need to decide how you're going to ask her."

"I was thinking of doing it at my big send off."

"Oh yay, I'll get to see it."

"Well it's perfect really, both our families will be there. I don't want to wait."

We have done so much this last week. The beach, shopping, Liv has spent lots of time with her family. We've been to my parents, had breakfast at Scott and Jen's. I took her up to Malibu in the Mustang, I let her drive and we lived to tell the tale! I think she has had the time of her life. I had my meeting and I'll be starting a huge job when we get back. Things have been great and with only a few days left, I'm trying to pack in as much family and Jen time as possible as well as getting organised to move.

We decided I would give my notice on the apartment just before we go. Then Dad has some time to make room for the spare furniture and there is time to get whatever I can't carry shipped. Dad is going to take over once we leave and sort everything out for us and he's going to oversee the sale of my truck. I haven't decided what to do about the Mustang yet. It's safely garaged at my parents' for now. I did some research and shipping it doesn't cost as much as I thought, but I would have nowhere to keep it in the UK. I have looked into selling it and I was really surprised. It would pay for a wedding and a house deposit! So I'm seriously considering selling her. I can't discuss it with Liv yet, not until she has the ring.

The jeweler called a while ago to let me know it was ready. I'll get it tomorrow, it's too late now and we have to get ready for dinner with Scott and Jen. They're having a big send off for me on Friday, but we decided to have a quiet night with them tonight as well. I tape up another box and jump in the shower. Liv is finishing her hair when I come out of the bathroom.

"You look beautiful," I say as I cross the room to my closet.

"Thanks. Someone called your mobile while you were in the shower, I heard the last ring when I switched off the hairdryer."

"Okay," I say going in search of my cell. "Do you know where it is?"

"It sounded like it was coming from the hall."

I find it on top of a box. There's a missed call from Brooke. What the fuck does she want? I clear the call list and shut it off, returning to the bedroom and heading straight into the closet.

"Anyone important?" Liv asks.

"No, just a cold call." I curse myself inwardly, that is the third time I've straight up lied to Liv about Brooke. I've done nothing wrong, but I feel like I've dug a big ol' hole now. The sooner I'm back in the UK the better. I'll be getting a new cell and I'll drop her on Facebook from a safe distance. I finish buttoning my shirt and return to the bedroom.

"Are you okay? You look little flushed."

"I'm fine, the shower was really hot; I should have turned it down." Fourth time I've lied.

"I'm ready when you are," Liv says as she puts her cell in her purse.

I splash on some cologne and follow her into the hall. "Let's go then," I say.

We arrive first at the restaurant. A couple of friends are sitting at a table outside, so we stop and talk to them for a moment. Then we head in and the waiter shows us to our table. Jen and Scott are not far behind and they join us, looking a bit stressed.

"Everything alright?" I ask Jen.

She looks at Scott and he nods. She looks back to me. "We got our fertility results through today," she says with a heavy sigh.

"Oh. So, what did they say?"

Liv starts to get up. "I'll give you guys a minute," she says sweetly.

"No!" says Jen grabbing her hand. "You're part of the family now. Please, stay."

I put my arm around Liv. "So?" I ask again.

"So, I have some minor ovulation problems that can probably be fixed with drugs, but…" She looks at Scott, again they exchange regretful smiles. "But, we definitely won't conceive without a sperm donor."

I reach across the table and hold Jen's hand. "God, I'm sorry. So what happens now?"

Jen shrugs. "We don't know."

"I told her, we start looking tomorrow," says Scott putting his arm around Jen.

"And I told him we need to talk about this. Having a baby we didn't make together isn't something we can do without some serious discussion," she says as though they've had this argument already today.

"It's just sperm Jen," he carries on regardless, "I'll be its dad."

"I don't really know much about this, forgive me. Will you have to adopt the baby if you use a donor?" I ask Scott.

"No," he says. "It's really simple. The donor signs his rights away when he donates and then the recipient mother states the father, me, on the birth certificate. Legally the baby is mine from day one."

"But how do you know you'll be okay with it when the baby comes?" Jen asks him. "You might feel completely detached and there won't be a damned thing I can do about it." She turns to us. "Sorry, we're killing the mood." Then she says to Scott, "Let's just leave it for tonight."

"I know, sorry guys," he says to us. "It's really fresh, we didn't mean to bring it out with us."

"Don't worry about it, it's us," I reassure them. "We're behind you, whatever you decide."

Liv shifts beside me and leans forward. "I know it's none of my business, but from personal experience, can I just tell you that biology has absolutely nothing to do with being a great dad. Trust me, I know." She gives Scott's hand a gentle squeeze and then Jen's. "You two will be great parents." Then she sits back. I give her knee a stroke.

"Thanks Liv," says Jen.

We manage to lighten the conversation and have a few laughs as we eat. I'm going to miss them so much, I hate to leave them like this. We order deserts and as the waiter walks away I freeze as I see Brooke walk through the door. She walks almost past our table and then stops and comes over.

"I thought it was you," she says to us all. "I'm outside with friends." She gives me her 'oh-so-innocent' smile.

"Danny, I tried to call you a little while ago, you didn't answer." My stomach turns over and I see Liv look at me from my peripheral vision. "I was wondering if I left my sweater at your place the other night."

My fingers dig into the palms of my hands as I feel Liv's silence next to me.

"No," I say, through gritted teeth.

"Oh, okay then," she says, all sweetness and light. "Well, you all have a lovely evening." She marches away to the restrooms.

I glance at Liv as she gets up.

"Excuse me," she mutters apologetically, placing her napkin on the table and walking away. I jump up and follow her, catching up with her at the door.

"Liv, wait," I plead.

She ignores me and heads out onto the sidewalk. She walks quickly away from the restaurant, with me behind her. I stop her at the corner.

"Hey!"

"What happened the other night?" she asks impatiently.

"Nothing," I sigh. "She came by and got upset, I sent her away."

"So what was all that about?"

"It's just a game. She's trying to mess with us."

She stares me down for a minute.

"No," she says, shaking her head. "You're hiding something from me." Shetries to walk away again. I pull her back.

"Okay," I relent. "Okay, but nothing is going on, I just didn't want to worry you."

"So?" she says, arms folded, tapping her foot.

"So, in Bruges when she called and I told her about you, she didn't take it well." I try to put my hands on her arms in an effort to help her see I'm telling the truth, but she shrugs me off. "The night before I flew back, she called me, she'd found out I was on my way home and called to see if we could hook up. I didn't answer. Then the next morning, she text me, saying that she'd tried calling, could she see me. We were eating breakfast together and I didn't want her to spoil our morning, it was bad enough leaving you."

"You said it was your mum," Liv spits, getting angry.

"I know," I sigh. "I didn't want to upset you."

"Well you have. Go on."

"Okay. Ten minutes after I get home, she's at my door, turning on the waterworks. She thought I would invite her in and, you know... I told her I was in love with you and I was moving to England to be with you. She cried and I had to get her a tissue, when I came back she'd come into the entrance hall. That's it. If she had a sweater, I never saw it. She's just trying to cause trouble and now she knows she has succeeded, because we're out here fighting." I reach out to touch her again, this time she doesn't stop me.

"Tonight, that missed call was her?" Liv asks.

I nod. "I'm sorry. After I didn't tell you the truth the first time, I just felt like I couldn't tell you the next time, without you losing confidence in me."

She scoffs. "And how did that work out for you?"

"Terrible," I admit. She thinks for a moment.

"I trust you Danny," she says reluctantly. "Just don't ever lie to me again."

"I won't," I promise, pulling her to me. I wrap her in my arms and hold her. I wish I could tell her about the ring, then she would know how sincere I am, but it's only another three days and I don't want to spoil it.

"They'll be wondering where we are," she says after a short while.

"Do you want to go back in, or shall we just go home?"

"No, we're not being driven away. But I'm not giving that bitch the satisfaction of thinking she's upset me. I don't want to walk past them looking anything but happy, do you understand?"

"Okay. What shall I do, tell a joke?" I ask.

Liv smiles, thank God.

"Just look happy, smart arse," she says sternly.

I put my arm around her shoulders and I'm gratified when she puts her fingers between mine as we walk in. Just before we pass Brooke's table, I plant a kiss on the top of Liv's head and in response she tucks her other hand in my back pocket. Neither one of us even acknowledges her and I hold the door open for Liv as we enter the restaurant.

When we sit back down, our desserts have arrived.

"Everything okay?" asks Jen.

Liv nods and gives me a brave smile.

"I was just giving Liv the explanation I owed her a week ago about this whole Brooke mess."

"Don't let her get to you," Jen comforts Liv. "She's just a sore loser."

"I know," says Liv. "I just need to be kept in the loop." She looks pointedly at me.

I nod in agreement and then Scott changes the subject. We finish our meal in reasonably good spirits and say our goodbyes.

Liv goes straight in and changes when we get home. I watch her as she takes off her makeup.

"Are we okay?" I ask quietly as I start to undress.

"Yes," she replies sullenly.

"Please don't lose faith in me."

"I can only trust you when you give me nothing to distrust," She sighs. "Until tonight, I trusted you implicitly. I'm just a little thrown by what you didn't tell me. I can see you did nothing wrong, but you certainly made it seem like you had something to hide."

"I know. I've been an idiot. It won't happen again."

"Make sure it doesn't."

She brushes her teeth and then I brush mine. When I switch off the bathroom light, she's already in bed, with the covers pulled up around her, facing away from my side. This is going to take time. I slide in beside her, but don't try to make any contact. We lie in silence for some time and then she turns over and faces me. Slowly, she lifts my arm and places it around her. So I follow her lead and wrap her up, relieved that she'll allow me that. I'll have to work extra hard over the next few days to make her trust me so that the proposal isn't tainted by this in any way.

"Goodnight," I whisper.

"Night," she whispers back.

Twenty-two.

As long as we're together.

Liv.

Danny drops me off at Grace's first thing and we kiss goodbye. He says he has some 'errands' to run, which is a bit vague for my liking. I'm still smarting from finding out a couple of nights ago the extent of the situation with that girl. But ultimately I do trust him, it's Danny, he's never let me down. I see why he hid the facts, it would have played on my mind, but I'm finding it hard to get past the disappointment that he lied to me. I just need to get over it, get home and forget the whole thing.

I'm pretty much packed, because we have so much still to do. I'm taking Matty to the beach this morning and then spending the afternoon at Grace's, just Grace and me. Mum and Connie are taking care of the children and we are having a pamper afternoon, in Grace's summerhouse in her garden. That way she's still on hand if needed. A bit of girlie time will do me good, I'll see what Grace thinks about this whole mess. She'll put me straight. I wish Max were here, I wouldn't feel so vulnerable if I had him.

Tonight is Danny's going away party; I'm meeting him there, so that I can fit in my time with Grace. All the family on both sides is joining us, so I'm just hitching a ride with my lot. Tomorrow, we're having a family day at Danny's parents'. Then we have to have an early night because we're flying home at ridiculous o'clock on Sunday morning. I really can't wait to be home now; it's so full-on here. I'm trying to fit in as much time with my family as possible, so is Danny, and it's keeping us apart, right when we need to be together.

Yesterday, he went out early and when he came home he looked shifty. I'm trying not to look for things, but I know a guilty look when I see one. I hate feeling insecure. It really isn't me. I snap out of it as I enter Grace's front door, and I'm mobbed by Matty.

"Livvy!" he screams and throws himself around my legs. He smells of sun cream and is wearing his beach gear. I hook my dress for tonight onto the doorframe and put down my bag.

"Help! The Matty Monster has got me," I say as I fall to the ground. Matty jumps on me and I grab him and tickle him all over. He squeals loudly and we are shushed from three different directions.

"Sorry," I giggle, getting to my feet. "Mia must be learning to sleep through this by now."

"Not Mia," says Grace, showing me that she is holding a wide-awake Mia. "Andy."

"Oh God, I'm not worrying about him."

"Thanks!" says Andy sulkily as he makes his way down the stairs, yawning.

I pull a face and laugh. Grace rolls her eyes.

"So," I say loudly. "I'm here to take Connie to the beach."

"No! Me!" cries Matty.

Ignoring him, I continue. "Now Connie, are you wearing your sun cream?"

"I am," she obligingly replies.

"No, Livvy, me!" Matty hops around at my feet.

"And do you have your hat?"

"Me, me, MEE!" Matty yells.

"I have," says Connie, perching Matthew's tiny Mickey Mouse cap on her head.

Matty goes into meltdown and pulls at my top. "AUNTIE LIVVY!! I'M GOING TO THE BEACH WITH YOU!" he screams.

"Oh!" I exclaim innocently. "Sorry, I thought I was here to take Connie."

"Silly," he says, fetching his hat from Connie.

Grace hands me a bag and shakes her head. "You cause such chaos."

"I know, but I wouldn't be 'fun Liv' if I didn't."

"That should be everything he needs," she says, back to business.

"Okay, we'll be back by midday, I don't want him out when the sun gets going."

"Here's the keys; remember, you drive on the other side of the road here," she says with a trace of humour, referring to the first time I used her car out here a few years ago.

"Thanks," I say sarcastically. "I think I have it all figured out now."

I pack Matty into the car and we head off for our beach fun. I love hanging out with him. It's always so simple.

We dig in the sand and build a hilariously inadequate sandcastle. Then we paddle in the sea. Next we go for ice cream. People watching with a bright toddler is such a joy. He makes cutting comments about all the posers on the beach, with no idea how funny he is. A couple of times I have to high-five him, he has me in stitches.

I take him shopping on the way home and let him go nuts in the toy shop. I know I shouldn't but I only see him once in a blue moon, why not? He also chooses a little bunny for Mia.

We roll back in, laden down with shopping, full of excitement and ready for lunch. I know we cause chaos, but I love to look at his happy little face. I've had such fun and I feel so much better after a couple of down days. I give Matty his lunch and then sing to him in his bedroom until he falls asleep. Then joining the others in the kitchen for lunch, I enjoy a much quieter cuddle with my gorgeous new niece.

I'm so grateful to have an extra tie to this place, in Danny. Because now I'm sure I will come back more, or for longer and get to enjoy these beautiful kids. I'm sure if Danny and I do have children he will want them to be citizens of both countries like he is. I shiver a little at the thought of our future. I'm still a little in shock at his revelation after the hospital last week, but this is the first time I've thought about it in a couple of days.

"So come on then," Grace says, settling into the recliner in the summerhouse. "I want to know everything."

"I don't know where to start," I admit.

"The beginning."

The beginning…I'm struggling to think of that now, with all that has happened in the last few days, but I give it a go.

"Well, he contacted me on Facebook and we chatted a couple of times. It was clear right from the first conversation, that we both still had some strong feelings for each other." I say sipping my drink. "Then after a couple of conversations, it got really heavy, really fast. I was feeling frustrated because I'd learned to stop thinking about him and here he was again, acting like he still wanted me, but so out of my reach."

"I can imagine," says Grace.

"Then he went quiet on me for a few days. I was really upset that he'd brought up all the old ghosts and then vanished." I think for a moment…I might have never heard from him again.

"Were you still with Mark at this point?"

"No, no, this happened right after that ended."

"Hmm, lucky." Grace smiles and reaches for her drink.

"Then he contacted me again and I was furious. I felt like he was messing with me and I told him I didn't see the point if I could never see him. I thought I'd put an end to it but then he replied, telling me I could see him if I turned around."

Grace gasps. "And was he there?"

"Of course he was there!" I laugh. "This would be the worst story of all time if he wasn't!"

Grace sighs, "That's so romantic."

"I know, so I'm totally swept off my feet. We tried to talk but it was just too emotional."

"So did you just shag?" Grace asks in her upfront way. It doesn't even surprise me.

"Yeah!" I giggle. "Completely out of character, I know, but I took him upstairs right then and we had incredible sex."

"Good for you. But then how could you not, he's spectacularly good looking and you've been in love with him your whole life."

"Exactly."

"So what happened after that?"

"That was about six weeks ago and things are great, he pretty much told me he loved me the next day, although I stopped him, because I was so frightened of getting hurt if he had to leave again. I made him move in, because I hated the idea of him sleeping at a hotel and not with me."

"God, Liv, you move fast!"

"I know, but it was just right."

"He said he loved me again after two weeks, when we went to Bruges, but I was ready to hear it then. That's when he told me he wanted to move over for good. Things have been so wonderful. I really love him Grace," I say, suddenly bursting into tears.

"Hey!" Grace says sitting up and putting her arm around me. "Then what's all this about."

I wipe my face with my fingers, until Grace produces a box of tissues.

"Oh, there's this ex-girlfriend causing trouble," I sniff. "It's silly really."

"How so?"

"When she found out Danny was no longer free to pursue their casual affair, she hit the roof."

"Hit the roof?"

"Yeah, just gave him a really hard time. We were away for the weekend and she called him after she heard that he'd gone off to England chasing a girl. I was there, it was so awkward." I wipe my eyes again; it feels good to finally talk to someone about all of this.

"So how are things now?"

I sigh. "Not great to be honest." I offer her a weak smile. "She tried to contact him again when she heard he was coming back and once again I was there. But for some reason Danny made out it was a message from his mum. Mark has been in contact a couple of times and I told him about it straight away, I just expected the same from him." I shrug. "He thought he was protecting me, but it really hurt."

Grace pulls a face. "I can imagine. Why lie about it?"

"I don't know, but that wasn't all he lied about. When he got back, she must have been waiting for him and she basically sobbed on his doorstep and tried to get him to sleep with her for old time's sake."

"God! She sounds mental."

"Yep. Danny was so worried that she would come between us that he hid it all from me. She kept calling him and then the other night, we were out with his friends and she just walks into the restaurant and casually asks him if she left her sweater at his place the other night." I let her digest this for a moment. "She knew she hadn't, but she knew Danny couldn't deny she'd been there and it would cause trouble between us."

"What did you do?"

"I waited until she left and then I walked out." Going over it makes me feel anxious all over again. "I was so upset, but I didn't want to give her the satisfaction of seeing it."

"Did Danny have a good explanation?"

"Well he came clean, but, to be honest, I'm still not sure why he felt the need to lie in the first place. He didn't do anything wrong, except not tell me the truth."

"And you believe him?"

I think about this. "I do, but I'm just rattled. I trust him, but now he's sown a seed of doubt in my mind, it's hard to shake it off."

"How long were they together?"

"That's the thing, they never really were. It was only ever casual sex when it suited them both. Prior to reconnecting with me, he hadn't even heard from her for a couple of months."

"I don't think you have anything to worry about," Grace ponders. "It sounds like she's the problem. He was probably just embarrassed. It doesn't paint him in a very good light, that's why he didn't tell you. He's happy to up and move to be with you and this girl won't be any problem once he does. I'd just try and put it out of your mind."

"Oh, I know. It's just everything was going so well until that point."

"You looked so loved up at the hospital the other day," she grins.

"We were." I think about our conversation after that. Through all of the uncertainty, this makes me smile.

"Why are you grinning?" Grace laughs.

I'm not sure I can tell her; it seems like a ludicrous thing for me and

Danny to be considering already, I feel I can't admit to it."

"Spill it Liv," Grace demands.

I laugh, still sniffing a bit from the tears. "After the hospital, Danny literally stopped the car in the road and told me he wanted us to have a baby!"

"What?"

"I know!"

"What the hell did you say to that?"

"I said okay," I say to deliberately provoke a reaction.

She looks at me like I've cracked.

"Are you crazy? You've only been together a month."

"Alright, keep your hair on!" I laugh. "We're not talking about doing it this week."

"God, I should hope not."

"We don't want to wait too long though," I add. "We've wasted so much time already." Voicing this defence seems to settle me. I hate the feelings I've had for the last two days, I want them gone, I want to spend the rest of my life with him. He made a mistake, but nothing has changed.

"Do you think you'll get married?" Grace probes.

"I don't know. We haven't talked about it. I'm not sure how important marriage is to him. He didn't bring it up when he said about having a baby, so maybe not."

"But won't you want that, if you're serious about the baby idea?"

"Erm, I don't know really. I haven't thought about it. I suppose so, but it won't be the greatest disappointment of my life if I don't get married, as long as we're together and have a family, I can live without the certificate." I consider this properly for the first time. I've never felt like I needed to get married, but that was always without Danny in the equation. The thought of being his wife, of walking down the aisle towards him and promising to love each other forever, no matter what life throws our way, gives me a flutter of excitement. But I remind myself to stay grounded, I'd be happy without it too.

Grace looks at me, grinning. "You're thinking about it aren't you?"

I roll my eyes. "Only because you brought it up."

"It doesn't make you a bad person to hold out a little hope Liv."

"I know, but I can take it or leave it, as long as we're together."

"I don't think you'll have to worry. I bet he pops the question when you least expect it. He seems the romantic type."

"He is." I muse, mulling over the idea of him proposing. I push the thoughts away; it's pointless getting excited about something that might never happen. I suppose we should discuss our intentions on that front. Right now, I just want to get back to normality after this Brooke issue. I'm certainly not thinking about marriage yet.

"Can you paint my toes for me?" Grace asks, changing the subject. "I haven't seen them in months, they're hideous."

"Alright!" I laugh.

"It'll happen to you one day," she says, defensively.

"Come on then," I say. "Choose a colour."

We spend the rest of the afternoon gossiping. I tell her some amazingly personal details about our sex life. I wouldn't normally do that but, she is my sister and she hasn't had sex in months, so she's a bit starved. She lapped it up.

Talking about my relationship with Danny, I can't help but realise how lucky I am. He's the love of my life and having reconciled myself with the fact that he was gone forever, I've got my Danny back for good. I suddenly feel overwhelmingly like I want to be with him right now. I'm supposedly meeting him at the party so that I can spend the afternoon with Grace, but I will admit it's also a little bit of petty punishment. It's such a stupid game to play and right now I have to close the distance between us.

"Listen," I say to Grace. "Andy knows where this restaurant is doesn't he?"

"Yes."

"I'm going to go home and get ready."

"Okay," Grace shrugs. "If that's what you want to do, we'll meet you there."

"I just really want to see him. I've been a bit shitty with him the last few days and I don't want to go to his farewell party with it still in the air.

I just want to tell him that I love him and I trust him." I feel it's so important to resolve this suddenly, so that we can start afresh.

"I think you should." says Grace, squeezing my hand. "Take my car."

"Are you sure?"

"Yeah, we only needed it if you were coming with us. We'll all fit in the big car without you."

"Thanks." I jump to my feet. I collect my dress and then kiss Grace. "See you at the party."

"Okay, see you later."

I hang my dress in the back of Grace's car and start the engine. I'm desperate to resolve this. I've been holding onto a bad feeling for two days, keeping Danny at a distance, and for what? I love him and I know I can trust him. It's not fair that I have made him think that I don't.

As I pull into the apartment complex my stomach is in knots. I hope he's willing to forgive my sulking. I want to move on. I jump out, leaving my stuff in the car. I have urgent business to attend to right now, I'll get ready later. Smiling to myself, I hurry for Danny's front door. The bedroom light is on and I can see him moving around through the gap in the curtains.

Freezing, I realise it isn't Danny I can see. Brooke is standing in Danny's bedroom, slowly removing her clothes. She's down to some slutty underwear and still going, smiling…at Danny obviously. I can't see him, but I know he's there. This is really happening. My world comes crashing down around me. I feel a sharp pain inside me, as the reality of what I am seeing hits home. For a moment I stand and stare, absorbing the devastation.

I realise I'm fighting for breath and I turn in a daze and run back to the car. Fumbling at the handle, I wrench open the door and jump in. I struggle to start the engine in my panic, tears streaming down my face. I throw the car into reverse and manhandle it out onto the road. I drive away recklessly and have to slam on the brakes as I almost collide with another car. Unthinking, I drive myself away without registering my journey, or how long it takes me. But, remarkably, I find my way safely to a familiar lookout point over the Pacific. I bring the car to a stop and stumble out just in time before I throw up.

I sob loudly on my knees in the light of Grace's headlights. Thankfully the place is deserted. I heave in fresh air, unable to regulate my breathing. But I feel nothing except for utter loss. Picking myself up off the floor, I feel my way back into the car, rest my head on the steering wheel and let go.

A while later, I've no idea how long, my mind begins to function again. What am I going to do? Danny has betrayed me. I can't feel anything through the numbness of the betrayal, but I know that what lies beyond is pure agony and I can't experience it here. I need to be at home with Max. I'm suspended in an awful state of nothingness, knowing that I will never recover from this and I just want Max. I weep again.

I glance at the clock. I don't know what to do now. I can't go back to Grace's. I can't face anyone. The party starts in an hour. I sit for an eternity, barely thinking, just surviving. I need to go home. All my things are in that apartment and I can never see him again. The pain of seeing him would kill me. I need my passport, but he can't know I'm leaving. I can't face confronting him about what I saw and I'm too weak to fight about leaving. Anyway, he doesn't deserve to know I'm gone, let him worry. The anger is fleeting though; I'm too devastated about the loss. I swallow hard, as I almost throw up again.

I gather my thoughts and force myself to think about what to do. I need to wait for him to leave for the party; Jen and Scott are picking him up. Then I have a small window to run in and grab my things before they all realise I haven't arrived with any of them. I don't want my family to worry, I'll let them know I'm leaving, but not until I'm safely gone. I can't risk anyone trying to stop me. Wiping my face, I reverse the car back onto the road and reluctantly head back.

I pull up in the complex, parking out of the way so that I can watch the door without being seen. I sit for a while, numb and vacant and then another car startles me. Suddenly I panic that she might still be in there, but surely he wouldn't take the risk, not with Jen due to arrive any time. I wonder for a moment whether it's just a last fling before he leaves. Then it occurs to me that he might be planning to leave me to be with her.

Shaking my head at the idea, I tell myself he's packing to go. In the end it doesn't matter.

Scott's car pulls up next to Danny's truck and Jen gets out. She goes in for a minute then they both come out. Seeing Danny is like being ripped apart, I can't stand the thought of never seeing him again. Despite the pain I feel, I want to run to him, I have lost my love. Fighting the emotion, I watch him get in the car and I know that is the last time I will ever see him. I wait as they drive away, watching until they disappear into the distance.

I shakily climb out of Grace's car and go to the door. With trembling hands, I let myself in and pause in the hallway. It all looks the same, but nothing will ever feel the same again. I make my way into the bedroom, but thinking about what happened here this evening, I lose again and just make it to the bathroom in time. I wash my face at the sink and catch sight of myself in the mirror. I look like a ghost. Taking a deep breath, I collect my thoughts. I can't be here and I don't have much time.

My case is packed, except a few things I still needed. I throw them in and fill my handbag with everything else. Checking I have my passport and purse, I pull my case out into the hall. I briefly consider leaving a note, but what would I write? I'm too hurt to give him what he deserves and I would rather he was sick with worry right now. I head to the door and turn to take one last look around; something catches my eye in the kitchen. A gift bag is sitting alone on the kitchen side. I cross the hall and pick it up. It's from a jewellers and it's empty.

He bought her jewellery! I heave, but quickly pull myself together. Screwing it up, I throw the box in the bin and kick it in frustration. I have to get out of here; I drop the spare key he gave me on the hall table and pull the door closed behind me. Loading my case into the car, I realise, it's Grace's car and I have to return it. I rifle through my handbag, certain I still have the number for the cab company I called last week when Danny was in his meeting and I needed to go out. Thankfully, I do and when I get my phone out to call them, I find I've a missed call and a message from Danny. I can't listen to it, hearing his voice will finish me. But I can't delete it without listening to it…my phone won't let me. This is unbearable. I clear the notification; I'll deal with it later. I dial the number and book a taxi from Grace's to the airport.

I shove the loose stuff I have in the back of the car into my case, except the dress. I bought it to look special for Danny tonight; I never want to see it again. I'll leave it there. Grace can have it. I drive over to Grace's house and pull up cautiously in case they haven't left yet. The car has gone, so I park up and go in the house. Leaving my case in the hall, I go in search of paper and a pen.

I quickly write a note to them all.

Please don't worry about me...
I've gone home. I couldn't stay, I'm so sorry. Please give Auntie Liv kisses to my babies. I'll call you tomorrow.
Liv x

I have to wipe fresh tears away as I fold the note and stand it in front of the TV, so I pull a few sheets of kitchen roll off to take with me, just as I hear the cab pull up.

The driver carries my case and I lock up the house, posting the keys back through the door. I walk away, there's no going back now.

"LAX," I tell the driver and he pulls away. We drive in silence and I think for the first time about Connie. I'm leaving her to fly home alone and suddenly I feel terrible but I know she'll understand. Then I realise I have a ticket I may be able to transfer, so I rummage around to find it in my bag.

It is difficult to read in the flickering streetlights as we speed along. I'll just have to see when I get there but I don't care if I have to buy a new ticket. I can't stay here a minute longer. The driver asks me which terminal and gets in lane. The airport is busy when we pull up, but I feel like the only person on earth, walking through the sliding doors. I desperately need Max now, but calling him will open the floodgates, so I have to wait until I see him.

I head over to the BA desk and exchange my ticket with no problem; it only costs a few pounds. The flight leaves in an hour and ten minutes. I look at my watch. They'll all know I haven't shown up now, panic sets in. This is the point where they might come looking and now I am stuck until I take off. I just have to hope they don't try to catch me up. I check my ticket, we board in forty minutes, and I don't think that is enough time to catch me. Drifting through security, I wonder what he's feeling right now.

I sit, scanning the crowd anxiously waiting for the flight to be called. I switched my phone off after I called the cab, so I have no idea if they have tried to call me. Finally, we begin boarding and, once I settle into my seat, I begin to relax. He hasn't followed me. I look at my ticket; I will arrive home at 14:50 tomorrow afternoon, UK time. I don't know how to begin working that out. My mind is so clouded. I just know it's a long flight and a big time difference. I rest my head on the back of my seat waiting for the rest of the passengers to find their seats.

Once the crew begins their safety talk and we push back off the stand, I know for sure I've got away. I'm also thankful that the flight is only half full and sitting in the window seat, I have two empty seats next to me. As the cabin lights go down for take off, I close my eyes and let go.

I step out of the cab outside the diner and pay the driver. Taking a deep breath, I push open the diner door and step inside. Everyone is busy so I head straight through, not seeing Max. I enter my code and open the door, but I am stopped in my tracks by Max's voice.

"Liv! Everyone's been so worried."

I turn to face him. His expression is a mix of anger and concern as he walks towards me and holds out his arms. I collapse into them, sobbing.

"Good God, Liv," he says, holding me tight. "What's happened?"

Epilogue.

Danny.

I have finished packing up the apartment and split the boxes into two piles: one for shipping and one for storing, to help my dad. I met a guy earlier about the Shelby, I think I've decided to sell, but I wanted to get it properly valued before I leave. The only thing I have to do is give notice on my apartment, I've typed the letter up but Dad is going to drop it in for me; I've simply run out of time.

I leave out my clothes for tonight, run the shower and glance again at the engagement ring. I'm feeling anxious about it now even though I know it won't be like last time. I wish we were going to the party together though, then I wouldn't have that 'what-if-she-doesn't-turn-up' feeling. But, in a few hours, I hope to have said goodbye to most of my friends, and be in bed with my fiancé. I smile at the thought as the hot water runs over me.

Deep in thought about how I'm going to put how I feel into words, I rub a towel over my hair and brush my teeth. Wrapping the towel around my waist, I stroll out into the bedroom. I stagger back as I come face to face with Brooke, dressed only in heels and her go-to underwear, lying on my bed. She smiles seductively at me.

"What the fuck!" I yell, so shocked, I don't know what else to say.

"Hey," she purrs.

"Brooke, what the fuck is this? How did you get in here?"

"I took your spare key," she says, twiddling it between her fingers. "I thought you needed a little persuading."

"Get out!" This isn't happening.

"Danny, you know you won't be happy leaving with that girl," she says softly. "We're good together."

"This has gone far enough, you're crazy! Now I'm going to say it once more, GET OUT or I'll call the cops." Brooke just looks at me. Not believing me for one second.

"I mean it Brooke, I'll call the cops. Harassment, breaking and entering, not great qualities for a teacher, you'd lose your job."

"You've changed," she strops, sitting up.

"Not soon enough apparently. Now, get your clothes on and get OUT!" Then, to make it perfectly clear that I mean what I say, I grab my cell from the dresser. I hold it up and enter the number. "I'm waiting Brooke," I say, hovering over the send key.

"Jesus Danny, I just want you to see what a mistake you are making with this girl," she says, getting up and half-heartedly picking up her clothes.

"I don't ever want to see or hear from you again, do you hear me?"

"Loosen up," she scoffs.

"GET OUT!" I yell and shove her towards the door as she slips her dress back on. "Key," I demand, holding out my hand. She stares at me in shock. "Stay away from me. I mean it, or I'll report this and you can kiss your career goodbye."

She fixes me with a deadly look.

"Fuck you Danny!" she screams and hurls the key at me.

I watch her stomp towards the front door and wonder briefly if I should report this anyway. She could turn it on me, say I did something awful to her, just to get back at me and I have no witnesses. Maybe the school board would be interested to know what sort of person she really is outside school. She isn't worth my time, I decide, as the door slams shut behind her. Turning my thoughts to Liv and my promise to be completely honest with her from now on, I pick up my cell again, deleting 911 and selecting her number. It rings a few times and then I hear her voice. 'This is Liv, leave a message'.

"Liv it's me, can you call me? I really need to talk to you." I try to sound calm so as not to worry her. Then, picking up the other phone, to keep my cell line clear, I dial Jen. I have to talk to someone about this. Jen calms me down and soothes my worries. I'll feel better as soon as I talk to Liv about it. I'm just desperate to see her, but it's almost time to leave. I expect she was showering or doing her hair when I called. I can hold on a little while longer. I finish getting ready and then pick up the ring in its bag and go into the kitchen. My mouth is dry from nerves so I quickly fill a glass with water and down it all. I pull open the bag and put the envelope with the certificates in the pile on the counter, it's all the important documents I need to take with me. I open the cardboard box and slide the wooden box out. Opening it slowly, I smile. Despite the crippling fear, I know she's going to love it.

Just then I hear Jen at the door. I check the spy hole to make sure it isn't someone unwelcome first. But I'm relieved to see it's just Jen. I pull the door open and she comes in, hugging me.

"Any more problems?"

"No," I say absently, returning to the ring. "Should I take it all packed up like this?" I ask her waving at all the packaging.

Jen comes over to see what I am talking about.

"Can I see it?" she asks, wide-eyed an excited. I open the box and show her. She gasps. "It's better than I remember," she squeals.

I grin. "So I should take the box, right?"

"Yes, put it in my purse if you like." She holds it open for me. I slip the wooden box back in the outer one and put them into Jen's purse, leaving the bag behind.

"Let's go then," I say, a flush of uncertainty washing over me. "She will be there, won't she?"

Jen gives me a little squeeze and nods as we head out to Scott waiting in the car.

When we arrive at the restaurant, my parents meet us. Needless to say, they were the first ones here. Jen has booked a private section for us with a huge table, but we stand with our drinks waiting for more people to arrive. The room slowly fills up and I watch the door anxiously, Liv and her family are the last ones to arrive, probably due to the kids. They're bringing them, because otherwise they couldn't all come, but that was fine with me. I start to feel uneasy, then, at last, I see Connie and Helen coming in, followed by Andy and Matthew then Grace and the stroller. I frown, where is Liv? I really need to see her now. Helen reaches me first.

"Sorry we're late, it's a logistical nightmare!" she winks, kissing me on the cheek.

"Danny darling," Connie croons as she too leans in for a kiss on the cheek.

"Where's Liv?" I ask them with a hint of impatience.

They both frown. "Isn't she with you?" asks Helen.

"No," I say, not really understanding the confusion.

"She left a little while ago, she said she would prefer you came together."

"I haven't seen her," I tell them, panic rising. "I'll call her." I pull my cell out of my pocket and make my way outside to try her again.

This time it doesn't ring, all I get is Liv's answerphone message.

"Liv, it's me, where are you? I'm worried," I say. Trying not to freak out, I dial the apartment, it goes to the machine, but I speak anyway, in case she's there and not answering. "Liv, are you there? Call me when you get this." I hang up. Trying my last option, I call Grace's, no reply there either. I head back into the restaurant.

"I can't get hold of her," I say to the group.

Grace looks worried. "I'll try her," she says, dialling. She puts her phone to her ear and blocks the background noise out by pressing her finger against her other ear. She pauses a moment, then says, "Liv, where are you?" For a second I think they are talking, but then she says, "Call me when you get this." My shoulders fall, when I realise nobody can reach her.

Jen comes over and puts her hand on my shoulder. "What's up?" she asks.

"Liv isn't here yet and no one knows where she is."

"She'll be here, don't worry." I look at her with despair in my eyes.

"Where is she?" I whisper. What if she doesn't let me ask her? I can't live like that again."

"Listen, don't start panicking. Let's go back to the apartment. She might be there."

I nod and go and tell Helen what we are doing.

"We'll go home and see if she's there?" she says, looking concerned.

"No, stay here in case she shows up. If she isn't there, we'll call you," I insist, trying not to sound too worried. Scott and Jen are ready to drive me back, so without apologising to my guests I quietly follow them out.

We pull up at my apartment and I jump out while the car is still rolling to a stop.

"Liv?" I call out as I open the door. "Liv?"

"Any luck?" Jen asks, appearing behind me.

"No," I sigh. I check in the bedroom, it all looks the same. Then it hits me. Her things have gone. I search around briefly but I know it's hopeless. I drop to my knees and put my head in my hands, this can't be happening.

Jen appears in the doorway. "Danny what's wrong?" she asks, kneeling beside me.

I lift my head and look at her with tears in my eyes. "She's gone. She's taken everything." Jen puts her arms around me and holds me tight. "It's happening again." I whisper.

Acknowledgements

I'm sure a publisher would tell me to keep it short, but I'm the publisher, so get comfortable!

To my babies...you are my sunshine.

To the remarkable women in my life, Mum, Gigi, & Nicola. Thank you for showing me the way. I wouldn't have my strength without yours. You are my inspirations. And to the tolerant, wonderful men who live with our strength every day, thanks for making us realise that it isn't weakness to let ourselves be looked after.

Steve, the love of my life and the funniest person I know. I only know how to write about this kind of love because of you. You have tolerated me being immersed in this story and held the fort, kept smiling and kept loving me. Even though I'm sure you thought I'd never see this through, the fact that you pretended I might has meant the world to me.

To my boys, Matt, Gareth & Kenny. You are so not who I thought I'd be thanking when I set out to do this. This is after all a lovey-dovey chick book, but weirdly it was you who ended up inspiring the bigger picture. Being friends with you has made me feel special, cherished and protected. I know you'll always look out for me even though I am a pain in the arse sometimes and I love you for it. I found the inspiration for Liv & Max and Danny & Jen's friendships from knowing you and it has made me realise just how lucky I am to call you my friends.

To my girls, you know I love you too. I have so much to thank you for, but the boys get this one! You know yours is coming.

Emma O, my original audience of one! I don't think you'll ever understand what you did for me when this all began. Maybe because you weren't bored to tears by my previous fifty hair-brained schemes, but your spurred me on. You single-handedly gave me the will to continue until I was so far in, I had no choice but to finish. I will forever be in your debt and you know you always have a place on the casting couch of my dreams. Remember, shirts off, its the only way we can make an informed decision.

Mel, you nutter! You did me a huge favour with the epic 'Spain read-through' and I have another manuscript sitting here waiting for sun, sangria and drunken annotations…I promise to tone down the erections!

Kirsty, you are the ultimate bouncing board! I hit you with a Q, you fire back an A. No messing!…..and NO BURGERS! The 'Quiet!' bit in Chapter 12 is just for you! You're welcome! ;)

Mum, Some of the discussions we have had over this book…I don't think I have ever laughed as much. It never ceases to amaze everyone what I can discuss with you and the depth in which we can discuss it, but I don't think it is weird at all, its just how we are, thanks for making me what I am and for being who you are…a pair of FIGJAMs!!! ;)

Amy, you're incredible, formidable and inspirational. The chalk to my cheese and yet the jam to my doughnut! I couldn't imagine being so different and yet so the same as anyone as I am with you. Your friendship and support has meant the world to me and not just in writing this book, but you know that.

And to my amazing Twitter Beta readers…Dana, Kat, Stace, Ava, Kelly, Puff…The SCARY girls of Twitter. The support, encouragement and love I have felt from basically a group of perfect strangers is incredible. You guys have made me laugh so hard. You have all taken time out to help me make this book better, you have talked me off the ledge more than once. You have opened my eyes up to some awe inspiring writers and I can't thank you enough. There is nothing I wouldn't do for you in return. Well nothing legal…I'm not #StuStalking for you D!!! I am so lucky to call you my friends.

To all the bloggers…I am only just getting to know some of you, but I think what you do for authors is just incredible, thank you. But a special thank you to Steph of Romance Addict Book Blog and Romance Addict Blog Tours. You are incredible, thank you for all your hard work and support.

Finally, Thanks to Kelly at Ultimate Proof for being a marvellous editor. You totally got what was I going for and I can't wait to work with you again.

Still Human
Kerry Heavens

Danny and Liv are back…

Danny loves Liv. He knows he loves her more than she loves him because she ran without a word when she saw their future mapped out before her. He knows he will never love anyone like he loved her and this time he doesn't think he can move on.

Liv loves Danny. She knows she loves him more than he loves her because he broke her heart in the worst possible way, right when things were falling into place. She knows she will never love anyone like she loves him and this time she doesn't think she can move on.

They needed a second chance because they just weren't ready for their first, but when events changed everything between them, they discovered they were just human after all. Now Liv and Danny have to find a way to survive being hurt by each other.

They doubted, they underestimated and they did believe the worst, but only because they were too young the first time and too vulnerable the second time. But now they have changed and if they are not the same, surely things can only turn out differently?

Autumn 2013

Kerry Heavens

Terrible wife, mediocre mother, appalling housewife,
Fashion graduate, wedding co-ordinator, Sex toy salesperson, shop manager, designer,
Font collector, romance addict
Fancier of nice men,
Ok, fancier of almost all men,
Awesome cupcake baker, Incessant singer
Film buff, friend
Writer

Website:
http://www.kerryheavens.com

Contact:
kerryheavens@kerryheavens.com

Facebook:
Kerry Heavens Author

Twitter:
@kerryheavens

Pinterest:
kerryheavens
Visit Pinterest to see my inspirations for the characters in my stories.

Thank you for reading! x

Made in the USA
Charleston, SC
25 June 2014